THE JOURNAL OF
DORA DAMAGE

BELINDA STARLING

BLOOMSBURY

First published 2007
This paperback edition published 2008

Bloomsbury Publishing, London, New York and Berlin

Copyright © 2006 by Belinda Starling

The moral right of the author has been asserted

Bloomsbury Publishing Plc, 36 Soho Square, London W1D 3QY

A CIP catalogue record for this book is available from the British Library

ISBN 978 0 7475 9325 6
10 9 8 7 6 5 4 3 2 1

Typeset by Hewer Text UK Ltd, Edinburgh
Printed in Great Britain by Clays Ltd, St Ives plc

www.bloomsbury.com

All papers used by Bloomsbury Publishing are natural,
recyclable products made from wood grown in well-managed forests.
The manufacturing processes conform to the environmental
regulations of the country of origin

For Mike

'Lady bookbinders are supposed to be heaven-born geniuses, who will bring back the old order of things. Those who fancy this are welcome to the delusion; we know better.'

The British Bookmaker vol 7, 1892–3, p. 7

'Improper books, however useful to the student, or dear to the collector, are not "*virginibus puerisque*"; they should, I consider, be used with caution even by the mature; they should be looked upon as poisons, and treated as such; should be (so to say) distinctly labeled.'

William Spencer Ashbee, introduction to *Index Librorum Prohibitorum*, 1877

Prologue

This is my first book, and I am rather proud of it, despite its obvious shortcomings. The red morocco lies unevenly across the boards, the corners have been poorly folded, and there is a grass-stain on the cornflower-blue silk front panel; the title on the cocked spine reads MOIV BIBLL; and across the leather bands, impressions of single letters entwine with a bough of botanical impossibility, sprouting pineapples amidst the oak leaves, acorns and ivy. I made it five years ago, when I feared what failure would have meant; today I cut and ploughed the pages, and discovered that at least they turn well, for the signatures were evenly sewn, and the headband is pliant but resolute. And now I am writing in it, and it will be the first book I have ever written, too.

My father used to tell me that before we are born, St Bartholomew, patron saint of bookbinders, presents our soul with a choice of two books. One is bound in the softest golden calf and majestically gold-tooled; the other is bound in plain, undyed goatskin straight from the tan-pits. Should the nascent soul choose the former, upon entering this world he will open it to find that the pages of the book are already inscribed with a story of an inescapable fate to be followed to the letter, and on departing it at the time of death, the book will have so deteriorated from constant consultation that the hide will be shoddy and the text illegible. But the pages of the latter book start off blank, and await inscription by the leading of a life of free will according to personal inspiration and divine grace. And the more one's destiny is pursued, the more brilliance the book acquires, until the binding far surpasses any hide, cloth or paper binding ever produced in the finest ateliers of Paris or Geneva, and is finally worthy of joining the library of human knowledge.

I have no such pretensions for what follows on these pages. This book is more likely to jump out of my hand, waggle its finger at me and tease me about the events I am trying to make sense of, and I shall have to stuff it into a bottom drawer amongst my stockings and smalls in an attempt to stifle its mocking. Or it may have a greater sense of responsibility, and less of a sense of humour, and reveal within it some approximation of the truth. For whatever one makes of its curious binding, it conceals the contents of my heart, as clearly as if I had cut it open with a scalpel for the anatomists to read.

Chapter One

It's raining, it's raining,
There's pepper in the box,
And all the little ladies
Are picking up their frocks.

I first realised we were in trouble when Peter vanished behind the curtain separating the workshop from the house just as Mrs Eeles came through from the street. She had visited the day before too, asking for him.

'He was here only a minute ago,' I said, 'tending the blocking press, or maybe it was the plane.' I looked to the others for confirmation, and they nodded. The ledger he had been working on for some politician or other was still lying on the bench, a naked manuscript being measured for its new clothes.

Oh, there were other signs, but I had chosen to ignore them until it was too late, until I was faced with too much proof that business was failing, that we were sinking into poverty, and would soon be destitute. It was like learning to read: one could pore over the incomprehensible scribbles of a book for years, until one sudden day the ciphers seem to rearrange themselves on the very page and yield their meaning at last. So it was with the trail left by Peter Damage, and once the truth dawned on me I could no longer ignore his swollen fingers; the empty tea-caddy on the mantel-piece; the hushed voices between Sven and Jack whenever Peter left the room; the cursing matches that took place, even in front of Lucinda and me. The most blatant sign was the one I had chosen most to overlook: that Lucinda's fits were occurring more often, and with greater severity.

Mrs Eeles had a long, straight nose like a candle-snuffer, which was wrinkling at the smell of glue and leather. Everyone who came in here did that, although I never knew why. It was a far better smell than the outside stench of London putrefying in the rain. She looked like a black chicken in her triangular mourning cloak, which dripped over the trestles. Her red face darted from under her veil as she pecked around the frames and presses with agitation, as if she might find Peter amongst the leather parings on the floor. She used to preen and offer him her cheek to kiss, and would call him 'Pete', or even 'Petey', and tell him to call her 'Gwin', and he would chuckle, and wrinkle his round chin down on to his neck out of bashfulness.

She was about to explain her reason for the visit, but as it was five minutes to twelve, a train rattled by outside our window, and Mrs Eeles raised her hands to command silence.

' "There is one glory of the sun, and another glory of the moon, and another glory of the stars; for one star differeth from another star in glory. So also is the resurrection of the dead. It is sown in corruption; it is raised in incorruption; it is sown in dishonour; it is raised in glory; it is sown . . ." '

We bowed our heads, and while I fingered my mother's hair-bracelet around my wrist, we waited for the rhythm of the train of death to cease rocking the foundations of the house. Five years before, in 1854, the London Necropolis & National Mausoleum Company had opened its Necropolitan Railway adjacent to Ivy-street, to shuttle corpses and their mourners twenty-five miles down the line to Woking, where they had constructed the largest cemetery in the world. I had heard Mrs Eeles had picked up the houses at the top of Ivy-street on the cheap, having unexpectedly inherited a small fortune from an uncle in the colonies. Whoever sold them to her had not understood her proclivities; a shrewder speculator would have charged her more for these houses, for they were to her as the apartments overlooking Lord's or the Oval were to a devotee of cricket. The train took the dead to their graves, but it took Mrs Eeles straight to heaven.

'". . . the first Adam was made a living soul; the last Adam was made a quickening spirit."'

For Mrs Eeles had an inclination towards death. I do not mean that Mrs Eeles lived in morbid sufferance. I mean that she loved death with a passion: she delectated in mortification. She loved death the way that a child loves sweets: it made her giddy, and giggly, and slightly sick.

'Pardon me for the disturbance,' she finally said when the moment of death had passed, 'but there's the small matter of the rent outstanding.' Her eyes swept over the shabby little room, which was harshly lit by two naked gas flames, because I had taken the lamps into the house to clean again. I hoped that she would find no cause for concern in the way we were keeping her property. From the battered benches, peeling wallpaper, greasy leather aprons and clammy air, one would be hard pressed to believe that objects of great beauty were produced here.

'The rent?' I said, with genuine innocence. Peter paid Mrs Eeles every quarter; they had their own arrangements, and an understanding that Damage's Bookbinders was not to lower the tone of Ivy-street. There had been a dreadful shindy only last summer, when Mrs Eeles let number six to a group of girls who claimed to be opera-dancers appearing at the Alhambra. She would never have considered that type as a rule, only that the house had a leaky roof and a draughty cellar, no matter how many workmen tried to patch it up. But when Mrs Eeles discovered they were what one might call gay, of the seediest type, she threw them into the street wearing nothing but their scarlet drawers, and hurled their fancy dresses after them. Oh, she could be a devil with her dander up, but she did see to the drains, unlike other landlords. Besides, I had heard that the late Mr Eeles, who had been a marble mason, used to throw his boots at her, so Peter always used to tell me that it was fortunate she had tenants to throw hers at. She and Peter had a special understanding, what with their obsessions with respectability and mortality: there was nothing that impressed Peter so much as the dignity enshrouding the payment of one's debt of nature.

'Apologies for the meddling of you into it, my dear,' she continued, 'but I can't find myself to catch your husband these days. Not that it's a worry to me, as you're honest souls, and I shan't be throwing you out on to the street, I'm sure, but it is now three weeks and two days behind.'

'Is it now? I'll get Peter to see to it at once,' I said.

'And how fare you, young master Jack? Keeping your feet nice and dry in here, I'll warrant.'

'Yes, thank you,' he muttered, continuing to glue down the grey moiré endpapers of a volume of plain, unvarnished calf, entitled, *The Law and Practice of Joint-Stock Companies*. Jack Tapster lived right up by the river, and was flooded out every other year, but the river had been his family's livelihood – or deathlihood – ever since his father ran off one night after a prize-fight and never came back. Mud-larks, they were, and turd-collectors. Mrs Eeles had brought him to us, as, though the Tapsters lacked respectability, they had not just the whiff but the stink of tragedy about them, which she could not resist. Besides, Jack was often called 'The Skull', not only from the black grimacing skull tattooed on his left bicep, but also owing to his skeletal appearance and his unusual cleverness, so to her he was a living *memento mori*, which may have had something to do with her favouring of him for our apprentice.

Mrs Eeles didn't care to look at Sven, who was German, despite him being the best finisher south of the Thames. It was a miracle he was still with us; he had come over on his

Wanderjahre in search of work and had never left. He was fine-tooling around a copper-plate let into the cover of *Rules and Articles of War (Better Government of All Her Majesty's Forces)*; second-in-command after Peter, he was clearly intent on not catching my — or her — eye.

'Peter must've forgotten, strange enough,' I said. 'He's been awful busy, Mrs Eeles, what with Christmas and things.' I became aware that I was blunting the needle on the wood of the sewing-frame, and Lucinda was clutching my skirt, pale as candlewax.

Mrs Eeles started to make her way towards the door. 'Ho, dearie, never need to worry about you Damages, do I?' she said heartily. 'You're a pattern young family.'

Despite the talk about her, I liked Mrs Eeles. She fussed about the wrong kind of people, but she never knew that I'd seen her from our box-room window, perched on her back porch, knees up outside her hitched skirts, smoking on a pipe. I could not tell her either, for I did not know how to without letting her know that I did not mind, that I thought she was quite the screamer for it. Sometimes she even came rent-collecting in her yellow curl-papers, when she must have thought she had already thoroughly brushed and fluffed her feathers.

I picked Lucinda up, and together we stood at the door and waved Mrs Eeles off into the gloomy drizzle. She lived round the corner from us, in the house two along from the workshop. Her empire only extended to the top ends of these two streets, where she could keep at bay the seedier folk that so troubled her sense of decorum, namely Fenians, Italians and Jews. On our side of the road was a terrace of fifteen houses, like a long line of dirty red siblings with the same narrow faces and familial features. Each had three floors with two rooms on each floor, one front and one back, plus a basement, except for ours, the first — or fifteenth — house, number two, Ivy-street, which had no basement but two small cellars, too small to use for anything other than storing coal and mixing paste. But the house did have an extra room off the ground floor where two roads met (and where a public-house should have been, were it not for a hiccup of town planning), and it was this room that became the binding workshop. So far, the neighbours had not complained about our industry, even though we could hear them plain as pewter through the damp walls.

I smiled at Nora Negley opposite at number one, with her saggy-dugged goat that always strolled into the parlour just when you were sat there having a cup of tea, and the widow Patience Bishop at number three who never liked visitors, or tea. Agatha Marrow was leading her donkey-cart up the road to number sixteen; I could see she had a new maid from the poorhouse to help her, for the last one was carried off by an ague even as she was stoking the range not long back.

'Marnin', Dara dearie.'

'Morning, Agatha.'

'Wet in't it?'

'Wet it is.'

'It is wet, oh, in't it wet?'

When times were better I used to give her our laundry, for although her children were the dirtiest in the street, it was a miracle the way the sheets came back from her without a speck of soot on them. But when I did it, no matter where I hung them, inside or out, the smuts and blacks from my hearth, or of the hearths of the city, would get to them some way.

I closed the door just as Peter re-entered from the house, somewhat sheepishly.

'I – er – I was looking for the unguent,' he murmured. 'It's gone from the pot on the dresser.' He started hunting for his spectacles, fists curled by his sides.

'It is gone, yes,' I said, equally quietly, with only the slightest raise of my eyebrow, not so as he could chide me for any impertinence, for he had dismissed it as quackery when I made it the previous winter, but that hadn't been such a wet one as this.

Eventually he found his spectacles lying on the binding primer. He picked them up carefully, but his hideous fingers were a sorry sight; it was like he was raising his glasses to his face with two cow's udders. I thought of suggesting a butter rub, but I held my tongue, for I already knew that the pennies in the tea caddy would not last the week, and Peter would scold me if there was no butter for his toast. We settled again into a grim, clammy silence; the only sounds were the puttering and hissing of the rain in the gutters and the gas in the pipes, whispering to us of the mysteries of the city, as if our very fates were bound into it, and which we could not hope to comprehend.

At two o'clock as usual I carried Lucinda back into the house, her legs wrapped around my waist, and she folded her head into my neck. Her smooth blonde hair fell about my shoulders like a pelerine of gold lace on a gentlewoman; indeed, I was all the finer for Lucinda. I was glad to leave the workshop and get on with the household chores while she rested, for I could smell the trouble, and I did not want her to have an attack.

The first time Lucinda had a fit she was but three days old. I still had no milk at the time, for it took a few days to rise into the breast, and in her fury and hunger she cried out sharply before convulsing, all twitches and purple. 'Hush, you angry thing,' I admonished, and, as if to punish me for my harsh words, her body flicked itself violently out of my hands, and almost into the fire. Her tiny tongue lolled from her mouth and only the whites of her eyes were visible, and she writhed and thrust herself close to the ashes, as if the devil himself were inside her and wanted to return to the inferno whence he came. I seized her and held her close, then laid her down on the chair and pressed my body against hers as her little fists and feet pummelled and thrashed my tender belly, until she lay still again.

I was frightened; I even called for the doctor, who told me she was having a teething fit, and gave her castor-oil, and told me to submerge her up to her neck in hot water the next time she fitted. But when the convulsions persisted beyond her full mouth of teeth I did not call the doctor again, for there was a fear greater than that from which I knew my daughter was suffering. I had grown to understand that my daughter was afflicted by the same disorder that ruined my grandfather's chances of a reasonable existence, and which saw him incarcerated in an asylum at the age of twenty-four.

I went to visit him once – old Georgie Tanner – with my mother when I was only five, just like Lucinda. I remember an old man more vividly than my grandfather, an old man crouching by his bed, tugging at his sheets, hissing, 'Your majesty!' at him. 'Your majesty. Can't be? Is't thou?' When we approached, he stood up with the sheets wrapped round his loins, the bones of his chest protruding out of his night-shirt, and pointed at my grandfather. 'Ladies of the court! His Majesty King George the Third!' He pulled a chair up for my mother, then turned to me, and clasped my hand to his chest. 'But mark you,' he whispered, nodding conspiratorially, 'it is my army that shall lead the rebellion, and then I shall rule the world!'

And when I looked around me to establish the whereabouts of the rest of his army, I caught the eye of another man, lying in his bed, who turned his face towards me and said, with a mouth as dry as skin, 'No food since 1712.'

It is possible that a five-year-old is better equipped than an adult when it comes to coping with such displays of mental peculiarity. That is not to say that insanity always turns an old fellow back into a child, but that children are of necessity constantly dancing in and out of the shadows of reason, and better at accepting displays of lunacy. Certainly my mother was more discomfited by the experience than I was, and had I not taken her as my example of how best to react in the circumstances, my sole memory of my grandfather would, doubtless, be a more pleasant one. Instead, I remember old Georgie Tanner more as she saw him: a cause for grief, smelling sour, lying inert, his rheumy eyes directed at the ceiling, and his mouth sore and dripping from the latest chemical solution intended to control his seizures.

He wasn't mad, even a five-year-old could tell that. He was just unlucky, for men don't often get locked up, not for madness, even though there are more mad men than women. Madness is a female word. 'It's a madness' they say, like it's a governess, or a seamstress, or a murderess. There's no male equivalent, no such word as 'madner'. I should start saying it, but then they might lock me up. Peter took me to see *Hamlet* at the Royal in our courting days, and when I saw Ophelia, I knew she wasn't mad. I wanted to cry out that madness isn't this pretty, with flowers entwined in her hair and ivy between her toes. It was Hamlet who was mad, carrying on to himself like that, and Claudius too, but who's brave enough to lock up a king and a prince? I wanted to tell the whole theatre, but they would have told me I was stirred by the heat, and that the gas-lights were hurting my head, which they probably were.

Lucinda wasn't mad either, but with the Falling Sickness one still had to be careful. We led a peaceful life, owing to the delicacy of her condition: she accompanied me each morning as I sewed and folded in the workshop; in the after-noons she helped me with the chores, and in the evenings we read books, made up fanciful stories, sang, or played the old cottage piano. In the winter, we nestled by the fire and sewed leaves of paper together to make simple, tiny books, bound with scraps of leather or cloth from the workshop; in the summer, we sat in our patch of a garden and sewed real leaves together, and then we placed our leaf-books under the spindly bushes for the fairies. I kept my anxieties away from Peter, as it was not right to trouble him with women's worries; but I also kept them away from the medical profession. I have many regrets, but that is still not one of them.

We liked being helpful to the bookbinders, Lucinda and I, for the sewing and folding was not hard. Occasionally I was privy to the books themselves, and had made several, not unheeded, suggestions for the casing design. I had enjoyed reading them: the legislative proposals, the academic theses, the histories, the memoirs of notables, and the primers for success in commerce (but Peter kept the medical anatomies away from me). I found them more edifying and provocative than the popular romances my sex was encouraged to read. Reading was my happiness: my father had described me to Peter's father, William Damage, as 'bookish' when our engagement was made, and while I knew he had not meant it entirely as a compliment, it boded well for my match with my father's apprentice bookbinder.

Surely one could forgive the daughter of a bookbinder for her love of books? But my father took no responsibility for my passion; he blamed my mother, who had been a governess before their match. She had, in his opinion, made the grave error of rearing me in the fashion of her superior charges, thereby expanding my intellect beyond the material station of any husband his income was capable of attracting. I would, he was convinced, remain not only a spinster, but entirely friendless, as I would be the intellectual, if not economic, superior of women of my own society. So I learnt the expediency of placing bell-jars, as it were, over my love of books, philosophy, politics and art, unmoveable as they were from the mantelpiece of my life, and I allowed them to become soot-blackened with neglect.

While Lucinda slept, I took the plants off the windowsills, shook out the muslin soot-stoppers, and washed the windows with cold tea – which would let in as much of the day's meagre light as possible, save our candles, and bring more cheer to the dim, north-facing room – and then I cleaned the lamps. I scattered yesterday's tea-leaves over the carpets, then swept them up again with the dust, and put them in the range to burn. My neighbours might have snubbed me for not washing the floor, but I was ever fearful of adding to the damp throughout the property and aggravating Peter's condition, so on my knees I worked only on the worst areas, scrubbing, wiping and drying in one motion. I swept black beetles, spiders and silverfish out of the corners of the kitchen, then I went down to the room where Peter made up his paste, next to the coal-cellar, and pulled some more water from the tap. I scrubbed the pans with sand, and set about cleaning the range, as the laundry dangled on my head from the clothes-horse on the grimy ceiling. Each time I turned my head, a damp trouser leg or shirt sleeve would slap my cheeks, as if a ghost were demanding intimacy with me. A lethargy set in as I toiled, and with it the familiar quiet anger, that this was my life, these were the walls of my existence, and the confines of my hopes.

It was not as if I were a particularly good house-keeper. For all my diligence, the house was never clean enough; I always fell short. My mother had been a veritable army general in the way she kept first our house in Hastings and then our So-ho tenement impeccably clean, but for me, I fear, it was a war I seldom won, and even if I were to wave a white flag of defeat, it would not be white at all, but a dingy grey flag, so no one would understand that I was surrendering. I spent the first years of our marriage waiting for Peter to realise that I did not wear a halo with regard to house-keeping; when he finally became aware of this, I felt continuously guilty for disappointing him so. If we were ever to have tipped one hundred pounds a year we could have considered employing a young maid-of-all-work in her first employ, but every year we never made it. We used to make do with a charwoman once a fortnight who helped with the heavy work and laundry, but now we could not even run to that. It was Peter's highest aspiration; not because he thought to ease the burden on me, but because it would have been proof of a certain gaining of station.

But my mother's favourite instruction to me, which she also taught the little girls in her charge (although never the little boys), was 'whatever it is that you desire, halve it'. Whether it be hopes for cake at tea-time, or a wish for a speedy recovery from an illness, my mother advised that if one halves one's expectations, one will never be quite so disappointed. And so I learnt that a polite little girl only takes half of what she really wants, and learns to settle with that half, and so I did, especially as far as Peter and our way of life in Lambeth were concerned.

My smock, apron, cap, face and arms were all wet and filthy, but it was four o'clock, and Lucinda was waking, so I shook all my dusty, sooty cloths, skirts and aprons into the dust-hole, then carried her downstairs and set her in her chair while I made Peter's meat-tea: eggs and forcemeat balls with potatoes. The wind raged outside, and I dared not leave the lid off the pan for too long for fear of soot being blown down the chimney.

'Are you making soot soup for Papa?' Lucinda said from behind me.

'No, love, I'm making smut stew,' I said, kissing her, and smoothing her hair, which was all ruffled from the bed.

'Yum, yum. And I'd like some black broth.'

'And so you shall have it. Just let's wait until Old Man Wind has blown some more blacks down the chimney, and we'll catch them in our pan and fry them up good and proper.'

But just then, Peter crashed in from the workshop in such a gammon I feared Lucinda would fall fitting. He barked at me, kicked the table leg as if he wished it were my own, and ignored Lucinda huddling in my arms.

'Where is it? We must have one somewhere. What have you done with them, woman?'

'What is it you're looking for?'

'A candle-stub, a candle-stub. Jack has failed to wax the cords of a casing. Again. And I must do it. Again.' Neither he nor I knew at this point that it would be the last one he would ever make; still I ignored the signs.

'Here you are,' I said, 'and here, drink this, before you head back.'

'Wretched stuff. Doesn't work.' But still, he downed it, and went back to his mechanics in the workshop. And he was right. Salicin never seemed to offer his fat old joints the relief that it was reputed to provide.

Where Peter was round, I was sharp: he used to complain that it was like sharing a bed with a carriage-axle. But I was not so much thin as muscular, all sinewy arms and bony shoulders, with no breasts or hips to speak of, and I knew that I lacked femininity because of my muscles. My snub nose and lank hair gave no beauty to my face, only my chin was round and stuck out like a bun put on the wrong side of a cottage-loaf. We were Jack Sprat and his wife, but in reverse. Maybe it was wrong of me to describe Peter's fingers as fat. They weren't fat, just as the pot-belly of a bag-of-bones Fenian isn't fat either, but the opposite: it's the worst sign of hunger, and Peter's fingers were the worst sign of something else, I didn't know what. He was born in the caul, his sister Rosie had told me, and drank his mother dry by the time he was four months old. Her tit gave up on him, and he on her, for she was rather partial to gin, and Peter had been an advocate of the temperate way of life since he could talk. But he could certainly drink water and tea by the gallon. He had already had nine cups of tea today, and would drink another six more before the day was out. Three to every one of Jack's; four to every one of mine. Still, tea wasn't costly, and left me with a fine bunch of leaves to sweep the dust up with each afternoon. Besides, it was his only excess, and I believed all men had to have one. He did not squander our money in the ale-house; I could forgive him his weekly pound of tea.

At half past six I aired Lucinda's nightdress over the fire, then put her to bed, read her a story, and heard her prayers.

'Mama,' she said to me, in that tone of voice which always preceded a difficult question.

'Yes,' I said.

'What if God doesn't look on me tonight, and something bad happens?'

'God always looks down on you, little one.'

'But bad things do happen too.'

'Yes, they do, but maybe they are God's will.' I didn't believe it, but it was said to me, and I said it to her, and she will say it to her children too, and so the conspiracy goes on. Besides, I did not have a better answer.

'But why would He want bad things to happen, if He loves us?'

'Some things He just can't help. But bad things won't happen to you tonight.'

'How do you know?'

'Because I know.'

'Because you won't let them?'

'That's right. I won't let them.'

'But what if a spider comes into my room, and wants to get into my bed?'

'You must tell it to shoo.'

'But what if the spider's mother had told him to tell *me* to shoo?'

'Then you must call me, and I will come and lie down with you, and then the spider will see that I'm bigger than its mother. Now, good night. And sleep well.'

'Good night.'

And as I left her bedroom I thanked the Lord as always that we had lived another whole day together, even if He does let bad things happen.

The clock on the mantel chimed seven as I descended, and I quickly scanned the parlour, which looked very dark tonight. The walls were papered with brown sprigs of flowers; the blue of the round tablecloth on the table was the only source of colour. Four ladder-backed chairs were neatly tucked in to the table, and a Windsor chair and an armchair with fatigued upholstery were turned towards the fire, on top of a faded floral rug. On the wall above the fire was an old print of *The Annunciation*, and below it on the mantel was a black marble clock, with a jar of spills on one side and a box of lucifers on the other. I heard Peter dismiss Jack and Sven through the curtain, so I checked that Peter's slippers were warm by the fire, and his pipe padded with fresh tobacco. I knew that Jack was helping him on with his overcoat, and I could hear the keys outside in the street as Peter locked the external workshop door.

Peter was just now standing and waving Jack and Sven off up Ivy-street, before turning to walk the few steps along the pavement to his own front door. He could, of course, have simply locked the workshop from the inside once his workers had departed, then entered the house through the curtain. He would have stayed warm and dry like that, but then, the good folk of Ivy-street would not have got their twice-daily glimpse of Mr Damage.

On cue, the front door to the house opened, and I was behind it. I relieved him of his coat, then crouched down to change his boots for slippers. I hung his coat and placed his boots by the fire, then pulled his chair out for him at the table and served him his tea without a word. He took off his round spectacles, and ate quickly and without pleasure. Between mouthfuls he lectured me about the arguments being bandied around at the Society for the Representation of Book-binders of South London.

'They laid off twelve men – *twelve men* – today at Remy's, including Frank and Bates. They've taken on twenty women

– or girls, I should say – since Christmas, and they're all staying. It's an outrage, an utter disgrace. And there's Frank with six children to support, and Annie dead of child-bed fever, the Lord bless her, and Bates on his knees, and on the street now, no doubt, with the rest of his family. Twelve men – *twelve men!* – with wives and Lord knows how many hungry mouths to feed.'

He waved his fork at me; a strand of egg twirled around it, splattering yolk in a circle.

'Why women? That's what I ask. They're not strong enough; nay, they are not *straight* enough. Bookbinding requires a linear mind, a firm hand, a sense of direction and rectitude. They cannot apply themselves to one task. They are used to the circular process of housework; an occupation to which there is no *end*.' For all his curves, Peter thought in straight lines. 'To *finish* a job is too great a burden for them. Granted, give them the lower-quality work, granted, give them magazines, if we must, and let them headband, let them mend paper, let them sew, let them fold, and let them even hammer sometimes, but let that be the end of it.'

And then he took another mouthful, and recommenced his talking straight after, all potato and spittle.

'Where's the security? Women are *meantimers*! "I'll get married soon but I'll work in the meantime." If that's not selfish, I don't know what is. And then to work beyond that, with a husband bringing in another wage! And then, even when they have a family! And what do they have? Children neglected by their mother, while the upright man with a dutiful wife and mother to several children struggles to feed them all on his solitary income!'

He swallowed hastily, and followed it down with a glass of water. Then he took another mouthful, but water seeped out at the corners of his lips, so he turned his head to one side, lifted his right shoulder and wiped his mouth across his shirt so he wouldn't have to let go of his knife and fork, and continued talking.

'Their standards are lower. They will sell shoddier work, for less. And their expectations are lower. They charge tuppence an hour! I need a shilling! And I would not *give* away the work which they sell for tuppence! It is inferior; it is not worth any amount!'

He stabbed at another potato with his fork, but it crumbled into floury chunks around the prongs. He tried again.

'Too many machines,' he grumbled. 'Machination equals *fem-in-i-cation*, but that's not to say it adds up. I've promised I'll go to the Society tomorrow to lend a hand.'

And one more failed stab led him to drop his fork, and as he struggled to pick it up again I saw him wince, and then he gave up entirely, rubbed his joints, and stumbled into an awkward silence, and the real reason behind his rage.

For his fingers were now fatter than the cigars he used to smoke at the end of a day's work before he took up the pipe. With his sleeves rolled up I could see the engorgement of his wrists and arms too; I could scarcely make out the joints between them. The urge crept over me to pierce him with a needle from my work-basket, not out of malice, but with just one prick, it seemed, the gallons of water trapped in his tissues would come pouring out and relieve him of his suffering.

It had rained constantly from January to November. Any other bookbinder would have rejoiced, as damp keeps leather moist and pliable. Peter certainly bemoaned the summer before, along with the rest of his trade, when I had to bring in damp towels every hour to drape over the books. It was unusually hot then, but despite the Great Stink it was a joy for us, as Peter's joints were for once at ease. But this year, we had had the wettest summer – and were about to face the coldest winter – we could remember. Peter's rheumatism had always been troublesome and fitted him ill for his chosen trade, but in this relentlessly damp city he had become a human sponge, and the pain was such, I knew, that he wished at times to be washed away in the daily torrents of grey sludge, down the sewers and into the sea, for a kinder end to his life.

I brought him his pipe, and lit it for him, as he drew sharply on it, and then settled myself down with my work-basket on the chair by the fire, and started to darn some stockings. Peter continued to sit at the table, puffing his pipe, and for a while we listened to the soot-saturated rain hammering the roof tiles, and the carriage wheels sluicing over the cobblestones. I pictured the men sloshing outside, heading towards the taverns to find a place around the fire where they could sit and steam, alongside other silent, steaming men, before limping back to lodgings where there was no wife – or an insufficient one – to look after them, no one to ensure they did not tumble in wet clothes into a damp bed. I often thanked my lucky stars not to have married a drinker or a philanderer, but Peter would tell me it was not luck, it was his modern values, and my reasonable house-keeping.

Then he groaned, put his pipe down and rubbed his hands. 'Dora.' He sighed, and I looked up. 'It perturbs me to mention the affairs of men's business within these four walls, and with my wife, but I fear I can keep it from you no longer.' When he spoke, he talked through his nose, as if it were swollen inside too. I put down my needle, and he nodded appreciatively. 'You are a good wife, and you have been of no small help to us in the workshop.' He picked his pipe up again, and winced. 'But we are in trouble.' His eyes searched my face to see how I was receiving him, then dropped to his swollen hands.

I had not expected him to look so downcast. The unkempt grey strands around his crown wisped out in all directions. I decided to let him speak further, then I would go to him and smooth his hair, and kiss his brow if he would let me. For all his aspirations, Peter never looked polished.

'I – I – I . . .' The sounds of wet London grew around us, as if trying to drown out the hideous impropriety of a man about to cry. 'I cannot work any more.' He pulled his chest upwards, and sucked the tears back on a sharp inhalation. His lips were red, wet and full like a baby's, puckering and pouting incongruously amidst his grey whiskers as if he were searching for something that lay just before his face. 'My hands hurt.' He sounded like Lucinda when she had fallen over, only graver.

'Shall I call for Dr Grimshaw?' I proffered. 'Perhaps it is time for you to be bled again, or for your bowels to be opened with a black draught.'

But I did not want to summon Dr Grimshaw with his black bag, his knives and his leeches. I could stare straight into his evil eyes and act as unruffled as a duchess, but inside I would be having palpitations in case Lucinda were to have one of her turns in his presence. Besides, we did not have the money for a night call. Even by daylight it would be two-and-six.

'This is not about my blood or my bowels,' Peter spat angrily. 'I can no longer work. These – these hands – will not let me. I cannot work. I cannot bind books.'

Still I did not understand. 'Jack . . . Sven . . . can't we . . . ?'

Peter batted off their names like flies. 'Don't be absurd. You may think, in your ignorance, that all one needs to bind books is a forwarder, a finisher and someone to sew and fold, but, quite frankly, it would be nothing short of preposterous to leave Damage's in the hands of an apprentice, a journeyman, and a – a – a – a *woman*!'

One thing that could always be said in Peter's favour was that he wore an apron alongside his mechanics.

He lifted himself out of his chair with a grimace, and started slowly to pace the floor. 'They cannot, Dora,' he finally admitted, his voice low. 'We tried today – we have been trying for weeks, in the afternoons, when you are gone – but they have not the skill. Jack has the strength for forwarding, but he is young and green. Sven is almost as fine a finisher as myself, but . . . well, Sven . . . he . . .'

The room felt chilly, and I noticed that the fire was low again. I wondered if Peter would find it rude if I tended to it while he was talking.

'Besides . . .' After a pause, he started speaking again, and his voice was even quieter, '. . . he is leaving us. Sven has seen the writing on the wall. He is too good for me now. He is off to Zaehnsdorf's, for twenty-five shillings a week. I offered him eighteen, and he spat on the floor. Damn that German. He spat on my floor!'

He sucked on his pipe and realised with distaste that it had gone out, so he manoeuvred himself painfully towards the hearth to rescue the spent lucifer from the stone. The fat, round ends of his fingers could scarcely grasp the slender piece of wood; his finger-nails, which might have given him some purchase, were buried deep in his flesh. I crouched down next to him and picked up the lucifer, placed it in the embers, then waited for it to ignite. We transferred it arduously from my fingers to his; I at least had to give him the dignity of lighting his own pipe.

Once it was lit, he could not stand up again. He could not lean on his hands to push himself up, or grasp anything to help him. I stood behind him for several moments, looking at his dishevelled head bobbing up and down, and listening to the puffs and groans. Suddenly my hands decided for me what to do, and did something my head would never have allowed. They slid into his armpits, and dragged him, with one sharp heave, to his feet.

I could not tell who was more surprised; the touch was a shock to us both, but Peter looked more startled by my strength. Perhaps he had never noticed how much I had to carry our long-limbed daughter around, or even that she was no longer a baby. It was as if he did not know that muscles could be made strong through the labours of housework or factory work, muscles that could rise up and crush the languid, unmuscled rulers of their sex. Did they not have to work an

22

eighteen-hour day and more, and tumble into bed at the end of it, too tired even to dream?

'What is to be done?' I ventured, softly, as if I could compensate for the hardness of my body and regain some semblance of femininity.

'What is there to do?' he railed back at me, still reeling from my touch.

Hire another journeyman, I wanted to say, angry at his anger. Is not this the obvious answer? But of course I stayed silent, and returned to the dying fire to draw up some heat into the room, embarrassed at what my hands had just done.

When he next spoke, his voice was solemn. 'We have not many books left to go into leather. We are not getting many more in. The booksellers are losing faith in Damage's Bookbinders. Herzina's won't buy from us. Chancellors have given up on us. Barker & Bobbs likewise won't touch us. Diprose is our only new lead, Charles Diprose. He has a fine line in medical textbooks, anatomies and so forth. There's no point my going to see him now, but I've heard he supports the unions.'

After a pause I said quietly, 'We could move.'

To any sensible person it would not have seemed too outrageous an idea. North towards the river or south towards the factories, it would have been less salubrious, but the drop in our rent would have been substantial. But so too, of course, would have been the drop in our status. Were we to move below the ten-pounds-a-year property threshold, he would lose his right to vote. We were currently paying twenty-five; a reduction of just five or eight pounds would help significantly.

'Preposterous,' was what he hissed back at me. 'Quite preposterous. Must I really trouble myself with instructing you, again, of the evils – the injury to our character and standing – which would be occasioned by such a descent? I beseech you to think beyond the capabilities of your sex and experience, and recognise what would be involved with the loss of our home and our station. It would be failure; it would be unseemly, un – un – un-*man*ly. No, we have a good name, and we must preserve it at all costs!'

But Damage was not a good name, and there was no use pretending it was. 'What's the damage?' some bookseller wag would say when they came to collect their bindings, and would think they were being original. And as for me, the moment I married Mr Damage, I became Damaged Goods. Damage? *Dommage*, my mother the governess said, and I knew now what she meant. Besides, it was never as if Peter seemed particularly anxious to pass his name on. On our wedding night he had led me to the bedroom, where he had prepared a tin bath, and waited outside the door barking instructions at me to scrub myself all over with carbolic soap and baking soda. When he was fully satisfied of my cleanliness, we managed the act during which Lucinda was conceived, but as it drew to a close he fretted that I was having a fit and that I, too, like my grandfather, was a convulsive. We did it twice more after her birth, both times again preluded with carbolic and soda, which may well explain my subsequent aversion to housework. I remember suggesting a third time, some months later, to which he replied in wonder, 'What do you want to be going and doing that for?' as if I had suggested we steal a hot-air balloon and see if we could fly to the moon. It was a wrongful disposition for a respectable wife and mother; I learnt to acquire an appropriate aversion. And if I dared to speak of wanting more children, Peter would silence me, and demand of me why I wanted to bring more children into this terrible world, before answering the question himself. He did not, he would say, desire me to die bringing forth our tenth child, as his poor mother did, leaving him and seven surviving others to be brought up by his long-suffering sister, until she went into service, when it fell not to Peter, Tommy or Arthur, the next in line, but to Rosie, who was only ten, to look after them all. But at least, by then, Peter had been apprenticed to my father's bookbinding establishment, and Arthur had started his ecclesiastical training under the Bishop of Hadley, who lavished favours on his family, which meant that life started to feel kinder to the little Damages.

Peter had been silent for a while. I did not imagine he was still contemplating my blundering suggestion. The truth was that Lambeth had not been what we had hoped for ourselves. We had chosen it with the best of intentions: Peter was apprenticed to my father at his workshop in Carnaby-street, where we lived on the floor above, and we continued to live there until we had to find our own dwellings because of the impending birth of our baby. And then both my parents died: my mother from cholera, which she caught from the notorious water-pump in Broad-street, and my father shortly after from pulmonary disease, although I suspect a broken heart also had something to do with it. I was four months pregnant. We could have stayed in Carnaby-street – we no longer had to leave in search of more space – but Peter was determined to whisk his precious wife and future child to somewhere cleaner. So we chose Lambeth, because its water was supplied by the Southwark and Vauxhall Company, and the pipes went down all the streets, into houses rich and poor, big and small. But the city miasma still wrapped around us here like a bonnet veil, and we might as well still have been in So-ho, for all the paupers and orphans and tollings of the workhouse bell. And we were little better than them; this was all we could afford, and all we were good for. As we traipsed around the Borough looking for somewhere reasonable, in the tiny stretch of salubrity between the river tenements to the north and the slums of Lambeth proper to the south, I clutched the words of William Blake's words to my bosom:

There is a Grain of Sand in Lambeth that Satan cannot find
Nor can his Watch Fiends find it: 'tis translucent & has many
    Angles

But in Blake's days, at Hercules-place, Lambeth was still blessed; for him it was the place of the Lamb. But for me, it was as hard as it was for Satan to find that grain of sand in Lambeth, and Ivy-street, and the protection of Mrs Eeles from the more sordid types, seemed to be the best we could hope for.

Peter still said nothing. Unthinkingly, but as if I were already recognising the need for further frugality, I rose and went over to lower the lamp. The room dimmed, and felt smaller as the flickering shadows from the fire increased. I looked at my husband, who was not looking at me, through the gloom. We spent the rest of the evening listening to the endless patter of rain on cobbles; whoever the gas was lit for that evening on the streets of Lambeth, it was not for us.

Chapter Two

What's in the cupboard?
Says Mr Hubbard.
A knuckle of veal,
Says Mr Beal.
Is that all?
Says Mr Ball.
And enough too,
Says Mr Glue;
And away they all flew.

Neither Sven nor Jack appeared for work the following morning, and Peter went out soon after they were due to arrive. I had hoped he had gone to see that Diprose fellow he had mentioned, the medical books man, but he didn't show up again, not even that night. Truth be told, I was quite grateful, for our food supplies had dwindled, and he was the main consumer. I spent the day increasing my already vigorous household thrift: the paper that I usually kept for twisting into spills, I sold instead to the rag-and-bone man, along with any old bones and scraps of cloth I did not need for dusting. I combined the contents of three biscuit boxes and two jam-bottles and sold them to him too, along with two pewter tankards. I would even have sold our left-over food to his friend the washman for pigswill, but we were eating every last morsel we had. I rushed to the door when I heard the bell ringing and the cry of 'Old clothes!'; it was the Jew with twenty hats piled on his head like the Tower of Pisa. I sold him Peter's summer hat, two of my three bonnets, a blanket and a petticoat, and a pint of dripping. And I scrubbed the house as best I could, and put the cleanest white cloth I could muster on the table that night. It was important to me that when Peter returned he could still have faith in his own fireside. In all the distress and unpredictability of his commercial life, it was here, amongst the household gods, where he would find peace and calm. For this want of work, I knew, would tax us sore, and would test the mettle of a worn man.

I trusted that tomorrow he would return with good news, and that I would not need to trouble him with women's worries, such as the price of groceries, or the state of my pans, or that Mrs Eeles had paid yet another visit just after the rag-and-bone man had left. Besides, I had long struggled to cultivate the air of resourcefulness and industry, cheerfulness and forbearance – I had even taken to serving Peter's bread cold and not quite fresh, to make the butter go further – and I did not want him ever to wonder if his poverty was due to my poor husbandry.

But when he did not return the next day, or night either, I started to think. I traced my hands over everything in the two bedrooms to see what we could lose – we kept the inferior stuff up here, as Peter wanted our social rooms to present our best face to the world. I collected a jug from the washstand in Lucinda's room, a soap-dish from our room, and one of the two toilet cans. We could not spare the chamber-pots, or the tin hip-bath, but I scanned the medical provisions with which we had tried and failed to keep Peter's rheumatism at bay – bandages, flannels, bloodletting ribbon, scissors, lint, spoons – and tucked the empty apothecary's bottles into the jug to give to the rag-and-bone man. But the rooms were bare enough already; there were no pictures to remove from the walls, no rugs of any worth. I knew, as I went downstairs with my haul, that I was choosing to ignore my parents' suitcase that hid in the box-room. I could scarcely remember what it contained, but, apart from the bracelet made of my mother's hair that I kept round my wrist, it was all I had left of them.

But sentiment did not entirely override practicality; I came upstairs again and went to the ottoman at the foot of our bed, and took out the yards of black crêpe. It was the veil that I had worn every day for the six months after my parents died, and it had since lain there for nearly five years. It had gone stiff, coarse and crackly, as if it had rusted all over, as crêpe is wont to do. I took it downstairs, and Lucinda helped me spread it out and inch it slowly over the steam coming off the kettle, and then we sprinkled it all over with alcohol, rolled it up in *The Illustrated London News*, and laid it by the hearth to dry. The next morning, when still there was no Peter, we unrolled it, aired it by the fire, and carried it out into the street.

We knocked on Mrs Eeles's door. She opened it cautiously, as if to check we weren't foxes coming to raid her hen house. 'You've just caught me. Come in, dearies.'

Without her mourning cloak she was formidable: she was wearing a shabby old black lace ball-dress, with sizeable frayed ribbons that picked her hems up in dramatic loops, under which splayed out sections of black gauze petticoats. On her nose were pince-nez eye-glasses, and on her fingers a selection of jet rings.

'Oh my, oh my, what is that you are carrying? Is that really? Could it be? May I have a look?'

We laid the veil out on the faded flowers of her couch. The room was surprisingly colourful for one preoccupied with mortality: the antimacassars were white, with a lavender lace edging; the rug had a deep blue pile, and every surface was covered in knick-knacks and figurines: two prancing china ponies; a trio of crystal owls; a miniature violin; a collection of thimbles; a selection of old silver tea-spoons with bone handles; a stack of prayer-books. There was also a chessboard, laid out ready for battle, which, along with a large number of framed photographs, was the only source of black in the room.

'What have you brought me, dearie?' Mrs Eeles asked.

'Finest crêpe, and I bought it new, too. Only wore it for six months. I was hoping – I was wondering – if this would be of interest to you.'

'Only one mourning?'

'Two actually. Overlapping.' I paused. I had presumed that the less wear the better; it had not occurred to me that successive grievings might have a cumulative effect, that sensations might linger and, indeed, one day, provide some sort of thrill. 'My parents, you know,' I added.

'Oh, you poor little darling. Bless your sweet orphan soul.'

'Would you – would you – consider taking this in lieu of rent?' I asked.

She fingered the crêpe thoughtfully, then bent her head down to it, and sniffed it noisily. 'Two months, I'll give you for it.'

I was so stunned it did not even occur to me to negotiate. 'Oh, thank you! Two months, yes, why, thank you, Mrs Eeles!'

I was still reeling when I heard Lucinda say sweetly, 'Oh, look, Mama, she's sleeping!' The photographs on a round side-table on the other side of the room had caught Lucinda's attention, but I was distracted, as I was wondering if it were too late to insist on three months. I twiddled my mother's hair-bracelet by way of an apology to her: I could never trade this, but would that Mrs Eeles were a pawn-shop, for I might even have got half a crown for it, and the prospect of redeeming it later.

'And this one, look, he's sleeping too!'

'Aye, sleeping cherubs, all of 'em. Look lovely, don't they? Especially seeing as they're gorn! Ye'd never know, would ye?'

'Gone?' Lucinda asked.

'Dead!' Mrs Eeles replied. 'Well, have they done your portrait yet?'

Lucinda shook her head.

'Of course not. Your mammy won't go to that expense until you're twelve or so, stands to reason. But if you passed over before then, she would want a record of you, you'd hope, wouldn't she?'

'Mrs Eeles!'

'Are they your children?' Lucinda continued.

'Lucinda!' I exclaimed. 'That's quite enough!' But, truth be told, it was Mrs Eeles I wanted to scold.

'No, dearie. Never had the luck. They're from my poor dear sister, and some cousins, and some more distant relatives, and a few tenants. All of them my acquaintance, mind. I knew of all of them, by letter or by conversation, otherwise it wouldn't be quite proper, would it now? Look at this one. Blew up on a steamship while her mother was waving him off with a spotted hankie. You should never use a spotted one, brings bad luck.'

'We really will be off now, Mrs Eeles. Thank you, indeed, thank you. Come along now, Lucinda.' I pulled open her front door, and from the top of her doorstep, I noticed she had a fine view directly on to the platform of the Necropolitan Railway, and into the waiting room for the Anglicans, though not the inferior one reserved for Non-Conformists.

'Right-ho, dearies. Thanks for popping by. You're welcome any time, you know. Lovely veil; what a treasure you are. I always knew you were sound, you Damages.'

And so we returned home, and still Peter did not return, and I troubled and feared for his safety. That evening I was starting to know the torture of a mother who cannot feed her own child, as I presented a plate of stale bread and cheese-rinds to Lucinda, who ate them as quickly as if they were apple fritters and custard, and I could only watch her in my emptiness, having peeled the crust off the loaf for myself sixteen hours before. I pretended to her that I was not hungry, that I had an ache in my gut, and that I had a few half-pennies to buy us something better in the morning.

As I put her to bed that night, a distant train left Waterloo station.

'Mama,' she said, in that same ponderous tone of voice that heralded the inscrutable question.

'What is it, darling?'

'A train has just gone past!'

'I know.'

'Mama?'

'Yes?'

'Is it a dead train?'

'Darling, go to sleep.'

'Is it a *dead* train, mama?'

I sighed. 'No, darling. The dead trains don't go at night.'

'But Mama, what if it was a special one, just for tonight?'

'I don't think that would happen.'

'It might do if lots of people died at the same time.'

'Well, yes, it might, but that hasn't happened today.'

'But what if it was a train without a ghost in it?'

'None of the trains have ghosts in them.'

'Just dead people.'

'Yes, and some living ones too. Now you be quiet and . . .'

'But Mama, what if the dead train left the station with the dead body in it, and all the living ones, and the death men, but the spirit got left on the platform?'

'Lucinda love, don't you be worrying yourself about scary things like that.'

'But Mama, what if that *happened*?'

I placed my hand on her chest. 'Hmm, well, now, that would be a tricky one. Let's think. Why would a spirit want to be left behind? Wouldn't it prefer to stay with its body until it got buried, and then it could go to heaven?'

'But Mama, maybe it doesn't like trains. Maybe it thinks trains go too fast.'

'But why would it be worried about that?' It would already

be dead, I wanted to add, so it wouldn't fear dying, but I thought that might be an explanation too far.

'Mama, do ghosts have to get tickets, or just their bodies?'

'I think just their bodies, but the living people have to buy their tickets for them.'

'So, what if the ghost couldn't get its ticket? It wouldn't be allowed on the train!'

'No. But I don't think . . .'

'And Mama, what if the spirit couldn't get on the train, and it didn't know where the train was going, so it couldn't follow it, and what if it came into my room through my window?'

'Now why would it want to do that?'

'Because it's nice in here and it might want cheering up, if it's just died and lost its family and that.'

'But I don't think that's going to happen.'

'But it *might*. And what if it does? Mama, will you come in here at once and show it the way out?'

'At once. I will ask it which wall it came in through, and I will send it back that way, with a map to the cemetery at the end of the line. And now, my love, you must sleep.' I kissed her again, and heard her whisper, 'Good night, Mama,' and I tiptoed out of her room.

The following morning, when there was still no sign of Peter, Lucinda and I went out again. The toes of our boots went in and out of our skirts like pistons, as we scuttled across the wet cobblestones, hunched and downcast against the rain. First we took stuff to Huggitty the hawker to sell. He was the type of dealer who supplied whatever he could get his hands on, and I had bought the piano from him a few pennies at a time. In our courting days, Peter would surprise me with the latest sheet-music, which he had bound up especially for me, and he would say that only lower-class parlours did not have a piano. Out of concern for his dignity, and for Lucinda's pleasure, I endeavoured to keep it. Instead we took to Huggitty the spoils from the bedroom, a *découpaged* umbrella stand, the embroidered antimacassars, the black marble mantel clock, and one of my two nice dresses. I even presented him with a description of the contents of the bookbinding work-shop, but although Huggitty was cruel and unscrupulous, and told me I was 'a proper jewel', even if I were to have found a hawker with more scruples, I knew that the antiquated frames, tools and presses were worth nothing, not since book-sellers expected one to have guillotines and sewing machines and whatnot nowadays.

We left Huggity's and steeled ourselves against the smells coming from the bakery next door, with the consolation that we knew he cut his flour worse than any of the bakers in Lambeth. And then through the drizzle to our next port of call – toes going in and out under our hems – which was the butcher's, Sam Battye. He let me put a sign in his window, advertising my services as a piano teacher, as I could not afford the rates of the *Lambeth Local Gazette*.

In and out, in and out, and I would watch our toes as if they were the only things I could depend on in life, although occasionally I would lift my head, and flick my eyes around for signs of Peter amongst the crowds, down the alley-ways, or slumped in door-ways. In and out in and out, a regular beat to counteract the gnawing of our stomachs and the fret-ting of the endless rain. I tried to distract myself by wondering what it must feel like to have one of those crinolines holding my skirts out, so nothing would be brushing past my legs. I shouldn't like that, I remember thinking, for my legs would have been colder than they already were. I'll keep my horsehair petticoat, I thought. Then I realised that I *could* indeed keep my horsehair petticoat, even if I had one of those crinolines, and wear it underneath to keep me warm, and it would have soaked up the splashes from the puddles, and no one would ever have known.

And finally all that remained for us was to head to the sign of the three golden balls and into the dingy interior of the pawn-shop, next to the gin-shop (as they always were), where we huddled in a cubicle and waited our turn to be served.

'You gave me eight bob for the gown last Friday! What d'ya mean only seven today? You know I'll be back Monday, I'm good as gold I am. What's it to ya?'

And we saw the broker shaking his head, and mouthing 'seven' to the woman with no hair and a black eye.

'But what about our Sunday dinner? Think of that! Or are you not a godly man?'

And then in lurched a man with a mouth full of broken teeth, who put two pairs of tiny little shoes on the counter, pocketed two shillings, and lumbered out again and into the gin-shop next door. Then in came another one, who took off his coat, his belt, and the very boots he was standing in, and watched as they were wrapped into a bundle and ticketed, and I could not help but stare as he hobbled away, his toes poking through the ends of his threadbare socks, holding up his trousers with one hand, and clutching his pennies in the other, and into the gin-shop he went too.

'He forgot to give me his handkerchief,' the broker said as he came to serve us. 'He'll be back later.' I shuddered to think what else he might be offered: the man no doubt would prefer to go home naked but with a bellyful of beer, if only the pawnbroker would accept his smalls and all.

'What we got 'ere then?' He whistled through the gap in his teeth as I laid out two solid-silver spoons boxed in red velvet, a silver-plated vase, a pair of pearl earrings, and a small, inlaid walnut music-box. He bit the pearls with his teeth, fingered the spoons and held them to the light, brought out a magnifying glass to the hallmarks, and checked the mechanism of the music-box.

'Ten shillings,' he said.

I gasped. 'For these? They're worth far more! I need at least a pound!'

He was unaffected by my outburst; he continued to look at the counter, for whatever I was saying, he'd heard it all before. 'The less you get, the less it costs you to get them back,' he said philosophically.

And so I pocketed ten shillings, which was better than nothing, and indeed my purse so chinked with coins that I pulled Lucinda into the better sort of baker's-shop and told her to choose whatever she fancied. She picked an apricot slice and a doughnut. I bought nothing for myself, but licked the sugar off my fingers once I'd handed her the sweets. I tried to fathom the extent of our debts, so I might know how much I dared spend on tonight's meal, but I feared the plumb line of my mind might fall short of the true depths of our penury. In and out more slowly now our toes went over the cobbles, dodging the dung and the rotten fruit as we rounded the corner past the Royal Victorian Theatre and into New Cut. I eyed the knife-grinders and tinkers, and the gypsy chair-menders sitting on their wicker-bundles in the rain like roosting fowl, and I wondered at their ability to forge a living out of nothing, and whether it would come to that for me. We picked our way amongst the stalls of shoddy clothes, shoes and hardware, solicited the kindest-looking costermongers, and picked up some stewed eels, a pound of potatoes, half a dozen eggs, some butter and the like.

We returned home with our victuals, which Lucinda unpacked while I set about scraping the empty coal cellar for something to rekindle the fire. But straightways there was a knock at the door, and whoever was there did not wait for me to come and open it, for the door snapped into the room and nearly caught me in the face, and a tall man with grey sunken eyes and a bristly chin set himself to pacing round the parlour sniffing at my furniture like a rangy dog looking for somewhere to spray.

'Mrs Damage? Weally, a pleasure. It's you who'll be owin' us, then. Wo' you got?'

'I beg your pardon? Who are you?'

'Now I be beggin' *yewer* pardon. Skinner's the name.'

'Mr Skinner.' I had heard that name before, but I could not remember where. 'And you are?'

'Acquain'ance of yer 'usband's. We've been, ah, workin' togevver, of sorts. 'E owes me. So you owe me nah.'

'Why? What's happened to him?'

'I'll let 'im tell ya that. But if ya want 'im back you gotta pay up. So I say agin, wo' ya got?' And then I remembered. Skinner was the most feared money-lender south of the river.

'Have you kidnapped him?'

'Naaa-ow. Dahn't be so silly.'

'I'm not paying you a penny until I speak to Peter.'

'So ya got some, then?'

'I'm not saying that.'

'Well, you better 'ad. Cos I can waise a bill o' sale on this place tomowwa,' he sneered, 'but fwom what I can see, there ain't enough tat in 'ere to make it worth the auctioneer's fees.'

'What does he owe?'

'Fifty pahnd plus sixty per cent in'rest.'

'Fifty! And sixty! He would never have signed to those terms! Why, he could have got a bank loan at seven per cent!'

'It's all here, in 'is own 'and. Wanna wead it?'

'No, I do not. I shall take you to the magistrate.' I started towards my shawl, gliding cautiously so that the coins in the purse at my waist would make not a chink and betray their presence.

'Aa-aww, is that how you treat a chawitable man?'

'Charitable! Why, you, you bully! You're nothing but a crook, and a brute!' I wrapped my shawl around my shoulders.

'No, not me, Miss. I'm a vewitable philanthwopist. Ask anyone up this stweet. Anyone who's been in any way

37

embawwassed. Like yer old man was. Go on, look, here's 'is own note of 'and.'

And I scanned the grubby paper he was holding, and read that a bill for fifty pounds was to be discounted, to be taken up quarterly in increments, with increasing interest, and saw the lawyer's seal, and the terms laid out, and Peter's signature at the bottom.

'This is my vocation, miss. I became a money-lender aht o' the goodness o' me 'eart. Sammy Skinner, Good Samawi'an, at yewer service. Come nah, I'm a lot prettier than the tallyman who'll be comin' in to give ya a good dunnin' if ya don't pay me.'

'Well, I'm sorry to disappoint you, Mr Skinner, but I don't have any money to give you. You will have to deal with my husband when he returns. You *will* let him return, I trust? He won't be able to pay you if he can't work, so it's in your best interests to let him go.'

'Do me a favour, Miss, and pay me nah.'

'I said, I have no money.'

'Forgive me laughin', miss,' he said, almost peacefully, 'but we both knows yewer tellin' little porky pies. I can 'ear it,' he whispered, 'chinkin' away, under yer skirts. Are you tellin' me I don't know the sahnd of money when I hear it? Wouldn't be a good money-lender if I didn't, nah, would I?'

I stood still, and looked at him in horror, and felt Lucinda looking up at us both.

'Come on, then,' he cooed, like a hungry man trying to get a chicken from a dog's mouth. 'Give it up. There's a good girl.' I put my hand to where my purse hung at my hip beneath my skirt, but did not put it inside. 'Come on, girl. Or do I have to go in there an' get it for ya?'

And so my hand slipped inside my skirts, and I untied the ribbon securing it, and made to tip the contents into my hand, when I saw Skinner shake his head.

'Just give it to me. None a' this cahntin'-aht nonsense. I

need it all.' And with that, he snatched it out of my hand, tipped its meagre innards out, flung the empty purse on the floor, and then he was gone, and with him my eight shillings.

I think it was fair to say that now, after the visitation from Samuel Skinner, having been too proud to ask for support, I had reached the point where desperation overcame pride. So the next morning, one of those awful ones when the water had frozen overnight in the pans, I left Lucinda with Agatha Marrow for as long as I dared, where I knew at least her stomach would be filled, and then in and out, in and out, my toes first took me back to the pawnbroker.

I waited in the booth while the man attended to a poor fellow whose face betrayed more misery than I dared to imagine. He handed over a blanket with a look of such sorrow it were like he were giving away a child, and took away a shilling for it. I wanted to run after him and check he had at least one more blanket left at home, but it would have served no other purpose than to make myself feel better in the face of his tragedy, and I feared the answer would have been no besides.

'My flat-iron, how much?' I asked as the door closed behind me.

'Four pence.'

'Four? But with the ha'penny gone to get me over the bridge that leaves me with next to nothing! I need at least sixpence!'

Still the man shook his head. 'Then you'll have to give me something else.'

'But I only want sixpence! Surely you can do a flat-iron for that?'

'I have twenty flat-irons back there,' he said, waving his hand at the storerooms behind him. 'All of 'em got four pence, nothing more. Here you go, here's a thrupp'ny bit and a brown.'

'But I need a tanner!'

'So, what else you got?'

'Nothing on me.'

'What about that ring?' He gestured towards my finger.

'No! I can't! That's my wedding ring!'

The man shrugged and turned away. I thought about going home, to get my own blanket, or one of Peter's waistcoats, which might raise nine pence, but I needed to get north of the river this morning, and I feared further delay would condemn me forever to the pile reserved for prevaricators and no-hopers.

'Please don't go! Help me! Raise me sixpence for the iron, and I'll bring it all back, I promise.'

'Not a hope, miss. I've heard it all before. Give me the ring, an' I'll give you what I think. If you redeem it soon enough, the old man might never know.'

And so I took off my wedding ring and handed it over. I looked down at the clammy white dented band it left behind on my skin, and waited for him to deliver his verdict.

'Three shillings.'

'You evil man! It's worth at least a crown! Do you spit on my husband's name?'

'Which is?' he asked, raising a pen.

'Damage,' I said meekly. 'Peter Damage, two Ivy-street, Lambeth,' as he filled out the ticket and handed me over the three silver coins.

Then in and out, in and out, my toes took me north across the marshes where the mud-larks – the tide-waiters, the beach-pickers, whatever name you want to give them – were wading over the shallows of the Thames in the rain for fragments of iron and wood, their children swimming alongside them waist-deep in mud, toes searching for lumps of coal and what-have-you dropped by the barges, to sell for one shilling per hundredweight. I scanned them for signs of Jack's family, and indeed, for Jack, for the Lord knew how else he might be spending his days and earning his living while he was not at

Damage's. And then I approached Waterloo Bridge, and gave a 'Good day' and a shilling to the toll-keeper. I waited for my eleven pence-ha'penny change and the clicking of the turnstile, then went through onto the bridge.

And then it was that I needed the in and out, in and out of my frozen toes more than ever to carry me forward. Once through the toll-gate, the hansom cabs picked up speed as if to make up for lost time, and I felt that if I lost the momentum of my pace I would be whipped over the side by one of them, or by the vicious wind itself, and over I would go to my icy, smelly doom. But I knew even as I thought it, that I would catch the sides on my way over and cling on. That would have been me, there, hanging on to the rim, all my remaining strength going into keeping myself hanging there. I could have stopped myself falling further, but I could not have found the strength to pull myself back over into safety. And besides, even if I could have, it would only have brought me back into the path of a cab, or another gust of wind.

The fog was dreadful on the bridge; it did not hang like a brown pall, but flurried and swirled in a fast-moving current, as if the bubbling brown Thames beneath us were a fantasy compared to the raging course of the fog-river through which we had to wade. Not for nothing was this called the Bridge of Sighs. I could hear through the wind the howls of lives spent along with their ha'pennies; the world looked so bleak from here that I would have bet my eleven pence-ha'penny on there being very few prospective suicides who had paid their toll and then asked for a refund, having changed their minds in the centre of the bridge. From up here, it was not possible to tell how much worse down there would be.

Then in and out, in and out to the city itself, where I hoped to find assistance; I would not call it charity.

First I visited the Institute for the Restitution of Fallen Women, where I waited in line for two hours with nothing

41

in my stomach to hold me up, but my fall being not a moral one, they had no time for me.

Next I went to the Guild of Distressed Gentlewomen, but, as I was not a widow, and lacked a whole cartload of children to support, my distress counted for nothing.

More hopeful was the Society for the Promotion of the Employment of Women, who told me I had the skills to become a fine governess, and so I could have been, had they not shuddered at my suggestion that my daughter attend me while I worked. But there was no other way: she would undoubtedly fall into convulsions at the prospect of long absences from me with only her invalid father for care. The harshest claws of poverty scratched like a mere kitten compared to that.

The rain started on my way back to Lambeth. In and out, in and out, I picked up my skirts so they would not wick up the water from the puddles, and wrapped my shawl tighter around me. In and out, in and out, I passed the heavy gates of the St Saviour Poorhouse, and my toes went in and out quicker than ever to carry me far from its reaches. More than an absent mother off playing the governess, the workhouse would have meant certain death for Lucinda.

I finally reached Remy & Randolph, the most advanced bookbinders in London, where the guard told me with a yawn that I would earn eight shillings – eight shillings! – for a fifty-four hour week as a paper-folder if I could bring a reference. 'They prefer girls to women, in 'ere, as girls are cheaper,' he warned my departing back.

I remember leaving the gates of Remy & Randolph as the lamplighters started their rounds, and I was fretting about all sorts: that Lucinda might have had a turn in my absence; that Peter might never return; that I had no choice but to find that old suitcase of my parents' in the box-room, and sell it, or at least pawn it, which might bring us enough money to last another two days. The evening chill was setting in, and

I scrunched my toes in my boots to squeeze out the cold from them. I walked like this down New Cut, past the two hundred costermongers, the vagabonds loitering in gin-shop door-ways, the five-year-old urchins collecting horse-droppings for the Bermondsey tanneries, in and out, in and out.

The rain had picked up even more, and my damp clothes quickly became saturated. The wool of my shawl was sodden, and my skirts were drenched by water hurled up from the cobbles by passing carriages. Soon, wool, flannel and horse-hair were all soaking, and I stank of wet animal. I remember trying to wrap my cloak tighter around me, and my hand failing to grasp one side of the flabby fabric, and as I clutched for it in the bitter wind I found my knees giving way, and I sank down on to the pavement, skirts billowing around me like a deflating hot-air balloon. My legs had nothing left in them to carry out my orders, not even the thought of Lucinda at Agatha Marrow's. My nose was streaming, but I had not the strength to move my arms to release my handkerchief from my cuff. I bowed my head so that my bonnet would disguise me from the scurrying swell of folk about me.

'Here's a pretty pickle,' an old voice croaked behind me. I dipped my head further into the chafing wet of my collar, and sank closer to the ground. 'Come, lovely. Down on your luck? There's a sorry story to hear, I'll warrant.'

I could see a pair of once-smart, heavily scuffed brown boots, and the hem of a brown tweed greatcoat. Then a gloved hand came down to mine, but I could not take it.

'Come with me,' the man said, his voice softer now. I wondered if he was one of those gentlefolk from the missions, who collect paupers from the pavements and throw them into church shelters for the night, only serving to delay for a few hours their inevitable demise in an icy puddle of gin and worse.

'Where do you live?' he asked, and the words formed on my lips, but it felt as if frost was spread there like a glass

43

cobweb, and would not let them out. Ivy-street, I wanted to say, by the Necropolitan Railway. Not far yonder, I can walk there. But he did not hear me.

Ivy-street. It might not have been one of the golden avenues around Lambeth Palace, or as smart as Vauxhall and Kennington, but neither was it one of the crumbling rows of tenements butting on to the river, or the slums of Southwark and Bermondsey. It was not as holy as Lambeth Palace to the south-west, nor was it as mad as Bedlam to the south. It was in a tenuous position, poised between two fates, just like me at that point. 'Ivy-street,' I finally managed to say.

But the man clearly didn't know where that was, for he said, 'Come now. Follow me, and there shall be some small salvation in it for you, I'll warrant. I know a place that's fine and warm . . .' I let him pull me to my feet, and when I wobbled for a moment, he grasped my waist through my cloak, and steadied me. Some keys jangled at his belt; I shuddered as the thought crossed my mind that he was Relieving Officer for the Poorhouse.

'. . . and better suited than the gutter for a fine-looking woman like yourself.' I dug my frozen fingers up my sleeve to find my handkerchief, but it was not there. 'Here, take mine.' I raised my hand to take the white cloth from him, but he had already started to wipe my nose with it, like a mother to a child. He was kindly, though, even if he were from That Place.

'Now, are you ready to walk?' He proffered his arm, but still I did not take it. I moved my right foot, and tried to transfer my weight on to it. I could walk, I was sure of it.

'Come, dear.' We set off walking together, side by side but not arm in arm, although I was grateful for his presence. We came to the end of the street and I raised my hand to bid him farewell and thank him for his assistance, for it was clear that I was going one way and he another.

'No, no, no, Mistress Pretty. I believe we have a misunderstanding. It is this way, comfier than the street and . . .' here he dropped his voice, '. . . cosier too.' His yellow eyes stared into mine, and he pulled his face so close that I could see the wax shining on the tips of his moustache. Beneath it, his dry mouth broke into a vile smile.

'So, what's it to be, you mischievous sow?' As he spoke, the clouds of air used by his words hung between us, as if I were to read from them the choice he was spelling out to me. 'So, what's it to be, then? Workhouse, or whorehouse?'

Chapter Three

Baby and I
Were baked in a pie,
The gravy was wonderful hot.
We had nothing to pay
To the baker that day
And so we crept out of the pot.

I'd have been lying if I'd said I didn't consider his proposal. I had often wondered how perilous life had to get before a woman would go to the bad, and now I knew. For it was not the word 'whorehouse' but the word 'workhouse' that sent a dart of power to my legs, and I stepped rashly into the street, into the path of a lurching omnibus, and hurled myself to the other side of it. The traffic was not heavy, but created enough of a slow-rolling barrier between us to prevent him following me. He stood at the side of the road and bellowed over the din, 'My money not good enough for you, eh? It'll be the workhouse for you, you whore! The workhouse, you ungrateful trollop!'

But I feared that his money *was* good enough for me. How hard could it really be, I wondered, to let this man lead me to his greasy bed and open my legs to him? I pondered it all the way back to Ivy-street, past Granby-street, which was notorious for its night-ladies. I did not turn in to Ivy-street, nor Granby-street neither, mind, but continued beyond, to the slums towards the river. No, I was not thinking yet of plying that trade. But I knew that there was no coal in the cellar, and no old log basket left to crumble into kindling, and I skulked along the shadowy streets where the tenements leered so far towards the centre that they almost met overhead. I met a woman in a door-way with a pinched face, eyes sunken and dead like coal, and, to my shame, I begged her for some wood. I could see from the rabble in her house that she was one of those who, at this time of year, actually become grateful to be living fifteen to a room, for the little warmth they could give each other.

I wondered if she ever let men take her for money. Not that I judged her to be a whore, but I wanted to ask someone who might know what it was like, how much to charge, how not to hate it, nor hate them, nor hate oneself, so.

She looked me over and said not a word, before going back inside. She must have read my mind, and I had offended her. I heard her growl something at a child; she was Irish. The little boy ran out of the house and past my legs, completely barefoot, his legs beneath his rags grey as a corpse. I began to turn to leave, but the woman grunted at me, and there was something in the sound that bade me stay. The scamp soon returned with a couple of thick sticks and a few lumps of coal, which he handed to me, staring at me directly with his dark, soulful eyes. There was a time when I wouldn't have touched a wretch like that even with fire-tongs. I found out then that sometimes it is the most miserable who are the quickest to help someone else in a similarly pitiable state.

I returned with my gifts to our little house, and pushed open the door, so I could ignite the home's warm heart and bring Lucinda safely back into it. In the gloomy darkness I could make out a shape on the rug in front of the cold hearth, and I could hear panting, punctuated with shrieks, like a monkey dancing to an organ-grinder.

'Who's there?' I said cautiously. 'Who is it?' I kept my foot in the door, despite the rush of icy air, in case I needed to escape. The shape fell silent. Then it started to heave and sob, and in the heart-rending sounds of misery I recognised Peter's tones. I let the door bang shut, dropped my meagre bundles, and sank on to the rug next to him, my hand on his back. He flinched, and scrambled to the corner like a chased animal, gibbering. But there were words amongst the incoherence.

'Hub- hub- hub- . . . Roo- roo- roo- Hub- . . .'

I followed him into the corner and crouched down, ensuring I was lower than him and looked up to him, and smiled encouragement.

'A – sp – a –, a – sp – a –, a – sp – a . . .'

I reached for his hands in order to hold them at chest-height as a kind of prayer of communication, but the moment I touched them he drew back and hollered in pain. But I had briefly felt the rage in his fingers, and feared for where he had been. It had not been drier than his home.

'Where have you been, my love? Tell me.'

'A – sp – a –, a – sp – a –, a – sp – a . . .'

'A spa? A spot?' I tried.

'A – sp – a – n –, a – span . . .' he continued. 'A sponge –'

'A sponge!' I seized upon the word, and he nodded, then shook his head, which added to my consternation. 'A sponge?' Did he want one? Was I to mop his brow? His face looked black in the gloom; I moved myself to allow the lamplight from outside to shine on him, and saw that it was bruised, swollen, and matted with blood both fresh and dried.

'I'm going to get a flannel from the press,' I told him slowly, but his protests mounted, and he continued repeating the word 'sponge' so I stayed by him, and tried to fathom his request. Eventually he sighed heavily and let his head drop to his chest, and so it went, and nothing was revealed, so I settled him into the Windsor chair and went into the kitchen. I let the draught into the range to draw up the heat, then went back to the parlour to lay the fire in the grate, before running upstairs to get a flannel, and returning to the kitchen to boil some water.

Then I cleaned his face as best I could as he winced and groaned, and I applied some salve.

'Here, love, drink some tea. You can tell me all later.' I poured him a cup and placed it into his beleaguered hands, then left for Agatha Marrow's house.

Lucinda was already asleep on a chaise amongst the piles of laundry and I picked her up and started to carry her home. Agatha said not a word, nor even smiled at me, but she laid a paper bundle on Lucinda's sleeping stomach, and held the door open for us to leave. Back home, I nestled Lucinda into her bed and felt a warm patch on her dress where the parcel had been. Inside the paper were four steaming cheese-and-parsley scones; it was as much as I could do to stop myself crying out and devouring them all there and then, but I scuttled down the stairs and presented them to Peter, who was still struggling to lift the cup to his lips. I broke a scone into pieces, and placed them into his dry mouth, trying not to let the errant crumbs straying from the corners down his shirt trouble me in their profligacy. I restrained my hunger until he had finished, and then I fell upon my own scone, and when it was gone I ran a licked finger around the paper to collect every last crumb, and thought about starting on those lingering on Peter's chest. I folded the other two up in a towel and put them in the dresser for Lucinda in the morning. It felt strange to be a recipient of such alms, but I was glad all the way down to my frozen feet.

'I was rooled,' Peter murmured finally, his mouth clagged with scone. 'Rooled up. In the sponging-house. Blades and Old Skinner had me done. Skinner skinned me. Got himself an arrest warrant for a shilling, threw me in the sponging-house. Blades too.'

Lucinda was turning in her bed upstairs.

'I only pledged twenty-five pounds. But the paper says fifty. It's got my signature on. And we agreed five per cent. Not – not –'

'How much?' I dared ask.

'Thirty per cent,' he lied.

'They charge what they please, don't they, those folk,' I said, numbly. Sixty, I wanted to scream. I saw it, Peter. Sixty!

But he proffered nothing further. There was nothing left in his voice, nothing left in him. He had become a veritable Dombey.

'How long have we got?' I eventually said.

'A week.'

'Will the bailiffs come?'

'If Mrs Eeles doesn't distrain it all first. We must – should we – can we bolt the moon?' For the respectable Peter Damage even to suggest this was a sorry sign of how far he had sunk.

I shook my head. 'No need, Peter. I've taken care of her. The rent's been paid for two months, love. Don't you worry there.'

'How?' He looked up at me in shock.

'I'll tell you another time.'

In bed that night I could not rest, despite my wearying day. I was hungry and faint, and sick for more food; my limbs were restless, and my sleep enervated. My dreams were haunted with spectres of my daughter, my husband and my father hovering around my mother's death-bed, but who was dead and who alive I could not tell, for all were grey with terror and privation, and all cried at me to save them.

My mother, Georgina Brice, died on 14 September 1854, twelve days after she went down with the cholera. She weakened quickly; her liveliness poured out of her with every filling of the chamber-pot. Everything about her was dry: her skin flaked under my touch, her mouth cracked not only at the corners but inside, at the roof, under the tongue. No matter how much clean water she drank, nothing would quench her. Soon she stopped passing water: she could not even cry tears, although she knew she was dying, and her face sometimes creased and heaved up and down, as if she were weeping dry.

The doctors said to give her salt, and more salt, to keep the water in her tissues, but it was too late, and I might as well have been embalming her for all the salt I shovelled into her. The fishy smell of cholera pervaded the house and the streets around the contaminated water pump in Broad-street. Even now, when I walk past the fishmongers' stalls, I am reminded of those dreadful days of death in our little tenement north of the river. Would that we had never left Hastings in search of the heart of the book trade.

She would ask me to sponge her face with water, then leave the sponge on her lips so she could suck it. But she was too weak, and the water just pooled in her mouth and dribbled down her chin. I was nineteen, and about to become a mother myself, but I was not ready to lose her, even though there are millions of wretches out there who lose their mothers as they draw their very first breaths, or in their tenderest years. I wiped her chin and neck, and I could see from her pallor that she was leaving, and that she did not know me any more. She opened her eyes wide one last time and stared at me, and she did not cry. She could not, the doctor told me, even if she had wanted to. She died like that, with her eyes open; her eyeballs had so dried out that it took me twenty minutes to close the lids, using my own tears as lubrication. Her body was not cold as marble, as the saying goes; rather, it was like petrified wood, so ravaged was her desiccated skin. As I washed her all over before dressing her, my tears dripped onto her and mingled with the water, and so great were the outpourings of my grief it was as if I needed not have brought the pail up. But tears are futile, and could do nothing for her dry old body, and so ashamed was I of my excess that I have not cried a single tear since.

Early the next morning, stiff-limbed, I picked the fire over for cinders to stoke up the range, and drew water into the kettle. As I set the breakfast things I ran my hands over the table, the chair backs, the piano. The knock at the door would surely come soon, and we would stand by stoically, relinquishing everything to the bailiffs, or the brokers, and be left standing in a bare little house. Where would Lucinda sleep, and how would Peter eat breakfast?

Yet it was a rare moment, for I felt a peculiar sense of freedom at the thought, as if furniture was merely tiresome and its removal a blessing, and I knew then what I had to do. Perhaps the answer had been inside me all along, but it took the prospect of release from my trappings for me to notice it.

So in and out my toes went again that morning, only this time the hem under which they went was edged with a slightly worn but still fine green ribbon, which contrasted with the pale floral cambric. I married Peter in this dress; it was the only decent dress I had kept from Huggitty, as if I knew I would need to look proper again one day, and it had a matching bonnet that caught the worst of the drizzle. I had left a note, assuring Peter I would not be gone long, but I did not state my destination. With luck Lucinda might not even wake before I returned.

I paid my ha'penny and scurried over Waterloo Bridge once more. It was still dark. I did not look over at Lambeth Marshes, but kept my eyes on my worn leather boots lined with *The Illustrated London News*, going in and out beneath my green hem. How hopeful the colour seemed, how fresh and springlike. I was such the innocent.

Occasionally I would glimpse the steamboats puffing underneath me, crowded with clerks on their way to Essex Street Pier, or Blackfriars Bridge Pier, or St Paul's Wharf, or Old Shades Pier by London Bridge, where they would disgorge their sombre-suited cargo. The air was oily on my skin: the breath of London.

The lamplighters were doing their rounds with their ladders, turning off the stopcocks at each lamp-post, and the pavements were already full of tradesmen, footmen, clerks, all wrapped up in thick cloaks. A few women were amongst them: maidservants in couples, wives tottering next to their tradesman husbands, the odd gentlewomen mantled and veiled to obscurity, with maids in tow. All were in pairs; I felt conspicuous on my own. I was stared at with impunity, especially by the men. Women are experts at the cross-gaze; why do men have to look directly? Was I overdressed in my finest, or not smart enough? Did I look like a lady's maid who had done away with her lady, or a prostitute, even? For, unaccompanied, I became a public woman, a term I used to reserve for those whose coquettish walks, kiss-me-quick ringlets, and slightly-too-trim trimmings sought to be noticed, and paid for. Oh, for an escort on to whose arm I could cling, to allay my fellow street-goers' curiosity and render me invisible.

Straight up Wellington-street I went, with studied nonchalance and directness of purpose, past Somerset House on my right and Duchy Wharf down to my left, and all the way up to the top where the road was bisected by the Strand. Then I turned right, trembling but determined, and increasingly immune to the gaze of men. I was crossing paths with journalists and hacks from *The Illustrated London News*, which had its headquarters hereabouts, and doctors from King's College, which I was just now passing. Through the shoppers I went, the gentlemen on fast business, the trolleys, crinolines, crossing-sweepers, hawkers, urchins, wheel-barrows, all weaving in and out of the irate, tedious crawl of carriages, cabs and buses. The noise was deafening: the iron-shod wooden wheels of the carriages rattling over the cobbles, the drivers of the omnibuses shouting their destinations, the thwarted haste of the red newspaper express, and at last I was anonymous, irrelevant, obliterated in the thickness of the crowds.

Soon I reached the church of St Mary-le-Strand, which marked the junction with Holywell-street. The traffic was at a complete standstill here, for the Strand branched into two strandlets, one of which was the narrow, dark Elizabethan lane of Holywell-street and its tortuous mesh of alley-ways, where I was headed. I could not see above the suited backs of the crowds ahead of me, so I raised my eyes heavenwards, to the overhanging tenements, the lofty gables and deep bay windows, under which hung wooden shop signs and figures, including a large carved half-moon which betrayed the mercery past of the street. The old lath-and-plaster houses huddled and skulked just like the people below, deprived of light and air but rich in dirt and disease.

At one junction with a fetid alley-way leading off into an unwelcoming labyrinth, I had to wait at a lamp-post to let people past. A notice was glued to it announcing the imminent demolition of Holywell-street and a blessed proposal of a new, straight thoroughfare to blast through the meandering pestilence and decay of this metropolitan anachronism, and bring order and circulation to the unregulated, crumbling relics of a bygone age. A gap appeared in the crowd, but before I started to move on again, I noted the sign was dated 'July '52'. It was the first sign I had of quite how tenacious Holywell-street was, how long it would hold out against the city-planners' drive for light, air and hygiene for all, how it determinedly clung to its own filth.

At another pause in my journey, I spotted a small grey plaque marking the site of a holy well, which once provided succour for pilgrims bound for Canterbury, its curative water giving them a taste of the holy wonders to await them at their destination and in the next world. As I inhaled the stale air I thought ruefully of my mother's death, and I fingered her hair-bracelet.

The signs intrigued me: 'Shampooing – Hats Ironed – Shaving – Books'; 'Boot Depot – Books – Sole Entrance'; 'Hawkers – Suppliers to the Trade', 'Removed Opposite', 'Punch – Almanacks – School Books', 'St Clements Stores Merchant – Books'; 'French American Spanish LETTERS';

'Bears' grease, freshly killed', and I shrieked as I came face to face with a very subdued bear – a real, live, breathing, hairy bear with a dry tongue – chained miserably to the railings outside the barber's, as if he knew he would be next.

Soon the crowds started to thin, and eventually I no longer needed to look up, but could scan across, into the windows. But straightways I wished I hadn't, for the first shop window stopped me directly in my tracks. Despite myself and my own feminine cross-glance, I looked directly through the small panes of glass of the narrow shop window, where the cobwebs were lit by gas-light, and the shop beyond lay gloomy and nefarious. Waiting for my perusal were lithographs, mezzotints, daguerreotypes, call them what you will, but their subject matter was plain: a girl greeted the morning sun in nothing more than her crinoline and chemise; another young lady laughed while gaily ironing an indeterminate item of clothing which she no doubt would presently put on; another made lemonade in such a manner that it was necessary to display her ankles; another shucked oysters with bare arms; ballerinas stretched their limbs along with their morals. I pulled away from the window, flushed, and saw a gentleman with yellow whiskers smiling at me, at my betrayal of interest, my forthright and shameless looking. My mother would have wept.

I stumbled on, averting my gaze and checking the card in my hand with purpose. I had taken it from the workshop this morning, and it read:

Mr Charles Diprose, 128 Holywell-st, London.
Purveyor to the Professions –
Importer of French and Dutch Specialities –
Books Bought.

Fortunately the subsequent windows between that print shop and Mr Diprose's establishment were less compelling: stacks of old and new books, prints of city streets and rural idylls, medical and scientific pamphlets, periodicals and broadsheets, second-hand clothes, old furniture. Many of these, like the print shop, I could not avoid, but now for more physical reasons: the shops tumbled forth their wares on to the pavement, and I had to step around crates of old books and dodge the swaying lines of old clothes.

I finally spotted the sign 'Diprose & Co.' swinging on its hinges underneath a small carved wooden figure of a negro sucking on a long pipe, wearing a wavy grass skirt and matching wavy gold crown, a gaslight directly beside it. I was at a loss to tell what it represented, but was relieved to see in the windows no arresting engravings. It was a smart but small shopfront, with a bright brass bell, on which I rang. It was quickly answered by a young man who enquired after my business.

'I should like to talk to Mr Charles Diprose, please,' I said sweetly.

'On what matter?' he asked, with a wobble of his head and a swagger not unlike mirth in his voice. Like Jack, he was a red-head, but his was that insipid washed-out orange colour one finds at the tips of a newly picked carrot, not the rich woody-coppery tones on Jack's bony skull, and his curled lips and the freckles stippling his skin were of the same pallid hue as his hair.

I was not prepared for interrogation at this stage. I had steeled myself for the actual encounter with Mr Diprose, and had not expected to fall before even offering my hand. I stuttered and stammered the words Damages – bookbinders – husband – business – Mr Diprose – at which the grinning assistant pulled back the bolts, delighting in my discomfort.

'He is out, but he will return presently. You may wait.' He ushered me in to the stuffy room, where two men were being served. I hesitated at the sight of them, but the assistant gestured to a chair in the corner on which I seated myself. The men raised their hats to me, exchanged a glance with each other, then returned to the books on the counter.

'But these are . . .' the man paused to look back at me, as he chose his words carefully, '*artistic* anatomy books.' I squinted and was able to make out the gold-tooling on the spines: John Rubens Smith's *A Key to the Art of Drawing the Human Figure*, and Pieter Camper's *Works on the Connexion Between the Science of Anatomy and the Arts of Drawing, Painting, and Statuary*. We had previously bound copies of both in the workshop when money was tight and expediency temporarily superior to principles, though of course Peter had never let me peruse them; I knew they were unseemly.

'The Camper is a fine edition,' the shop-keeper argued. 'A reprint of the 1794 English translation from the Dutch.'

'But I require *medical* anatomy.'

'Ah, *medical* anatomy, of course. I have several copies of Quain's, and a splendid edition of the Gray's, quite the modern thing. Or if Aristotle and his *chef-d'œuvre* would be more to your liking . . .'

'Young man . . . Have you no sense of . . . I have never . . . ! Good day!'

And thus the two men turned to leave, raising their hats to me again, as another gentleman appeared hurriedly from within the shop behind the brown curtain. He was a paunchy, round-shouldered man with a purple face and black beard. Both his skin and hair were shiny, and his silk hat greasy; even his sombre black frock coat seemed damp. I would have said he was trying to be a gentleman, and knew enough of them to have influence on him.

'Who were they, and why did they leave?' he said, in clipped, hushed tones as he removed his hat.

'Proper ones,' mouthed the assistant.

Just then, the purple and black man caught sight of me. He half-turned to the assistant, while continuing to look at me, as if trying to ascertain my station and purpose there, and what response of his would be appropriate.

'This is Mrs – Mrs – ah . . . Damson? Damsel?' said the assistant.

'Mrs Damage,' I said.

'Mrs Damage?' the gentleman repeated, more warmly, but still with reservation. 'Mrs Peter Damage?' I nodded. 'Mrs Damage,' he said again. 'Charles Diprose.' He took my hand, and kissed it. If I had been a lady, and wearing gloves, I would still have been able to feel through the kid that his hands were clammy. The kiss left a trail on my skin like a snail. He gestured to his assistant to bolt the door.

'I have not had the pleasure of meeting your husband, but I know of his work, and his contribution to the unions. *Il se porte bien*?'

He must have assumed my delay in replying was due to my not understanding French, rather than my uncertainty as to how to answer, so he asked, 'Is he in good health?'

'Passing good, sir,' I finally said. 'Yes, sir.' The assistant was standing by the window, peering out into the street, as if keeping watch.

'And his apprentice, Jack. How fares he?'

'Passing well, sir, yes, sir. Jack is a fine apprentice.'

'And of course, Sven Ulrich.'

'Yes, indeed.'

'I hear he is no longer with you. Hard to keep, the Germans. They are so very precise, such fine craftsmen. One cannot keep them without paying the price.'

I looked at him but found no answer; my jaw was slack with horror. What else did he know? What had he heard from others in the trade? Of course they all talked to each other; they all knew each other's business. He must have known how rude and surly Peter Damage had become; how no one wanted to work with him any more; how his standards of work had deteriorated and that he was no longer fit to call himself a Master Binder; that he was facing bankruptcy, and poverty.

'So, your business here?'

'Peter – Mr Damage – sent me.' Regardless of what this man knew of our circumstances, I had to try, at least. 'He would have come himself but, well, he's been laid up with a hurt leg and cannot walk. He has given me his full consent for coming here; nay, it was his very suggestion. His hands are fine, though, you see. He can still get the books up.'

Diprose was smiling at me. I had to keep going. I thought that he vaguely resembled William IV, although not so much that one might accord him any more than a modicum of respect.

'I couldn't help noticing, sir, that a few weeks ago you sent your card to my husband, but I fear you received no reply.' His smile didn't flicker. 'At least, I assume you received no reply. It's our errand boy, see, proved difficult and, frankly, unreliable, and . . . Well, whatever your purpose was with the card, he would like to help. If it's work you're wanting us – him – to do, he still can.'

Diprose pulled a chair up, and sat down. I noticed he had some difficulty bending at the waist, so he eased his trunk down to the point at which his knees would bend no more, then toppled backwards into the chair, with a grunt. He folded his arms, and said nothing, but gestured to me to continue.

'Is it work? Or, or maybe it's nothing any more.' I was uneasy now, and could not stop my mouth from overworking. 'Pardon my troubling you, sir, it's just that, he doesn't like to ignore his customers, and seeks to provide a tip-top service to booksellers and libraries and purveyors, who furnish him with, with . . .'

Diprose held his hand up, and turned his head stiffly away, while holding my gaze with his eyes. I bit my lip as I watched him gesture to the assistant, who leant over to receive a whisper in his ear before disappearing behind the counter into the back room. Mr Diprose was still looking at me, arms folded. Unnerved, my eyes flitted across the wood panels and display-shelves, as if they would help me know what to do next. I smoothed my skirts, and had just about decided to stand up and slip away into the anonymity of the London streets, when the assistant returned with a fat manila envelope.

He handed it to Diprose, who gave it directly to me. It was surprisingly heavy. I looked down at it on my lap, then back up at him, and then down again.

'A Bible,' he said.

'A Bible? I thought you did medical books.'

'We *do* all sorts of books in here, Mrs Damage,' he said, mocking me. He had his head on one side, as if he were trying to measure me. 'Do you know Sir Jocelyn Knightley?' I shook my head. 'I mean, do you know *of* him? Have you not read, in the papers, of his triumphant sojourn amongst the tribes of Southern Africa? *Ma chère*, he is an eminent physician: *un peu* scholar; *un peu* scientist; *un peu* adventurer. His dramatic exploits on the dark continent have caught the attention not only of the scientific community, but also of the Church. The Bishop of Reading, no less, has proposed the establishment of a mission amongst these savages. Which is why Sir Jocelyn has commissioned from us a new manuscript, printed first in Latin, then scribed *à la main* in the local tongue, to present to the Bishop, in honour of his support. Tell Mr Damage to give me something simple, classic. Shall we say, a representation of God's bounty in tropical climes. He has three weeks.'

'Thank you. Yes, sir.'

Diprose clutched the arms of his chair and leaned forward as if he were about to rise, but his body stayed firmly on the seat of the chair. I thought he was again having difficulties with the manoeuvre, in reverse. But he opened his eyes wide at me, as if to engage me in his actions; I realised he was expecting me to stand up first, so he could too.

But still I sat. 'Sir. I am unfamiliar with the usual procedures involved, but . . . In order to pay for the best materials for the commission . . . Would you perhaps see yourself towards advancing Mr Damage a small sum?'

'*Je vous demande pardon?*'

The man was no more French than I was; my audacity grew in direct proportion to his persistence in a tongue he believed I did not understand.

'You must pay him first.' Was that my mouth from which those words escaped? I did not like the man, but I desperately needed his custom. I could feel something clamour in me like a workhouse bell, and I struggled not to reveal my desperation. 'Three weeks is a long time before payment.' I felt my cheeks flush. 'I presume the Bishop will require the finest morocco, and substantial gold-work.'

He did not release his grip on the arms of the chair. 'Most peculiar,' he said. 'It is not our practice to advance. It does not tally with our book-keeping.' He kept looking at me, but said to his assistant, 'Pizzy, I believe the tree up which we were barking is most definitely the wrong one.' He reached out for the envelope. 'Madam, we have made a mistake with your husband. I bid you farewell, before I waste another minute of your time.'

Had I handed the envelope back to him straightways, the future of my family might have been very different. But, as I continued to clutch it to my bosom, needing a moment's pause to gather my thoughts, he seemed to revise his attitudes, for he waved his hand towards a box of paper I had not noticed, in the corner behind my chair.

'Finest Dutch, surplus to my requirements. Take it, and tell Mr Damage to use it as he will. I will always buy blank volumes. There is a fine market for ladies' commonplace books, pocket-books, journals, albums, *que voulez-vous*. I'm sure there are countless other ways to describe a sheaf of papers bound daintily and prettily according to the fancy of *les femmes*.' He nodded at me knowingly. 'Mr Damage should be able to knock a few of those up in less than a week. I shall pay him on receipt.'

Pizzy the assistant blew the dust off the top of the box, and picked it up, then he turned to me, and paused.

'Ah.' He seemed unsure of whether he could hand me the box. Perhaps it would have been deemed improper, too heavy, too inappropriate. I would have none of it; those were my papers, my ticket out of the insolvency courts. I took the box from him, and bade the gentlemen good day.

'*Au plaisir de vous revoir, Madame,*' Mr Diprose said, bowing.

The box was indeed heavy, as I found before I even reached Waterloo Bridge. The drizzle was flecking my face, causing the blacks settling on my bonnet to dribble on to my ears and streak down my neck. It was not yet ten o'clock, but the world was out in force. It felt as if I were going the wrong way over Waterloo Bridge as I weaved my way through the relentless wall of tradesmen. There were butcher boys in blue-and-white striped aprons, with brown hunks of meat oozing beneath the black-spotted wax paper on trays carried on their shoulders. There were baker boys too, their wares more appealing, wafting sweet smells across the odours of horse-dung and sewer construction. Even the milkmaids, in their white smocks, with covered pails swinging from the yokes like extra pairs of strange arms, were heading north, as if they were all fleeing Lambeth, their course determinedly set by the north star, towards Westminster and the City, where people and pickings were richer, and they only returned when they were empty-handed. With my box of Dutch filling my hands, I couldn't help but feel I was going the wrong way.

I pushed the door open with my foot, and placed the box down just inside the door. A sense of peace pervaded me; I was home.

'Where have you been?' Peter's voice thundered with more force than I had expected, given his state only yesterday. 'Where?'

'I – I –' I stood up straight and flexed my fingers, to iron out the stiff red and white creases.

'Where?'

'I will explain . . . I was going to explain . . .'

'Explain? Explain what? Explain how a mother can leave her house, her husband, her child? With no *prior* explanation? How dare you? Do you know what you have done – to me, to her?' With that, he pointed to the heap on the rug by the empty fire; it was Lucinda, with a blanket cast over her. The blood fled my frozen cheeks.

'What's happened to her? Tell me.' But his words had to follow me as I flew to her side. She was sleeping. But I knew – as only a mother can, before even taking in the set of her face, the colour of her lips, the grip of her fists – that she had had a fit in my absence.

'How do you expect me to cope with – with – *that*?' Peter spat. 'How was *I* supposed to know what to do? How could you expect me to step into the breach left by her – her *mother*? How could you do this to me?'

'How did it happen? How did she fare?' I wanted to know everything; if it had come on slowly, or if she had woken and fussed to find I was gone, and if he had attempted to soothe her, or if he had taken leave of his senses first, giving her no bedrock of stability; an infection, as it were, of ill-temper.

Peter did not seem to hear me, or perhaps the questions – being, as they were, about someone other than himself – were too hard for him. 'You – you – you irresponsible harlot,' he raved. His eyes were crazed and delirious, yet he did not frighten me; I felt distanced from him, as if I were watching a lunatic through a window. I turned back to Lucinda. My heart was pounding, but I knew she was safe now, and the danger had passed. It only served to confirm to me the importance of my presence; however I was to earn a living and support this family through this difficult time, it had to be with Lucinda by my side. It gave me the courage of my convictions for the task of persuasion I had ahead of me.

'There, now,' I said to Peter. 'I'm back where I belong. I won't be going anywhere again, I promise.' It was as if I were crooning into Lucinda's ear, not a grown man's. But beneath his livid exterior was relief that I had returned.

I went into the kitchen to draw up the range, and to make up a little bed in front of it for Lucinda. We were, I could tell, going to have to start living out of one room for warmth, like the poor unfortunates who had no choice but so to do. When I came back into the parlour, I found Peter fingering a piece of Dutch paper as if it were a leaf of gold.

'What is this?' He was too awed to be enraged.

'Handmade Dutch, heavyweight, ivory, with an interesting watermark, that I haven't examined properly yet but it appears to be the letters L, G and . . .'

'I will ignore your insolence. I repeat, what is this? What is it for? How did you come by it?'

The time had come. 'I have a suggestion, Peter. Just a small one, which has arisen out of the inspiring example you give to me daily as you toil on our behalf. I was wondering, and was hoping you would agree, that –'

He stood up, and held the paper up to the light to examine the watermark.

'– under your jurisdiction –' I continued.

'Linen fibre, too,' he muttered to himself.

'– you would let me assist you in the workshop.'

He turned to me. 'I beg your pardon. Did you say something?'

'Yes, Peter.' I was not going to gabble like I did with Diprose. 'Do you not think that together – by which I mean, you leading me – we are capable of continuing to work the shop?'

Peter snorted. 'We shall do no such thing.' I took the paper from him; he was about to launch into his opinion, and we could not afford to lose even one piece of paper. I laid it back in the box. Peter's mouth seemed to be grabbing at air, as his mind formed his words. 'I shall not have you adding to the many vulgar examples of your sex who steal from honest workers and their poor families, and who threaten the very structure of family life upon which England became great.'

'But Peter, I will only be, as it were, your hands, instructed by your brain, and the commands from your mouth.'

'You! You – will be *my* hands? When you have *quite* returned from the leave you have evidently taken of your senses, you will understand the absurdity of assuming that these little hands of yours are capable of lifting a hammer, let alone landing it accurately and with due force. The absurdity of assuming that you have the capability to learn what it takes seven years to teach an apprentice, and a lifetime to perfect! Or the discernment to know which approach should be best taken for the range of bookbinding problems that are brought to me daily, or to determine a noble from a shoddy binding, or to ensure that margins are straight, spines curved, lettering precise, backs strong. Do you understand? Hm? Do you?'

'Yes,' I answered. 'No.'

'What brain fever afflicts you, child? What troubles you so, that you dare to degrade my house so? Today you have visited a man, with no other escort than your own conscience. My reputation, I presume, you cast to the pigs.'

'Must you ask? Peter, you are sick. Peter, we have no money. Peter, we are cold and hungry, and the bailiffs will be knocking in six days. Six days. We have a box of fine paper and an African Bible. Shall we burn them for heat, or shall we make something out of them?'

He chose not to hear me. He seemed to be addressing the print of *The Annunciation* on the wall beyond me. 'You delicate creature,' he said, with a feeble smile. 'You – you are too good for manual labour, too precious for the arts. Let us pity those poor women who are forced to make their own way in the world and earn their own keep, when they should be husbanding the wages of their menfolk.' His eyes were starting to glaze. 'Let us praise your dependent existence, and work to your strengths, that of embellishing the house and cheering the heart of your husband. Think of our loss of character.' Here the light came back into his eyes, and he turned to sear them onto me. 'Think of how they'll talk of us! "There's the man who wasn't enough of a man to keep his woman." "There's the woman who wears the trousers beneath those skirts." Think of it, Dora. It would be worse than hanging, or, or transportation, even! Think of it, Dora! Have you anything to say to that?'

And so he gave me the perfect opportunity to hang him with his own argument.

'Indeed, Peter. What if I, truly, went out to make my own way in the world at large? Here you are right, for they would point, and say, there goes the shame of Peter Damage, as I walk to the factory or the market or my mistress's mansion. Him who's in prison for debt. Him who lost his house and let his wife and child go to the poor. But this way, Peter, won't it be best? You are sick. I am offering you a solution that saves your face. We can bring Jack back into the fold. He's indentured to us; he's breaking the law now by not being here. And you will tell us – you will tell us always – what we are and are not to do. I will not be your brain, but I will be your hands, your arms, your muscles too, for the Lord knows I have them. I have sat in bookbinder's workshops all my life listening to every instruction first my father and now you breathe upon your mechanics, and I have heard them all. And if you don't help me, why, Jack and I shall muddle through this ourselves! How hard can it be?'

I could not tell how he was receiving me. He seemed to be holding his breath. His face was red, but through anger or shame I did not know, and I feared what might issue forth from his pursed lips and his clenched fists. But I had to continue.

'So, are you happy for books to leave this establishment with your name on them, but in which you have had no part, and let them flutter amongst the Strand and Westminster showing everyone your prowess? With you or without you, I am binding books. From tomorrow morning, Damage's Bookbinders is open for business. So, Peter, let us keep this within these four walls. Let us keep the name of Damage strong. Let us allay our public shame. And use me to do that. Try me. Try me, for we have no other choice. Try me, and if we fail, we fail.' My, I realised, here I was becoming a veritable Lady Macbeth. 'But screw your courage –' Did I dare continue? Peter would never recognise the quotation, and I had no other words of my own to use '– to the sticking-place and we'll not fail.'

But like Lady Macbeth, was I leading my lord into an evil trap? Was I unsexing myself, or worse, him? I looked over at him and was surprised to feel only scorn. He had already unsexed himself. He was impotent. And we had nothing to lose.

'Well, I never did see such a manner,' he said, on a vicious exhalation, 'from the likes of a wife.' He pulled on his coat and scarf, and placed his hat on his head. He tried to squeeze his hands into his gloves, but the pain was too great and he gave up, casting them onto the floor with a disdainful look, and stuffed his hands instead into his pockets. I watched him go over to the front door.

I had failed. I wondered to which devil he was going, to which money-lender, den of crooks, whorehouse, or even drinking-house, in his rage. At least he had not struck me. The thought crossed my mind that the door would slam behind him and that I would never see him again.

'Where are you going?' I asked croakily, and raised my hand as if in farewell.

He turned to me surlily, one eye-brow cocked. 'To the river, my silly wife,' he said, 'to find out which gutter Jack's lying in.'

Chapter Four

Hush thee, my babby,
Lie still with thy daddy,
Thy mammy has gone to the mill,
To grind thee some wheat
To make thee some meat,
Oh, my dear babby, lie still.

We had enough paper to make two albums – one quarto and one octavo – and two duodecimo, two sextodecimo, two vigesimo-quarto and two trigesimo-segundo notebooks, and several smaller frippery books for young ladies to write their secrets in. And still we would have sheets left over. But rich in paper as we were, we were paupers in leather: we had little more than half a sheet of morocco, which would never cover ten albums of varying sizes. The Bible, of course, would have to be full-leather, but we knew without conferring that we would have to wait until we had been paid for the volumes before we even considered its binding.

'Could we bind them in half leather?' I suggested. It would have been a jigsaw-puzzle of a task, to cut ten spines and forty corners from the half-sheet we had, but by eye it did not look impossible.

'Certainly not. We cannot use cloth over paper of such quality. Don't be ridiculous. Besides, I need Jack here to help; it is monstrous to presume you and I can proceed without him. This is all quite, quite ridiculous.'

Jack had not been in his house; Peter had barked at Lizzie,

his long-suffering mother, who had simply shrugged her shoulders and offered him tea, which he refused because it would have been made with pestilential river water, and gin, which he refused on principle.

'What is the world coming to?' he raged when he returned. 'Where is the respect for age, and experience, and professionalism? She should have begged and pleaded with me not to report Jack to the magistrates for rupture of indenture. I was surprised, Dora, nay, I was angered, at her insolence. He is our charge and our apprentice, and he is in serious breach of contract.'

I chewed my lip as I looked down at the half-sheet of morocco, trying to solve both the problems that were presenting themselves. I wondered if it might be best for me to take the trip to Jack's house and speak to Lizzie myself. The nuances in her speech and manner might have betrayed something to me to which Peter had been oblivious.

But just then I heard Lucinda calling from the house, so I left Peter in the workshop alone and scooped her up in my arms. She sang me a little song, and started to plait my hair, and I drifted round the house holding her and pondering how to overcome the first hitch in my master plan – that we did not have enough leather. I ran my hands over the books in the case by the fire as if the touch of those bindings would inspire me, but their old leather gave little away. We had a good collection of books, and there was not one I had not read cover to cover several times. They were all ragged now, for when she was smaller Lucinda used to occupy herself with pulling them out of their shelves and heaping them on the floor. The casualties of childhood delight were sorely in need of a re-bind, but none of the editions were special enough to merit the effort. We had a Bible and *Pilgrim's Progress*, and several volumes of poetry, and it was here that my hands lingered, as if I were looking for a few lines, a cheering couplet, that would provide succour or inspiration. William Blake, of course. Keats. Wordsworth. But my hands did not pull one out at random; neither did the pages fall open at some words into which I might have read some meaning. We left the books behind, and we climbed the stairs to fold and press the laundry together.

But Wordsworth came with us in spirit, for as I smoothed the shabby sheets and checked for damp patches, I remembered reading somewhere how his sister Dorothy would cut up her old gowns, and use them to bind the early volumes of his poetry. I had never seen one, but I could imagine the pretty faded floral fabric enfolding his pretty floral poems with the colours of Grasmere, and protecting them with a woman's love. But without the genius of William's writings within, Dorothy's dresses would not have been worthy enough of gracing a gentlewoman's writing-desk as required by Mr Diprose. We needed something finer. But still the notion persisted, and I remembered too a tale of royal libraries, of the magnificent bindings manufactured from Charles I's own waistcoat collection. But I had no regal waistcoats to hand or to spare in my linen press. I only had my one fine dress – my Sunday dress, my wedding dress – which I had worn the day before and which was still muddy and drying in the kitchen.

And then I remembered my parents' suitcase in the box-room. Dared I see what was inside? From what was I hiding? I pulled it out, laid it on the bed, and opened it.

On top were a few keepsakes: a gold ring the size of a shilling tooled on to a scrap of red morocco; a piece of folded card decorated with pressed violets and clover leaves, which contained within two locks of pale yellow hair, which was not mine, but of the sickly twin brothers I had never met; a pair of worn-out boots with lop-sided tongues and split edges, which were too small for me to bother mending. I pulled open the tops and traced my fingers around the insides where my mother's ankles had once been. I wondered how much I could get in the pawn-shop for them, and if she would have minded.

Underneath them all was a dress, laid up in lavender. It was nothing special, but it was silk, and a most excellent, strong silk at that, which had scarcely worn at the elbows and where the sash rubbed, despite the fact that it was over forty years old. It had been given to my mother by the lady of the house where she was governess, who had never worn it. It was markedly of the fashions of the twenties, and my mother had tried in vain to update it to suit first her, and then me. I had worn it twice, on the summer evenings when Peter took me to Cremorne and the Vauxhall Pleasure Gardens, and always felt clumsy and outdated in it, but I loved the way it felt against my skin, and the colours – a plain, cornflower blue, with a yellow silk underskirt – were charming.

I knew immediately that it would do. I wondered why I had not thought of selling it to the Jew, or Huggity, or even taking it north to the clothes traders off the Strand, but I was grateful to the guiding heavens that I had not. Its purpose was now more than as a dress to a gentlewoman or a poor unfashionable bookseller's betrothed. This was not a dress whose time was over. It was several books whose life had only just begun.

Lucinda helped me unpick every seam with care, and we reserved the thin strips of cream lace around the cuffs and neckline. Even the tiny triangles of silk from the darts around the bust and waist I saved, thinking I could use them for appliqué. I only had to discard a square panel from the back of the skirts, where there was an indelible grass stain.

Then Lucinda and I teased out whatever coloured threads we could find from my workbasket, chatting, and laughing even. Over the years I had kept the remnants of every head-band I had ever sewn, and like any good housewife I had a variety of colours and textures, silks, cottons and linens. The pinks, golds and creams I laid on top of the blue silk; by that evening they had become embroidered flowers. The silver purl I laid on top of the yellow silk; this found its way to being plaited and stitched on in elegant curls. Also in the suitcase was a patterned twill that was interesting enough of itself, and could be transformed into a handsome desk book, striped with the delicate burgundy leather off-cuts – the ones pared off from spines and edges that would be considered too thin to use – which I would learn to chase and *répoussé* with a simple scroll design, running from the raised bands of the back to within a half-inch of the fore-edge. I even cut up a cushion, which, once I had discarded the shabby trimmings, would become a purple velvet album, embroidered with gold thread and coloured silks in a rose and thistle design, with ornate gilt corner pieces, and pale pink ribbon ties.

Lucinda and I brought them back to Peter in the workshop, and watched his face carefully as he fingered through them, and laid them out with care.

'It is just as well you have found these. I have come to the conclusion that the journals must all be half-leather, and you have done well to find the material for the front and back faces,' Peter said solemnly. 'Furthermore, we must continue without Jack. I fear we have no choice.'

Lucinda clapped her hands. 'We have worked hard, Papa! It was fun!' I smoothed her hair and kissed her; I too was relishing the prospect of the next phase of work.

First Lucinda and I folded and rubbed the papers with polished bone while Peter soaked his hands in Epsom Salts, and then I worked out the various stitches that would be required for each type of book. Peter had always been happy for me to do this: he asked my opinion on everything from tacketing to tape-slotting, kettle-stitches to meeting-guards, whether thongs should be raised or recessed, the difference between oversewing and overcasting, and which thread would work with which paper.

'May I go and play in the street, Mama?'

'Of course you may. Thank you for your help, you useful

girl. I shall be in here if you need me.' I rigged up the old sewing-frame, and started to sew the various sections together and on to the main cords for the books.

So recently thrown into the pits of peril, I was at last starting to feel sunshine on my face as I laboured in our own cause. My carpet-needle wove in and out between the pages of the sections and the vertical cords of the frame, and through its regularity I tried to convince myself that we were back in the old days when money was less of a worry, and that when I had finished sewing, there would be only a minor amendment to our usual practice, which was that I would be doing Jack's work instead of Jack, and Peter's work instead of Peter.

Despite a short break at midday to prepare lunch for Peter and Lucinda, I had sewn all the books and albums by one o'clock. I stood by the chair where Peter was dozing under his newspaper.

'I'm ready for the forwarding, if you wish,' I said. Then I went back into the workshop, punched the holes and prepared the vellum thongs for the tacketing. Soon he was by my side, scanning the assorted piles of naked pages.

'But we cannot use any of these. It would be a waste of finest Dutch! Have we not some inferior paper upon which I can instruct you? This is going to be difficult, if you have not even the brain to determine something so fundamental.'

'We could disband an old volume of ours. The *Pilgrim's Progress*, or the Scott?'

'Possibly. You are thinking, at least.'

'Or . . .' I started rummaging in the scraps drawer. '. . . here, would this do?' I held up an old set of papers, yellowed at the corners and torn here and there, but soundly sewn, approximately two hundred pages thick, uncut and unploughed.

'I asked you to make that years ago, didn't I? I believe I instructed Jack on it,' he said wistfully. 'It will do, but it needs re-hammering first.'

And so we began. I took Jack's leather apron and wrapped it over my pale blue work smock. I heated up some glue as Peter laid out the leather and marked out on it ten shapes of varying sizes.

'We are in luck, for once, in this sorry situation. There is just about enough left over to use on your mockery of a journal. So we shall have one trial run, before starting the serious matter.'

Once the glue was liquid, I painted a thick coat into the back and stippled it between the sections, cut the strings a couple of inches above and below, and started to round, groove, and back the book. But it was harder than I had anticipated, and Peter was not forthcoming with assistance. He simply asked, as I hammered unevenly, 'Did you ask Diprose how he likes his spines?'

I shook my head.

'Idiot,' he said. 'What if he's one of those dreadfully fashionable flat-spine men? Let me see what you've done. Move it over here. Now turn it over.' He stayed silent for a while, the air hissing between his teeth, which he clenched whenever he was concentrating.

'Not quite a third-of-a-circle, but not flat at least. The first rule. Never over-round your spines. And why? Why?'

'Because . . .' I looked up into the corner of the window frame as if I could read the answer there. 'The spine won't be sufficiently flexible. The margins will be reduced by the extreme curvature. If forced beyond its capability the spine may spring up in the centre of the pages like a ledger. This could strain the sewing.' I may not have been the student, but I had attended the lessons, which was little solace when it came to struggling with the clamps of the press, cutting the millboards with an unwieldy saw, and making holes with a bradawl. When I pared the leather, my hand shook, and although I will not exalt the paring knife by claiming it had a mind of its own, it certainly did not wish to follow the instructions of my mind, and the resultant scrap was pitted and uneven, too thin here and not thin enough there.

'Peter, please, I am failing.'

'Indeed,' came his reply.

And so I took the grass-stained section of the skirt, and cut it to size, and smoothed it over the front and back boards, and then rounded the leather onto the spine and the joins, and smoothed and rounded and smoothed and rounded, but still it was lumpy, and a shocking revelation to me of my inadequacy for our plan. I was angry at Peter's refusal to help: could it really have been more important to him to confirm that I, as a woman, was unfit for such work, than to extricate us from the trap of debt?

My troublings were interrupted by the rattling of the external door to the workshop, followed by a pounding, then a voice.

'Mr Damage. It's me. Mr Damage. It's Jack. Please –'

Peter strode to the door, but he could not grasp the key between his bloated fingers. I unlocked the door for him, but hid behind it as I opened it so that Mr Damage's full worth could fill the vacating space and greet the street.

'I'm sorry for my leave, Mr Damage. Please –'

'Hush your excuses, boy,' Peter bellowed. 'Get in here. Stop making your fuss so public. Have you no courtesy?'

I closed the door behind Jack, and turned the key in the lock again.

'I'm sorry, Mr Damage,' Jack started up once more. He certainly looked as if he had had a rough time. His eyes were dark and sunken, and his hair was so lank and greasy it hardly looked red any more.

'Sorry?' Peter's voice had calmed, which was possibly worse. Jack glanced over to the old birch cane in the umbrella stand, on the receiving end of which he had been too many times. I winced at the thought, and knew I would have to excuse myself before the walloping began. But Peter simply said, 'No need to be sorry. A month's wages is apology enough.'

Jack gasped, and looked with horror from Peter to me, and back again. He had only been gone eight days. I should say something, I thought. I must defend the poor lad. But I had already taken all the power I dared from Peter. I was not boss of the workshop yet. I stayed silent, coward that I was.

'A month's wages from the lad whose inefficiency has sorely cost my business. You'd better scrub your face and pull up your socks, my boy, because of the trouble you've caused. Never let it be said that Damage's isn't good to you, giving you a second chance and helping you mend your ways.' Peter headed towards the curtain into the house. 'I'm going to mix up some more paste, and when I'm back I want you to make it clear you're grateful, boy. It's not often a master will take back a scrap who's lost him so much respect in the trade.'

Jack hung his head, but one eye peered up at me beneath his curls, before scanning his bench for the work I'd been doing. We shared a small smile. I loved Jack, almost in the way I loved Lucinda. He wasn't much younger than me, really, but he seemed like a child still. He never seemed interested in girls, never had a sweetheart. He would have had a handsome face, really, if it had only had a bit more meat on it. Poor little scrap, I couldn't help thinking. He was too fine for the slums; he was like a skeletal silver birch, which glows even in mid-winter, when all the rest of the trees look like dead twigs.

I handed him his apron, which he took from me without a word, then he ran his finger over the hinge I had been making on the book in the press.

'What's this, Mrs D? You tryin' to do my job?' he said.

'Needs must, Master Jack. What do you think?'

He wrinkled his nose. 'It's not the best I've seen.'

'No, me neither,' I rued. 'I'm glad you're back. I need to concentrate on the finishing, if we're to make a go of things.'

'Well, I'll see if I can't sort out the mess you've made, so you can at least use the spine to practise yer toolin' on.'

'Thank you Jack,' I whispered, as Peter returned with the paste. 'It's good to have a friend in here.'

By nightfall a row of blank books of various sizes waited on the benches, drying out, and we were still on the bottom rung of the ladder down to the poorhouse, but at least no lower. We knew we were racing against time, and the knock at the door of the bailiffs, the debt-collectors, or the police, for whatever was in the house at the time of their arrival would legitimately be theirs. Even Mrs Eeles was within her rights to claim her back rent by distraining everything we owned; she would then have a mere five days to take it to the broker.

But I was determined that nobody would get their hands on my beautiful albums, nobody except Charles Diprose and his clientele. Peter could go to prison first, I found myself thinking, before they would interfere with our work. That night, and every night after, before I went to sleep, I took the books up carefully, one by one, and laid them out on a board under our bed, until they were ready to take to my Mr Diprose.

The morning I was due to deliver them, the mud had finally dried on the skirts of my floral dress; I brushed the crusts off into the garden, and then sponged the remaining patches where the dirt was ingrained. On my return today they would be just as filthy, but I could not arrive at Mr Diprose's with them already in such a state.

I wished I could have done the same with my hands, which were wrinkled, stained, red-raw, and clearly betrayed the fact that I had been working. A pair of gloves would have hid them from Diprose, but I had not even a cotton pair. The family for whom my mother was governess used to say that if one cannot afford kid gloves one should not wear gloves at all. They were right, in a way, gloves being a menace to clean and costly to replace, so one should not wear them if one is the type of woman who has to do even the smallest bit of dirty work, but today I would have settled for cotton. I would never look like a lady, besides, kid gloves or no: I had no waist or hips to speak of, my arms were more built up than Jack's, and I'd never seen a society lady with my snub nose, my grey eyes, my brittle hair. And so my cold, chapped hands, red with work and yellow with pressure, were clear for all to see as I carried the box of books back to Mr Diprose.

'Well, well, Mrs Damage. What a delight it is to see you.' Pizzy greeted me at the door, and relieved me of the box. Diprose came through from the back room.

'I presume by this return visit that Peter's foot is still ailing him?' he said, and he and Pizzy shared a smile that excluded me. I cannot say how long we chit-chatted, for all I remember was the moment I was asked to open the box and reveal its contents, and Charles Diprose's first, 'very nice', followed by an, 'I'm impressed'. And I could see at last that the books were indeed very nice, and impressive. Possibly I had known it all along; but his verdict allowed me to believe it. Similarly, I cannot remember how much he paid me for the books, but it felt like both a king's ransom and an insult to a pauper. Simply to have earned the smallest amount of money in those days was a great achievement, and yet reminded me of how much more we needed in order to harbour in a safe place. I was pleased, and proud, and scared, all at once.

When I left him, I walked due north-east through unfamiliar streets, through heckles and shouts, for close to an hour, to Clerkenwell, where I found my way to James Wilson, fabric merchants. Emboldened by Diprose's favourable receipt of my cloth bindings – or rather, his lack of complaint – I was going to investigate whether it would be worth our binding the Bible in weave rather than in hide, to save a few pennies. The smell of dyes and fabric treatments got up my nose in the warehouse as I fingered the samples of cambrics and buckrams. I stroked the leather-look cloths, and listened as the assistant told me how suitable they were for use on everything from books to bonnets, curtains to coffins, but the prices startled me.

'You want cloth, you gotta pay for cloth, love,' he told me. 'It's the Yankees. The cotton famine. There ain't no cotton to be had, scarce as honour right now. What you are, then? A hat-maker? A seamstress?'

'My husband's a bookbinder. Too busy to come out today. Apprentice is sick, you know what it's like.'

'Well what's he doing sending you 'ere then, when he could've told you 'isself and saved you the journey? Didn't he know? What's he been using all this time, then? Papyrus?' He chuckled at his own joke while I flushed at my ignorance. Damages was not an industrial binders mass-producing cloth bindings. 'It's worse than the bloody Crimean, now, I'll tell you,' he went on. 'See this. This is best quality Charles Winterbottom cloth. Used to be seven pence a yard. In the war, it cost you four shillings sixpence. Now you can't get it for less than six shillings. Why else do you think they've all had to go back to binding in plain boards? Nothing to fret about. They'll become historic artefacts in a few years, them books.'

But I realised, as I mulled over bindings becoming casualties of war, and the prospect of Damages suffering the same fate, that I also had been frightened to go where I really needed to go. It was safe for me, a woman, to buy cloth. Leather was different; the tanneries terrified me.

But I set off again, this time due south-east, through the heart of the City, and over London Bridge. Each strike of my feet on the pavement was sending aches up through the very bones of my legs, and I was weary, and in need of a sit-down. The houses were miserable here, and as much in a state of disrepair and despair as their inhabitants. The closer I got to the broad, low tannery buildings, the more the cobbles beneath my feet were stained gules, and matted with clumps of fur, trod-in gristle and wool, like a peculiar red and brown moss.

This bloody carpet thickened underfoot as one neared the source of the vile smell, which had a pungency that stirred the guts with the fearsome rawness, not of death, but of the slow, putrid rot that follows. It stuck to the wheels of the wagons and vans, and to the wooden clogs of the workmen; one dared not slip, for fear of closer contact with the decaying, deathly slime. There were rickety wooden bridges over the series of tidal streams that condemned this district of London to its awful trade, providing sufficient new – one could not say clean – water twice daily for the tanners and leather-dressers. And where the river did not reach, pools of greasy brown water bubbled menacingly with poisonous gas, like pustulous, open wounds, and reeking of putrefying animal. Small boys with red legs squatted amongst them with sharpened sticks, scavenging for meat, which I hoped they would sell to the cat-meat man, and not the pie-man. Wandering amongst them were some older boys carrying buckets of dog turds, to take to the tanneries to cleanse the skins once they were out of the lime-pits; they'd get eight pence for a bucket of pure. The boys' faces were sunken, their noses pinched, as if they had been bred to minimise the mephitic air entering their bodies.

I walked past the warehouse of Felix Stephens, for I knew we owed him, and found the sign of Select Skins and Leather Dressings. I hesitated at the door, then sidled in, to find thousands of hides stacked ceiling-wards, and a considerable number of men shouting prices, writing notes, and exiting briskly with rolls of leather under their arms.

'You lookin' for summink?'

'I am,' I said with false confidence. The man's voice may have been youthful, but his skin was as leathered as his wares, and his arms as strong as an ox. I told him my purpose, and he pulled out for me several fine moroccos, some pigskin, and some calf, and let me peruse them all.

'What's this?' I asked, pointing at a line running across the hide.

'Prob'ly a vein. Too reg'lar to be a scar.' He pulled out some inferior hides from another stack, and showed me flay marks, fighting scars, trap scars.

'Is it cheaper like this?' I asked.

'Depends,' he shrugged. 'These are beasts, wild beasts, who've lived their lives, and all the better for it. Might seem imperfeck to you, but it's beau'iful to summun else.'

'What's this?' I asked, pointing at a white patch on one of the moroccos, which was otherwise relatively unblemished.

'We call that a kiss mark,' the youth said, without relish. 'It's where the hides have touched each other in the pits, so the tanning agent couldn't get there. Just meant someone didn't rock the frames properly, didn't do their job. Prob'ly a Paddy.'

'Will you accept less for it?' I asked. It was of a lovely quality besides, and I knew I could disguise it somehow.

He thought for a while. 'A'right.'

I bought just the one skin: a skin of such quality, without a kiss mark, would have cost me two shillings and four pence, but I took it away for just one shilling and sixpence, which I estimated would be sufficient to bind eight crown octavo books.

My journey home was not far, through the fog and the Borough, and as I walked I wondered how much I dared spend on food tonight, or whether it would only be scraps again for supper. I buried my nose in the scroll of leather – it smelt better away from the tannery – and let the magnificent smell of dead beast nourish me. Would that I could have bought its flesh, too. But Diprose's coins still danced in a pouch beneath my skirts, and I felt something akin to, but not exactly like, hope.

Jack marked round the Bible, and cut out the leather. He snipped the corners and spine spaces off as accurately as a surgeon, laid it on the marble slab, and pared away the dermis, grading it thinly towards the corners and top and bottom of the spine. It must have been hard for Peter, watching Jack's hands on the knife he would not have been capable of gripping, paring with precision the leather he could only have destroyed.

'A pea of paste, a pea, no more!' Peter ordered, as Jack damped the leather on the front and worked the paste into the reverse, then smoothed it firmly but not tightly across the millboards. He folded the leather over around the tops of the boards, and tucked it in around the head-band, using the bone folder, then started to form the head-cap on to the leather, when I had to leave to settle Lucinda for her nap, and collect the water in the pails, before it was turned off again. When I returned, Jack had repeated the whole process with the bottom of the boards and spine, then the sides, and finally the angles of the corners, which met in a perfect mitre. Jack was skilled, but he had learnt from an expert. Then he inserted the boards and books between flannel and tin, and put them into the press.

At least twelve hours had to pass before it was ready for finishing; I needed as many of those hours that Lucinda and the house could spare me, and then I would need to be ready for the finishing, too. Its permanence daunted me: unlike a hearth or a doorstep that could be gone over repeatedly should one miss a mark or a stain, gold-tooling cannot be erased or painted over. The finishing announces excellence and nobility, from the gold itself to the pleasing hand-tools, which, like dainty but solid bits of jewellery, feel satisfying in one's hand. I heat Peter's hand-tools on the stove, and my spoons and pans look dirty and ugly by comparison. I whisk up egg white and water to make bookbinder's glair, and I am an alchemist; I whisk up the remnant egg yolks to make omelettes, sauces, custards, and I am a curmudgeon. Finishing is the way the book presents itself to the world and gets noticed; the forwarding is more like women's work, for one never notices it unless it has been shoddily done. Twelve hours, and the task, the honour, the responsibility, would be mine.

Chapter Five

I'll tell my own daddy,
When he comes home,
What little good work
My mammy has done;
She has earned a penny
And spent a groat,
And burnt a hole
In the child's new coat.

'MOIV BIBLL,' Jack read over my shoulder. 'Moive Bibble. Who's she? The police officer responsible for offences against spines?'

'No. She's the Patron Saint of Bad Toolers.'

'What's it meant to say?'

'Holy Bible.'

'Ah. Never mind, Mrs D. You'll get there. That's not half bad for a first try. I've seen plenty worse.'

It had not been the easiest of mornings. We had started with a discussion of the brief: 'a simple representation of God's bounty in tropical climes'. Peter had no pineapples, no fig-leaves, no palm trees, amongst his tools. The closest he had come to the tropics was binding *The Reports for the Year 1856 of the Past and Present State of Her Majesty's Colonial Possessions*. I wondered why Diprose had even thought of Damages for this brief. For all his curves, Peter was a rectilinear sort of man; his fillets were the straightest in London. His idea for this would have been a geometrical diaper pattern across the front cover, with a border of straight lines of varying thicknesses.

'But you are not capable of the discipline of regular diaper tooling,' he told me bluntly. 'You are clumsy. Let us not even consider it.'

Yet he would not consider anything else. I had painted watercolours on some rectangles of vellum, too small to make more than a book for a midget, but each one was too sensual, or too beautiful, or too dangerous for Peter to contemplate turning into a tooled design. I had designed Biblical scenes for Peter before in this way: the Annunciation, countless Miracles, the Crucifixion. But when asked for God's bounty in the tropics, I found myself time and again in the Garden of Eden, the Tree of the Knowledge of Good and Evil, serpents, fruit, and the innocence of nakedness.

'No fruit. Too suggestive, too much a woeful reminder of the fateful apple,' he would say. Or, 'Fig-leaves? A representation of the civilised – by which I mean, clothed – appearance of Western missionaries, would be more appropriate than their naked and barbarous brethren.' And finally, 'Are you attempting to incite my wrath with your border of snakes, or are you merely stupid?'

'Diprose has asked for simplicity,' he went on to explain. 'Diprose is a man of the times. Not for him this endless gold filigree, this vulgar excess, this florid lack of taste. Nor for me neither.'

My paintings were also too elaborate for me to convert into tooled gold. I could have embroidered them in coloured silks and silver and gold threads, onto the purest white satin, with the most elaborate border of beasts, birds and fish, but both Peter and I knew I could not hope to gold-tool them.

'It is quite apparent,' Peter eventually said, 'that we must start with establishing of what you are capable, and work the design within those meagre limitations. A simple diaper is what it must be. A leaf will do.'

Peter had several leaf tools, but they were the ash, the oak, the sycamore, the chestnut, not the palm, the baobab, the gingko. 'God's bounty in tropical climes,' I muttered, as I played with the tools. A tentative pattern was forming in my mind. I selected a small crown tool, a miniature diamond, and a triangle. I sketched it on a piece of paper, and showed Peter my idea. 'Imposs –' he started to say, before sucking in his lower lip and nodding, slowly.

I practised on the half-leather of the woefully bound journal with which I had started and ended my forwarding career. Peter showed me how to draw up the template on paper, and fix it in place over the half-leather. Then I warmed the tools on the stove, and went slowly over the pattern. My dwell was insufficient here, and too much there, the crown was not straight here, and the diamonds did not align there, but slowly the leather became covered with indentations that represented tiny, imperfect pineapples. The crowns were the leaves, and the diamonds and triangles the matrix of the skin. I was still tooling blind; we could not waste a speck of gold dust on practice.

'Now for the spine.' Peter showed me how to grip the book in the press and prepare the lettering. I selected the type for 'HOLY BIBLE', warmed them too on the stove, and pressed them into the leather. It would not yet pass muster with Charles Diprose, but even Peter knew it was an admirable start. Some of the letters were skewed, I had dug in too deep in places, and held the tool at the wrong angle so that one side of the letter went deeper than another, but it was just about legible.

'Never mind. We must pursue our goal with determination. You have had enough practice with the – the – that – *pine*apple, and we will have to hope for the best.'

With a ruler I marked out a paper grid with the precise location of each tool, and affixed it to the front cover of the Bible. Then we took the book over to the booth in the corner, along with the tools. Jack locked the external door and pulled the door curtain across it, stopped up the bottom with the felt draught-excluder, and pulled the curtain across the internal door and around the booth.

I tooled the design through the paper, removed the paper, and heated up the tools for the first round of blind-tooling. I painted the design with glair using a fine sable brush, and let it dry. I repeated it, another thin coat. Then a third time, on Peter's insistence. Finally, I took the gold out of the strongbox below the bench, greased the impressions, laid the gold on, and heated the tiny branding irons.

It was unbearably slow, and the irrevocable nature of the work was daunting: I could burn the leather, or cut it, or get the tool in the wrong place, or tool unevenly. When it came to putting the gold down, there really was no return. I kept holding my breath, and becoming giddy.

'Your hands must not shake,' Peter insisted, but my hands were not shaking, and both of us knew it. 'Where the iron touches, the gold sticks for good,' he murmured, but I was getting it right. My pressure was still uneven, but I took the time to rock the tools, which increased the amount of light reflected from the gold. 'Give the pattern dignity. Slow and steady.'

But soon he stopped instructing me, and finally conceded, with discernible sadness, that I did indeed, and most fortunately, have a steady hand. He left after a while, to find some salicin or take a rest, I did not know. I paused while he moved the curtains, and ensured the gold was not disturbed by any breeze. When he had gone, I continued.

Give the pattern dignity, slow and steady. His words still rang in my ears. I continued – four, five, six, seven more pineapples. I was almost halfway down the front cover. Then, despite myself, my focus shifted from the present tooling to the ones I had yet to do, and back to the ones I had done before, and I congratulated myself on how good they were, and gained from them a false sense of confidence. Then in crept the thought that Lucinda would soon be ready for some food, and then her nap. Was that her I could hear, wandering around in the house saying 'Mama, Mama'? She knew better than to come in and disrupt the folds of the curtain, but what if she did? I lost momentum; my mother's brain took over, my hands rushed and tried to do their usual several things at once instead of the one task in progress. And so I made two errors simultaneously: I burnt the leather, and I mistooled, which meant the ghost and the final impression would not sit squarely on each other. In an attempt to rectify it, I dampened the leather and picked at it with a pin to try to lift the impressions, but I only scratched the leather and made more of a mess.

I stood back, hot and breathless, and looked at the central row of pineapples. Not just one but all of them were out of kilter and at odds with each other, strewn like children playing in the fields, rather than neatly serried ranks of pupils in a schoolhouse. I stopped, and wondered why I had ever been so hard on Peter for only being capable of doing one thing at a time.

I did not allow myself to despair for long. I simply left the workshop behind me to see to my child, and do what at heart I knew I was best at. I did not return to the workshop at all, but busied myself about the house to thwart the worrying. And when I heard noises later coming from the workshop, I did not dare descend to see what Peter was up to. There was swearing, and shouting, and a bench leg being kicked, followed by puffing, and panting, and sobs. I trembled in bed and cried myself to sleep. I knew I should have got up to confront the responsibilities that I had ensured were now my own, but I decided to let the man be, for a while. I must have fallen asleep at some point, for I woke with a start as the church bell tolled five, and my hands were still gripping the top of the counterpane tightly. Peter was soundly asleep next to me. I took the chamber-pots and descended, then rifled through the fires for embers to put in the range. Only then did I go into the workshop.

It was as I had left it. The bench leg did not betray the kicking it had received, nothing was lying on the floor or out of place as if hurled to vent its master's spleen. Cautiously I pulled back the curtain around the gold-tooling booth, and saw my Bible lying there much as it did yesterday, only the centre of the leather on the front cover of the binding was gone. Someone had, extremely skilfully, cut around my mess in a perfect rectangle, and lifted it clean away from the cover. In its place was another perfect rectangle of soft cream vellum, inset into the red morocco. Someone had tooled some perfectly straight lines all the way around it, as if it were meant, as if it had always been part of the majestic, celebratory design of God's bounty in the tropics. And on the vellum was my original watercolour of the Garden of Eden, all palm-trees and coconuts and fountains and cicadas and monkeys and lusciousness. Below it lay an expanse of red morocco, still waiting for its pineapple diaper. I smiled, and found that I could not wait to get to work.

But first I swept the floor, dusted the furniture, cleaned the hearths, set the fire, made the porridge, drew and heated the water, and aired the washing. I left Peter in bed: the night's escapades had nearly been the end of him. He did not get out of bed until eleven, and only then because the phial of salicin by his bed was empty. So I bound his hands up tight in bandages, in the hope that they would force the fluids to be reabsorbed by his body, then I raided the tea-caddy for our last remaining pennies, and headed out to the market and the pharmacist with Lucinda by my side.

Finally, at half-past four that afternoon, I started work.

Peter did not ask to see it, but once it was finished I brought the book to his bedside, held it out for his inspection, and turned it on all sides. HOLY BIBLE, the spine read, clearly and evenly. He was lying on his left side again, head tucked in and knees drawn up like a baby, his swollen hands pressed between his thighs. He raised his head slightly, nodded, then closed his eyes once more. I wrapped the Bible in soft muslin, and took Lucinda back to Agatha Marrow's with a kiss and a promise, and set out for Diprose's for the third time in as many weeks.

'Hello, Mrs Eeles,' I said as I reached the top of Ivy-street.

'Hello, dearie.' She wasn't wearing a veil today, but an enormous black bonnet, which looked as if someone had tipped a coal scuttle over her head and left it there. A sallow, bucktoothed boy of about ten years hovered by her side. 'His mam's just died, I'm taking him in for a bit,' she said mawkishly. ' "Stand we in jeopardy every hour; in the midst of life we are in death." Say hello, Billy.'

'Hello,' Billy said, not looking at me.

'Hello, Billy,' I said. 'You must play with my Lucinda while you're here. You'll meet her in the street soon enough.' Billy nodded, preoccupied with the expanse of black bombazine around his temporary guardian. I looked longingly at Mrs Eeles's black gloves; they weren't fine and white, like a lady's, but I could have done with them today. My fingers were stained with leather dye, and cracked all over, as if they too were becoming leather in the process. Oh, the irony of it, that ladies got to wear smooth white gloves over their smooth white fingers, yet the ones that needed them most, the hard workers of the country, couldn't afford them, and even if we could have, we wouldn't have been allowed to wear them, or we would have been called fast, or gay, even. Mrs Eeles got away with it only because hers were black, and she was eccentric besides.

Mr Diprose himself greeted me at the entrance to his shop, took the Bible from me, and unwrapped it. He would, I feared, be displeased with the design or execution of the binding, or worse still, would find me out, from the stains on my fingers, or the shoddiness of the handiwork. He was silent in consideration for several minutes. His lips were a tight, thin line, and his face flushed the colour of port, like Peter's did when he was angry.

'*Vous me troublez, Madame,*' was all he eventually said, and expressed his perplexity by rising and ascending the bare wooden staircase to the floor above.

I must have sat there for well nigh on fifteen minutes. Not a soul entered or left, but there was muted activity upstairs, footsteps, hammering, machinery. I peered through the curtain into the road, and through the windows I could see clerks, businessmen, errand-boys and -girls, street sweepers, racing pell-mell down the cluttered streets in their droves. From the remarkable silence of the shop interior it was as if I had turned deaf, for the plate-glass was thick and its sealings magnificent in their design. It kept out the smells as well as the sounds, and as I relaxed into the aroma of well-bound books, leather dressings and neatsfoot oil, I inhaled my own odour and realised, as Mr Diprose descended once more, that I was foul.

'You have struck me, Mrs Damage.'

I did not know how to answer such a strange remark. 'Beg pardon, sir?'

'You have quite struck me, madam, today.' My thoughts danced with smiting Mr Diprose's corpulence with a boot, or a book, or even just my poor hands. I wanted to giggle, but I dared not. I think I smirked at him. 'I asked for a simple representation of God's bounty.'

'In tropical climes,' I added, to be polite.

'And your husband has not taken me at my word.'

'Oh, hasn't he, sir?

'No, indeed he hasn't. He has surpassed the brief. A more complex, and, dare I say it, feminine expression of God's bounty I have not seen. I was told your husband was a man of lines and angles, of form and function, whose bindings spoke of the probity and order to be found within. He is a Parliament binder, is he not?' I nodded. 'I do not wish to embarrass you, but I had heard your husband had fallen on hard times. I consider myself to be something of a philanthropist in the book industry. I took pity on the unfortunate man, knowing that he must have a dear wife and a host of children to feed. It was compassion, Mrs Damage, which led me to give you that Bible for your husband to bind. It was not an important commission. But he has made it so. *Vous m'avez frappé*, I will say it again, Mrs Damage, by presenting me with something so beautiful.'

I think I flushed, and for an instance was unaware enough of myself to clap my unseemly hands together.

'That is not to say I am altogether pleased,' he cautioned. 'The inset piece makes it vulnerable; it will not wear well. But then, one has to wonder how many Bibles this Bishop already has. Let us presume he will not be taking this one in his luggage on his next trip to Oojabooja-ville. And, Mrs Damage?'

'Yes?'

'The work may be lavish, but I can furnish your husband with no more than the standard fee.'

I had expected no more, but I skipped home with the few coins jingling merrily in my purse, although through my excitement I tried to hold in my head the sums that needed paying – to Skinner and Blades; to the grocer's and the coalman; to Felix Stephens and the other suppliers, and for food – and the fractions of each I could get away with paying this week to keep everybody happy for a while, and how much would be left over to buy some scraps of leather and silk to work up some more notebooks from the remaining Dutch paper. I knew I would always be able to sell them to Diprose, but I was also planning to make up a particularly fine book and tout it around some of the other booksellers who hadn't been overly prejudiced or directly affected by Damage's recent troubles. There were a few of Peter's old clients, too, to whom

I hoped to return with the news that Damage's was open for business, with the same management, but new staff.

But when there was a rap at the door of the workshop the following day – a particularly sharp, unfriendly knocking – my heart jumped into my mouth like a frightened child and I was sure we had run out of time. I did not think of the sight that would greet the person at the door, of a woman on her own in a bookbinder's workshop, hard at work, but simply flew to the door and opened it, hammer in hand, before whoever it was knocked it down and knocked us up for obstructing seizure of property.

At first I did not recognise him; his gloves were faded tan with dark brown stitching, and he was holding a large, flat briefcase that partially covered his face, but the oily sheen on his black silk hat gave him away. He lowered the briefcase to reveal his black beard, below which was a purple neck-scarf stained with grease.

'Mr Diprose!'

'*Bonjour, Madame.*' He lifted his hat to me. 'Forgive the intrusion. I have brought your husband two new manuscripts. I trust he will be pleased.'

'You – he – oh!'

'May I not come in?'

'But certainly. How rude of me. Do, please.'

It would have been permissible if the paper had been newly folded and strung up in the sewing-frame. It would just about have been acceptable if the sewn sections had been lying on the bench being curved. We would have got away with it had Jack been here, had I not sent him out to deliver our trade card to a stationer's in Holborn. But to someone who knew, like Mr Diprose, it would have been apparent, from the hammer in my hand and the jar of freshly made paste on the bench, that I was doing men's work. Of course, I was not breaking the law for doing this, but I knew better than to publicise the fact.

I put the hammer down quickly, and was about to gabble a concocted story about where Peter and Jack had disappeared to, when Peter entered in disarray from the house. His hair was ruffed up like a duck's tail, and his face was crumpled like the sheets he had clearly just left. The bandages binding his hands were grimy and frayed, and Diprose saw them straight away. Our visitor's mouth and eyes had widened into three silent 'o's; his cheeks percolated glistening beads of sweat, like dew.

'Mr Diprose. May I introduce to you my husband and proprietor of Damage's Bookbinders, Peter Damage.'

'How do you do?' Mr Diprose said, and put out his hand, before retracting it nervously, staring at Peter's dressings.

'Mr Diprose, what an honour. Pleased to meet you indeed,' Peter said earnestly, as if to compensate for his lack of hand-shake.

'Tell me,' Diprose muttered, unable to take his eyes off Peter's hands, 'am I interrupting something?'

'No, no,' Peter said blithely. 'We were just – nothing that can't wait.' He said something about the work coming through the workshop, the state of the book market at the moment, the lamentable quality of modern paper. 'To which I add my deep gratitude at your gift of the fine Dutch paper. A delight, a positive delight, to bind. I trust the journals are selling well?'

'You trust correctly,' Diprose said slowly, preoccupied now with the globules of newly dried paste covering my hands like hideous warts. I excused myself, seized a duster, and went into the kitchen to make some tea. I could hear them continue in hushed, but urgent tones.

'And you a union man too, Mr Damage. How long have you been in breach of them?'

'There are no regulations yet, only proposals,' Peter said meekly.

'It is hypocrisy.'

'It is expediency, Mr Diprose. My hands will be mended soon.'

I could not hear the next exchange, but then Mr Diprose must have walked further towards the kitchen, for his words, laced with menace, were unmistakeable.

'I could cause a lot of trouble for you, you know that.'

'And will you?' Peter replied. He threw those three words to Mr Diprose like a challenge; I was proud to see there was still a man within him.

I wished I could have seen Diprose's face in the pause that followed. He held all the power; possibly he was measuring whether Peter was victim or worthy opponent. He took his time, as if the decision were momentous to him.

'*Je suis un philanthrope*, Mr Damage. I heard a union man had fallen on hard times, and I ventured to help. I believed you to be rewarding me well, but you have deceived me.'

'Surely deceive is too harsh a . . .'

'My most important client, Sir Jocelyn Knightley, has likewise been deceived. You have put me in an embarrassing situation. I promoted you to him using the Bible, and he is now much taken with your work. He has since bought a commonplace book and an album for his wife, with which she was delighted. She gave much praise to the embroidery, and the elegant but unassuming way it harmonised with her salon. It was as if she had commissioned it. He already has plans to send you further work. And now I must let him down. You have most embarrassed me.'

'If he is that taken with my work, what matters a woman's input? Dora is only my hands while mine do not function. She has no head for the work.'

'Sir Jocelyn is a scientist, Mr Damage.' Mr Diprose sounded exasperated. 'He needs a binder for his life's works. His area of speciality is ethnography. Primitive peoples, Mr Diprose. His mastery in the fields of phrenology, physiognomy, and, ah, the baser urges of mankind, have led him to a far greater understanding of the savage nations than anyone has heretofore achieved. He is feted in the Scientific Society. But, really, must I impress upon you the dire consequences of exposing literature of that ilk to women? *La donna è mobile*. It will addle their brains and disturb their constitutions.'

'I am in complete accord . . . I had not appreciated . . . My dear wife . . . But, Mr Diprose, there is no reason why we could not continue with more Bibles, and journals, and the like?' Peter had started to plead. It did not make pleasant listening. 'Bland stuff? *Women's* stuff? And when my hands are healed, I can satisfy the wishes of this eminent Lord Knightley. Please. Mr Diprose? I should be most . . . most grateful.'

Diprose gave pause; the pleading no doubt swelled his philanthropic nature. I heard the click of his briefcase, and a rustle of papers.

'It troubles me to see the vine of talent and dedication withering in the stony soil of tribulation. I like to reach out to those in desperate circumstances.' I wondered to myself if Mr Diprose might be a bachelor, or a widower, for he would have made a fine match with Mrs Eeles, neither of them being able to resist the whiff of desperation. 'I have here a small prayer-book. It is in the same type as the Bible, and again, first in Latin, then hand-scribed, but it is to be folded smaller: it is, as you will see, vigesimo-quarto, instead of sextodecimo. It must form part of the same set.' There was another rustle of papers, and the sound of an envelope being ripped open, followed by a chinking of coins. 'An advance for the commission,' he said. 'It was to be two manuscripts, unfortunately, but the second is of the sensitive nature I have previously described, and I deem it inappropriate to leave with you.' He counted out some coins, then poured the rest into his coat pocket.

'And you – you won't breathe a word of this to the union, will you?' Peter begged, as Mr Diprose got up to leave.

'So, you are asking me to keep your secret. Good day, Mr Damage. And *bon chance*.'

Peter tumbled into the kitchen, sucked of strength, and lay on the cold floorboards. I went into the workshop, counted the coins, and ran to the pharmacy.

Chapter Six

Old Boniface he loved good cheer,
And took his glass of Burton,
And when the nights grew sultry hot
He slept without a shirt on.

'You are most fortunate to be married to a modern man like myself,' Peter announced between bouts of vomiting. The ipecacuanha was taking effect, and his guts were retaliating. 'Most members of the weaker sex are never permitted to be seen beyond the confines of their houses. If they have to go to market, they go straight there, then return home directly. If they do not have to go to market, the tradesmen come to their doors.' But he was wrong. A woman's life could never truly lack visibility, no matter how low or high her rank: women who went to market were exhibits; women who never went to market were exhibited at balls and parties instead. Still, I nodded politely, and held his hair back from his head as he suffered a particularly violent retch that would have come from his very bowels, had they not recently been purged with calomel. 'You are blessed indeed to have a husband with my nature,' he said again, spitting strings of bitter gastric juices from his mouth. I agreed with him.

The emetic exhausted him quickly, and he took to his bed, with strict instructions that he was not to be disturbed. But I was anxious without his guiding eyes. The prayer-book might have been smaller than the Bible, but the expanses of red morocco that required regulation diaper tooling taunted me, despite my relative success with the Bible. I feared I would make a mistake on the first row of pineapples, or the last, which could not feasibly take a vellum insert. Jack was still teasing me about Moive Bibble, which did nothing for my confidence, and I knew Lucinda was suffering from my absence. She was more than capable of amusing herself, of course, but a child needs her mother in ways far greater than a workshop needs its binder, a house its cleaner, or even a husband his wife. Not to mention that the river ran in both directions: I was suffering from Lucinda's absence no less.

I fretted over the binding all day as I went about my chores; I did not trust myself to start work without Peter. But the following day he refused to assist me again, so I determined to settle on a design that played to my strengths and the materials available to me. It was to be a half-binding of red morocco, using the remaining soft yellow silk for the front and back, embroidered in the same colours as the watercolour on the front of the Bible. Then I planned to paint a biblical scene on a piece of Dutch paper, which I would use as a doublure. I was bending the brief so far that it was likely to snap, but I had to trust that by remaining true to its spirit, the books would still qualify as 'matching'.

However, I needed not have worried all those long days. When I finally returned to Holywell-street and presented it to Mr Diprose, he looked over it with disinterest, his forefinger curled in the furrow between nose and upper lip, and his thumb stroking his beard.

'Fine, fine. Hmm.' He spun his chair round away from his desk, and thought some more. '*Bon*. I think we should go now.'

'Go, Mr Diprose? Where?'

'I informed my client, Sir Jocelyn Knightley, about the unfortunate matter of your sex, and much to my horror, it does not seem to perturb him in the slightest. On the contrary. He seems to take delight in the fact. He wishes to continue relations with Damage's. It goes entirely against my better judgement. Your timing is felicitous. We can see him this morning.' He clipped his vowels and spat his consonants; it was as if the vowels were dangerous, open spaces, which needed to be reined in and ordered by fixed, predictable consonants, which dictated the confines of the vowel.

He pulled on his coat and hat and led me outside. We walked quickly to the Strand, where he raised his arm and hailed a hansom. He let me ascend, then followed me in, although he was ungainly and creaked, as he would have found bending difficult. I dare say we would have been quicker walking, at the pace the cab lumbered along in the slow-moving Westminster traffic. As we headed westward, the horses and carriages thinned, but the pace of those on the pavements was slower: swells and high-bred ladies strolled in the streets towards the daffodils of Green Park; dubious dandies and demi-reps laughed in the spring sunshine; the perfume of fashion and the gleam of grooming abounded around us.

'Tell me about Sir Jocelyn,' I said to Mr Diprose.

'Is one anxious that one will reveal oneself to be something of a *parvenue* in the face of one who is the *dernier cri*, the *ne plus ultra*, of the elegantly patrician world one is now entering?' He chuckled at his facetiousness.

'I have no pretensions even to being a *parvenue*, Mr Diprose. I was not aware that I had recently arrived somewhere of note.'

'Oh but you have, my dear, now that you are in the employ of Sir Jocelyn Knightley.'

'I thought we were working for you.'

'I am little more than a hawker,' he said with a wryness that implied that he considered himself nothing of the sort. 'A procurer, if you will.' He pouted his lips on the second syllable. 'And I have procured you for Sir Jocelyn, against my better judgement, I hasten to add. You will continue to work for me and through me, but he is our client, and it is him to whom we both report.'

'You are unhappy with this arrangement?'

He sighed and shrugged his shoulders.

'It remains to be seen. There will be plenty of commissions coming your way: rare books, curiosities, literary *arcana*. You are most fortunate. We shall do well.' But his tone betrayed that he was not altogether delighted with this happy turn of events. 'We shall see. *Vigilate et orate*. We shall watch and pray.'

'What shall we see?'

'I wish I shared Sir Jocelyn's confidence in his plan. You are, after all, a woman. Where there is trouble, *cherchez la femme* . . .'

The hansom took us to the west side of Berkeley-square, and pulled up outside a grand white building. We had to ascend seven broad steps, wider than my kitchen; two ball-shaped miniature trees in square planters stood sentry on either side of the door. Diprose rang the bell, and immediately, a tall, grey-haired butler answered the door.

'Good morning, Goodchild,' Diprose said.

'Good morning, Mr Diprose,' Goodchild replied with the slight nod of the head which, I was to learn, he reserved for those who were not of the upper set, but were nevertheless due certain recognition. His voice was low and soft; it was the tone one would use in a reading room conferring on a book, not standing on a door-step in one of the finest squares of the metropolis.

'May I introduce Mrs Peter Damage.'

'How do you do, Mrs Damage. But Lady Knightley is not receiving today. Would you care to leave your card?'

'No, Goodchild. Would you be so kind as to tell Sir Jocelyn that the bookbinder is here, and that we have the leisure to wait?'

Goodchild stepped aside to let us in. Behind where he had stood was a waist-high Negro boy, alarmingly life-like but blessedly inert, holding a white wire birdcage up with one hand; on the other perched three exotic yellow birds. His loincloth drooped precariously down towards his right knee, but his decency was preserved, as well it might have been, for there was no hitching up to be had of bronze and glass. I wondered if Diprose had stared, like me, on their first encounter, or whether he had always thrown his coat on him as he did now.

A piano was playing somewhere as we climbed the soft, carpeted stairs, and I presumed it was being played by the hands of Lady Knightley. They would be smooth, milky hands, not like mine. We padded quietly behind Goodchild up to the top of the stairs; there was a large panelled door directly in front of us, on which he knocked.

'Come in,' came the voice. Goodchild held the door open for us.

It was how I had pictured a gentlemen's club: stale, dusty and smoky. A man stood up from a large burgundy-covered desk in the far corner of the room, and strode towards us with handsome grace. He was tall and languid, like those elegant men who danced quadrilles at Cremorne on the covers of my sheet-music. He had fine long fingers, and long feet in polished brown shoes. He took my overworked hand in his, much to my shame, and despite myself I found myself looking up at him. A shock of honey-streaked brown hair flopped over his forehead, and I imagined Lady Knightley's delicate fingers sweeping it back over his head. His eyes were a lustrous brown, like a bear's, and exuded a sense of fiery righteousness. In flagrant defiance of fashion, his bronzed countenance boasted close aquaintance with the sun, and his face, I was relieved to see, was a kind one. But there I was, looking too long; I dropped my gaze.

'Mrs Damage,' he said, kissing my hand. His voice was languid too; it oozed downwards and filled the room, even though it wasn't loud. It was deep and liquid, and I found it soothing, like liquorice, if a bit sickly. I pulled my hand back from him, for I was losing myself.

I searched for Mr Diprose for help, but he had settled himself in a worn leather armchair with a glass of whisky in his hand. There was another chair facing him, on the other side of the fire, and in between was an exotic, low leather couch draped in a fine red Persian rug and embroidered cushions. I wondered if I was meant to sit there. But no one asked me to sit down. Still I kept searching, for what I did not know. Sir Jocelyn moved to my side, bent his knees so that his head was at the same level as mine, and followed my gaze, as if he wanted to see what I was seeing.

The room was brown, very brown. The furniture was all rich mahogany, dark oak and chocolate leather, with wine-coloured brocades; the walls were the colour of tea. But despite this gloom, there were glimmers of wonders, and I could not help my eyes from flitting from this to that with alarming promiscuity.

I was afraid of what I saw, and it was fear, more than anything, that rooted me to the spot. For the animals that seemed so elegantly unusual in Lucinda's picture books, or at a distance in the circus, were terrifying to me in proximity. Their skins, heads and tusks leered out or up at me from the walls and floors, and even though I knew they were dead, it was as if they might suddenly take to breathing again once they sensed my presence and smelt my fear, and would devour me on the spot.

In between the heads hung the paraphernalia of the hunter and adventurer: plenty of instruments – sextants, I imagined, and telescopes, compasses, microscopes and all sorts of meters – and between their dials and the heads on the walls hung a variety of firearms, some tribal spears, beaded headdresses, and shields.

I was on safer ground when my gaze fell on the stretch of bookcases filled with endless volumes, beautifully bound in finely lettered, gold-tooled leather of all colours; the wall behind his large leather-topped desk held several glass-fronted cabinets, some filled with books, others with medical implements or exploration equipment. I peered over my shoulder at the bookcase closer to hand, where several volumes by Richard Burton were grouped together: *First Footsteps in East Africa*, *Personal Narrative of a Pilgrimage to El-Medinah and Meccah*, *Complete System of Bayonet Exercise*. Next to them was Livingstone's *Missionary Travels*. So Knightley did not catalogue alphabetically. Maybe this was his 'Africa' section.

And indeed, next were the anatomy books, which fairly made my pulse race, so fine a collection had he. Peter would have swooned to see such masterpieces sharing the same shelf. There were two books of Galen: one was a crisp, modern *Oeuvres Anatomiques*, the other an ancient, crumbling *De anatomicis*. There was Bourgery's great, four-part *Atlas of Anatomy*, Cheselden's *The Anatomy of the Human Body*, Quain's and Gray's. But the most precious, esteemed book in the whole collection I knew to be the large black and gold folio, entitled *De humani corporis fabrica libri septum*, by Andreas Vesalius, the founder of the science of anatomy. On the Fabric of the Human Body.

'You have an eye for the Vesalius, madam?' Sir Jocelyn said.

'Yes, sir,' I answered. 'I have not seen one before. Actually, I have not seen any anatomies,' I hastened to add, 'but I have heard of the most famous.'

'And deservedly so. The man was brave enough to risk imprisonment by stealing a corpse from the gallows itself, in order to dispute Galen, and prove that Barbary apes are not anatomical equals to humans.'

I looked aslant at him, for I was not sure how he was expecting me to react; it was not usual practice for intelligent men to talk to women such as me in such a way. And it was then that I spied the most disturbing item in the room, out of that cursed female corner of my eye. It fascinated and repulsed me, and I could not work out what I was looking at, and eventually I found myself looking at it head-on. I felt

Sir Jocelyn leave my side, and creep over towards Diprose, but still I could not change the direction of my gaze. It was like a grotesque sculpture of a human torso, like the marble classical sculptures of old, with truncated arms and legs (which, incidentally, I never knew was deliberate or not; whether the sculptors had deliberately chosen to focus on the torso, or if the head, arms and legs had been knocked off over the centuries). But this one was different. The surface had been painted to resemble flesh, but in places the meat was missing. It had one beautiful, perfect breast, with a shockingly real nipple, but where the other one should have been was an orange, pitted cavity. Every separate hair on my own flesh stirred in horror, as I realised that what I was beholding permitted a vision of the interior of the body.

'See how she looks so,' Knightley whispered, and I tried to flash my eyes away from the hideous cast. I met Diprose's eye, which felt uncomfortable too, so I dropped my gaze to the fire, which was lit, despite the heat in the room, and from there to the couch, and then back to the poor semi-form in front of me.

'Indeed, Sir Jocelyn,' Diprose hissed back. 'Which is why, with all due respect, I advise we proceed with caution.'

I did not hear Knightley's reply, but knew he was continuing to watch my struggle with placing my gaze. Eventually I determined to face them both and wait for them to address me, which I did for a while, but they continued to observe me, as if I were some scientific curiosity, so I dropped my gaze and found my eyes wandering back to that thing, where they could penetrate beyond the skin to the marvellous inner world of the body.

At length Sir Jocelyn went over to the statue, and put his hand on its shoulder. His other hand he held out to me. 'Come. Would you like a closer look?'

I think I nodded, and my legs started to walk towards him. But I was about to step on a dead tiger. I hesitated, heard

Diprose snigger, then planted my foot firmly on the skin. It yielded softly, and I felt as if I might slip.

'I will warn you, Mrs Damage, that this is not usually considered a suitable object for women to peruse. Hitherto, I have not shown it to many. Indeed, have I shown it to any? Good lord, this could be a historic day. But I have been told by my advisers —' here he smiled benevolently, '— that you show special qualities which prove that you are not like the rest of them; hence.'

And here, with his own finger, he pointed out to me what I was looking at. 'I picked it up in Paris. It's *papier-mâché*, made by Auzoux.' He dug his hands right into her cold flesh, and pulled out pink cushions and tubes and curiously shaped lumps, and told me that this one was the liver, and these were the kidneys, and this the oesophagus, and I couldn't follow it all and felt my insides turn right over several times in sympathy. He asked me if I wanted to touch it, but I shook my head.

At that moment, the door opened and Goodchild brought in a tray of tea and cakes. I felt the old familiar gnaw of hunger to which I had grown so accustomed. 'Have you met my wife yet, Mrs Damage?' Sir Jocelyn asked as we walked back towards the fireplace. 'She was hoping to see you at some point.' Again, I shook my head. 'She was thrilled to find a bookbinder she can inveigle into her pet cause. Her charming Nigger philanthropy. Don't take it too seriously. I don't. Still, I should consider myself blessed that she did not choose temperance as her pet time-waster. Or the vote.' Good-child left, and Sir Jocelyn himself bent down to serve.

'Tell me, Dipsy,' he continued, 'does it strike you as strange that, having so benefited from slavery for centuries, our conscience should only stir when more profitable methods of sugar production are discovered? How happily we erase past shame with present virtue, as long as it continues to serve us. It is nothing but humbug. Humbug, hypocrisy, and self-interest.'

Diprose chuckled. He had nothing to add to the argument; possibly he had run out of foreign words to drop into his conversation. He simply nodded his concurrence with Sir Jocelyn's assertion that it was market forces, rather than morality, that led to the abolition of the British slave trade.

'Bless my dear wife. She still drinks tea unsweetened, despite loathing the drink so in its natural state. What about you, Mrs Damage?' he asked, pouring the tea into a china cup. And then, as he tipped one, and then a second, spoonful of sugar into the cup, he asked me, 'Sugar?'

'Thank you,' I said as I took the cup, and watched as he put a slice of lemon in the one he handed to Diprose, but did not have one himself. Instead, he lit a cigar, which was monogrammed with the letters 'JRK'.

Diprose took his tea, and muttered something I didn't understand, but I heard the word '*kaffir*', which I had heard before around Lambeth market when there had been a fight. So he had found a foreign word to use after all. I think he was trying to be funny, but Sir Jocelyn didn't laugh.

' "*Kaffir*", Dipsy, comes from an Arab word, "*kafir*", which means "infidel". It may indeed sound like the Cauzuh word "*kafula*", which means, "to spit upon", but the word you are using is a continent away from those to whom you are refer- ring. If you are to use a term of abuse to describe a man of colour, please choose a geographically correct one.'

He stretched out his legs to reveal silk stockings and a pair of monogrammed slippers. I could imagine those legs wading through crocodile-infested swamps and sticky jungles. I could see him clubbing a man-eating tiger to death while singing the baritone aria from *Don Giovanni* and ripping her apart with his bare hands in order to assuage a week-long hunger. I could picture his strong body laid low with dysentery and malaria at times, but not for long.

Suddenly he stood up. 'Mrs Damage, you are perfect for our requirements.' My cheeks reddened to match the rose-coloured bloom of the light on his desk. 'I can tell by your pert little nose.' No one had ever called it that before, only 'snub'. 'You have a nose for discretion, and an aptitude for business. And your delightful chin tells me you are quick to learn, and are creative and spontaneous, without abandoning caution. Your brow tells me you have a sense of fun, and are quite flirtatious. But interesting features are all very well, as far as they go. It is how one chooses to inhabit them, to manifest their qualities in life, that makes the difference.' He picked up a black leather-bound file, pulled out from it some drawings, and handed them to me. They were sketches, made in charcoal, of all the bindings I had constructed for Diprose. 'Are we correct in assuming you designed these yourself?'

I nodded, for my mouth was too dry to speak, despite the tea.

'*And* executed them?' It would have been impossible for me to lie, but I did not know then whether a lie would have saved me. I nodded again, and then managed the words, 'Jack did the forwarding.'

'Ah yes. Jack. We shall come to him. But you were the finisher?'

'Yes sir.'

'Excellent news. I believe that problems often arise in book-bindings when there is a division of labour. It is as if intelligent thought is lost in the gap between designer and maker. Is it fair to say, Mrs Damage, that you give a plain binding the same attention to detail and commitment as a more elaborate one?'

'Oh yes, sir. My prices vary only according to the size of the book and the amount of gold required.'

'Indeed. And your father Mr Archibald Brice, late of Brice's Bookbinders, Carnaby-street, died of pulmonary disease, 28 September 1854? And your mother Georgina, likewise, of the cholera, 14 September 1854? No surviving siblings? Your husband, Peter, was apprentice first in Hammersmith at the workshop of Falcon Riviere, and next at your father's, after Riviere died a year into his indenture?' I nodded. 'You married in June 1854? Peter took over the binding business, and moved it to Lambeth in November 1854? He suffers from rheumatism? Now an invalid?' I nodded again and again.

'I presume he has been taking salicylate, and probably quinine too, and that neither have been efficacious? And various other splendid embrocations too, no doubt, all with trifling success? Any signs of gout? Sciatica? Pleurisy? Periosteal nodes?' I had long since ceased nodding, for I simply did not know, and he waved his arm dismissively.

'Let us get back to the point. Jack Tapster, apprenticed to you since December 1854, of Howley-place, Waterloo. Any trouble with him?'

I shook my head. He sat down at his desk and picked up, not a pen from the well, but a gold pencil with a large coloured jewel embedded in the end, and added something to the notes.

'Thank you, Mrs Damage. You may go now. We shall contact you soon with regard to our full intentions for you. Good day.'

I put down my tea, stood up, and the gentlemen both stood up too, and I went over to the door on my own. No Goodchild appeared to open it for me. Behind me I heard Diprose gather himself together with a start, and he commanded me to wait. 'I suppose I should take you back now,' he said, and he took the door from me and ushered me through.

We found our own way to the stairs, and started to descend.

'Well, that went sufficiently well, under the circumstances.'

'Should I not have said all that about Peter and his rheumatism and the like?' I said anxiously. 'He knew it all, it seemed. I couldn't have lied, could I? Not like I did to you at the beginning. Should I have? I knew I should've.'

'Come, come, my dear. You have fooled no one. Sir Jocelyn has bestowed you with the blessing of his approval, and, *malgré moi*, you and I have no choice but to consent.'

I wish I had known then why the man had such an aversion to me. I did not know if I shamed him, or tempted him, or repulsed him, or all three at once, but for something about these feelings he chose to dislike me.

We hailed another cab and returned to the shop. He bolted the front and back doors, and gathered some manuscripts about him.

'First, Boccaccio's *Decameron*.' He held it close to me, without proffering it, and I could smell the sourness of his breath. 'It has some fine illustrations; *c'est à dire*, they are of the more exuberant variety.' He was agitated, and his eyes refused to meet mine. 'You must render their spirit on the binding, if not their detail.' He sighed, and added, 'You will be very busy. I will have the first books to you as soon as I manage to procure them from Amsterdam.' It did not occur to my troubled mind to question the whereabouts of the books, whether they were enjoying the sights and sports Amsterdam had to offer or whether their purpose there was strictly business, innocent such that I was. What sudden reversals were to befall me.

'And here. You will need this.' He handed me a weighty implement, like a large bookbinder's tool or stamp. I examined it carefully: it seemed to be a peculiar coat of arms. In the centre was a shield, divided into four by two straight overlaying chains: in the top left quadrant was a dagger; in the top right, a clarion; bottom left, a large buckle as from a belt; bottom right, a crowing rooster. The shield was supported by a rampant elephant on the left, at the foot of which was a cannon, with a pile of three balls waiting to be loaded, and on the right, a satyr, also rampant, leaning against a column around which curled a serpent. Above the shield a beacon burned from a castellated grate, with bunches of grapes descending from its lower basket. And across the middle snaked a ribbon with words on, in undulate, which I could not make out in reverse.

'The Knightley coat of arms?' I asked.

'*Les Sauvages Nobles,*' Diprose replied, but I did not understand. 'The majority of books will need this on the rear cover, or occasionally on the front when the design so warrants. You shall receive instructions.'

'And what about payment?'

'Mrs Damage. *Virtus post nummos*, indeed!'

But the blackguard's insult only emboldened me. 'Mr Diprose. You know I have not yet the means to purchase materials appropriate to the task.'

'I will send you a few things to help you out,' he said with irritation. Then he creaked his torso forward at me and placed his hands upon his thighs, so that he could stare directly into my eyes. 'Tell me, child, the definition of "discretion".'

I swallowed. 'Prudence,' I blurted out. Then I thought harder. *Discernere*, to perceive. 'The ability to discern.' My mother, the governess, delighted in setting me word games like this. 'Circumspection.' *Circumspecere*, to look around on all sides. She would have pushed me harder still. I could hear her voice now, but I was grasping for my own words. 'The adoption –' I was getting into my stride, '– of behaviour appropriate to the situation.' I paused. 'Which errs on the side of caution,' I added.

'It will be required,' he replied. 'Payment will be handsome once discretion has been proven. You certainly have need to assure that *je ferme ma bouche*. How tidy, that we are now keeping each other's secrets. We have *un arrangement*?'

I nodded. Satisfied, he reached for my hand, helped me to my feet, and placed the Boccaccio in my hands. I made to move towards the front of the shop.

'No, Mrs Damage,' said Mr Diprose. 'You must leave now by the back entrance.'

I looked at him blankly.

'Are you scared of ghosts, Mrs Damage?'

'Ghosts?' Was he testing my mettle, as a member of the fair sex?

'Ghosts,' he repeated. 'For there is reputed to be a ghost of Holywell-street. Will you permit me to shiver your senses with the story?'

'Please do.' I stood by the back door and waited.

'Once upon a time, a young man – let us call him Joseph – came up from the country – let us say, the wilds of Lincolnshire – to earn his living in the big city – let us say, he was a printer. Joseph was abandoned one night – perhaps he had been drinking with some other printers – in the darkness of Holywell-street, but knew it was a journey of only a few short yards back to the main thoroughfare of the Strand. He went one way, then another, then took a turn, then another turn, and found himself staggering down more and more winding alleys, and soon became lost.'

'What became of him?'

'Many have guessed, but none will confirm. You and I can only imagine what cruelty lies in these irregular alley-ways. His body was never found, but his spirit was unable to find the same freedom. It is said that his ghost still haunts Holywell-street, still wanders round and about the narrow lanes, never quite reaching the Strand, and constantly going back to the beginning of his journey, where he has to start his quest over again. But you, Mrs Damage, seem skilled at finding your way out.'

Then he drew a small map of the back alleys on a scrap of lining paper. 'Go here, then turn – here – and – here. Look sharp, head down, and quick pace.' The route he was suggesting would take me out into the daylight of the Strand rather than back into Holywell-street. 'You must return this way too. *En cachette*. Three sharp knocks only on the back door. It is preferable for you that way.'

I ran through the twisting lanes as instructed, and blessedly did not meet another soul, living or otherwise. I told Peter little of the day's events on my return, only that Mr Diprose had decided to furnish us with more books. I did not wish to burden him with the details, for they troubled me, and I was stalked in my dreams that night, not by the rangy Sir Jocelyn and his stiff Mr Diprose, but by an animated, malevolent anatomy model. It chased me around the benches and presses of the workshop, its pink open throat cackling at me and issuing threats, until, at the door to the kitchen, I turned and stood my ground. The model became still and calm too, and let me stroke its painted skin, and I placed my hands inside onto the organs, which were not cold and hard, but soft, warm and wet. It giggled as I fingered them, weighed them in my hands, held them up to the light.

To know the inner workings, to understand the inside, to see within: I would put up with the cigar smoke, and the men who looked, and the animal heads, and the back alley-ways, for that. Or so I believed, in those days.

Chapter Seven

Speak when you're spoken to,
Come for one call,
Shut the door after you,
Turn to the wall.

Dear Mrs Damage

These choice materials are not meant as a replacement for your creative eye, whose cleverness and ingenuity at selecting unusual yet appropriate couvertures has already been noted and appreciated. I bestow upon you the final freedom to choose, whether it be silk, skin, fur, feather, or que voulez-vous. I entreat you, notwithstanding, to select with care. Just as some colours flatter particular complexions, and some bonnet styles suit certain shapes of head, so too must you consider the colours and styles of your binding according to the nature of the book. Sometimes I will require the most excellent bindings, in hue, texture and execution, to arouse and induce a primitive – c'est à dire, carnal, rather than cerebral – reaction. Sometimes, on the contrary, I will command the most plain, unobtrusive binding to act as shackle and protector for the more mischievous literature, to prevent it leaping off the shelf at the less knowledgeable reader. I trust we have an understanding; that it is the responsibility of you, the binder, so to clothe the texts for me, the bibliophile, in suitably pleasing habillé, *and that you will prove quick to instruct.*

As an aside, it is with some ennui *that I must inform you that our visitation to Berkeley-square did not go unnoticed by Lady Knightley, who labours under the illusion that her husband's activities do not escape her. She has sent me word that she wishes to meet with the little lady bookbinder with an eye for sentiment and fingers for finery; my speculations are that this is an innocent invitation without any basis in that green-eyed mistrust a lesser woman might display for a less-adoring husband, but that you are female is evident to her, and I propose to you that it would be* contra bonos mores *not to attend to her request as soon as possible. She receives on Tuesday and Thursday in the afternoon.*

Most sincerely yours, &c.

Charles Diprose

Encs.

Assorted leathers: 4 x alum-tawed pigskin, 1 x black sealskin, 2 x maroon crocodile skin, 2 x grey and white snakeskin, 4 x Japanese embossed leather (2 x floral, 2 x seaweeds and sea creatures)

Assorted silks, silk brocades and silk satins

Gold eyelets: sizes, various

2 oz gold

The paper may have been perfumed with vetivert, but the writing was spiky and stiff like the man himself, and unlike the soft wonders awaiting me inside the treasure chest. I unpacked the contents, and laid them out on the bench.

'Ooh, Mama, show me, show me!'

'Where have you been?'

'Playing in the street with Billy.'

'Billy?'

'Mrs Eeles's boy.'

'So your hands won't be clean.'

She held them out to me, and flapped them over and around. 'Spotless.'

'Black as a pickaninny. Come and let me wipe them.' I took her through the curtain back into the kitchen, dipped a sponge into the pail, and cleaned right into the lines of her palms and under her finger-nails. Then she dried them on a towel, and followed me back into the workshop.

'Oh, Mama! It's like the elves and their shoemaker! Can we be the shoemaker, can we? Can we cut little patterns out and leave them for the elves to make by morning? Look, this would make a fine jerkin for a goblin king. And he could have breeches of this, and boots of that. And he would marry a royal elfin queen, and she would be draped in this!'

'That's enough now, Lucinda. I am as excited as you, but we must be careful with Mama's work materials.'

'But can I help you?'

'Yes. You can help me choose the right ones, and tell me how I can cut them, and combine them, and inlay them, to make the most beautiful clothes, but for our books, not for any elves or goblins.'

'But Mama, what if they're goblins *disguised* as books? And when we go to bed they leap up off the workbench and go to the goblin ball?'

'Wouldn't that be exciting? Only I hope they would promise to be home by midnight and not soil their breeches in the mud before I get a chance to give them back to Mr Bookseller.'

'But what if they don't?'

'Then we must rap their bottoms with an emery strop and tie them to the bench with trindles.'

'I'm tired, Mama.'

'Perhaps you should lie down and have a little rest. Are you feeling peculiar?'

'A little. But not too much.'

'Would you like to sleep in your bed?'

'I'd like you to put me in front of the fire in the parlour.'

So I carried her through, and made a space for her on the rug in front of the fire, at the feet of her father sleeping in the armchair. She rested her head on the cushion which I took off the Windsor chair, and I brought a blanket down from her bed and wrapped it around her. Her eyes started to sink into her, and it looked as if she was starting to doze off. I was impatient to get back to the leathers and silks, and to get Jack started on the backing boards. I kissed her on the forehead; in retrospect I should have waited longer, but she seemed drowsy enough.

In the workshop I re-read the letter, and pulled the manuscripts out from the bottom of the box. And then Peter shouted from the sitting room, and his shouting was pained and anxious, and I knew what had happened even before I heard her small body writhing on the floor and hitting the table legs.

'Where are you, woman? For the love of – !'

I rushed in and moved the two dining chairs away in one gesture, and kicked the table towards the wall with my foot, before rolling Lucinda on to her side and placing my hand on the small of her back in the slow wait for her to find calm. Past experience should have taught me that she always would, but each time it felt as if she had cast off into the unknown, and might never drift back to my shore. Her skin was grey, and her breathing fast. But eventually she fell into a deep slumber, and her breathing grew more regular, and I picked her up in my arms and buried my head into her neck, and wished I never had to let her go from this hold again.

Peter uttered a couple of 'humphs' before picking up an old newspaper. He considered it improper to fuss over anybody else's health, except, perhaps his own. All that he wanted, always, was for Lucinda to keep herself quiet and out of his way, and he had neither the energy nor the inclination to engage with her childish whims; if the needs of others were not subordinated to his own, he sulked. But this was ever the wife's challenge: to look after her children, while making it seem as if she put her husband first.

I took Lucinda to bed, and sat darning clothes by her bedside for an hour, until I could be sure she was safe. Her fitting, coming so soon after the excitement of the parcel in the workshop, felt like a bad omen. I wondered if I should simply repackage the box and instruct Jack to take it back to Holywell-street, with the announcement that Damage's would have nothing more to do with Diprose's, but we were in no position to look this particular gift horse in the mouth.

I kissed her hot cheek, and descended. Peter was agitating his crimson fingers and muttering ungodly curses beneath his breath; it had not escaped me that the seams of his moral suit of clothes were becoming somewhat unstitched as his health deteriorated, abandoned as he must have felt by the good Lord.

Back in the workshop, as I wondered what to do with the dangerous contents of the crate, I discovered something I had overlooked beneath them all. It was a large apothecary's bottle, with a hand-written label, which read, 'Patient: Mr Peter Damage, 2, Ivy-street, Waterloo. Under Specification of Dr Theodore Chisholm, Harley Street. Triple Strength Formula. Not for General Sale.' I uncorked it and examined the contents: it was a brown, syrupy liquid, which I took to be a laudanum nostrum, not unlike Battley's, Dalby's or Godfrey's. I took it back in to Peter and read him the label.

'I'll get a spoon,' I said, and left it on the table next to him, but by the time I returned, he had already swigged from the bottle. I re-corked it and put it on the dresser, but only a few minutes later I noticed a strange smile creep across his lips, and his eyelids were heavy. Unlike me, he slept soundly that night.

*   *   *

The illustrations to the *Decameron* were indeed unusual. At first I could not work out what they were about, but when I did, I said 'oh!' and quickly closed the book. I paced around the workshop for several minutes. I arranged the papers in a more perfect pile. The tools, always left in neat rows, were made neater by my agitated hands. I chipped the wax drippings off the candles and laid them in the melting tray. Only when there was nothing left for me to straighten and order did I return to the unusual volume with great trepidation and care. But as I still was unable to view the pictures for long, I turned to the relative safety of the text, and did what I normally did when I felt flustered: I read.

I read of creatures – I could not yet consider them people – who performed acts without shame such as that they would be sent straight to hell, and with good reason. I trembled at the wantonness within and searched for shelter for my soul against the certain apocalypse that would befall them for doing it and me for bearing witness. My shame would protect me, I believed. At least, it always had done; we women wear it like a veil.

I read into the night, a hundred marvellous tales of fortune and the plague and truth and lying – and the other kind of lying. And oh! The women dressed as men! And my! The heart consumed! And then when I could feel my place in the text encroaching upon the stiff paper of an engraving, I was at least prepared, and could accept that the illustrations made sense in the context of the whole, and were another way into, or a different angle on, the startling feelings elicited by Boccaccio's masterful tales.

And I could feel the familiar sensation of a design for the binding forming in my head. As the public face of this very private volume, it had to be something ambivalent, sensual and evocative, which only hinted at the surprises inside. My yearnings that night were not for the strange joys Boccaccio wrote of, but for the skill to execute a binding that would do them justice.

In the morning, Peter, dull of temper, instructed me somehow to raise eighteen shillings, as Skinner was due to call later that day. So Lucinda and I took his Sunday suit to the pawn-shop, and got a solid pound in return, which felt satisfactory. As we rounded the corner of New Cut, two half-sovereigns in my purse, we passed the theatre, where a group of the better-to-do ladies and gentlemen of Lambeth idly watched a performance by some minstrels blackened with burnt cork.

'Look, Mama! Let's go see.' I was going to lift Lucinda up to get a better view over the crowd, but her wily smallness wheedled its way through the skirts and trouser legs almost to the front, and I found myself in the midst of the crowd some way behind her. A lady stood in front of me whose golden curls shook about her ears as she laughed at the musical jokes. A gentleman had his arm around her tiny waist, and when the songs became maudlin she leant her head on his shoulder, crushing her perfect curls on that side.

Something fell to the ground between us. I waited for a moment, then cast my eyes down, and slowly stooped to pick it up, hoping she wouldn't notice the movement to her right side. It was a fine gold earring, inlaid with four garnets. I hesitated for a moment, and looked at my lady's ears. They were graced with simple diamond studs. I scanned the rest of the group to find the lady with the naked ear to whom I should return it. I saw her; she was directly by my left arm, but she had not cared to look at what I had collected from the pavement. In an irreparable instant, I curled my fist over the earring. I waited a few moments until the end of the song, and then in the midst of the applause I reached forward between two gentlemen and tugged gently on Lucinda's braids.

'Come now, little one,' I hissed.

'But Mama,' she wailed.

'Hush your moaning, child. We must be off. Hurry, or I shall tell your father.'

The garnets would be perfect for my design. I had become a thief.

I showed the earring to Peter, who did not ask me how I had come by it, but straightways set himself to troubling how to provide a firm setting for the garnets. I bit my lip as he held the piece on the palm of one hand, and prodded it with a bloated finger-pad of the other hand. It was going to be a painstaking piece of work for him, and I meant that literally.

That afternoon, after Mr Skinner had come and gone with one half-sovereign and eight shillings and very little trouble else, Peter found solace for his resultant nerves in the laudanum bottle again. I put Lucinda to an early bed, wiped the brown spittle off Peter's chin, and stayed up until midnight disbanding and cleaning off the backs of the sections of the old binding of the *Decameron*, and mending the holes in the folds with pared paper. It was an arduous and fragile process, but I trusted that the mends, which seemed invisible by candle-light, would be likewise barely perceptible in the light of day. My eyes were heavy by the time I rigged up the sewing-frame, but it was a simple enough layout – octavo, with blank first recto, engraved frontispiece on first verso, title page on second recto – and I sewed all the sections together and left them on Jack's bench in time for his half-past-seven start. Despite my empty stomach, I slept soundly at last, well nigh oblivious to Peter's moans of pain and fitful snores.

In the morning I let Jack in, settled Lucinda with some sewing in the kitchen, and returned to the workshop. Hands on hips, I stood looking at Jack, waiting for him to look up at me, but he did not; he continued to prepare the cords and boards. Then he snorted, as if trying to suppress a laugh, and I giggled at the sound, and soon he was chuckling too. Finally he turned his back on me to fiddle with the laying-press and said with a guffaw, 'I thought I'd seen every-thing, me, living by the river!' I grabbed the duster from the rail and wiped down the bench with what felt like alacrity, and Jack turned his head round and winked at me. I cocked my head and my hip towards him in one motion, and grinned.

'But what do you reckon, we don't show the old man?'

'Mr D? Do him the world of good!'

'Hark at you! Vile little river-scamp! Be the end of him, more like.'

'Nah, keep him busy in there.'

'Impudent lad! Give your red rag a holiday, Jack-a-dandy.'

'Beg pardon, Mrs D. Didn't mean no harm.'

Now it was my turn to wink at him, and he beamed across his wicked freckly face like a sweet urchin.

'Hush thy mouth, Jack,' I added quietly, 'because thy lord and master will be amongst us this morning.' Jack struck his brow with his fingers in a mock salute, and the tattooed skull on his forearm grimaced at me as if it wanted to warn me that this was no laughing matter, when the only funds that had come in had gone straight out again, and every knock at the door put a terror into us. Truth be told, I was rather troubled about how Peter would fare, not only with the garnets, but with the mischievous book itself.

I need not have worried. The garnets took so much of his concentration that he never once so much as asked the title. As far as he was concerned, it was another fancy lady's book, of no interest to him, all shimmering gold flowers and flagons, scrolls and swags. I adorned the back with the crest of *Les Sauvages Nobles*, and tooled the word '*Nocturnus*', as instructed by Diprose, beneath it. And the four stones studded the corners like small pools of blood.

When the book was finally finished, the three of us gathered around the wine-coloured volume, silent with satisfaction. 'The *Decameron*. Bockackio,' Peter read from the spine. The lettering was perfectly even – Moive Bibble had packed her bags – although Peter said nothing about my handiwork.

I gave it to Jack to deliver to Holywell-street, with the map on the scrap of paper to guide him in the back way. He left at midday, and I spent the next few hours scrubbing the workshop. I cleaned the windows and oil lamps thoroughly, and garnered together every last trace of gold-dust to take back to Edwin Nightingale. Then Lucinda and I made griddlecakes for our tea. Still Jack was not back, and the clock was chiming four.

Finally, just before five, he rollicked in with a nose as red as his hair, a wet patch down the front of his coat, and a large brown-paper package in his arms.

'Look at you! You're bung-eyed, Jack!' I scolded, and whipped his behind with a kitchen towel.

'And you're lovely, Mrs D.'

'Where have you been?'

'At the sluicery.'

'I can see that. What have you had to drink?'

'Why? You offering me some more?'

'No, I am not. But go on, then, tell me what happened, but hush you now, before you wake the squire.' I took the parcel from him and placed it on the table; it felt like more manuscripts.

'He was chuffed to pieces, Mrs D, to pieces. You won't believe what he gave me. This.' He opened his fist to show a handful of silver and brown coins. 'Nah, that's not it. Well it is, or it was. It was a friggin' coach-wheel, Mrs D!'

'A crown? He gave you a crown?'

'Aye he did, and I said to him, I said, am I to give this back to Mr Damage, and he says no, Jack, my boy, it's for you. It's your tip, young lad, he called me.'

It was as much as I could do to restrain myself from snatching them out of the sot's hand; the injustice of it stung my cheeks. Here my child was starving while Jack went out drinking on my employer's gratuities.

'And this is for you, he said it was.' He waved a brown

envelope in my face. I grabbed it, and felt inside to find a sovereign. It was more than I had handed over to Skinner.

Jack whistled. 'A thick 'un an' all. Crikey. And go on, open the parcel, Mrs D, when you've stopped dribblin' over the balsam.'

I prised open the seal, and found inside several thin manuscripts and a letter from Mr Diprose.

Dear Mrs Damage,

I enclose twelve books which I would not trouble you to persue at any length. Their literary merit is scant; they belong to that subset of facetiae *known as* galanterie, *and they are nothing but the simplest examples of that genre. Despite their gaudiness, I ask you to dress them with understated elegance, as one would make a lady of an opera-dancer. On the back of each must be the crest of* Les Sauvages Nobles; *underneath, one each of the following noms de plume, in the order in which the manuscripts are stacked herewith:*

– Nocturnus
– Labor Bene
– P.cinis It.
– Monachus
– Vesica Quartus
– Beneficium Flumen
– Praemium Vir
– Clementia
– R. Equitavit
– Osmundanus
– Clericus
– Scalp-domus

Yours most sincerely, &c
Charles Diprose

* * *

123

I chose to ignore Diprose's suggestion that I should not read the books, for I felt it important to distil the essence of the book on to the binding. But he was correct about their merit: they were sentimental novelettes with little thought of style, characterisation and plot, and I only managed to wade my way through the first three of the twelve.

The first was rather fancy in its descriptions of marital passion, and the protagonists preferred to do the act *en plein air*, as Diprose no doubt would have said.

The second made me blush even more, for the activity, although occurring inside the house this time, was not inside the marriage, and described with a bit less restraint.

By the time I reached the third, I wished I had taken Diprose's advice more seriously. I knew not how to clothe these naked bodies in the binding of a book.

Eventually I restored to the language of flowers. In the centre of each front cover, I wove a wreath of ivy leaves, as a symbol of wedded love and fidelity, and these poor souls needed all the help they could get. How appropriate, I thought at the time, that I lived in Ivy-street. And within each wreath of ivy, I placed a different bouquet of flowers according to the requirements of the story.

For the first, fern, for shelter from the elements.

For the second, marigold, for the health and vigour the protagonists clearly required.

For the third, euphorbia, to represent persistence, the key value praised therein.

And may the Lord bless my naïveté, for I made sure that the discerning booklover could delight himself with the discovery that, in each circlet of ivy leaves, every third leaf was in fact a heart.

Chapter Eight

When I was young and in my prime,
I'd done my work by dinner time;
But now I'm old and cannot trot
I'm obliged to work till eight o'clock.

'You are skimping on the household,' Peter shouted at me from upstairs as yet another parcel arrived at the workshop.

This one seemed innocuous enough at first glance: an Apocrypha, a Litany, a *Paradise Lost* and a *Regain'd*, an *Areopagitica*; two reprints of Michael Drayton's *The Nymphidia* and *The Muses Elizium*; M. Felix Lajard's *Cult, Symbols and Attributes of Venus*, published in Paris in 1837 and in need of a re-bind, a minute-book for a Turkish Bath company; several collections of correspondence; two Visitors' Books, four blank account ledgers; twelve black journals; and various short anthropological, medical and anatomical tracts. Most were to receive the coat-of-arms of *Les Sauvages Nobles*, especially the blank ones, which would display it on the front cover, not the rear.

'Smell that?' Peter shuffled into the workshop as I was reading Diprose's accompanying letter. ' 'Tis an ill bird that fouls its own nest. You haven't cleaned the range properly for days, and the house forever smells of burnt fat.' I knew I would have to scrape it well and rinse with more than vinegar, but it was the least of my worries. If the business coming through Damage's doors were only half of what I had wanted,

I thought to myself, my initial desires must have been truly excessive. And Diprose was reminding me in his letter that Lady Knightley persisted in her wish to meet with me.

But Peter was right. I was keeping the windows in the workshop scrupulously clean to help our work-weary eyes, but I had not cleaned the windows in the house since January, so it looked gloomier than ever. A thick layer of grime had settled over everything, and I knew I performed every task – the laundry, the cooking, the scouring of pots, the cleaning out of the grates, the filling of the coal-scuttles – in a manner that became more slapdash by the day. I rarely had the time in the evenings to sit and mend clothes, so holes grew in Lucinda's frocks and my smocks. Peter, fortunately, rarely changed out of his nightclothes these days, except when some of Dr Chisholm's precious mixture spilt down his chest. Washing days – when I used to have to get up at four to start heating the water – had started to drift over now on to other days, so each morning I would treat only the dirtiest of the linen for stains, put them in to soak, pummel them in a snatched morning break, then try to rinse them some time in the afternoon, and hang them out to dry in front of the fire overnight. By morning they would always be speckled with soot and dirt from the coal fire, oil lamp and candles. But they were still cleaner than they would have been if I had hung them outside on the line.

Peter was also right about housework being circular and endless, but he was wrong that it was best suited to a woman's disposition. That is to say, it was not suited to mine. I always found myself eager to start work in the workshop despite the pressure of household chores, for in binding books I faced a result, an object that I could hold, and of which I could be proud. I could see little purpose in taking pleasure in the whitening of a doorstep or the making of a plum pudding: both would vanish within minutes, along with all proof of my toil.

Peter's scolding that morning only made me feel cooped in a cage. To avoid facing the mouting workload and more of his wrath, I decided that today I would visit Lady Knightley in Berkeley-square.

I put some sand to heat in a pan over the range, beat and sponged my floral dress once more, and set about making myself somewhat more presentable. A hard task, or so I thought, until I ran a brush through my hair and looked in the glass. Are my weary eyes deceiving me, I wondered, or have my grey hairs disappeared? Where could they have gone to? I looked younger, more like myself as I was a few years ago. Could it be that I was actually thriving on this new regime? But alas, it was not my eyes, but my hairbrush (and the dirty glass) that played tricks on me. I had not washed either for weeks: filthy from the constant grime snared by my hair, the hairbrush blackened my hair back again every time I brushed. I smiled at my own vanity; I was meeting a lady today.

I went back to the kitchen, transferred the hot sand into a calico bag, brought it up to Peter, and tucked it in at the bottom of the bed where his feet lay.

'Where are you going?'

'To see a lady about some books.'

'I need nursing.'

'I will be back soon. What do you need?'

'Some beef-tea.'

'I will get some gravy-beef from Sam Battye on my way back,' I said. I knew already that I would lie and say that he had none, not that we had not the pennies for it. I would make him some arrowroot, or toast-water, instead.

I walked quickly from the dingier part of the metropolis to the more delightful one; I could not be away from Lucinda, or my bindings, for long.

It was not Goodchild who opened the door between the plant balls today, but a short, squat woman who looked as if she had been accidentally crushed in one of our presses, which had crumpled her face and body latitudinally before some kind mechanic had noticed and unscrewed her. She was a series of wide horizontal folds: her forehead bulged low over her brow, her nose over her chin, her chin over her neck, and her breasts over her gut, somewhat like the old Tudor tenements in Holywell-street or by the river.

'I'm here to see Lady Knightley, please.'

'Card?'

'I have no card.'

'Name?'

'Mrs Damage.'

She closed the door in my face, and the latch clicked shut. I stood looking at the fine brass door-furniture on the black-painted door for a moment, before turning to face Berkeley-square, with its enormous trees, and close-cropped grass, in which not a weed dared grow. Then I turned back again, and the door was still closed, so I started down the steps. A wasted journey, but at least I could say to Diprose that I had tried. I crossed the road and stood on the verge of the grass. I crouched down, and reached out to touch it. It felt illegal.

'Mrs Damage!'

I pulled my hand back and stood up as if I had been stung by a bee in the non-existent clover, but I did not turn round.

'Mrs Damage! What are you doing?' It was that maid again, calling from the top of the Knightleys' steps.

Head bowed, I hurried back across the street so I would not have to shout my feeble explanation. Touching the grass. I'm ever so sorry. We don't have grass like that in Lambeth, see.

But before I could speak, the woman called again, 'I'm to take you up to see Lady Knightley,' so I ran up the steps for fear that the door would close in my face once more, and into the hall, and was taken aback again by the statuary

Negro lad, at whom I nodded by way of apology, and followed the maid up the stairs. We went along the plush, carpeted corridor, past the lion's den of Sir Jocelyn's office, and stopped outside another door.

The maid opened it, but before she could show me through she rushed inwards, saying something that sounded like, 'Let me help you, ma'am.' The door swung back towards me but did not quite catch: was I to push it open with my fingertips and peer round to show my presence, or was I to wait until it was re-opened for me? I stared at the strip of light between the jamb and the door. I heard panting as the maid plumped cushions, a lady sighed, a drink was poured.

'Where is the girl?' the sighing voice enquired. Footsteps approached the door again. From the maid's face as she pulled the door open, I realised I should have been bold enough to follow her in initially. A less polite girl than me would have thought of a name for that woman, even if she would only have hissed it under her breath to her on passing.

The lady, lying on a mauve chaise-longue, was as graced in charm and sensitivity as her maid lacked it, but that, then, is because she was the lady, and not the maid.

'Thank you, Buncie,' she said, by way of dismissal to the maid, and turned to me. 'The little bookbindress!' she exclaimed. 'Come, sit here by me. Let me see you!' But it was her I wanted to see – and not be seen by – and this glorious chamber too. It was a paradise of femininity and sweetness; she was not the only treasure in it. Everywhere was silken, shiny, smooth and soft: fringed shawls bedecked with roses and peonies were draped over the backs of chairs and occasional tables; the mantel was pelmetted with pink and green tassels, some so deep I feared they would catch fire. The sound of birdsong was such that I had never deemed possible to hear in London – it seemed louder even than when I had stood in Berkeley-square itself – and the dried spiced petals in bowls gave off the smell of roses so strongly it was as if every fabric in the room had been rinsed only yesterday in pure rosewater. Everything beckoned 'touch me', but the moment I entertained that thought the room seemed to shriek at me, 'but not with those grubby common little hands!' and so I swelled and shrank my way round the room by turns.

The walls were papered a tender duck-egg blue. The gold beading between the panels glimmered as if they were nothing less than solid strips of real gold. The buds on the chintz looked as if they could burst into flower at any moment, and the blooms as if they could have been picked off the sofa and displayed in a vase. And from the ceiling hung three enormous, glass gasoliers, cleaner than my common gas-lamps ever were. There were wide window-seats in the vast windows, which offered views that were paintings in themselves: trees, and a sky that was so blue it could not have been the one I had left outside in Berkeley-square, and certainly not the one that hung over our heads in Lambeth. Here there was an abiding sense of purity about the room, a luxuriance, a peace.

I glimpsed my journal lying on her desk next to a charming blotter and inkstand, pen-tray and paper knife. It was the one bound in blue silk embroidered with pink, gold and silver flowers, and it did, indeed, match the décor of the salon. Then the lady patted the chair next to her again, and I saw her hands, and curled mine under in shame.

The cuff from which her hand appeared was finely embroidered in red and blue threads, as were her hems, and round her waist was an elaborate sash dripping with red and blue beads. Her face was not exactly beautiful: her features were meaner than the expansiveness of the room would have suggested, and she had small, almond-shaped eyes that did not seem to see me. Her mouth was thin, and when she smiled at me it was close-lipped and practised, but at least, as my mother would have said, she smiled. Descriptions such as 'enigmatic' and 'wan' would no doubt have pleased her. Her complexion was such as one of our modern painters would have delighted in; like the room, she had a subtle gold-tinged glow about her.

'So you are my fine bindress!' Her voice was quiet, but had a hard edge, as if used to speaking only sparkling wit and clever sarcasm. 'Let me look at you. I can't tell you what a stir it put us in when Charlie told us you were a *woman*. Tell me, Mrs Damage, you must be frightfully clever to carry it off. Is it dreadfully hard work?'

I cannot for the life of me remember how I replied. I believe I answered her with simplicity and timidity, and that she did not seem to notice or care. I do remember taking especial care with my pronunciation.

The conversation flowed reasonably well, coming as it did in the main from her. She spoke in short sentences, as if otherwise she would, rather bothersomely, run out of air. But she was not sparse in her compliments for my bindings and indeed revealed her veritable passion for the subject. She directed me here and there around the shelves of her room, asking me to take down this volume of poetry, that volume of diaries, and bring them to her. But her shelves were filled too tightly, so it was hard to ease the books out using the sides of the spine cover; many a headband had been viciously ripped in the pursuit of a book. I was also anxious that my hands would sully the bindings, and wondered if I should ask her for a cloth to protect them. I did not stop to notice the absurdity of the bookbinder who feared that her hands, which bound books daily, could not then hold a finished book for a few seconds.

She certainly did not have the same reservations, for she rubbed her hands over the leathers and silks in the same way that I would season the skin of a chicken before sending it to the bake-house, and she opened the books with such a vile crack she could have been instructing me on how to spatchcock the fowl. The number of spines she broke during my short visit to her that morning would have kept me in business for days, not to mention the headbands. I could solicit her for work, I thought, should the trade from Diprose ever dry up. Furthermore, although there were a handful of fine or rare bindings in her collection, I saw nothing to which I could not aspire; indeed, I noticed a few books that would never have been allowed to leave Damage's in their state, and started to realise that already I could consider myself a reasonably competent binder, with capabilities beyond my own doubts.

'Have you been to America?' she asked suddenly. I told her that I had not. I tried to think of something appropriate to add, but felt that she would not wish to know that the only long-distance travelling my family had undertaken was when Peter's great-uncle was transported to the colonies for political radicalism, and took his cousins with him. Peter, out of a sense of moral rectitude, had chosen not to share the details with me, and I in turn kept them from my patroness.

My silence was filled by her sigh, for something was clearly troubling her. She closed her eyes again, and asked me if I was familiar with the activities of the Ladies' Society for the Assistance of Fugitives from Slavery. I had to disappoint her again.

She was, she explained, a founder member of the Society, which reported to the British and Foreign Anti-Slavery Society. She told me, with increasing rapidity and shortness of breath, of her initiation into the abolitionist movement as she entered womanhood, when she felt the burden of frivolous society being lifted from her slender shoulders and replaced by a meaningful crusade, which would weigh heavily but not crush her.

I finally accepted that I did not have to be poised with something interesting to say. As I listened I let my gaze roam around the room again, and this time I saw a framed hand-bill, depicting a figure not unlike the boy in the hall, only kneeling and chained. I could just make out the inscription, 'Am I not a man and brother?'

'I will tell you,' she went on, 'of the horrors our dusky brethren still have to suffer in America.' And she did, and she was right in describing them as horrors. Yet I could not help thinking of our own workhouses, which sounded similar enough: wives taken from husbands, and children from mothers, and sickness and hunger and those girls whose bodies were found and everyone knew it was the master who had done it, but no one could say anything, because they were nothing more than his plaything, as they all were, even the little ones. So as she sounded forth about whips and bodies on trees, I couldn't see much difference, although I am sure she could have found me one. I was relieved when she cut to the purpose of her summoning me to her, which I feared she had started to lose sight of, as I was unable to fathom it all this time. I was even starting to think that perhaps this was what ladies of her station did for pleasure: call for some hapless poor woman, and torment her with ghastly stories of what people of our colour did to people of other colours in far-off lands.

'One of the Society's main activities, aside from our endless campaigns for abolition, is sponsorship. Each year we raise enough money to assist a handful of fugitives from slavery in their flight, and their establishment in a new way of life. It is hard to live as a free man even in a state where slavery has been outlawed. It is safer in Boston than in Virginia; it is safer in Canada than Boston, yet it is safer still in Europe. The lucky ones find safe passage here, and here we can help them.

'There is one slave in whom we have been particularly interested. Lady Grenville was visiting friends in Virginia last year, and was so struck by a certain young man that she raised a large enough sum, from teas and bazaars, to purchase him from his owner. Lady Grenville has since, sadly, died, and it has fallen to me to deal with the matter. We placed him as a porter for Messrs Farmer and Rogers in Regent-street, but they have unfortunately removed him, due to tardy habits. He deserves a second chance. I have been hoping to procure him a more stable position, in a more intimate, family business, to earn himself a living, and ultimately relieve his dependence on the Society.

'The inevitable fact is, that he is a man. We were all rather startled, my dear, when we discovered that our little bookbinder's is run by a woman, but . . .'

'. . . you can only have half of what you desire.'

'Excuse me?'

'Oh, I beg your pardon, madam. It just slipped out. It's something my mother said. "You can only have half of what you desire". Not meaning you, that is, but . . .'

'I see. Yes.' She seemed to weigh this for a while. 'A peculiar sentiment. But yes, in this situation, one can only have half of what one desires.' She nodded slowly. 'I see you are not of the ordinary sort, so I imagine you will be capable of managing this peculiar servant.'

What could I possibly have said to her? Did I not have more than enough on my plate than have to mother a vagrant fugitive slave as well? What of the millions of poor souls on my doorstep in Lambeth who also deserved a spot of employment? And what if the work were to dry up? Jack and I could manage at present, but what of the day when my efficiency had increased so much that I could bind a book of twice the beauty in half the time? It would not have occurred to Lady Knightley to ask if this suited my own ambitions for the business, or whether trade was healthy enough to sustain another employee.

And then she swept away all my fears and appealed directly to my lowest nature, which, due to desperation, was very receptive. 'The Society will provide you with a substantial subsidy. We do not expect you to cover the costs of training and settling from your own pocket. You will receive an initial sum of five pounds, followed by twenty-five shillings a month.'

Five pounds! I could not refuse. I knew I had little choice anyway, but the money swept away my doubts. A rudimentary plan was already forming in my head: the new clients to approach, the efficiency of a renewed triumvirate in the workshop. Besides, he might have been a man, but he was as desperate as I was, and would no doubt be grateful even to do women's work: I could hand over to him all the folding and sewing.

'You will keep a tally of any damage to property or goods, and we will cover this too.' Oh my, I thought, and the doubts flooded in again. Had I agreed to take on a wild animal? 'I said you were not of the ordinary sort. By doing this for me you are proving to be altogether rather remarkable.' I did not feel it. I only felt foolish. But five pounds, Dora, and a guaranteed turnover of twenty-five shillings a month!

At some point she must have finished talking, for she rang a little bell which sat on a silver platter by her chaise, and looked at me with a fancy smile, and we waited in a small silence, before Buncie appeared at the door. I rose and made to leave.

'And Mrs Damage.'

'Yes, madam?'

'Don't mention this to Jossie. He will surely try to intervene. I cannot tolerate another lecture about slavery.' She closed her mouth and looked away.

'Oh.' I paused, and heard Buncie huff behind me, so as only I, and not her mistress, could hear. I thought of the file he held on me. 'But he ... he ... knows all about what happens in the workshop.'

'Well, he doesn't have to know this, does he?' she snapped.

And so Buncie led me out into Berkeley-square again, and I ran home, intrigued by yet one more pact with another strange, luxurious person, suspended in her magical chamber, in a city full of secrets.

Chapter Nine

Miss Polly had a dolly who was sick, sick, sick,
So she called for the doctor to come quick, quick, quick.
The doctor came with his bag and his hat,
And he knocked at the door with a rat-a-tat-tat.
He looked at the dolly and he shook his head.
He said, 'Miss Polly, put her straight to bed.'
He wrote on a paper for a pill, pill, pill.
'I'll be back in the morning with my bill, bill, bill.'

Despite the curious turn of events and the promise of a new worker, the rigours of the daily round ground the memory of my visit to Lady Knightley out of my mind almost as soon as I returned. I worked hard in the workshop until late in the afternoon when Peter awoke and began crying for me. Every cavity of his face was swollen: the folds of skin under his eyes looked like bags of blood, dark like kidneys on the butcher's block, and his mouth was blistered and puckered.

'I had a b – b – bad d – d – dream.'

'Did you, my love? What was it that so scared you?'

'I, I, I'm not scared. Sit me by the fire.'

I settled him with a blanket and a cup of tea, before returning to the workshop to finish the botanical gold-tooling on the twelfth book. I was glad I had developed the motif of the ivy-wreath, for there had never again been a wedding ring on all those roaming hands. Jack was forwarding *Cults, Symbols and Attributes of Venus*, and Lucinda was rearranging the leather off-cuts into pretty shapes on the floor.

The only interruption I expected was Peter, with some complaint or other. So when we heard the sound of hooves and wheels stop outside the very door of the workshop, we were caught unawares. Jack opened the door to reveal a shiny black brougham, with bright red wheels, gold lamps, and a coat of arms on the side, pulled by a single chocolate-bay horse, and I was so startled when I saw who descended from it that I had to look away. And when I did, I saw Mrs Eeles, and Patience Bishop, both with arms folded and eyes watching, and behind them Nora Negley peered amongst twitching curtains. Some of the children had even stopped their playing to watch.

He was an even more wonderful sight than his carriage, I will admit. Quite the pink of fashion, as he stood there in his fine black frock coat, with his red cravat, gold eye-glasses, and heavy gold watch-chain across his vest. He held a silver cane, topped with a large round ball of red glass, like the largest ruby I'd ever seen. I almost forgot I was in my smock, with not a moment to change into my good cap and collars. At least I had my old ones on; I was not caught bare-headed by Sir Jocelyn Knightley.

He reached for my hand, and I proffered it, and he kissed it, even though it was stained with dye and gnarled with dried glue, and I bid him come in.

'Why, what a neat, well-kept workshop you run, Mrs Damage. And ah, that succulent, gamey smell you get in only the finest bookbinders' establishments.' It was the politest way yet anyone had ever described it.

'Good afternoon, Jack,' he said, before I had a chance to introduce him.

Jack stopped what he was doing and came to the side of the bench, made a little bow and said, 'Good afternoon, sir,' before going back to his work.

'And you must be little Lucinda,' he said to my daughter, and ruffled her hair. She scowled at him. Then, from beneath his frock coat, he produced something that looked remarkably like a tiny baby. He held it by the head, and its body hung limply from it, its limbs dangling independently, so I surmised it could not be a doll. I gasped in shock, and Lucinda screamed, 'Mama!' and ran to my skirts where she buried her face.

'What's the matter, Lucinda? Don't you like your new friend? If I am not mistaken, she is in need of some care.' He held it closer to her, and I could see the sweetest porcelain face looking at her, with rosebud lips and feathery eyelashes, and yellow curls painted over the smooth scalp. But if this really were a doll, I could not fathom why its body was not stiff, not all one with the head. Then he held it upright, both hands encircling its chest, and squeezed. A noise like the in-breath of a victim of pulmonary disease ensued, followed by the sound of a goat bleating: a high-pitched, 'Maaa-maaa'.

'Fancy that! She even calls you Mama. Here. What are you going to call her?'

I took the doll from Sir Jocelyn and crouched down to Lucinda. It astounded me: I had never seen a doll that was pretending to be a baby. All the dolls I had ever seen were dressed as miniature ladies, only even stiffer. I turned this one over in awe and lifted her cambric gown with as much care as if she had been a real baby: she had jointed limbs and a flexible chest that seemed to be made from india-rubber, and real little boots on her feet, tied with a green ribbon.

'Maaa-maaa,' she moaned back at me.

I couldn't help but giggle. 'Oh, my! Isn't she quite the little one!' I tried to press her into Lucinda's hands, but she refused, preferring to peek over my upper arm. 'I fear Lucinda wishes to be her elder sister, and not her mother.'

'Which seems to suit you perfectly, madam,' Sir Jocelyn remarked, and I blushed in an unseemly fashion for I knew he was teasing me.

'Will you show me around, Mrs Damage?' Sir Jocelyn said.

He had started to stroll around the workshop, so I stood up quickly, and laid the doll gently on the bench, as if rough handling might hurt her.

'I'll leave here for you, if ever you feel like it,' I whispered, and indeed, as I turned to follow his roaming frame, I saw, out of the corner of my eye, that Lucinda had stealthily taken the thing off the bench and was investigating it at closer quarters.

I barely reached his shoulders, for he was a big man, yet he moved around the benches with perfect balance and agility, and I knew from the flashing and glittering of his eyes that he was taking in every detail, down to the absence of my Peter.

'I congratulate you on the cleanliness of the place, Mrs Damage. I imagine that is not as easy task in Lambeth. Sometimes I loathe city life and yearn for the open veld. Or if it must be a city, make it Paris. I was born there; my father was French, did you not know?'

'No, I did not. Is Knightley a French name?'

'His name was Chevalier. I was orphaned young, and brought up in Worcestershire by my aunt, who decided to anglicise it. So, Knightley. But Sir Jocelyn Chevalier has a ring to it, does it not? You have been to Paris, Mrs Damage?'

I shook my head.

'The air affords wondrous clarity; the city rings pure. It is to the hideous opacity of London as heaven is to hell. I resent the return to London. I notice its stench most when I do.'

It was as if I mattered to him, and I knew I was succumbing to his derring-do and dash.

He picked up one of the books on the table, and ran his finger over the ivy-leaf wreath. '*Hedera helix*. Not the gentlest of plants. A hostile assailant, with quick, hardy runners; it deprives its host of sunlight, with a resultant loss of vigour, and eventual demise. I should recommend it to the Foreign Office as an emblem for the construction of Her Majesty's Empire.'

'You are too harsh on the plant, Sir Jocelyn,' I said. 'Pray tell me, what does not injure that to which it clings?'

'A very good question, Mrs Damage. I see you are no stranger to the philosophies of love.' He pretended to ponder, as we shared the joke. 'Woodbine,' he finally answered, with mock triumph, and returned to the ivy wreath. 'Your tooling is excellent,' he said. 'Strange to think we find such beauty in the posthumous scarification and gilding of an animal's hide. Like a tattoo, on dead skin.' Then he ceased his musing, seized one of my hands, and turned it over to stroke the palm, like a fortune-teller at a fair. 'Do these delicate hands really do all this hard work?'

I nodded, and he started to chuckle.

'Why are you laughing?' I asked, slightly indignant.

'Why, Mistress Binder? I will tell you why. Because you make me happy. And why do you make me happy? Because of your ingenuity, and your creativity, and your bravery.' He waited before delivering each attribute to me, like a gift on platter. 'Ah, Mrs Damage. You delight me. You are the fresh air we need in this stale old business. These are sumptuous, supple bindings, for men like me, who do not wish simply to read and shelve our books.' Then he added casually, 'Did you enjoy the *Decameron*?'

'Yes, thank you, sir.'

'Translated by John Florio, 1620. It's about time someone did a more modern version. With all one hundred stories. I pity poor Alibech, whose tale of putting the devil back into hell gets left out every time. Possibly I should . . . why, there's a capital idea! You see, Mrs Damage, what purpose science without its application to human existence? On my travels through the Orient I have gained wisdom of the sensual side of human nature, which has informed and transformed my scientific study, such that my purpose is now the liberation of our oh-so-corseted society from the restraints of decency and prudery as an urgent matter of health and well-being. Is this not a far greater, and more necessary, import to this country than tea or sugar or pineapples? The sacred texts of the East, along with, of course, the buried classics of Greece and Rome – buried by priggish translations and expurgated editions, I mean – and more recent works such as the *Decameron*: these are works which captivate, and which liberate, and no, that is not a semantic impossibility, and it is what England needs. Our literature is chaste and ailing, because we as a society are chaste, and ailing.' Here he leaned conspiratorially towards me, and said in a stage whisper, 'And were not your husband's bindings terribly chaste, Mrs Damage, and is not he ailing?'

'Chaste, Sir Jocelyn?'

'I knew his work, of old. It was not his fault; he, and every-body else it seems, was only operating within a tradition that exalts the terribly dull, the ineffably boring, the tediously prudish. But you: your bindings are as beautiful, as sensual, as arousing, as full of vigour as ... well ... as *you* are, Mrs Damage.'

I mewed involuntarily, and quickly made a show of looking at Lucinda's doll.

'What are you going to call her, Lucinda?' I said, hoping my voice did not quiver.

'Mossie,' she said.

'Mossie. How lovely.'

Oh, but he was dangerous, and I was not immune to his charms, for all that I could see through them. There would be too many ladies who loved him already, too many dandies scouting the style of his coat, the angle of his hat, and his fashionable turned-down collar. And even as I considered the demise of the stock and high-pointed collar that would surely become general because of Sir Jocelyn's example, I was sensible enough to know that even my new status as Mistress Binder did not justify the way in which he spoke to me, and so immured was I by the boundaries of class, age, and education, that I was determined that my head would remain resolutely level in my transactions with this rogue.

Which was just as well, for, having so skilfully unlocked me, he cut to the purpose of his visit.

'Lucinda.' The bolts slammed shut again inside me. 'At the risk of indiscretion, Mrs Damage, am I right in thinking that Lucinda suffers from Epilepsie?'

My eyes widened in alarm, and I reached for Lucinda and she for me in the same moment. Jack put down his tools.

'I beg your pardon?'

'Does she have convulsions? The Morbids? Falling Sickness? Oh, but I did not wish to alarm you in the slightest. I applaud your wish to exclude the authorities. I am not an advocate of institutions. Some may call me a radical, and they may well be correct, but I can safely say that not all doctors wish to lock people up. May I ask Lucinda a few questions?'

There was terror in Lucinda's eyes, but the nobleman knelt down to be at her level. He was as disarming of the daughter as of her mother; he was gentle and teasing, and soon had her giggling. He smiled at her, and she smiled back; and despite myself, my cold loathing of doctors melted somewhat.

'Now, Lucinda. A little frog came to my window the other night, to tell me that his dear old friend Lucinda sometimes comes over a bit peculiar. Is he correct?'

She chortled and exclaimed, 'A frog!' Then she nodded.

'The frog was unable to tell me what happens to her when she feels like this. Can *you* explain it to me?'

'Yes. I feel strange.'

'Strange. Anything else?

'And I feel like lying down.'

'Lying down. And do you?'

'Sometimes.'

'Anything else? Does your head hurt?'

'Yes, and my eyes too, cos sometimes it's like candles are flickering in them, but they're not really there, cos we never have so many candles lit at once, and then sometimes I been sick, and then I wake up and there's a fog inside me although I'm better.'

He listened intently, all the while crouching down at her level. He held his finger up. 'Do you see my finger? I'd like you to blow on it as if it were a candle, *but*, you are not trying to blow the candle out. You must blow slowly, as if you want the candle flame to *lie down*. Now, inspire deeply, and take care that your shoulders don't rise. Now breathe out, and make that flame lie down.' She obeyed. 'Well done, Lucinda. What a good girl you are.' He ruffled her hair with his hand. 'Whenever you feel funny, I want you to ask your mother to hold her finger up, and blow on her candle.

'Now, observe. This peculiar contraption is called a pair of callipers. They are like the pincers of a crab.' He showed her how they opened and closed. 'But look, they are a most discerning crab. They will not snap at pretty little girls. They may tickle, but they are friendly callipers.' She let him measure her head, and then he felt her head all over with his bare hands, and she watched as he made some notes in a tatty little book in need of a re-bind. He looked in her mouth, her ears and her eyes, and wrapped a tape-measure around her skull, and her neck, and her chest. He listened to her heartbeat, he tested her reflexes.

'Would you help me, Lucinda?' He opened his large black bag. 'Do you see all these phials? They contain pills and powders. There are so many of them! But we are looking for the most special phial of all. It has a brown cap, with a piece of string tied around it. Can you see it?'

'Here! Here it is! Shall I take it out?' she said gleefully.

'If you would be so kind. Good girl. Now this —' he took off the lid and shook most of the contents out onto a large piece of paper '– is something that is almost magical. Do you like magic?'

She nodded, as he tipped the rest into his palm.

'And can you count to twenty?'

'Yes I can. One – two –'

'Excellent. You must count out twenty grains – like this – and you may mix them in some water first, or eat them off your palm.'

'What will they do to me?'

'Nothing. Not a thing. For that is their magic, Lucinda: they will simply act as a preventative. You will not feel quite as strange as you used to; you will be safer and less tired. But you will not know that, unless you remember how you used to be.' He folded up the paper and gave it to Lucinda. 'Give this to your mother to keep safe for you.'

'Thank you, Lou,' I said as she handed it to me. 'What is it?' I asked Sir Jocelyn. But something most strange was happening to him. For all his athleticism, he was struggling to pull himself up to standing from where he had been kneeling on the floor. He held on to the side of the bench, and he grimaced, just as Peter did whenever he made the slightest movement. He reached for his side, and pressed it in as he hauled himself up.

'I was attacked in the Kalahari,' he puffed, by way of explanation. 'Got a spear in the ribs, and some residual damage to the intercostals.' He was tugging at something on his person: at first I thought that he was trying to get his watch out of his pocket, but then his waistcoat rose up with the movement of his arms, and he was pulling at his crisp white shirt underneath, which came clean out of the waistband of his trousers, and I realised to my utter horror that I could see his woollen undershirt, and that he was unfastening the buttons about his middle.

'Sir Jocelyn,' I started. 'No . . . !' I clutched Lucinda to me with the hand holding the paper of grains, and buried her head in my skirts so she should not be victim to the horrid sight. Jack moved closer to us, but clearly did not know what to do either.

But the man continued, as if this were the most normal practice in medical, scientific, epileptic, what-have-you circles, and soon he had peeled apart his undershirt, and I caught a degrading glimpse of his navel, all curly hairs and bronzed skin. I covered my face with the hand that was not holding Lucinda, and whimpered.

'Mrs Damage, do I alarm you? Come now, permit yourself a moment's viewing.'

'But my modesty, Sir Jocelyn!'

'Your modesty, my good woman? Your modesty will not be compromised by a look! Come, Mrs Damage. Come, *Dora*, if I may. Dora, you may look, and still be virtuous. You, why, you have a scrutinising gaze that belies your inner wisdom. Look, I entreat you, so you may better understand me.'

I did not remove my hand from my face, but separated my fingers somewhat, and turned my head back towards him. I lowered my gaze, all the while partially obscured by the Vs of my fingers, but kept Lucinda's face pressed into my legs. And where his fingers were pulling apart the fabric of his undergarment, I saw a fuzzy blue shape, like the spokes of a wheel radiating around his navel.

'What – what is it?' I asked, despite myself.

'The sun. A tattoo of the sun.' He was already buttoning himself up again, tucking his shirt back into his trousers, pulling his waistcoat neatly down over his waist again. 'A minor deity, I must have seemed to them, I'll warrant, or how else was I to have survived their vicious assaults? The Sun-God, I fancied. I had myself marked accordingly by a sailor on the return boat.'

I released Lucinda, but could not remove the image of the blue sun staining the skin around the dark hole of his umbilicus. I heard Jack exhale heavily, busying himself in his work once more.

'I have left instructions in my will to bind my complete works with the skin from my torso, with the scar left by the spear resplendent across the back panel, and the tattoo round my navel on the front. What do you think of that, Dora?' But he pursued beyond my dumbstruck silence. 'I shall call my memoirs, *Afric's Apollo: Helios in the Bushveld, or Travels of a Latter Day Sun-God*. Is it not a fine way to achieve immortality?'

There was no answer to that. The paper of grains he had given Lucinda offered me a diversion.

'But the grains, Sir Jocelyn? Tell me about the grains, please.'

'Potassium bromide,' he said, as he arranged the tails of his coat. 'It will significantly reduce the incidence of her convulsions, but it may increase her appetite and urination, and affect her co-ordination somewhat.'

'Is it safe?'

'Completely. It has had tremendous efficacy in a large number of cases of what we call hysterical – or menstrual – epilepsy.'

'But she's five years old, Sir Jocelyn!' Still I could not look him in the eye, or anywhere else.

'She has suffered from convulsions since birth. Do you wish to wait until puberty to be rid of them? It will be a blessing for you both.'

Then he turned back to Lucinda with an 'A-ha', as if he had forgotten something, as if he had no awareness of the gross breach of propriety he had just committed in front of her. I wondered at this world he inhabited, where convention was to be broken up and trampled over in fearless pursuit of a better world, cheeks flushed and moustaches rippling in the warm breezes of progress. 'In here, look.' He pulled a small blue bag from his pocket and instructed Lucinda to hold out her hand. He counted out one, two, three small, brown, rolled sticks into her little palms. Then four, five. She dropped one and laughed, and held out her skirts to catch some more. Soon she had ten sticks.

I knew what they were: crude opium. I felt a flash of anger; the man was surely insulting me. I could have bought these from any pharmacy by the pennyworth or tuppenny-worth.

'Give them to your mother again, please, but these are for your father. And tell her from me, Lucinda, that I bestow them upon her for the simple reason that a lady of her responsibilities and industry has precious little time to run to the pharmacy.' Oh, but the man was so persuasive he could talk a paddle-steamer out of slapping the water as it moved.

'Now, run along, and play with Mossie,' he said to Lucinda, 'and tell her about your magic grains.'

'I will!' And she lifted up her doll to him, too struck to thank him, and I was too gone to make her, and we watched as she waved good-bye and ran out into Ivy-street to show Billy.

Sir Jocelyn folded my fingers over the sticks of opium in my palm with his broad hand, and grinned. 'Besides,' he continued his explanation, 'I believe your local pharmacy only stops Bridport's best, which is nothing compared to pure Turk. And before I forget –' he pulled a small brown apothecary's bottle from another pocket, '– here it is already made up, so you do not have to wait until your own preparations are ready.'

'Thank you, Sir Jocelyn. That is most thoughtful of you.' I moved away from him and placed the sticks in a box on top of the cabinet.

'And for you,' he added, 'a different sort of pure Turk.' He took a square wooden box out from his case, and opened it to reveal what looked like a slab of pale yellow jelly divided into diamond shapes, beneath a thick white powder. '*Rahat Lokum*.'

'I beg your pardon?'

'It is Arabic for "contentment of the throat". A sentiment I salute. Do try one, Mrs Damage.'

'With my fingers?'

'Is there anything better?'

With difficulty I gouged one of the diamond shapes out from amongst the others, and placed it in my mouth. Instantly the powder tickled my nose from within, and although I did not sneeze, my eyes watered and my throat closed up. The texture of the confection was cloying; it adhered to my teeth and the roof of my mouth as I chewed, and to my tongue as I tried to extricate it from where it was stuck, and I dared not swallow for what it might do to my throat. Contentment of the throat?

And the taste! It was like eating a rich lady's too-strong perfume in solid form! But it was sweet, oh so sweet, like honey from the spoon.

'Do you like it?'

I shook my head and then nodded; I could not speak; my eyes and nose were streaming. And in truth, I did not know the answer.

'I am helping to finance an old school chum who is opening the first Turkish Baths, right here in London,' he continued as I struggled. 'The city needs to have something to recommend it, doesn't it? The Iznik tiles arrived yesterday . . .' and so he went on, as if I were the type of person who would be interested, or would have the leisure to attend the Baths, and went on about his own travels through the Ottoman Empire with the same school chum, the aromas and colours of Izmir and Latakia, the pashas, the beys, the sultans, the women. Then he paused, as if to take in the furious action of my jaws, and smiled languidly. He stroked his chin with his long fingers, leant forward to me and murmured, 'Can you guess why the *lokum* is so fashioned, my dear?'

I shook my head again, chewing.

'The diamond shape,' he whispered, so that Jack would not hear, 'may be pressed between the outer lips of a woman's nether orifices by her lover, then licked out of her. It drives them both mad with untold delight and desire, or so I am told.'

I choked, and spluttered white and yellow confection into my hands, as Sir Jocelyn leant back to enjoy my reaction.

'Can you taste the jasmine, Dora?'

I nodded, finally able to free my tongue. Soon, I thought, I might dare to swallow the dangerous sweetmeat; it was not safe in my mouth or my throat.

'I trust it delights,' he probed. 'That is its sole purpose. It was especially commissioned by Sultan Abdul Hamid the First, for the delectation of the women in his harem. He had far too many to keep satisfied, so the sweet was designed for the appeasement of wanton ladies craving solace in the arms of their only man. Which reminds me: a favourite book of mine about a rather infamous Turk is in need of repair. I shall send it to Diprose and he will get it to you. You might enjoy it.'

I believe now, although I dared not admit it at the time, that he actually winked at me. He bent down to collect his bag, then adjusted his hat on his head.

'Good day, Jack,' he said.

'Good day, Sir Jocelyn.'

I opened the front door to him, and his driver dismounted, to open the door of his brougham.

'Good-bye, Mrs Damage. It was a most satisfactory visit.'

'Good-bye, Sir Jocelyn,' I managed to say, after swallowing particularly violently.

He stood for a moment in the damp chill outside the work-shop, as if he wished to savour the full flatus of Lambeth one last time before departing from it. Then, when he seemed to have breathed his fill, he looked me directly in the eye, and, with the kindest of smiles, said, as if in passing, 'You look after my books, and I'll look after little Lucy.'

'Who was the visitor?' Peter enquired from his place by the fire as I was taking Lucinda up to bed. His feet were propped on the Windsor chair opposite him: brown knitted socks were stretched over the lower part of his feet, but scarcely made it to the wide, red, ankles, which looked, each of them, like the neck of a hardened drinker.

'A client,' I said. 'Would you like me to cool your feet?'

'Which client? He was dressed in too much finery to be a bookseller.'

'My love, do not strain yourself to talk. Why, look at you.'

'I need some more draught.'

'You're nearly through it.'

'Get me some draught!'

'I will be making you some Black Drop. I have some sticks,' I said, then added hastily, 'which I bought from the pharmacy.'

'I must go to bed. Take me to bed.'

I sent Lucinda up on her own, then pulled the blanket off his knees, and he leant on me as he hobbled over to the stairs. He seemed shorter now, and older. His legs were bowed, his feet splayed, and every part of him sagged with the weight of invalid tumescence.

'Did he bring books?'

'No. But he brought the promise of them.'

'Of what ilk?'

'Foreign stuff, mainly.'

'With what purpose?'

I thought hard to phrase this correctly as we climbed. 'I believe he informs on the behaviours of the communities at the outposts of Her Majesty's Empire.'

'Ah. Foreign Office.'

'Possibly. Probably.'

'Good, good.' We reached the bedroom. 'Put me down gently, woman. I do not bounce, despite this villainous cushioning.'

Over I went to the little table and picked up a pot from amongst the lint, the tape, the scissors.

'No, not the embrocation! A poultice! Blister me!'

'I must see to Lucinda first. It will not take a moment. I can hear her undressing.'

'You must not leave me! Give me something, anything, to help the pain!'

'But the draught is almost finished. I shall make some Black Drop tonight, but it needs to ferment.'

'Get it!'

And then I remembered the bottle Knightley had given me. I raced down to the workshop where Jack was still hard at work. I took in the pile of books with one look, calculated the cost of candles against the number of bindings we would get done in the time, and came out once more in favour of the books.

'Four books to get up into leather tonight, Jack,' I shouted at him as I grabbed the bottle. 'Can you make it?'

'Aye, aye, Mrs D,' he said to my departing back. At least he didn't have to provide his own candles, which he would have had to in one of those larger, commercial bookbinders, like Remy & Rangorski.

I took it back upstairs. I would not let him gulp it from the bottle; he had to wait while I poured it out into a spoon. He spluttered at the vicious taste.

'That will help. Now, I will wash Lucinda, and I shall hear her prayers, and I shall return as soon as I can.'

He was not best pleased, but I had to manage my household as well as I could. I wiped Lucinda with a cold flannel, helped her into her nightgown, and hugged her – and Mossie – tightly as she said her prayers to us.

'Mama. I think the angels are God's babies.'

'Are we not all God's babies?'

'Yes, but they're the ones who stay up with Him in Heaven.'

So I kissed her, and padded downstairs to make up Peter's poultice. I stirred up some bread and water in a pan, and when it was piping hot, laid out the boiling paste on a clean rag. Then I hurried back upstairs to find which extremity Peter required it on tonight.

'No, not now,' he moaned. 'Not any more. Come to bed. Come, comfort me.'

And so I slipped off my smock, but instead of pulling on my nightgown I lay next to him in just my chemise, placed his head on my upper arm and stroked his cheeks, while he muttered at me. 'Stay with me, nursie. Don't leave me, nursie. Don't go back to work, Dora.'

So I extinguished the candle, and lay still, in the darkness, listening to the chuff and pull of Jack's saw in the workshop below. When Peter's snuffles turned to snores, I extricated myself from his heavy head, pulled on my smock once more, and tiptoed downstairs. The clock was striking ten, and the night air was chilly.

Jack and I worked together, illuminated by a single candle stuck in the ridges of the book press, until he left me as the church clock struck midnight. I stopped as it was tolling two, extinguished the candle, and went into the kitchen where I cleaned the knives by moonlight with soda crystals and emery paper. I couldn't have left them soaking overnight, for the steel blade would start to rust, and the handles would rot. I was tired, but I decided to set the Black Drop to brew there and then, as it would take several weeks to ferment: the mixture of opium, verjuice, yeast, sugar and nutmeg was my mother's trusted recipe, only she had never had the privilege of pure Turk in her concoctions. Finally, I raked out the kitchen fire and laid it ready for the morning, and counted out how many candles we had left to see us through the foggy gloom of tomorrow.

And oh, those candles, with their tongues of light, lapping up our oxygen and our pennies. What tales they could have told of the pages they illuminated, night after night, in a little corner of Lambeth, in the depths of the sordid city!

Chapter Ten

Doctor Foster is a good man,
He teaches children all he can:
Reading, writing, arithmetic,
And doesn't forget to use his stick.
When he does he makes them dance
Out of England into France,
Out of France into Spain,
Round the world and back again.

The gardens of my bindings were not well trimmed, neatly bordered rectangles of perfection. They rioted and teemed; herbaceousness burst its borders; beds sprung with flowers that leapt instead of slept under the reader's gaze. Flowers flourished together that should have been continents apart, but they seemed to like it like that, and so did I. My lawns were long and unkempt; they would tickle one's ankles and one's fancy as one walked. And after all, in a literature in which, I was to learn, 'putting Nebuchadnezzar out to grass' was a euphemism for the sexual act, I thought it kindest to give the old Babylonian King some long, luscious grass that was worth feasting on.

I found it hard to believe I was the only binder working with such designs. I imagined Diprose had others, like me, concubines in his harem, although I assumed I had the dubious honour of being the only woman of the lot. I could not help but wonder whether I should feel jealous of his divided attentions and how long my bindings would keep me in high favour. However many there were of us, our time had only recently come: I was to discover there had been a change in law only three years previously, when the Obscene Publications Act – better known as Lord Campbell's Act – declared that it was not illegal to own immoral literature, only to publish and disseminate it. And so, as ownership was no longer a crime, the owners could commission bindings that were more flamboyant, exuberant, and, if the fancy so took them, demonstrative.

Before this, the dull bindings so berated by Knightley were necessary so as not to incite undue interest from the uninitiated. Some collectors would go further with their disguises, and put them in plain bindings, with a simple cross on the cover and a 'Book of Common Prayer' or a 'Testament' or an 'Apocrypha' on the spine, despite containing within pages most ungodly. Stories were legion of the auctioneers who, getting their hands on the estate of a deceased nobleman, would sell – without so much as a second thought or a scant perusal – the large number of plainly bound but less than innocent Bibles and prayer-books that lurked in the palatial library, to many an unsuspecting purchaser.

I had never considered myself a true innocent: I was aware of naughty goings-on, and naughty drawings thereof, and I was no stranger to the newspapers' incessant debates about the development of photography and the possibilities for its misuse, but, despite having been brought up a bookbinder's daughter, in So-ho of all places, I had never imagined that there would be such things as naughty books; there would be no need, I assumed, for a modern-day Paul to encourage those of the curious arts to burn their books. I had heard of the Vice Society, but had always thought that the members were proponents of the thing itself, that is, the vice. If a Bridge Society was where one played bridge, and a Bird-Watching Society was one that facilitated bird-watching, what, pray, was a Vice Society? Dedicated to the discussion and development of carpenter's clamps, for all I knew.

Its full title, according to Diprose, was the Society for the Suppression of Vice, founded at the turn of the century by the Church of England (presumably embarrassed by having purchased one too many fake Bibles from house clearances). It supplied the Metropolitan Police with information regarding the sale, distribution or exhibition of obscenities – after which a search warrant could be issued, and obscenities seized and destroyed unless their innocence was proved in court – but I never imagined that I would become part of the chain of supply they sought to crush.

Three guineas a volume was the price at which the volumes on which I worked would sell, or so Diprose told me. Three guineas a volume. Or three pounds and three shillings. Or sixty-three shillings. Or 756 pence. These were not books for the common man. Lord Campbell's Act was a ruling only for the rich; the lower classes, presumably, would not have known what to do with such literature, and if they had, the excitement in their loins would have driven them to storm London's own Bastille, and a revolution was not what Lord Campbell or anyone else up there wanted.

No, these were rich men's books that came into my house, and their owners certainly seemed to take great pains not to make me feel like a common woman. Not only did the next hansom to stop on our cobblestones bring several crates of books and manuscripts – which I had to store in the parlour for want of space in the workshop – but also a pale blue parasol trimmed with point-lace, a tortoiseshell hair comb edged with gold filigree, and a black-and-purple feather fan.

It was Jack who spoke sense to me. 'What you gonna do with them? Strip 'em and use 'em to fancy up your bindings?' And he was right. Whenever would I use these superfluities? 'Be careful, Mrs D,' he said. 'Be careful of the roses. It's always the nobs who cause the most trouble.'

And again, he was right. The roses were not just the ones who bought the books. They had lead roles in them, too. The men in these books were not street-sweepers or sewer-flushers, closer though they might be to bodily functions: they were kings, dukes, barons, and in the literature that had Knightley's stamp on it, caliphs, emperors, maharajahs, and the Dey.

Ah, the Dey. *The Lustful Turk, or Scenes in the Harem of an Eastern Potentate* was the fine 1828 first edition promised to me by Sir Jocelyn, and it told me more than I ever needed to know about the dark Dey and the white women whose legs were at first forcibly, and at length willingly, opened to him. My mother, the governess, had taught me to keep mine closed all the while, and my husband had furthered that lesson. What had I been missing?

The answer to that was the most extraordinary feature of the Dey's anatomy. It troubled me greatly that the poor women he seduced at first considered it an object of terror: it was, variously, 'that terrible instrument, that fatal foe to virginity', 'the instrument of my martyrdom', 'my stiff virgin-stretcher', 'his dreadful engine', 'the terrible pillar with which he was preparing to skewer me', and 'the enormous machine buried within her'. But then it became, to those very same women, once they had succumbed to their apparently pleasurable fate, 'the uncontrolled master key of my feelings', 'nature's grand masterpiece', even 'that delightful instrument that attunes my heart to harmony'. Such a change of attitude to 'this wonderful instrument of nature' is simply, I learnt, the passing of time: it is the 'terror of virgins, but delight of women'.

But this was not simply a story of passion awakened time and again: the Dey may indeed have converted many a terrified virgin into a hedonistic woman, but that was not to be the end of it. For what a reduction befell his mightiness at the end! After his attempt to deflower one of his new harem girls (not in the way that nature intended, but in the hellish, secondary, dark orifice), the girl took her rightful revenge by cutting off the organs most vital to the Dey's manner of exis-tence! I considered this a curious exaltation of those parts of his anatomy; I could not for one moment see the appeal to Sir Jocelyn in a story that left the central male character so emasculated. But, ah me, the Dey so loved his two English girls that he gave them his 'lost members preserved in spirits of wine in glass vases', and sent them back to England with them, where they bestowed them upon a girls' boarding school, to be shown 'as a reward for good behaviour to the little lady scholars'.

I was spoilt for imagery to put on the cover of this extraordinary volume, but did not know how bold I dared be for Sir Jocelyn. On finishing the book I could not shake the image of the parts in glass vases from my fevered brain, but, much as I relished the disarmament of that terrifying weapon, I felt Sir Jocelyn might have accused me of focusing on the wrong part of the story. Instead, I paid homage to his previous visitation to my humble workshop, and settled upon a central minaret shape surrounded by intricate geometric tile shapes, within which basked a beautiful woman, whose finely embroidered robe slipped fetchingly about her shoulders. And between two slender, white fingers, she held rather suggestively a solidly gold-tooled, diamond-shaped confection, which explained the enigmatic smile on her face.

And on the back, the insignia of *Les Sauvages Nobles*, with the word *Nocturnus* underneath, betwixt two ivy leaves.

It was always my endeavour – my very point of 'modernity', according to Diprose – to distil the essence of the book in the cover design. Yet nowadays I scarcely had time to read most of the manuscripts before binding them; I would simply scan them briefly, and, for the most part, this was a blessing.

So, when I opened *Fanny Hill, or Memoirs of a Woman of Pleasure*, at the point where she describes the impressive member of a young fellow as 'not the plaything of a boy, not the weapon of a man, but a maypole of so enormous a standard, that had proportions been observ'd, it must have belong'd to a young giant', I could not help but select a glorious vermilion morocco, and tool down the centre a maypole, prodigious in size but innocent in nature, around which a single voluptuous woman danced, clutching two ribbons in her joyfully outstretched hands.

Ovid's *Ars Amatoria* was bound in dark-green hard-grain goatskin with scarlet silk doublures. I blind-tooled the edge with hearts, stars and butterflies, and gold-tooled in the centre a beguiling Venus extracting a myrtle leaf and some berries from the garland binding her hair (as she does at the beginning of Book Three), to give to Ovid along with her pearls of wisdom in the womanly arts. Her instructions were most novel and intriguing to me.

> One must lie on one's back, if one has a beautiful face and attendant features.
> But if one's rear is better, better to be viewed from the rear.
> But if it is the breasts and the legs which cause delight, one must lie across the bed beneath the beholder . . .

I had never beheld these parts of my body in this way, unfamiliar as they were to me as far-off parts of the globe. For the first time in my life, I started to wonder about my best angle.

Another book, a slim, anonymous volume, which intrigued me, mentioned in passing an extraordinary, magical place, called the Clit-oris. The author was unspecific as to its exact co-ordinates, but it sounded as if it should be in Africa, or Xanadu, or Timbuc-Tu, so elysian were its qualities, especially for the female of the species. As it was an adventure story of sorts, I gave it a spine of grey snakeskin, and on the black silk cover I embroidered an ornate compass, surrounded by waves, islands and fishes in gold, silver and coloured threads, and on the back a naked woman rode a dolphin towards foreign shores.

But, what to do with the new edition of *Venus School Mistress*, or *Birchen Sports*, amongst plenty others similarly entitled by a certain Mr R. Birch and others? Before spring 1860, I had lived twenty-five years assuming that the cane was something to be feared, and its use avoided through good behaviour, but I learnt soon enough that there was many a person in this strange world who were zealous disciples of the birch, and indeed, myself became extraordinarily learned in its occult pleasures, in word if not in deed. I could now instruct one on how to keep a supply of birch in water to ensure its freshness and suppleness, and of wooden, metal and leather instruments of torture that surpassed the birch in their ability to scourage, fustigate and, verily, phlebotomise. I discovered that those who lived too deep in the country to frequent the flagellation brothels in the metropolis were blessed with natural wonders that far exceeded the birch: the holly brush, the furze bush, the butcher's bush and, oh, most joyfully, in summertime, green nettles. I learnt of the eminent noblemen who regularly go for a salutary whipping in order to reap its extensive health benefits (it warms the blood), and how those who called for the banning of birch discipline in educational establishments were depriving an entire genera- tion of the pleasures and passions awaiting them in later life, the taste for which would be developed in youth. 'What a treat in this seminary for the idolators of the posterior shrine!' exclaimed one character in one of the dusty manuscripts, and indeed the seminary to which he was referring could have been Damage's workshop at one point, so replete was it with flagellatory tracts.

And so it was, with such intriguing information at my fingertips, that I reached for Peter's old birch cane with as much menace as I could feign, and called sternly for my little boy Jack, and when he arrived, sweating, together we spliced it, sanded it and re-varnished it, and then we inlaid it in sections, four reinforced struts running down the front and back covers, and I was to understand it raised more than a chuckle back at Diprose's establishment.

Harder to develop a design for were the collections of plates with brief introductions but otherwise few words that already had their own visual style, and not always to my aesthetic. For these, I resorted once again to the language of leaves, flowers and herbs; from the 'secret love' of acacia to the 'remembered friends' of zinnia, I had something, no matter how fragile, behind which to hide. Lilies were safest, due to their ambiguity, but the temptation always to resort to the cautionary oleander, and to eschew the lustful coriander, was great.

Sometimes I was repelled, sometimes charmed, but always arrested, never bored. How strange the models looked, all tangled limbs, enlarged appendages and gaping orifices! Not one single image was anything like any amorous picture I had hitherto imagined; they were love unromanticised, but for that reason, possibly more authentic. One particular plate was entitled 'cunnylyngus': in it a man was behaving to a woman as a dog to a bitch, sniffing her crotch, and licking her with his tongue. My sentient mind screamed, Iniquity, diabolism, bestiality! until it heard a quieter, but similarly reasonable, voice in my head argue that it had never seen an animal behave in this way, licking another with such concern for the pleasure of the other. Something in me responded to this sense of transcendence, that in these pages there were higher, and not lower, energies at work. Even the most unwholesome of them, which inverted the tenderest act between a man and a woman into a display of violence and viciousness, held up to me what I had often felt underpinned my whole existence as a woman, but for which I had previously no visual representation in this world of convention and delicacy. I had not known that men could feel this way about women, but now that I saw it, dare I write that I felt gratitude to the images I was seeing for helping me make sense of foundlings and baby-farms and fallen women?

But as I was never intended to be their audience, what mattered my response? I thought of the artist, cross-hatching away at his shady visions, and the models performing for his art. Were these personal masterpieces for him, and the height of his aspirations? Or was he a hack-worker, scratching a meagre income from other people's lusts? Did he see the luminous beauty, the curious honesty, in these human forms, or were they as vile to him as the daylight world said they were? Possibly he was just like me, in it for the money, and doing what he was told.

There was no place for shock, I learnt, if I was to get on with the work. The easiest were the tawdry novelettes and galanteries, which soon left me untouched, but eventually even the more vulgar literature ceased to raise a flush in my face: I started to find the endless litany of bodily parts rather tedious. The day soon came when I no longer had to wonder about euphemisms such as 'visits to the dumpling shop' and 'sewing the parsley-bed'. I learnt entire new languages: I accepted words such as *gamahuching*, *firkytoodling*, *bagpiping*, *lallygagging*, or *minetting* as if they were my mother tongue. My world became tinged with unreality; such literature placated with its tone, written with such levity, good humour, civility and incoherence. It came to be endearing, childish, and meaningless. In fact, I came to realise, it was rather like the whimsical poems filled with nonce words that I read to Lucinda at night, only a bit wetter.

But my amusement was my protection, for in truth I was deeply discomfited by some of what I was confronting. To justify my role as Mistress Bindress in the obscene underworld of the book trade, I had to convince myself I was fashioning, as it were, the pearl around the grit in the oyster; I was making something beautiful out of something ugly. And at times, what was so ugly did not embarrass me, or shame me, but sometimes gently, sometimes forcibly, led me to my own ugliness, my own grit inside my hard white exterior, to which I had little desire to go. They were places for which my upbringing and society had not prepared me, and I was angry both at my ignorance and at this rapid acquisition of knowledge that was both against my will and counter to my expectations. The books told me of strange spices and savoury fruits I yet knew not of; I read words of love uttered by fortunate tongues that had tasted its bittersweet juices, and they led me into the dark caves of sin, and left me there in torment and confusion.

Over the following weeks, we bound scores of books with the insignia of *Les Sauvages Nobles*, plus one or other of the inscriptions. I started to notice a pattern emerging: twelve English names cropped up amongst the letters, the treatises and the accounts more often than others, and I could soon connect them to their particular Latinate expressions. They were names that I had seen in the pages of newspapers or heard talk of in the streets: names of noblemen. It did not take a genius to work out the correlation.

The first time I tried to go up to Peter to talk to him about them, I found him rocking in his chair, his pink legs trouserless, flesh quivering in fear.

'Leave me, leave me,' he was moaning. 'Go away, you vile woman! Get off me!'

'Me, Peter? I'm not on you, love.'

He had to swallow the spittle in his mouth before he could say anything more intelligible. 'Dora! Get her off me, Dora! Get her away!'

'No one's there, Peter. Tell me what you see. Who is it?'

'She's monstrous! She's the devil!'

'No, she isn't.'

'Can't you see her? Look at her red face, see how she drips blood. Clean them, clean these sheets. She's dripping blood all over them. Get them off! Get her off! Clean me! Look at her teeth, her fangs. Catch the blood. Catch the blood before it falls on me. Catch it! Remove her! Scrub them clean!'

'Peter, you're not in bed. There's no one here. There are no sheets. There's no woman.'

But it was all in vain. His cries continued, so I raced to the dresser for the Black Drop. He guzzled at the bottle, then wiped his mouth with the back of a swollen hand that appeared as one with his swollen arm. He laid his head back on the antimacassar, and was calm for a while. He gazed out of the window to where our daughter was playing, but I doubt he saw her.

'I need – I need a cup of tea.'

'I shall bring you one.' I made a pot, but Jack needed me to advise on margin widths and flyleaves, so I could not stay with Peter much longer.

It was a few days later, when Peter expressed an interest in the activities of the workshop, that I decided to distract him with my queries about these men.

The first one, '*Nocturnus*' or '*Nightly*' I kept to myself, for I already knew it to be Sir Jocelyn Knightley, our host to this strange biblio-ball. But I listed the other guests to Peter.

'Lord Glidewell.'

'Ah yes, Valentine, Lord Glidewell. He is a judge. One of our finest.'

'That's right. I remember seeing his name on a broadsheet handed out after the hanging of Billy Fawn Baxter.'

'Must you mention that dreadful affair? He murdered his mother, didn't he?'

'Father.'

'Unnatural,' he shivered. 'And so, Lord Glidewell must be . . .'

'. . . *Labor Bene. Labor* – to slide, or glide.'

'Ah, I see. That's how it works. Who's next?'

'Dr Theodore Chisholm. I presume he's an eminent physician;

his name is all over a lot of these medical tracts. And on those bottles they send you.'

'Why, he's on the board of the Royal College! To think, my prescriptions are personally authorised by such a man. And his Latin name?'

'I'm not sure. I can't work it out. Let's leave him until later. Now, Aubrey Smith-Pemberton. Who's he?'

'He's a Member of Parliament. I bound for his office on the Yale affair, several years ago. He presides over the committee that regulates the Cremorne Pleasure Gardens. The sooner he shuts it down, the better, as far as I'm concerned. It represents all that's loose about today's society.'

'But we had such fun, there, Peter, when we were courting!'

'Child, must you?'

'I'm sorry. So, Smith-Pemberton. This was the hardest one. It's usually written "*P. cinis It*". I only managed to work it out because I found it written at the end of a poem as "*Aubretia Malleus P. cinis It*". "*Aubretia*" being the flower, which is obviously Aubrey, "*malleus*" is a hammer, so, I thought, related to a smith, then a "P", followed by "*cinis*", which is ash, or ember, and then "*It*" is not "it", as I first thought, but one ton. So, Aubrey Smith-Pemberton.'

Peter seemed bored with my puzzle-solving; he was tired, and I feared I was wearing him further. Possibly I was being too pleased with myself.

'Next?'

'Dr Christopher Monks.'

'Headmaster of Eton – no, Harrow, actually.'

'A-ha. And he, therefore, is . . .' I pretended to fret over the Latin names in front of us, and waited for an age for Peter to get there first.

'*Monachus!*'

'Oh yes, you are right, Peter! How clever!'

'Next?'

'Sir Ruthven Gallinforth.'

'Governor of Jamaica.'

'Ah, I thought as much. I have only recently bound some of his richly colourful accounts of the Caribbean islands; he has some shocking tales to tell of the tensions between the British and the plantation workers.'

'It must be hard, dealing with such indolence. They are not natural workers.'

'Is that so? I was not . . . So, I struggle here too . . .' And again I waited. 'Hmm, I wonder. "*Vesica Quartus*". I don't know what "*vesica*" means, but "*quartus*" is "fourth", so presumably . . .'

'Next.'

'Archdeacon Favourbrook. Jeremy, he is referred to in one of the letters.'

'Yes, he is an archdeacon, of somewhere. A venerable man. So, let's see, do you have any words there that mean favour, and brook?'

'I think we must. Do you suppose "*Beneficium Flumen*" would be that?'

'Precisely. Next.'

'Hugh Pryseman. I've heard of him. He's heir to the Viscountcy of Avonbridge, and he must be . . . "*Praemium Vir*". Prize man.'

'Next.'

'Well, the rest don't seem to be as important. They haven't written anything I've bound, and they don't feature as much in the texts or correspondence. There's Brigadier Michael Rodericks, of the Royal Artillery, the Reverend Harold Oswald . . .'

'A clergyman.'

'Indeed. Then there's Captain Charles Clemence, of the Bombay army of the East India Company.'

'*Clementia*.'

'Of course! And finally, Benedict Clarke, who seems to be in industry.'

'I know not of him. But the others are clearly all eminent individuals. Members of Parliament, churchmen, dignitaries, noblemen.'

I showed him the coat-of-arms.

'Why, they must all be members of the same club,' he said, not reading the inscription of *Les Sauvages Nobles*. He nodded heartily. 'Oh, Dora, this is magnificent news. I'd been touting for the off-trade from White's ever since I got the Parliament contract. My dear wife, I must confess to underestimating you. You will save the Damage name yet. Keep up the good work. Now, be a good girl and bring me my draught, for I must sleep.'

But I could not rest easily that evening, as I thought of Jocelyn, Valentine, Theodore, Aubrey, Jeremy, Christopher, Ruthven, Hugh, Michael, Harold, Charles and Benedict. I could assume the intimacy of their first names in the dream-creations of my workshop, as I, mistress of their dreams, knew their fantasies probably better than their wives. I thought of Sir Jocelyn, with his beautiful, clean new wife, Sylvia, and wondered how he could leave her to breathe not just the fetid air of my Lambeth but the miasma of sin emerging from these pages. I thought of the others: as I tooled the spines, I tried to imagine what rooms they would look down on, from what shelves. And if the pages had faces, whose faces would they see looking back at them? What acts would they bear witness to? These were not the sort of novels to be read around the hearth by father or mother to the rest of the family. These were solitary pleasures, not read at bedtime or in one's chair, but under the bed covers, or with the chair in front of the door, yet such precautions would never suffice. It was as if safety could only be had if the head that read them could be sliced open, and the books secreted inside the cavity of the skull itself before suturing the incision shut, for these books were temporary balm and permanent antagonist to the needs, twists and wounds of an already tortured mind.

But until medical science had progressed to this point, the books would have to be held in furtive hands, which no doubt would have preferred to have been free to whip the nether regions into a similar torment as the mind. Was it really, I had to ask, possible to have *fun* in this manner?

Chapter Eleven

Who's that ringing at my door bell?
A little pussy cat that isn't very well.
Rub its little nose with a little mutton fat,
That's the best cure for a little pussy cat.

Measurements and weights of paper, margins and gutters, rectos and versos marched across my brain even while I was sweeping the floor, shaking the mattresses and banging the rugs. Crimson orifices and their myriad descriptions, endless and ever more extraordinary plays on the word 'cock', and the more absurd euphemisms for sexual congress danced round my head as I served supper, aired our nightgowns, and shooed the beetles out of their dusty hideyholes in the kitchen. My husband slumped in his bed, my daughter frolicked in the street, and my hands, feet and shoulders permanently ached; I never sat, except to sew. But I did not complain, even when Jack found me asleep among the paper-shavings as he lit the candles at seven the next morning. For this pestle-and-mortar existence, hard though it sounds as I write it, was not in fact grinding me down. It was refining me.

The summer was over before we even realised, and the first cold, foggy, September day meant the leather started to feel more supple in the workshop. But otherwise it was a day like any other. I rose at five, riddled the cinders, drew up the fire, unpegged the linen, put the kettle on, cleaned the range, whipped around a sweeping-cloth, steeped the washing, made the breakfast, and set to soaking and boiling enough ingredients to cover the day's meals.

Then I ran into the workshop, and cleaned it thoroughly, making sure to collect every last grain of gold-dust to sell back to Edwin Nightingale, and to continue my war against mites and silverfish. I ran a wet cloth over the windows, but the autumnal fog hung like a pall around the house, so I might as well have left them alone for all the light we gained. I let Jack in at seven, but my chores still weighed over me, so I returned to the house. I counted out twenty grains of bromide for Lucinda, which she took before her bread and milk.

'Mama, I'm still hungry,' she said once she had finished. She had taken to saying this, since starting the bromide.

I took Peter his porridge, tea and toast in bed, but he would not eat until he had had his first dose of Dr Chisholm's laudanum. While he toyed with his food, I emptied the slops, cleaned the outdoor privy, and rinsed the chamber-pots with hot water and soda, before returning them to the bedrooms, when I collected Peter's tray, and handed it over to Lucinda to finish. His appetite was decreasing as hers was growing, which at least balanced the household bills.

Throughout the morning I would go into the workshop to sew a few signatures, but run back at times to stir the copper, to check the row of bottles of Black Drop fermenting by the fire, and to turn and shake the mattresses. At eleven, Lucinda and I went to the market, but through the soupy yellow fog we could scarcely make out the market stalls, and we returned with only a basket of milk, eggs, bread, butter, ham, apples, and cheese, and our mood was as dark as the day itself.

As we walked slowly back up Ivy-street through the dingy mist, we could just make out the shape of the perambulating pot-man and his large wooden frames, pulled by a mule, by the workshop door. 'D'ya want any, lady?' he said to me as we approached.

'Jack?' I asked, who had joined us at the door. Peter had never allowed alcohol on the premises, nor drank it himself, being temperately inclined, but I couldn't help but worry at all the water in his tissues. I knew it was a practice in most of the other binding workshops to wet their whistle daily. The men had to have some perks, I thought.

'Up to you, Mrs D.'

'What have you got?' I asked, peering at the frames through the gloom.

'English Burgundy, heavy brown, porter and stout.'

'I think we'll have a jug of the burgundy and one of porter, please.'

'Regular, or just today?'

'Make it regular. We could do with a bit of liquid to keep us going in the evenings.'

'Right-ho, Mrs?'

'Mrs Damage.'

'Alrighty, Mrs Damage.'

A train rattled past us, and as the man started to fill the jugs he asked, 'That the stiffs' express?'

'Yes, it is,' I said, and could not help but laugh.

Truth be told, and I never would have said it to Peter, but I was all in favour of a spot of beer. The pump in Broad-street from which my mother contracted cholera also served Golden-square, Berwick-street and St Ann's, which is why mother caught it from the water at the Ragged-school where she had started to teach, for in Carnaby-street we never would send to Broad-street for water. It impressed me that none of the seventy men working at the Broad-street brewery died; most of them confessed to never drinking water at all, only beer. And when one remembers that over six hundred died then, there's a lot to be said for never drinking water again. They opened up the pump-well and found a cess pool was leaking into it. Since then, I've always had a sneaking suspicion that water wasn't good for one, but I could never say this to Peter.

Lucinda and I took our purchases inside. I put the apples in a bowl, and the eggs, cheese and ham on the marble slab, then poured the milk into a pan and left it to scald on the stove to keep it fresh. Once I heard the pot-man rattling his frames over the cobbles, I nipped back into the workshop to instruct Jack about the brown diamond shapes I wanted him to inlay into some black morocco.

And then it was that there was a knock at the door, and there, when I opened it, stood a small, nervous gentleman. The fog was so dense I could not see if there was a carriage behind him; but out of a darker-seeming patch of fog looming below the lintel, a tall shadow stepped forward, revealing itself to be another man. The man in front cleared his throat, but made no introduction of himself. Instead, he announced his companion, with a certain flourish and a swelling of pride.

'I present to you,' he said in a high voice, like the scratching of an insect's wings, 'Mister Ding.' Mister Ding did not step forward, but waited as the smaller man continued. 'Who is also, of course you need no prompting to remember, both a man and a brother to us all.'

'Er. My name is Din. Din Nelson.' His voice was deep and coarse; his accent cut through the fog like the tolling of an unfamiliar bell.

'Ding,' said the little man in front.

'Din. As in noise. Din. With a "nuh".'

'Din-nuh.'

It was as if the fog around Mister Din cleared as the words passed over me, and my skin prickled with shock. It was not because I had forgotten all about his impending arrival – which I had, things being as busy as they were – but because I had not quite appreciated, strange though this must sound, that the ex-slave, to be stationed at Damage's bindery by Lady Knightley's Ladies' Society for the Assistance of Fugitives from Slavery, would be black.

Oh, of course my rational mind knew that he was a slave,

and that slaves were Africans, and Africans were Negroes and Negroes were black, but when I had agreed to take him on and settle him in the workshop, my brain had not taken the necessary step of envisaging a black face behind the sewing-frame. Fortunately the shock did not paralyse my movements or my manners, and I managed to smile politely and extend my hand to him. The little man nodded approvingly, and the black man took my hand and bowed deeply, as if I were a lady.

As he stepped into the workshop his nose twitched, just like everyone else's.

'It's leather and glue. It always smells like that, especially when we're busy. Books only smell nice when they're done up.' I started to gabble as he was not looking at me, so I could not tell if he understood. But then I saw Jack's nose wrinkle, and I smelt it too, and I was abashed, for it had to be our visitor himself who smelt so horrible.

''Ave yer left summink on the stove, Mrs D?' Jack said, as Lucinda ran in through the curtain.

'Mama, Mama, the milk!'

'Oh, Lord! The milk!' And I twisted my way between the stranger and the bench, pushed aside the billowing curtain, and snatched the pan away. Where the milk had scorched on the hot surface, it looked as if it were caustic, as if the metal had bubbled and rusted underneath.

'That's another pan for the rag-and-bone man,' I sighed.

'Don't worry, Mama. I'll clean it up,' Lucinda said.

'No, don't *you* worry, little one,' I said as I kissed her on the nose. 'I'm afraid it's ruined.' But in truth, I felt like crying, for I was tired, and I wasn't able to concentrate on more than one thing at a time, and I didn't know how to get rid of that strange man in my workshop. I was tight like a string, stretched between the worlds of domesticity and commerce, and blurred in the centre, too, from the constant twanging. But I fingered my mother's hair-bracelet, and kept it all in; I hadn't cried since she died, and I wasn't going to start now.

Back in the workshop, the little man was buzzing and fussing with envelopes of money and contractual papers, which I counted and signed, but soon he disappeared and all was quiet again. I closed the door behind Mister Din Nelson, and did not know what to do with him. It was hard to look him directly in the eye for a while, until I realised that so I must, in order to establish my place in the workshop to him, but once I did, he was not able to reciprocate. One eye seemed to be interested in the air around my left ear, and the other drooped.

I did not even know where to put him. I could only think of the milk on the stove, and the glue that needed making up, and the dirt on the oil lamps that prevented us from working efficiently.

'Come over here, mate. Let's have a look at you,' Jack said, and he reached for Din's arm, and led him over to his bench. The man walked with a limp. 'Tell me, what're your skills? What can you do with those 'ands then?'

Din shrugged, and his eyes seemed to straighten up a little. 'I been woodworkin'.'

'What did you make?'

'Wagons. Furn'ture. Fences. Gates. Houses.'

'You good?'

Again he shrugged.

'What else?

'Tree fellin'. Fruit pickin'.'

I tried to catch Jack's eye and roll my own at him, as if to say, what have we taken on? But Jack wouldn't engage with me. He listened and nodded his head, and started to show Din around the workshop. He gave him a hammer, showed him the boards, opened a press for him. The man wasn't clumsy. He looked at home behind the bench. He was a good listener. But I didn't want him there. I wanted him to leave Damage's and never come back.

But I wasn't being honest with myself, for this was nothing

to do with Din. I wanted to find fault with him, but only because I found too many in myself. The presence of the stranger was forcing me to accept the transgressive nature of my business. I could not simply announce to the poor man that he was now working for someone who bound rude books for rich men; neither could I let him discover the fact on his own. That he had come from Knightley's wife was irrelevant, especially as I wasn't even allowed to mention that to Knightley in my defence. Oh Lord, the secrets I was keeping from both husband and wife; I was bound to them both.

And, lingering behind these thoughts was everything I had heard about the African; he would, I feared, be idle, servile, lacking in loyalty and discipline, and, in short, nothing but trouble in the workshop. My only consolation was the envelope of money I still clutched from Lady Knightley's Society, which I tucked into my waist before joining Jack in his instructions of the strange new fellow.

We started with sewing, but Din's thick fingers and one slightly maimed hand did not respond naturally to my demonstrations. I was a little irritated, and anxious at the hours I would waste teaching him. We needed another sewing-frame, so I could continue to work while he watched and practised. I chewed my lip in thought, then ran through into the parlour and collected a dining chair.

'Where are you taking that?' Peter growled.

My haste was an excuse not to answer him, for how was I to explain the new arrival to the man who was still the proprietor? It was not for me to make changes to our staff without his say-so; and who was to say how skin colour and background would prejudice his reaction further? Lowering the tone of Ivy-street, indeed. I would be in great disfavour; from him, and from Mrs Eeles, too, no doubt.

'Some more brew, my love?' I asked, uncorking the bottle for him, before fleeing with the chair.

Back in the workshop, Din watched as I tied four lengths

of binding string tightly from the cross-bar above the seat to the cross-bar beneath it, the same distance apart as the cuts Jack had made in the back of the book. I took a flat board from the laying press and placed it on the seat of the chair against the cords, laid the first section of the book on it, and fitted the four cords into the cut lines. I showed Din – on his frame, with what would be his needle – how to open the pages and put the needle through from back to centre, between the pages, and bring the needle out again to the back at the next cut, pass it behind the string, and reinsert it, and so on. He then laid a new section on top, and reinserted the needle directly above where it emerged from the first section, and repeated the process. When he had finished this, I showed him how to tie the two loose ends above each other together, and to start the third section with a completely new thread, and how to make a kettle-stitch between the second and third sections, before placing the fourth section on top. And I made sure, always, that he sewed textual manuscripts only; those with mischievous prints I reserved for myself.

His hands moved well with the needle, and he learnt quickly how to pass it through the paper without scuffing, and the exact tension required on the strings for optimum page-turning. I relaxed in direct proportion to his gaining prowess, and peculiarly, found my churning anxieties about the reactions of Sir Jocelyn, Mr Diprose, Peter and Mrs Eeles being replaced with one over-whelming curiosity. What, I kept wondering, as I watched every move of his fingers, the backs of his hands, his wrists, doing the job that I had done for so many years, what did it feel like, to have skin like that? To see that colour on one's outstretched hands? And how different would it feel from my own?

My mind raged on this thought, but he hardly said a word, which was most courteous of him. Soon I was able to continue with my own sewing, and the two of us worked side by side well into the day, by the end of which we had sewn twenty-three manuscripts.

But my, if only we had needed twenty-three manuscripts sewn that day! Six blank bindings had been waiting for me in the gold-tooling booth when Din arrived, and by the time we waved goodbye to him at seven o'clock they had been joined by a further four. I was getting behind; and I would get even further behind if I did not learn to continue with the usual line of *facetiae* in the presence of this dark stranger. But it did not feel proper so to expose this uncertain person to the true nature of my business.

Oh, he would never notice, I tried to convince myself. He would not be literate, of course; and besides, the number of illustrations, prints and photographs in the manuscripts were so few, and my cover designs were never so explicit or obscene, merely suggestive. But my inhibitions persisted. I knew I would often have to dismiss Din early, so that Jack and I could work unencumbered into the night.

The following morning, when I unlocked the workshop door to let Jack in, I heard a group of children further up the street laughing and cheering. The sun was managing to shine through the misty sky, and it felt to us all like a late reminder of summer. I looked up the street to see what was happening.

At first I noticed the children on the edge of the circle, for there were several who were holding themselves back from whatever the attraction was. In the midst of the main crowd was Din's tall figure. He seemed to be telling them a joke, or singing them a funny song. He pulled something from the ear of one of the older boys, and there was a general exclamation of delight. But there were mothers watching uncertainly; Agatha Marrow marched out and pulled her twin girls back inside, another boy got a clip round the ear.

None of us was unfamiliar with the sight of black people; but we seldom had one up our street. It was, no doubt, Mrs Eeles's influence: Peter had approved of her insistence on the Englishness of her territory, said it was a sign of gentility. I watched as Din approached, and knew that a whole street was watching me. I could not help but smile at him as he raised his hat to me, and sidled past me into the workshop.

'Good morning, Mr Nelson,' I said loudly, before I followed him inside and shut the door. Was I mistaken, or did his one good eye look at me?

I was about to settle him to cleaning the oil-lamps, when I heard a carriage draw up in the street. Through the glass I could see it was Charles Diprose himself, in a battered old hansom.

'Quick! Hide!' I hissed at Din, and without a pause he hurdled over the bench to the corner of the room. He moved fast, despite his limp. Lord, I thought, did he think that his old slave owner was after him with a band of mercenaries? He was heading to the gold-tooling booth, which was a sensible enough place, considering the curtains, but he did not make it in time. Diprose had already pushed open the door and was smiling at me, but his smile fell as it saw Din behind me, and his sweaty face went pale.

For all of our sakes, I made a hasty decision to land the one person in it who was least likely to be punished. It was also the truth, a quality that seemed to be somewhat lacking in my business these days.

'Mr Diprose. Allow me to introduce Mr Din Nelson, our new apprentice, who has been placed at Damage's through Lady Knightley's what-not, you know, the um, the Ladies' Society, for Runaway Slaves from, from America, I think it's called.'

Diprose's eyebrows arched viciously and his eyes bulged beneath, like two greasy spoons. He addressed not a word to Din, but grabbed my arm, and walked me stiffly towards the door so that Din could not hear his words.

'Does Sir Jocelyn know about this?'

'I believe not, sir.'

'He will be told. I warned Sir Jocelyn of the risks of hiring an *ingénue*; it appears you are labouring under a gross *mésconnaissance* of the severity of the situation.'

'What am I to do? I am under orders from Lady Knightley.'

'Does she pay your wages? Does she put food on your table?'

'But, Mr Diprose, with all due respect, the man was a *slave*. It was the least I could do, the least any of us can do, to let him have this job. And I need the help; with all the work you're bringing me, it's too much for the two of us, and, really, how much harm can he do?'

'That is not the point.'

'Shall I talk to Lady Knightley?'

'With difficulty.'

'Why?'

'She is *enceinte*.' The word seemed to leave an unpleasant taste in his mouth. 'She ceased receiving visitors back in August. She certainly will not be permitted to undertake any work for her "what-not" while she is expecting.'

'So we are stuck with him. We shall make it work somehow.'

'Your optimism *ne vous sied pas*, Mrs Damage. We know nothing about the man.'

'That can't be hard. You seem to be admirably capable of gathering information.'

'Do not pass on to me your dirty work. You agreed for him to be here; you must find out about him.' It was a remarkable feat, the way he spoke in such a murmur with barely a movement of his lips, but managed to load every word with menace. 'You must report back to me on everything you find; and you must use whatever means necessary to procure his discretion.' It was not just laziness: I was presenting him with the opportunity he had been waiting for, and he would use this, I knew, to topple me from my place of preference with Sir Jocelyn. 'And, if you do not,' he concluded, 'I shall see to it personally that you end up lower than the gutter in which I found you.'

'Surely it is simple, Mr Diprose,' I ventured. 'Here, look.'

I rummaged in the files to find Jack's indenture, pulled out the crumpled piece of paper with the lawyer's red seal, and showed it to him. 'Look, please. ". . . the said Apprentice his Master faithfully shall serve his secrets, keep his lawful commands everywhere, shall gladly do Shall do no damage to his said Master . . ."'

'Oh, *ben trovato*, Mrs Damage, *ben trovato*,' he said, with sarcasm. 'What a clever girl you are. Considering that the legal limit is one apprentice per every four journeymen, and oh, a-ha, I see, with one apprentice, one woman, and two large empty holes where the skilled workers used to be, *ergo*, you are already in breach of those limits . . .'

'I am not suggesting, Mr Diprose, that we draw up an apprentice's indenture. We simply require a legal document that says as much as this, that says, as here, let me find it, here it is, "either of the said parties bindeth himself unto the other". Surely, this is exactly what we need – "bindeth himself" – do you hear that, Mr Diprose – "bindeth himself unto the other by these Present . . ."'

'It would have no legal substance, but if you have the money to cover the fees of a decent lawyer, Mrs Damage, please go ahead. But I suggest that either you keep your doors closed to every charity-case that comes knocking, or you find the wherewithal to ensure *sa loyauté*. You do indeed need to find a way for both your said parties to *bindeth* yourselves unto each other, but not like this, with *un morceau de papier*. I suggest you start thinking.' Then he raised his hand to his beard, and rubbed it vigorously so that his chins shook. 'Besides, a legal document does not overcome one insurmountable issue with regard to the man's origins.'

'I beg your pardon?'

He dropped his hand in disgust at me. 'Have you not noticed before? The indelicate nature of some of our literature?' He was so exasperated now he was almost spitting. 'The anthropological thrust, the *ethnographic* bent of it?'

'I had not thought . . .'

'I shall ensure some comes your way soon enough, and then we shall see where your allegiance lies, and how a flimsy piece of lawyer's puff helps you then. Good luck, Mrs Damage. I, for one, shall not be heart-broken to see the back of you.' Then he marched outside with his characteristic creaking, upright haughtiness.

'Help me, would you, boy?' he shouted at the driver, who looked as unwilling as if Diprose had asked him to run up the Himalayas. The boy yawned, slid down from his seat, and climbed inside the carriage like a cat looking for somewhere to curl up. He did, fortunately, emerge again, with a large wicker box in his arms, and bore it into the workshop.

'Books?' I asked, with some misgivings, thinking of our workload.

'No. *Personnel*. Not from me, *je vous assure*. Open it later; you've got far too much to be getting on with to be distracted by this.' He climbed up into the cab, and passed me two large hides through the doorway. They were an exquisite, dull, Venetian-red colour. They looked aged, but I could tell by the feel of the leather that they were very fresh and moist.

'What is this?' I asked. 'It's beautiful.'

'Goatskin,' he said, 'from the Niger territories, or the Congo, or somewhere *maudit* like that, dyed by whichever set of natives they'd be, with a tree-bark, or the like. A secret process, to which, no doubt, our Empire will get the recipe before long. Put them inside, then come back for the books.'

I dodged the cab driver at the door, then went into the gloom of the workshop and laid them on the bench. Din was staring out of the rear window into the yard; I did not address him, but returned to the street as instructed. I spotted Nora Negley peering round the shabby side of the carriage, Agatha Marrow was beating a mattress further up the street, but certainly not fast enough or loud enough to interfere with her ability to hear what was being said.

'*Les voicis*,' Diprose said, holding a pile of large, heavy books, which he handed to me one at a time. 'Three volumes, all in need of a good re-bind. The first is what you might call anthropology; a foray into rites, practices, folklore of certain curious cults.' There was no title on the old binding, so I opened it to read the frontispiece. 'Oh, please,' he hissed, in exasperation, 'do you have to open it in front of me, and in the street of all places? It really isn't suitable, you know. Don't make it any harder for me. If I had my way you wouldn't be working for us at all.'

It was called *Des Divinities generatrices ou le culte du phallus*, and the design of the frontispiece was an enormous disembodied phallus reaching to the sky, penetrating some clouds. I closed it quickly.

'And in case it is not evident to you,' he muttered, 'our conversation today must not reach the ears of Sir Jocelyn. I do not wish for him to know about your currish slave, at least not until you have proof of his loyalty; his wife's goings-on are not exactly his *cheval de bataille*. And neither must you reveal to him my threats to you,' he added, rather more casually, as he suddenly became rather interested in the curling endpapers protruding through a corner-tear of the cover. 'I am, unfortunately, bound to him as you are to me.' Before I could ask how, he had continued, 'We must, I suppose, find a way to muddle through –' the tip of the endpaper crumbled between his fingers, and he rubbed them together to get the paper off '– much as I would relish putting a plug in your rather mediocre sink-hole.' If he were expecting a reaction from me, he did not receive one. So he gestured at the book I was holding. 'Paris, 1805. I want the three as a kind of trilogy, and this will be the first one. Here is the second. A classic from 1786 by Richard Payne Knight, the grandfather of priapus.'

It was *A Discourse on the Worship of Priapus and its Connection with the Mystic Theology of the Ancients*. I knew it well, if only by its extensive referencing throughout other works I had bound.

'And the third?'

'*The Satyricon and Other Priapic Writings*. Imagine, if you will, a series of bindings dedicated to the great God Priapus. May I suggest to you that the cover design to unite the three should be, what one might describe as *emblematic*, if you understand my meaning. I need these quickly; they must take priority over the rest of the consignment. *Au revoir*, Mrs Damage. Ill met by gas-light, as ever. I will not bid you good day.'

Oh, but he was poisonous, but poisons could be avoided, or purged, or antidoted. I returned to the workshop, closed the door firmly behind me, and chose to worry not about Diprose's contemptible chaff, but about how to occupy Din today, and whether Lucinda was getting enough to eat, and how on earth I was to gold-tool three 'emblematic' designs without Din noticing.

I gave the books to Jack to disband and clean, but I could not help but steal a peek at the wicker box before I settled to my own work. I gasped, and had to open it fully when I saw its contents.

'Blow me dahn!' Jack said. 'Bellytimber!' It was a hamper of exotic foods: Danish tins filled with sticky pastries, jars of French jams and preserves, a large, spiced ham studded with cloves and pineapple rings, two bottles – one of port, one of champagne – and two cheeses wrapped in wax paper. Tucked down one side was a brown-paper parcel; I opened it to find inside a cream silk ladies' scarf, cool and smooth as soap, and a child's navy-blue wool coat, warm and soft and snug, like my Lucinda herself.

Also for me was a pair of bronze kid boots, with a pointed toe, a dainty heel, and laces all the way up to the top of the boot, which curved around my calf. I could not help but try them on straightways. They were a perfect fit, as if they had been made for me. How had they known the angle of my toes, the arch of my soles? But the heel was so high that I stumbled, and I cursed the gentleman and rubbed my sore ankle; how badly I needed a new pair of boots, but how useless was a pair I could not walk in!

I took them off quickly, and returned them to the hamper. I closed the lid hastily; such distractions would turn my head today. I would leave them for Lucinda to discover. I returned to work, ashamed at my excitement and angry at the profligacy of a gift I could never use.

I situated myself in the draught-proof booth to plan my designs. Din could see me from here, but if I angled my work correctly he would not see what I was doing, and besides, once the gold-tooling had begun, the curtains would be closed.

And so to the frontispiece of the first book: a phallus complete in itself, not appendaged to a body. I copied it, and experimented with suspending it in a fine-tooled oval of ivy-leaves. It felt curiously normal for me now to be doing this, despite the fact that I was a wife, and had only occasionally seen my own dear husband's 'emblem', and that woefully long ago. I entertained myself by wondering what his reaction would be were I to announce to him that I needed to disrobe him for the purpose of research. His seemed to belong to an entirely different species from Fanny Hill's maypole or the Dey's masterpiece; neither did I remember his throbbing with ammunition like a flesh-coloured trebuchet, or 'at full cock' like a loaded gun, or erupting like Vesuvius. But then again, at least, that meant that I had never been the silent victim of bullets, shrapnel or lava either. Perhaps that was how men preferred their women; what a disappointment I must have been to my husband, for not being a docile and willing conduit, a physiological sewer, to the pourings-forth of his mighty Jupiter Pluvius.

Perhaps the simple answer was that Diprose was right, and it was not I who should have been reading these things at all.

Chapter Twelve

As I went by a dyer's door,
I met a lusty tawnymoor;
Tawny hands, and tawny face,
Tawny petticoats,
Silver lace.

'The devil has come upon us!' Peter shrieked.

I was just coming up from the cellar with some fresh paste, so I rushed to him, anticipating the discovery of my child on the floor: it had been so long since she had fallen fitting, but still I feared it daily. But Lucinda was nowhere to be seen. Peter was standing in the doorway between the kitchen and the workshop, clutching the hem of his nightshirt around his crotch like a boy who has had a bad dream, and wobbling a purple finger in the direction of the benches.

'Take him away!'

'Peter, my love, may I introduce . . .'

'Take him away!' The bloodshot folds of skin hung from his face like an ornate gold and red brocade curtain, which quivered as he shouted, as if someone was hiding behind them shaking their swags and festoons.

'He is working for . . .'

'Give me my draught,' he pleaded, suddenly.

'Peter, there's nothing to be afraid of. This is Mr Din Nelson and he's going to be . . .'

'Give me my draught now!'

I uncorked the bottle and handed it to him, and he swigged it gladly, and sat quivering in his armchair by the fire once more. So I never did introduce him properly to Din, and he never mentioned the man again either. I instructed Din to stay in the workshop at all times, and never to come through into the house even to make paste, and the curtain was kept closed from hereon in.

The same group of children escorted Din to work each morning; it was the mothers pulling them inside who varied, according to the daily rumours of his good nature or malevolence. It was a struggle between respectability and convenience, for there was no doubt the man was entertaining their children, which was always a blessing when it kept them out from under one's feet. Besides, there was something jaunty about Din's striding limp, and every morning he would raise his hat to the women, and each day he met them – and they him – with an increasing firmness of eye.

In the evenings he would stay until six, when he folded his work, swept up the threads below his seat, gathered his coat, and bade us good evening. He never enquired, as a more diligent employee seeking promotion might, as to whether I might require him to stay longer; he never waited for my dismissal every evening. But I was hardly bothered by this; what concerned me more was his fourth day, a Friday, when I darted into the house at five o'clock to serve Lucinda up some pancakes, and when I returned, Din was nowhere to be seen. He had cleaned up his mess, put away his work, and taken his coat an hour before time, and all without Jack's noticing. I thought no more of it, aside from a minor indignance at his insolence.

It rather suited us, because we needed to get on with the Priapic Trilogy, and due to Din's absence, we could start on it an hour early. We were planning to experiment with *répoussage*, whereby the design is modelled into relief from the underside of the skin. Jack dampened the leather and, while he held it taut, I cut halfway down along every line of the design, with a knife sharper than paper, and with scarcely a breath between us. Then we coaxed the three proud *peni* into tumescence: with the point of the bone folder and the agate we made the incision bulge and rise, before filling the hollows with a mixture of *papier-mâché*, sawdust and glue. Jack and I were so absorbed in the vulnerability of the procedure that we soon forgot the subject matter at such close quarters; we could just have easily been performing *répoussage* on a nose, or a chin. And at around ten o'clock, when Jack and I beheld the first of the three finished books, we could see that we had created a veritable masterpiece of the nether regions.

I heard a shouting from upstairs, and raced up to find Peter kneeling by his bed, grimacing, in a puddle of urine. He had knocked his chamber-pot over, and his nightshirt was soaked.

'Give me some draught,' he begged. 'Give me some Drop.'

'I will, love. Let me clean you up first.' I rolled the wet portion of his nightshirt up into the dry bit above, then lifted it over his head. I found a clean one from his cupboard; it hadn't been aired, but there was urgency in his nakedness, so I dressed him quickly and got him back into bed. He dosed himself straightways, and sank back into the bed and into himself, as I soaked up the rest of the puddle with the old nightshirt, tucked it inside the chamber-pot, and took the whole lot downstairs.

Back at work, I fretted about Peter, and wondered if I really were doing the right thing in my new trade, with my leather penises and the like. They certainly made a change from the books a woman like me was meant to be reading, which seemed to demonstrate over and over again, with a million minor variations, that women are untroubled by desire, and that on their purity and domesticity depends the moral state of the entire nation. I thought of the books I had loved, rather than those that set out to belittle me. I tried to imagine Jane *firkytoodling* with Rochester, which was not hard, given that they only made love once he was a cripple, and I had bound plenty of literature which dealt with that topic. Or Cathy and Heathcliff, with Edgar watching, or, better still, a *ménage à trois* powered by the passion of hatred. It surprised me how easy it was for me to imagine this, but then again, I had always found more genuine passion between the pages of *Jane Eyre* than between the sheets of *The Lustful Turk*. I empathised with Jane: her lack of hope for her life, her minimisation of her desires, her ability to knuckle down and do whatever it was that needed to be done. After all, I was the daughter of a governess who had never hoped to marry either; and, like Jane, I never felt that I was included among the fair sex.

But then again, the women of Lambeth on a Saturday night could not be described as the fair sex, either. Women who shrieked and fell, and showed their thighs from the gutter, all the while laughing from the drink. Women who sold their babies to the baby-farmers, who were all women too, to do away with them because they couldn't bring themselves to do it with their own hands. Women who gave over their own daughters to the men who refused to pay for the old crone any longer, women who could do this to their own girls, to avoid hunger, rather than throw themselves off a bridge first. What on earth was fair about that? Fair sex, what poppycock, I thought, before remembering that I couldn't use the word 'poppycock' any more, not now I knew what else it could mean. No, we were the *un*fair sex, and yet what was really unfair was that if we went to public hangings, or public libraries, or public anythings, we received a scolding for not protecting our purity.

When the church clock chimed midnight, I laid down my tools, took off my apron, and didn't even bother to check the kitchen fire. I left the kitchen dirty, and I looked in on my sweet Lucinda, only I didn't kiss her cheek, as I was dirty too, and I took off my dirty smock and put on my dirty chemise. But I could not take off my shame and lay it on the chair by the bed. That would never go away, and I lay down next to Peter in an uneasy sweat of tiredness and dirt, in a stew of dirt and shame and anger, and I knew it would still cling to me in the morning when I woke, like a clammy shawl, like the London fog.

The following day was Saturday, and I was ready to speak to Din, not about his reasons for leaving us an hour early, but in an effort to find some way of binding him to the workshop. I had not planned my questions wholly on behalf of Mr Diprose; I confess to a certain curiosity about the life he had lived, before circumstance and rich ladies conspired to throw him up on my shore.

'Where do you lodge, Mr Din?'

'In the Borough, ma'am.'

'Your exact address, please, for my records.'

'The Lodging House for Transient Male Workers, ma'am, on the High-street.'

'And your landlord?'

'Mrs Catamole.'

'You have been there how long?'

'Eight months, ma'am.'

'And before that, you were where?'

'At a flop-house.'

'Excuse me?'

'A beer-stop.'

'Why did you leave?'

'Them places is only temporary, ma'am. The Ladies' Society for the Assistance of Fugitives from Slavery wanted to find me better straight off, and cheaper too, so they sent me to Mrs Catamole.' His accent was enchanting: thick, and syrupy, with an evident American twang, but with something else, too. Like his step, his speech was jaunty.

'Is it to your satisfaction?'

'Yes, ma'am. The bed is comfortable, and the board whole-some and pleasant. I never expected so much, nor hoped for it neither.'

'How long have you been in England?'

'Eleven months, ma'am. Nine months in London.'

'Where were you in the interim?'

'In Portsmouth. The Ladies' Society for the Assistance of Fugitives from Slavery got me safe passage with a Dutch ocean-liner. They dropped me in Portsmouth.'

'And where did you lodge in Portsmouth?'

'I didn't.'

'So where did you go?'

'I walked, and took lifts where I could.'

'And where did you sleep?'

'Rough, ma'am.'

'I beg your pardon?'

'On the streets. Or in boat-yards, or fields. I got to London soon enough, ma'am. I took myself to my benefactress, but she had been unwell, she died.'

'Ah, yes, Lady Grenville. You must have thought your luck had died with her.'

'No ma'am. I make my own luck. I was expectin' nothin' more from the Ladies' Society for the—'

'Yes, yes, I know who you mean.' How quick he was to subdue, from my rude interruption! I bit my impatient tongue, then said softly, 'You may continue. Pray, tell me, how did you get to be here?'

'I knew of another American fellow like me, who had run the railroad for a while before the price on his head got too high, and he ran to England. I heard he was in Limehouse. So I took myself there.'

'Did you find him?'

'No. But I found those who knew him. Americans, lots of them, all of them Negroes. Another runaway, too.'

'So how did Lady Knightley find you?'

'Lady Grenville's girl asked me to leave an address. The only one I knew of was this one I was headin' to in Limehouse. I had carried that address with me for years.'

'And Lady Knightley found you there,' I said.

'Yes. The folks there told her they might find me on the floor of a Chinaman's rooms some streets away. And there she did find me.'

The vision this presented was remarkable. Lady Knightley, driving around from place to insalubrious place, in search of a man she had never met, from a country she had never been to. I bowed my head; if she had been present I would have dropped to my knees in humility and respect.

'And she took you to the flop-house? And thence to Mrs Catamole's?'

'Yes ma'am.'

'And how have you found the English to be, Din?'

'Mighty helpful, ma'am. Civil as they could be. They do not trouble me while I walk the streets. When I hail an omnibus it stops. At table Mrs Catamole asks me how I find the fare. That never happened at home, even before I was caught.'

'You were caught?'

'Yes, ma'am.'

'Did they send you back?'

'No, ma'am. I was caught in the beginnin'.'

'Forgive me, Din. I am not understanding you.'

'I was caught by the tradin' men, when I was a boy. I was free before that.'

'You – *became* – a . . .?' He had not used the word to me; I did not know if I could say it to him. 'You were how old?'

'Fourteen, ma'am.'

I wanted to clarify what I was hearing, and to find out more, but I was straying into dangerous territory, and the man wasn't revealing without my questioning. I picked up my pen and resumed what I thought was an official line of enquiry.

'Next of kin, Din? For my records, again.'

If I had thought this was a safer way of interrogating I could see from his face that I had got it wrong. I did not know then that a man of his colour could turn pale; it was a fearsome sight, and was as unfamiliar to me as the paleness of desert sands to those smeared with city grime.

'None,' he finally said. 'My mamma and pop are dead, ma'am.' His voice was resuming its previous courtesy, despite my lack of it. 'I had two brothers and two sisters, but I won't be seein' them again. And no, ma'am, I leave no wife or children behind me.'

'I am sorry to hear that, Din' I replied. 'Thank you for answering my questions.'

'Pleasure, ma'am.'

I closed my notebook with a snap and turned sharply on my heel in the desperate hope that something lay on the bench behind me that could occupy my industry for a few moments. Eventually I moved into the gold-leaf booth and the day's tasks. I watched him from here, and weighed his polite answers in my head. Throughout the morning I found my gaze falling on him when I no longer wished to gold-tool another innuendo-laden title, or *répoussé* another penis.

And instead of the lists of body parts and sexual practices my brain used to litanise, I turned to the planning of my argument to Diprose about how Din could not possibly be a threat to anyone, for he was polite and gentle, and that after a man had been through what he had, and suffered the loss of his family, what cared he a few smutty stories?

He left again an hour early on the following Friday, and the next.

'We must watch him next week, Jack,' I said, 'and see if he still gives us the slip.'

'Aye aye, Mrs D.'

But each week, we would forget to stand guard, and when

I remembered, something would distract me. Peter would summon me in to cut his nails, or Lucinda would ask for food, or the pot-man would arrive and fill our empty jugs, which always seemed more important than Din stealing a mere hour from us.

Eventually I asked him about his life in America before setting foot on English soil. He told me he had been born there, which banished the images I had envisaged of a small boy being transported from the tropics in the fetid hold of a vast ship. I asked if his parents had been born there; again, the affirmative.

'So how old were you when you realised you were a – a – when you realised that the choices available to others were not available to you?'

'As a Negro, I knew it all my life, even before I was captured. But it was a different kind o' captivity. We knew the evils of captivity in the South, but even the scorn we got in the streets, the curfews, the segregation, told us we were free, at least. When I was caught, it all changed.'

'Had you escaped?'

'No, ma'am, not until recently.' His courtesy was impeccable in the face of a woman who was not understanding him.

'So when were you captured?'

'July first, 1846.'

'Which made you how old?'

'Fourteen, ma'am.'

'Please explain,' I begged, when my obtuseness became unbearable even to me.

Finally he spoke without using my questions as prompts, and I hung on to every word for fear his flow would dry up.

'I was going to a conference of preachers in Washington DC with my pop.'

'Your father?'

'Yes. Pop was a minister, a Methodist preacher. Mamma was a nurse. We lived just outside Baltimore, with my brothers and sisters. So, we were going to DC. It was goin' to take us two days to get there. Only we got ambushed, by poachers. They took us south an' auctioned us in Virginia.' He spoke coolly.

'Who bought you?'

'Master Lucas. He was local to Virginia; Pop went to a Texan, a ranchman by looks of him.'

'You were separated?'

'Yes. You look surprised. I don't wish to shock you, ma'am, but they take babes from their mothers. Least I was grown.' I heard his tone: do not pity me, it warned.

'Did you ever see him again?'

'No.'

'So how do you know he is dead?' I had never asked so many questions of a man, but the evenness of his honesty emboldened me.

'Mamma told me.'

'So you saw your mother?'

He paused, and looked down at the floor with a quiet puffing of breath. He had had enough of me and my questions. I wished I could have erased them all, but there were still so many I wanted to ask. How did he meet his mother again? What of his siblings? Where was the law in all this? Could not the police have helped? If his kidnapping and sale was unlawful, why could they not prosecute, convict, liberate?

But there were really no answers, only the cruel unfurlings of history against which this man was powerless. We sat with our silences for several minutes, listening only to the sound of Jack's hammer, which resonated a soothing sense of solidity and reliability throughout the workshop.

And then came another shout from inside, and still I thought it might be my Lucinda in danger, less likely though it was these days. It was, of course, Peter, lying far back in his chair, his eyes glazed, his throat rattling. He looked as if he were dying: I felt his brow, and patted his cheeks, but his vital signs were good, his circulation still vigorous. He was not close to death, I surmised, but it was if he had lost his way through the valley of the shadow of it, and was not enjoying the scenery.

'There it is,' he gurgled, and a long string of brown, laudanum-scented spittle descended from his mouth and onto his chest.

'Is it?'

'There she is.'

'Is she? And what does she look like today?'

'She's got g – g – g – green sk – sk – skin.'

'Is she a ghoul? A ghoul-ess?'

He nodded. 'She's suck – suck – sucking my s – s – soul from my – my – my –'

'Your . . .?'

'M – m – m – my m – m – mouth!'

'It's the opium, love. It just makes you worse.' I spoke slowly and softly, as if to a child. 'It takes the pain away, but it brings you these dreadful women. It's a choice you have to make.'

'No, no, no. Stop! Stop!'

His hooded eyes rolled towards their horror as if compelled. But no matter how terrifying she may have seemed today, nothing would stop him from taking his draught of laudanum tomorrow, and as often as possible thereafter.

I might, in the years prior to Din's arrival at Damage's, have agreed with Cardinal Manning and others that opium addiction was slavery. But would the most reverent gentleman had made such an equation had he met a man like Din? Or known that William Wilberforce himself was slave to the poppy? That, unlike sugar, poppies were cultivated by those who earned a wage and lived in far better conditions than in the chains of the plantations, farms, and homesteads of America?

'Have those men been back?' Peter drooled.

'No, love, they haven't.' I wasn't sure which men he meant, but then his eyes opened, then narrowed into slits, and he started to mutter.

'Indolent dandies . . . Turkish baths . . . degenerate . . . British Empire . . . just like the Roman Empire . . . look at the Ottoman Empire . . . bawds . . . lechery . . . villainy . . .'

And I knew which men he meant, and I knew that he knew, and I could say nothing more, only leave him to his rantings, which flowed forth with surprising vehemence for one floating on a laudanum cloud.

I was sorry for him. His manliness had all but gone from him; he could only watch as his wife made an admirable living from his business, working on material to which he felt she should not be exposed and from which he could not protect her, and which further served to remind him of his failure as a real man. My husband had become a molly, a milksop; but it was not his fault.

I tapped the window-pane to catch Lucinda's attention as she played in the street, and waved at her. Then I returned to the workshop and to Din, and I was surprised to see that he was ploughing the pages of Ovid's *Amores* under Jack's supervision.

'With care, with care,' I cried. 'Do not cut away the margins! You will make an octavo of that quarto without care!'

Wordlessly, Din took it out of the plough and handed it to me to check. The print lay near perfect in relation to the spine and head. I fingered the paper-shavings and held them to the light, to make my redundant point. The man was good.

'These are pieces of history. This paper is a hundred years old.' I should have stopped, but I could not help myself. 'What of these crisp edges, when the discolouration of time is removed? Old books need the most cautious handling.'

I handed the book back to Din, and I could see Jack smiling out of the corner of my eye. No doubt he was remembering the time when Peter asked him if he were making a collection of margins, or whether he had been enervated by the author, so profligate was he with the plough. Jack received ten of the best after that, but I doubt he felt touched by the birchen mysteries. I was still daunted by the plough; Din had done very well, and was now demonstrating to me, not without pride, how well the pages opened.

I struggled to find some words of praise to follow my tirade, so I simply nodded in appreciation, and watched Din continue to open and close the book. Then it occurred to me that he was flicking through it, as if he were looking for something. It was mildly comical, but I was not going to laugh at him, not after his earlier revelations to me. I waited for him to finish. For the first time, I noticed the mark on his upper arm, protruding from his rolled-up sleeves. It was a word, written with the same fuzzy dark lines as Sir Jocelyn's tattoo. 'LUCA●', it said.

Suddenly I heard him exclaim, 'Here it is,' and he cleared his throat, and said something that I didn't understand. I wondered if he was speaking in an African tongue that might have been native to his family, a language they possibly spoke at home.

'I beg your pardon?' I said, and he repeated it, but I was still no clearer. 'Let me see,' I asked, and held my hand out for the book. He gave it to me, and I scanned the page for the quotation, but I was lost. His finger stretched across the paper to show me the line I was after.

'You can read?' I asked, unaware in my amazement of how rude I sounded.

'You mean, can I read *Latin?*' he corrected.

'And you can.'

'Yes, ma'am,' he said, unmoved by my insolence. 'I can't be a preacher's son and not read.'

I tried to focus my eyes to where his finger pointed, and slowly read it out loud. ' "Suffer and harden: good growes by this griefe, Oft bitter juice brings to the sick reliefe." But this is not Latin, Din. This is Christopher Marlowe's translation.'

'I prefer the original. Marlowe was trapped by his couplets. Ovid is tellin' us to endure, for some day our pain will benefit us.'

'Say it again, Din,' I prompted, still confused.

'*Perfer et obdura: dolor hic tibi proderit olim.*'

'And your translation, again, if you will?'

'Suffer and endure, for some day your pain will be of benefit.'

'Some day your pain will be of benefit,' I repeated, dazed. I stared at the page for a moment longer, before closing the book and giving it to Jack to place between the boards of the standing press. I did not know what else to say. I turned slowly and quietly to Din and said, 'Your father taught you?'

'No, ma'am. My mamma.'

'Your mother.'

We lapsed into silence, until finally I could not help myself. 'When did you see her again, Din?'

'I been wonderin' when you'd ask.' He grinned, good-naturedly. 'You women. She did what a mamma does. She waited until her children' – he pronounced it 'chillen' – 'be old enough to care for themselves, then she came South to find us. Bad choice, it was, but I can't be blamin' her. She didn't find Pop. She heard talk that he be dead. She found me though. She found me.'

'That must have been remarkable.'

'Remarkable, yes, ma'am. And no, ma'am. She found me, an' Master Lucas found her, and said that, she bein' on his land, she might as well join the rest of his sorry family. She worked in the fields for him until she fell down dead. Then I left. I'd been plannin' on runnin' all the time I'd been there. I'd helped hundreds hit that railroad, but I couldn't run and leave Mamma, and she weren't well enough to run with me. I helped hundreds of others to run, though.'

'How did you help them?'

'Bein' a reader, and a writer. I wrote hundreds o' letters an' free-papers to be carried, documents that said things no one could prove. That's why they called me Din.'

'Din? I don't understand.'

'Dudish Intelligent Nigger.' He was smiling; was he playing with me?

'Is that really why?' I began, but it wasn't an important question, not compared to what he was saying.

'An' I was goin' to run once she died, but Master Lucas knew it, an'kept me chained and covered by dogs wherever I went. I wanted to go to New Orleans an' stow on a boat to England, I wanted to get to England all along, but then I caught the eye of Lady Grenville, and she paid Master Lucas three times more than I was worth to any folk back home, so I got here anyways.'

'How fortunate.'

'Fortunate, yes, ma'am. But they was goin' to do me in anyways, owin' to my writing those letters. Master Lucas was goin' to take the money and use it to put a price on my head. They all wanted me done, as they all knew it had been me who wrote the letters.'

'Couldn't anyone else have done it?'

Din snorted. 'You think they had a happy bunch o' niggers who could read and write? Niggers are folk with no letters, ma'am. We don't have no books, don't get no schoolin', don't *need* no learnin'. What were tough – almost tougher than not bein' back home in Baltimore – was not the work, or the disrespect, it was the not readin'. I had to hide it from them, or they woulda pulped me so hard I woulda lost most o' my brains and been more use as a vegetable for the pot. If you was a white boy, and you was found to be teachin' a nigger, you'd be fined fifty dollars and thrown in jail. If you was a nigger boy and you did the same . . . Well, but anyways, there weren't none of them kinds of white boys where we lived, so some boy had to do it.'

He paused, as if he were wondering whether he had taken out too much time and should be getting back to work. I just wanted to keep listening to him. It was as if a window had opened between us, and we could hear each other breathing the same air in our separate rooms. Jack's hammer was beating, so I slipped inside its regular sound, and waited.

'So I come to England,' Din resumed eventually. 'I come to England, where Mr Isambard Kingdom Brunel be buildin' his railroads, and tellin' folks he wants all his drivers not to be able to read, cos only them who can't read pay mind to things. Why, there's some truth in that, ma'am. I don' see no disrespect there. Words can be traps, ma'am, and drivers don' be needin' traps. But I see the traps *an*' I can read.'

He spoke with pride. It was only later that I wondered whether I should have taken it as a warning.

'And now you have come to a place where you can have all the books you could wish for,' I said.

'Ain' it the strangest ol' world, ma'am.'

'Ain't it just, Din.'

'I'm losing you, Dora,' Peter said that evening, when his perturbing visions had left him.

'No, you're not.'

'Then I'm losing my mind.'

'No, you're not,' I said again, but with less conviction. For the pain in his brain was nothing compared to the physical torments of his joints without the ease of laudanum, which was taking his mind with it.

'Don't take the bottle away.' But I did, and I put it on the dresser. He closed his eyes, so I took his sore body into my arms and rocked him like a baby. I wished I could have remembered what he looked like when I first met him. Was his nose ever sharp, or was it always this round? Did he always have this porous, pitted forehead, or was his skin once smooth and taut? I had not expected then that it would come to this. I knew the hazards of bookbinding; bookbinders died young, I knew, of pulmonary disease and the like, from all that leather-dust, like my father. But what mattered Peter's lungs now, when his very flesh was drowning?

At times like these I would catch myself thinking that what he really needed was for me to show him what pleasure really felt like, to distract him for a moment from his pains by straddling him and giving him the sweets of my body, or unbuttoning his breeches and taking him in my mouth, for this is what I discovered *minetting* actually means, from the French (and, incidentally, I had learnt by now that the clitoris is not in Africa). But it would have killed him, I knew. How many times had I read of lecherous men shuffling on a crimson cunt and shuffling off the mortal coil? Now there's a story to pass on to Mrs Eeles, I thought to myself.

But wasn't it strange that my professional life should have been so devoted to a morass of seething sexuality, while my husband, the one person I was legally entitled to *firkytoodle*, was slumped in the corner, oblivious to the writhing bodies of my work and my imagination? No, in many ways it was not strange at all.

Then came the challenge from Holywell-street. I did the first thing I could think of: I dismissed Din, but only temporarily.

'Din, you may go. I won't be needing you today.'

'As you wish, ma'am.' He put down his mug of English Burgundy, and gathered his coat.

'It is no indication of your progress – and, indeed, prowess – in the workshop. I am pleased with your work to date. Still, I won't be needing you. I trust you will find something to occupy your time suitably?'

'You trust correctly. I thank you, ma'am. I am grateful for the liberty; I have business to attend to.'

'Business?' I smiled, presuming that this was a joke. 'Just for today, mind?'

He smiled back at me. 'As you wish, ma'am,' he repeated.

I think my heart started beating again once the door shut and his whistling receded up Ivy-street. I had been tense since I opened the crate and recognised its contents for what they were; I knew that my immediate instinct to get rid of Din was correct. I tried to pretend to myself that I was only carrying out Diprose's wishes: the man had not yet been verified, and was still not to be wholly trusted. But I defy anyone to have seen what was on those pages and not have dismissed him too.

Each stack of paper was a collection of several hundred photographs. They were to be bound as a series of catalogues, each of a certain theme. The preface for the first read:

This volume is for neither the prurient and perfidious, nor the ignorant and innocent. The artist of discernment, who professes the pursuit of truth, the liberation from taboos, and the continued supremacy of Britannia, as the higher motives behind his representations, will be best served by its contents. The nature of such an endeavour compels the reproduction of extreme imagery, which is a triumph of the technology of our age.

I flicked through. Here, on page 21 entitled: 'The Negro's Revenge. Young wife violated by Negro in revenge for cruelties by master'. There, on page 45: 'Untitled. Stupration of mulatto daughters by father.' Later on, on page 63: 'African maid circumcises female word.'

The precious reader, artist or not, was not sufficiently warned by the preface. For these were by no means the worst. I picked up the second, then the third stack of papers, and scanned them all, until I was so stunned that the papers slipped from my hands and back into the crate, crushing the corners where they landed. I stood up slowly, then ran into the house and out to the privy where I vomited savagely.

Even Jack was subdued. We talked in low tones, and noticed

the trembling of each other's cheeks. Once we had decided on the bindings, and trapped the images between suitably stiff endpapers, we didn't turn the pages again.

Hyperion to a satyr; antidote to a poison; this contrary world threw up to us a clash of perspectives, and Damage's was the point of collision. For the following morning we received a package of an altogether different kind, shortly after Din arrived back for work with an innocent smile, as if to say 'all well, ma'am?'

But all did not look well with him either. He was walking stiffly, and his limp was more pronounced; his arm did not seem to move effectively, and he had a wound somewhere about his neck, which I did not notice at first, but which oozed on to his dirty collar throughout the morning.

'Good morning, Din. I trust you had a pleasant day off.'

'Thank you, ma'am, most pleasant.'

'Are you in trouble, Din?' I asked him, as he struggled to sit down without pain.

'No, ma'am,' he replied, and that was the end of the matter. I dared say nothing more, out of decorum.

And then the aforementioned new package arrived, so I sent Din to make up some paste, and stood for a while, picking at the dry skin on my upper lip.

'What's in it, Jack?' I eventually asked, nodding towards it. 'Do you want me to have a look?'

'Yes please.' I pulled at a flake of skin, which stretched my lip away from my teeth.

'No pictures,' he said first. Then, 'this one looks all right. And this one.' The fragment came away from my lip. I pressed my bottom lip against the top, and tasted blood.

'All manuscripts. Seven of them, all the same. They look pretty safe to me, Mrs D. You can look now. It's all right.'

And so I sat, and read, wetting my lips with my tongue to ease the smarting, as Din came in with fresh paste.

My dear Mrs Damage

It seems a tremendous while since we first met. And how tedious my life has become since then! Jossie has been a frightful bore about my condition; it seems I must rest around the clock. I have missed everything worth seeing this summer, and I fear I shall miss the Mistletoe Players' Production of Uncle Tom's Cabin *at the Phoenix if the baby does not appear until after Christmas. Still, I am blessed to be married to the finest physician in London, and am nearing the end of my confinement with as much good grace as I can muster!!!*

My activities with the Society continue apace, notwithstanding Jossie's disapproval. And here I come to the purpose of my letter. You may have heard of Mr Frederick Douglass, Mr William Wells Brown, Mr Josiah Henson & many others; if you have not, I assure you their names will soon be unforgettable to you, for their stories are certainly! Many is the lecture I have attended given by these eminent former slaves, and I wish I could share with you now the eloquence with which they captivate their audience: they terrify & enthrall, & elicit copious tears, reverent anger, & inspired action! Many are the panoramas I have viewed which have reinforced to my eyes what my ears had witnessed, illustrating the horrendous conditions under which they are forced to live and work! Many are the torture implements I have touched & shrunk from, &c., which they exhibit at these events! And many are the narratives I have purchased after such an experience, & of that ilk is the document which I am proud to enclose.

It is entitled My Bondage and My Freedom, *by Mr Frederick Douglass. Herewith are seven copies, all still in their trade paper bindings. You will see it is already in its fifth edition!!*

*I & several of my Society colleagues would like to
have them personally re-bound by you for the Society
with the Society's emblem and motto centre-top, for
which I have enclosed the appropriate tools. Centre
itself requires an engraving of Douglass's profile; I
enclose some recent portraits of him for reference.*

I also enclose the appropriate sum for your pains!

*After my confinement I shall be visited by Mr
Charles Gilpin, publisher of William Wells Brown's
narrative, & will recommend to him your furnishing
for the quality end of the market. William Wells
Brown sold 12,000 copies in 1850 alone, when I was a
mere girl. We need our treasured copies beautifully
bound for longevity & as a mark of respect for their
noble contents!*

*In the hopes that this letter finds you and the dear
dark boy well*

Yours &c.,

Sylvia, Lady Knightley

The change in patron, author and subject matter came as a
tremendous relief. Jack went out to buy some leather, while Din
and I removed the trade bindings and the old stitching, and
sewed through all seven manuscripts. When we had finished,
we took a copy each, and settled down to read, he in the sewing
chair, I in the gold-tooling booth, as Lucinda sat at the bench
and drew pictures.

We paused for a mug of beer at lunch-time. 'How do you
fare, Din?' I gestured towards the book, to make it clear I
was not talking about his injuries.

He weighed my question for a while, then casually dropped
it on the floor.

'You don't cry,' he said. 'In America they say the ladies of
England increase the ocean between us with their tears for
us. Are you not moved?'

'I asked you a question.'

'An' so did I.'

'Would tears convince you of emotion?'

'No. I am an innocent, ma'am, in the ways of English women.'

'And so am I, Din, so am I. In the ways of English men, too. But I wish to know your reaction to what you have read.'

'An' I wish to know yours.' He sat back in his chair and folded his arms as best he could.

But there were no words I could use. What mattered my reaction in the face of his human defiance of human monsters; what purpose his reaction, having been treated inhumanely himself by the inhuman?

'Tell me, instead, how this compares to your life. Is this what it was like for you?'

'There are similarities,' he returned, 'both bein' captive, an' escapers, an' fugitives. But his life is not mine. You can't know one by knowin' the other.'

'Have you thought of doing this, Din? Of writing your own narrative?'

He shook his head.

'But I'm sure you could. You are intelligent; you can write. It might help you fathom it.'

He shrugged. 'Why would I need to?'

'It would certainly make money.'

'What do I be needin' money for?' he asked. 'I have a job, don' I?' It sounded as if he were mocking me. He rested his hands on his knees and leant forward, as if to get up.

'How about the cause? It would raise money for the abolitionist cause.'

'You mean your society o' ladies?' And now he was rounding on me, for sure.

'You have something to say about them?'

He paused. His silence was beguiling. What was he withholding? He was smiling to himself, and his head was cocked.

'Come now, Din,' I cajoled. 'I have no allegiance to them.

You wish to tell me something?' I smiled and beckoned; he grinned back at me, then nodded to himself.

'All right, ma'am.' A secret; he was going to tell me a secret. He placed his hands on the back of his head, stretched and winced, pondered for a while, then wound me towards him with his words.

'Let me tell you, ma'am,' he said, with deliberate intrigue, 'about what they have bought.' He stopped.

'You, Din?' I prompted.

'That's right. But how they be usin' me!' I thought he half-winked at me, but it could have been the tremors of a bruised eye.

'How, Din?'

He was quiet again, smiling.

'Din!' I shrieked. 'Tell me!'

'They send for me, ma'am.'

'When?'

'When the fancy takes them.'

I giggled nervously like a young girl. 'And?'

'And . . .' He was still weighing up how much he could tell me.

'I want to know *everything*, Din! Don't do this to me!'

'And . . .' And then he was off. 'They take me into this room, ma'am, this red room in her house, an' they put the pelt of a tiger round me, an' a spear in this hand an' a shield in that, an' ask me to stand about like a Zulu warrior. "Ooh, a Zoo-loo, a Zoo-loo," they cry, an' wave their arms.'

'Oh my! Din!' I cried. 'How monstrous!' But how fabulous, too! What knowledge!

My reaction encouraged him further. 'I'm their dandy Zoo-loo. An' so I stand, an' I wait, an' they look at me, like they seen nothin' like me before, an' treat me for a fool.'

'How degrading that must be for you!'

He shrugged. 'They the ones degradin' themselves. They the fools.'

'What else do they do?'

But he would not answer. He simply sat and smiled. So I moved slightly closer to him. A question burnt my lips; I did not know if I dared ask, until it spoke itself for me. 'Do they touch you, Din?' I said quietly.

He paused, and held my gaze, still grinning. 'Oh, Lor', do they touch me!' He whistled through his teeth. 'They stroke my arms, an' they kiss my brand –' here he pulled up his sleeves to show his tattoo '– an' they cry tears over me, an' they say, "Oh, Sylvia, how his skin shine!" an' "Oh, his teeth be so white an' fright'nin'!" They keep me there so late, sometimes, they send me to climb out up by the coal cellar so I don' be scarin' the neighbourhood.'

'Do you mind?'

And he shrugged again, and laughed wryly. 'It ain't how I choose to spend my evenings, no, but it ain't pickin' cotton neither.'

A thought crossed my mind. 'Is this where you go, Din, of a Friday?'

His temper changed. 'No, ma'am.'

'Where do you go?'

'I ain't gonna be tellin' you.'

'That is fair, Din. If it is half as humiliating as what you do for the ladies, you should be keeping it to yourself.' What else did they do to the boy? *My* boy, I was already feeling.

'And indeed I will, ma'am,' he said, tapping his finger to the side of his nose. 'Shall I be waxin' the cords now, ma'am?'

I handed him the candle-stub, and we shared one last smile as he took it from me. I wandered slowly back into the booth, warm with conspiracy, to plan the new design.

I laid out all the portraits of Douglass. He was a handsome man: his large hair was swept over neatly in a parting to one side, and on the other it rose upwards like an irrepressible spirit. His brows were arched, and met in a deep furrow over his strong nose, and he had a wide chin. None of the pictures

– even the line-drawings – were simple enough to be transposed on to leather, so I started to sketch my own version, with the right balance of strong and weak lines according to the tools available to me, and my own level of skill at using them.

Yet I could not get it right. I drew face after face, with increasing agitation, and the more I drew, the more I feared Din would come over to ask me something. For every face on every scrap of paper bore little resemblance to Frederick Douglass, with his large hair, and straight nose, and looked every inch like our own Din Nelson, hairless, with precise, heavy brows, a broken nose, a thick lower lip, and an uneven gleam across both cheekbones, which I could only guess betrayed the damage he had formerly suffered. I could not get the eyes even, the nose straight, the cheeks level.

I worked on the gold-tooling throughout the following day, only vaguely aware of the hammerings, the planings, the sewings around me. It took significant quantities of gold, for I decided that the hue of his skin would best be portrayed by solid gold, rather than just a gold outline, and Lady Knightley was paying me well. I finished the binding around five o'clock, and emerged from the gold-tooling booth in a state of confusion and embarrassment. For, try as I might, the face that glistened back at me and the rest of the workshop from the cover of *My Bondage and My Freedom* was Din's, not Douglass's.

Was it that his Negro features dominated my perception of how a black man looked, in the way people claim to be unable to tell one Chinaman from another? Or was it that I preferred his unbalanced features to Douglass's more perfect ones? I had never previously stopped in my tracks to admire a man of his colour in the way that I (I had to confess) admired Sir Jocelyn Knightley, or even Peter, once upon a time. I found beauty in the man, beauty where I least expected to find it.

'Let me see, Mrs D,' Jack said, ambling over from his bench.

'I – no – it's not quite –' I scanned the workshop hastily. 'My, where's Din?'

'He was 'ere just a while back. Has 'e given us the slip again? I don't believe it.'

But he had; somehow, from our very midst, while we were deep amongst the millboards and gold-leaf, he had managed to escape us.

'The cracksman! What yer gonna do abaht him, Mrs D? It's not as if it's the mornin' after pay-day, when you'd expect a few sore 'eads, even in Mr D's day.' But still, Damage's had never been a place of unexplained leave, except in cases of severe illness or domestic disaster. I wondered what disciplinary procedures the Society would approve of.

'You are right Jack. It is unacceptable.' But it was not for me today. I showed Jack the book.

'Nice,' he said, 'and, by the way, forgot to tell ya, Select Skins asked me to pass on a message, that you still ain't settled your credit, an' they're gettin' a bit crusty abaht it, to say the least.'

Even Lucinda, when she came bounding into the workshop, noticed nothing. I had expected her to stare at the book and ask why Din's face was on the cover. But she didn't; she simply ran her finger over the Society's emblem and said, 'That's pretty.' It was clear, or so I was able to persuade myself, that any resemblance was a figment of my untrustworthy imagination.

And so our brief respite had ended. Douglass's wonderful work was like Jack amongst the turd-collectors, a gem sparkling amidst excrement. The crates kept arriving from Diprose. They were getting worse, too, or so Jack told me as he riffled through their contents, and I shrivelled into myself as he told me what was inside. More photographic catalogues – 'Nah, ya really mustn't looka' these, Mrs D. Not for you, not for you, Mrs D' – but also more stories, prints, and the like, the titles of which Jack read to me.

'Choose one for me, just so I can see for myself.'

'All right, Mrs D,' he said doubtfully, and flicked through a few manuscripts, most of which he hastily put back in the crate. 'All right, here's one, but I have warned you. Scientific nonsense, again, I think.'

It was entitled *Afric-Anus*, and subtitled, *A Scientific Foray into the Size of the Negro Rectum in Relation to the Penis; followed by an Essay on the Libidinosity of Women of Colour*. I opened it to a page that depicted the prodigious posterior and pendulous labia of the Hottentot Venus.

And that was it. In an instant, I knew that I would have to find my employment elsewhere. I had other ways of feeding my family, and of providing to Messrs Skinner and Blades, and to Mrs Eeles. I was a fully fledged bookbinder now, and I would ply my trade elsewhere. Diprose, Knightley, and the lot of them could go hang.

Chapter Thirteen

How many miles to Babylon?
Three-score and ten.
Can I get there by candle-light?
Yes, and back again.
If your heels are nimble and light,
You may get there by candle-light.

On Monday morning I knocked on Agatha Marrow's door, Lucinda at my side. She clutched the Danish tin, which still contained a few of the pastries, and which I had topped up with some bon-bons and marshmallows, by way of thanks. I knocked again.

'How strange. I don't think she's there.'

'But I saw Biddy and Bitsy, at the window!'

'What, this one?'

'No, upstairs. Maybe they don't want to play with me today.'

'I don't believe that.'

'*And* we've got a present for them, and it's still not even Christmas.'

But the door remained shut, so we walked back up Ivy-street to our house. Jack was hunting for a clean cloth in the kitchen.

'I can stay here with Jack, Mama. Can I? Can I?' Lucinda asked.

'There isn't one, Jack love, I'm afraid. You'll have to make do with this one.' I threw him a dirty brown rag.

Lucinda started to jump up and down. 'Can I, can I?'

'Yeah, she can stay 'ere wiv me, Mrs D. I'll keep an eye on 'er.' He was looking disdainfully at the rag; I prayed he did not sniff it. I was ashamed; he could not use it on the books, and yet there was nothing else.

'Are you sure, Jack?'

'I'll be no trouble!'

'I know you won't, little love.' And I meant it too; she had become so easy, so compliant, recently. It was as if, now her fits had gone, she had nothing to question. She slept more, she ate more, she pottered around alone more. Maybe she was just growing up.

'And you can keep the tin of pastries. Only don't eat them all.' I stood up and said in a whisper to Jack, 'Make sure she doesn't eat them all.'

I put my head round into the workshop and scanned the towering crates of unbound books, the stacks of manuscripts sewn and ready to be forwarded, and the heaps of blank bindings waiting for me in the tooling booth. It was overwhelming. And then I saw Din, who smiled at me as usual, only one of his teeth seemed to be missing, and he looked for all the world as if he had been in a fight. Lord, I thought to myself, I hope he's not getting roughed up every night in the Borough. I wondered if I should say something, but his head was bowed and he was already working away at the sewing-frame. I kissed Lucinda good-bye, and told her I wouldn't be long. And then I made a hasty decision: I ran back into the workshop, trimmed a rectangle of card, and scribbled something on it.

'I'm going to make this easier for us, Jack,' I said over my shoulder as I left the house.

A train was rattling past, and whilst it was not that of the Necropolitan Railway, I could not help but think of it, and I wondered what sort of world this was in which we were living, and what of one to where we were destined, where bodies take the direct train from Waterloo to Woking, while souls are doomed to wander, lost and mapless, through the cruel streets of the city for ever. I walked south for a while, past the gates of Remy & Rangorski, then knocked on the door of a little cottage further up the road with a sign saying 'Rooms Available', and handed the proprietress a card. She looked at it, and agreed to place it in her window. I watched from outside as it went up against the glass, and read it again to make sure it said what I wanted it to.

> Wanted. Girl skilled at sewing, folding, invalid nursing and
> domestic chores, to present herself at Damage's Bookbinders,
> 2 Ivy-street, Waterloo.
> References required.

Then I turned, and headed north again, up to Waterloo Bridge and Holywell-street.

I had no intention of walking away from Mr Diprose entirely this morning; I simply wanted to draw a line, and give him its exact co-ordinates on the wide-ranging map of his literary stock, so that he would no longer attempt to push me over it into the more unseemly territories of his kingdom. By way of example, I took with me the worst of the first lot of photographic catalogues; I was going to give it back to him, and state simply that I was not to receive any more commissions of the kind.

Apart from the knavery – the villainous way the photographs had been so constructed to convey the worst imaginings between human beings – I was also rankled by their lack of honesty, for all their pretensions to integrity. These were not images for anatomical study and pictorial accuracy: the printing alone would have cost more than Jack's monthly wage, and their weighty bindings would push their cover price far higher than anything any 'artist of discernment' could ever afford. Neither were they lickerish little morsels for a spot of harmless titillation; nor were they Paphian offerings to the mighty Aphrodite. They were far, far more dangerous, and far beyond anything I could understand.

I found my way through the back alleys to the peeled-paint door at the rear of Diprose & Co, and rapped three times. The bolt was pulled back by the assistant, and he took my hand gently in his.

'Mrs Damage.'

'Good day, Mr Pizzy.'

'At your service as ever. Call me Bennett, please. Have you brought us some wonders from Waterloo?'

'I must disappoint you there, Mr Pizzy. I have come to speak with Mr Diprose.' There was another man in the room with us too, wearing a red-and-white spotted neckerchief, and a grubby checked shirt. He scarcely acknowledged me; he was too occupied with chewing a pencil, and rivers of grey saliva coursed from the corners of his mouth. He had another two pencils stuck behind his ears, presumably for when hunger struck later.

Mr Pizzy bolted the door behind me, and went to the front of the shop. I heard low murmurs, and the bolt being drawn closed across the front door into Holywell-street. Mr Diprose emerged from behind the green curtain.

'Mrs Damage.'

'Mr Diprose.' Oh, but there was no love lost between us.

'Please be seated.' He lowered himself stiffly into his chair; he really was incapable of bending in the middle. 'I trust you have come to furnish us with information about your inky labourer. We have been hoping for an assurance that you have secured his loyalty.'

'Indeed, Mr Diprose, I have managed to find a fair bit about him, and am convinced he will be of no danger to us. That is not my purpose in coming here today, but I can assure you Mr Nelson does not concern himself with our activities.'

'Your certainty intrigues me. Please explain how you came by it.'

'He is not like us, Mr Diprose,' I attempted. 'He has suffered things we can only imagine. His past is all horrors, and his present a mere distraction. It may be useful for him to work at Damage's for the time being, but he is not committed. He will move on when the time is right . . .'

'Forgive me, Mrs Damage, but your airy sentiments are not convincing to me. If he is not committed, where is his loyalty?'

'He is not *interested* in what we produce! It does not concern him. His thoughts are elsewhere. We – you – are *irrelevant* to him!'

'So, you are telling me, that the only reason I should feel safe that the most unlawful literature in the land is daily surveyed by a man of whom we know nothing, is that he considers it an irrelevance.'

'Yes! No, I mean . . . Mr Diprose, I will be confronting him myself. He is an intelligent man. I will tell him straight out about our shady business, and inform him that he must not speak a word of it to anyone.'

'And you presume I will be happy with the word of the man.'

'Won't you?'

'You may be a *gobe-mouches*, but I can not be so easily duped. Tell me, what *do* you know about him?'

'He was born in Baltimore. His father was a preacher; his mother a nurse. He was abducted from them – he was taken at the tender age of fourteen, separated from his family – and sold into slavery. They are all dead now. He has no roots, he has no homeland. He is drifting free . . .'

'Mrs Damage, the answer is staring us in the face. I congratulate you upon unearthing it; your ingenuity becomes you. You are telling me that if the man ever becomes a trouble to us, we shall simply *send him back*! *Merveilleux*.'

'Why!'

'This is perfect. And we could probably get a pretty penny for him too. *Nous y gagnons*! Presumably you have threatened him with this?'

'No!'

'Then that is what you must do immediately. Mr Pizzy, would you escort Mrs Damage back to her workshop and see to it personally that she delivers her ultimatum to her Mr Nelson?'

'You are monstrous, Mr Diprose! You dishonour me, and discredit yourself, not that you seem to care much of that. Here. I return these to you. I will not bind work of this nature.' I placed the stack of photographic prints on to the table with a hefty thud. Diprose looked down at them, without moving his head. One eyebrow rose quizzically, and he looked up at Mr Pizzy. Even the noise of pencil-chewing ceased momentarily.

'What is it about them to which you so object, Mrs Damage?' my interlocutor said eventually. I could sense – I could feel – Mr Pizzy's smug smile broaden behind me.

'Do you require me to spell it out to you?'

'Yes. Yes,' he said whimsically. 'That would be most enjoyable.'

'Mr Diprose, they are vicious, unwholesome, and downright horrible.'

'They offend you.'

'Yes. They do.'

'And you do not like your sensibilities being offended.'

'No, I do not.'

'You do not approve of them.'

'No.'

'So Mrs Damage doesn't approve of them,' Diprose announced, as if to his men. 'Do you think, my dear girl, that that matters to us? Do we look like we care?'

'I do not wish to bind them.'

'Why on earth not?'

'Because . . .'

'Because they offend you. Forgive me, Mrs Damage, but I do not see the connection.' One of the men laughed. I wanted to ask him if it had escaped his notice that there was a black man in my employ, but then, I knew that that was what he wanted me to say.

'And which particular ones do you find most offensive?' He lifted the pages up from where I had left them on his table, and started to turn them over one by one. He did not look up at me, but, of course, he lingered on the abominable pictures he suspected caused me most distress. 'Which ones, Mrs Damage? This one? Or this?'

But I would not rise to his goadings. It was not only the ones that contained the vengeful Negroes. They were all vile.

'Mrs Damage, I am *un peu fatigué* of this subject. You assume I am a man of leisure, that my life is one of *dolce far niente*. Let me put it simply: you have no choice over what you do and do not bind.'

'Then I shall take the matter up with Sir Jocelyn Knightley.'

I had never seen Diprose laugh before, and it was not a pretty sight. His silver-rimmed glasses bounced up and down on his purple nose with each chuckle, but he held my gaze with his eyes throughout. The mirth of Pizzy and the pencil-man was more abandoned and hearty, even when the pencil snapped between the latter's teeth, and he tried to rub his tongue as he continued to laugh.

'I fear you will not find his reaction as generous as ours.'

'Is there not one decent fibre in the whole ungodly lot of you?' I raised my voice, but still I did not dare shout. I felt like a schoolmistress, enraged but powerless amongst sniggering children; and then it was that I came to the horrible realisation that my anger was delighting them. I was one step away from Mistress Venus with her birch rods, and I suddenly realised that her disciplinary procedures were nothing more than an artificially bestowed power, handed to her temporarily by the men who so yearned for chastisement. Mistress Venus was just another job for just another brow-beaten woman, just another task to fulfil, along with cleaning his slippers, filling his pipe, and being the cushion for his rage.

'What *troubles* you so, Mrs Damage? Are we to remind *you* of where your loyalties lie? Or do I detect a certain *penchant* – some desires *contre nature* – for *les hommes de couleur?*'

'I think you've got it, Charlie,' Pizzy sneered. 'She's in love.'

'We thought we were doing you a favour. Rather like sending Pauline Bonaparte to Haiti. It is quite extraordinary, the number of seemingly respectable women who lose all sense of decorum at the smell of black meat.'

'Black meat?' Pizzy said. 'Cup of tea: hot, black and wet. Is that how you like it?'

'You must have greatly appreciated the last book we sent you,' added Diprose. '*Afric* –'

'You blackguards! You sons of Satan!' I finally snapped.

'Hark! Thus speaks the lover of the son of Ham.'

'It's sweet,' Pizzy said, 'the way you talk of your dusky dandy with such tenderness.'

'Why!'

'Is it true, then, Mrs Damage, what they say about the nether parts of monkeys?'

And I screamed. I opened my mouth and reached down into the ancient soil, far beneath the flimsy foundations of the building, below the sewers, below the holes opening for the Metropolitan Underground Railway, and summoned from it a scream for which I did not know I had strength. I saw Diprose's eyes pop from his purple head, and Pizzy's apricot-coloured whiskers bristle around the wet 'oh!' of his lips, and still I screamed. I hurled the pages on to the floor and kicked them, then stood on them with both feet, and my legs wobbled like a new-born fawn over the hideous photographs, spreading across the floor distant images made up of nothing more than ink on paper, black and white and grey, and I crouched over them, and sobbed without tears.

Pizzy's hand grasped the flesh on either side of my mouth, Pizzy's palm formed a seal around my lips. At the same time, a child raced in from the alley-way like a dirty streak of effluvium.

'Rozzers!' he cried. His two front teeth were missing. 'It's a bloody *razzia*.'

Diprose was standing up. 'Silence,' he hissed at me. 'Get the girl up.' He tugged at his waistcoat, and turned briskly towards the front of the shop.

'Knife it!' Pizzy whispered at me. 'Or you will live to regret it.' But my screams had stopped. We heard Diprose's voice switch to controlled charm as he unbolted the front door and greeted the new arrivals in the shop.

A girl – or rather, a woman – had rushed in with the boy, all long ragged hair and faded orange dress. Pizzy handed me over to her, and she gripped my waist with one hand and the back of my head with the other, and led me to the rickety stairs. The pencil-man had already reached the first floor; Pizzy was busy handing him boxes, stacks of books, brown-paper parcels, up the staircase. The gap-toothed boy was scurrying around, quiet as a girl, gathering goods. The stairs brought us out into another dingy room, clearly the centre of Diprose's enterprise, with its printing presses, blocks of type, and stacks of paper. Pizzy was up with us now, flitting around the room, collecting this and that, and whisking it up a second flight of stairs, which we too climbed, along with two men who had been tending the printing press, their faces pricked with grey stubble like burnt fields of corn, moving silently, jerkily.

We reached the attic, where there was an opening in the far wall, curtained with cobwebs; we climbed through it, and into a wide, dusty room in the roof-space of the adjacent building. An older woman was already in there, waiting for us.

'All right, Bernie?' she hissed at the woman who was leading me in.

'All right, Mrs Trotter,' Bernie replied.

'Is Alec in?'

'He's coming.' Alec, it turned out, was the young lad, Mrs Trotter's son.

And then – once the room was full of the salvaged contraband, three men (two printers and the pencil-man), Alec Trotter, Mrs Trotter, Bernie, and myself – the opening was closed, and I did not stop to wonder how it looked from the other attic, or where Mr Pizzy had gone to, but I guessed that this was not the first time the room had been used in this way.

And we sat like this, in almost total silence, in the darkness and dust of the attic, for what must have been close to five hours. We heard the sounds of doors opening and closing in the houses below and around us, and footsteps, furniture being moved, cabinets opening and closing. For a while the noises were louder – closer – and I imagined the activities had reached the first floor.

We waited and waited, the unproductive hours slipping past, mocking us in our abeyance. The only movements were the shadows through the cracks in the plaster, crooked sundials marking the progress of the day outside. I tried to avoid the stares of my other cell-mates through the miserable gloom of the attic, and occupied my mind with different thoughts: of Lucinda with Jack, and whether she would notice how long I had been gone; of all the books I could be binding, the food I could be preparing. The inactivity was unfamiliar to us all in that attic. It was as if someone had told a joke that had fallen flat, and we were doomed to linger in the awkward after-moment for eternity. We were inoperative, null and void, useless, like seven phlegmatics trying to compete on idleness, or seven lie-abeds waiting on Providence, seven lotus-eaters feasting on lethargy, seven workers going rusty through lack of use. It was as if we were procrastinating, but had quite forgotten what action it was that we were deferring.

And then we heard footsteps nearing us; they climbed to the attic, and spoke loudly outside our hatch, and we dared not breathe.

'She's not 'ere. There's no one up 'ere.'

'Where could she've got to?'

'You sure you 'eard a woman scream?'

'I'll swear it.'

I prayed silently to my Maker. I had neglected Him for too long, and I promised Him anything, anything, if only He would get me out of here and safely home where I could feel Lucinda in my arms. I would go to Church more, I would sing hymns around the house, I would keep the house clean, I would not read any more illicit books before binding them, I would refuse to carry out any design that was too 'emblematic' . . .

'Could've been out in the alley, s'pose,' one of the men said. 'If she'd screamed lahd enough.'

'Must've been. C'mon. Better get back wiv ve uvvers. Nice pickings today.'

And then they descended, and the place became quiet.

In time the torpor started to lift. It started with the inescapable fact that our bladders were in varying degrees of fullness, and we could not help but fidget. A chamber-pot was passed round; it was shown to me, its sulphurous contents threatening to slosh on to my skirts, but I shook my head and declined its use.

'What d'ya expect? She's the toff's toffer,' Bernie said. It was the first time any of us had spoken for hours. 'Laced and marbled good and proper.'

'D'ya think she's even got an arse?' Mrs Trotter replied.

'Oh, sure she has. But she likes it blacked.'

'Does she now? Like a good blackleading, do ya?'

'Got a voice on her too. If she had kept 'er pretty mouth shut we wouldn't be risking our skins like this,' Bernie added. 'Did you hear 'er holler?'

'Shut up,' the pencil-man said. 'We gotta wait til Pizz-pot gets up 'ere.'

And so they lapsed into silence once more, and we waited. The shadows were fading; it was getting dark outside, and cold. We could no longer stare at each other's shoes, or scrutinise the worm holes and cobwebs in the beams above us. We sat in the stink of each other's urine, and waited.

And then, at last, the hatch shifted a little, and then some more, and Pizzy's head, illuminated by a candle, emerged into the room.

'You can come down now,' he said wearily. His tie and top buttons were undone, and his clothes all creased.

One by one, we stretched our legs, rolled on to our knees, pulled on to something to bring ourselves to standing. Bernie reached her hand out to me; I took it, and she pulled me up.

We went down to the first floor. I could not tell if the room had been ransacked; it looked fairly orderly to me, but the others were wandering around it, opening drawers, assessing the damage.

'How much was it, Ben?'

'Four hundred books, nine hundred and fifty prints, and eight hundredweight of unsewn letterpress. All the Gamianis went.'

'Will they be destroyed?' one of the printers asked.

'Oh yes.' He looked tired; he ran his hands through his hair, then rubbed the back of his neck. 'But at least we saved some of it. Thanks to young master Trotter.' He ruffled Alec's hair, and the boy ducked out of reach.

'I really must go, Mr Pizzy,' I said, like someone who had stayed too long at a christening. 'It's been a long day, and I must get back to my daughter.' Some food and beer was brought out from underneath a table.

'Nobody leaves,' Pizzy replied. 'Not till it's safe. And certainly not a fine lady like yourself, Mrs Damage.' He smiled with his mouth closed. 'You must stay here the night; I will get Bernie to make a bed for you upstairs. You will be quite safe, I assure you. Alec, go down and guard the door.' He handed me a glass of beer, and I took it, but I could not drink, despite my thirst.

'So, what 'appened, Pizz?' said pencil-man.

'Remember the nob with the black cane who came in last week?' Pizzy said. Pencil-man nodded. 'Vice Squad.'

'So was it the constable today?'

'Yes. He was a give-away the moment he walked in the door. "Do you 'eppen to 'ev any prints by A*ckillees* Deve*reer*?"' Pizzy said, imitating the policeman's artifically polished accent. Someone laughed. 'And Charlie played it so straight. "A*ckillees* Deve*reer*?" he said back to him. "Are you, perchance, referring to the French illustrator, Achilles – *Asheel* – Deve*eria*?" And the rozzer said, "Er, why yes, perchance, oi em." And blimey, his glasses fell off at the sight of them!'

'Which ones did 'e show 'em?'

'The lithos.' I knew them. They were a sequence of lithographs on the history of morals under Louis-Philippe. 'And when he could finally shut his mouth, he said he was going to seize the prints, and any more like them in the establishment, and take him before the magistrate, under the authority of Lord Campbell's Act, and then five of 'em came bursting through the door like a rum rush, grasping everything they could get their sordid, hypocritical little hands on, and dragged our Charlie off to Bow Street!'

'Will he go to prison?' I asked.

'If he does, he'll be out within the week, Mrs Damage,' Mr Pizzy rejoined.

'Why so sure?'

He laid a finger on one side of his nose, then said softly, 'Contacts.'

'Where?'

Slowly and with satisfaction he said, 'A Noble Savage. In the Home Office.'

'Really?' I raised my eyebrows.

'Charlie once had a two-year conviction with hard labour, and was out in three weeks with hands soft as butter. Nowadays they don't even bother to convict him; they just hold him for as long as they dare before getting their fingers rapped. They just do it to get their hands on a bit of filth which they enjoy for a bit then burn it.' And again, he roared with laughter, until his face fell suddenly, and he said solemnly, 'We did lose a fair bit of stock and press, though. That's not so good.' Then he seized his pipe, threw up the sash-window, and leaned out of it. He unscrewed the burner of the gaslight, and vicious flames flared up from it, nearly scorching the wooden figure of the African, but he nevertheless managed to light his pipe from it. And when he pulled himself back into the room, having singed his whiskers and blackened one side of his pipe, he started what seemed to be a well-aired speech about the burning of books at Ephesus, the fiery purge of Don Quixote's library, and the flame of freedom that would burn out hypocrisy. '*Nihil est quod ecclesiae ob inquisitione veri metuatur*,' he told me assuredly. Then he slumped in his chair once more, and sucked thoughtfully on his pipe, before reaching over and clasping one of my hands on my lap. He clearly enjoyed his master's absence.

'Dora, Dora. It's a shame these cases hardly go to trial any more!'

'Why would you want them to? Would you not get done?'

'Oh my yes, or no, we wouldn't. Only the trials are such merry sport! By rule of law, each obscene item has to be categorised and described, and read out as the list of indictments in court. Item one, clay phallus, in the style of Pompeii. Item two, daguerrotype of naked woman in congress with a horse. Item three, print of Hyperion fucking a satyr up the arse. Oh, it cheers the heart of a radical *obsceniteur* to hear such words spoken in a court of law by an upholder of the law. Is that not the heart of the matter? Have we not won, then?'

'Won, Mr Pizzy?'

'Yes, won, Mrs Damage. Please call me Bennett. Do you think we are in this for the money? This is a moral crusade! My father started it all. He was a true radical, part of the Cato Street Conspiracy. Suspected, but never proven. Clever man. He was one of many radical publishers – based, as they all were, in Holywell-street. They were freethinkers. *Splendore veritatis gaudet ecclesia!* They published tracts on politics, religion and sexuality, and they did this –' he waved his hand around the room '– only to satirise the aristocracy and the Church. And to raise funds for more radical press, of course. Now, take me. Chip off the old block as far as politics are considered, but no bloody hope of a revolution round the corner. My challenge is to Lord Campbell's vile Act (oh, he who could show you a few vile acts, I'm sure!); the radical cause I champion is the distribution of obscenity to the working classes.'

'Working classes, Mr Pizzy?' I retorted. 'Mr Diprose pays me more per binding than my husband earned in a week! And I assure you, that if the man in the street were to chance upon the princely sum of three guineas, he would not beat a path to your door to spend it.'

'Unfortunately, Dora, for I prefer to call you Dora, you are indeed correct, but the situation is only temporary, while I earn enough to fund my radical ventures. It is not only a mighty lucrative scene you and I have fallen into, but one that provides me with remarkable fodder for my ambitions. Think of the hypocrisy: these lords take their families to the Cremorne Pleasure Gardens on Saturday by day, their mistresses (or, indeed, rent-boys) on Saturday night, and spend the rest of the week legislating against Cremorne's vices!' He pulled a file out from under the floorboards. 'Look.' Here he showed me a host of pamphlets and unbound manuscripts, like yellowbacks, but less mustardy and lurid in hue, although not, I was to discover, in content. I cast my eye over the stories.

The old familiar characters were there, differing only in name: the Right Honourable Filthy Lucre, Lord Havalot Fuckalot, Lady Termagent Flaybum, the Earl of Casticunt, the Comtessa de Birchini. I picked up one entitled *Reasons Humbly Offer'd for a Law to Enact the Castration of Popish Ecclesiastics*, then put it back down again.

'Is this not the key to the health of the nation? This is where Sir Jocelyn and I find common ground, in the free discussion – and unbridled practice – of sexuality.'

'But is not Sir Jocelyn from the very class you seek to overthrow?'

'Indeed, you are right. But he is a rare 'un. The fellow is more a man of the people than he lets on. Don't you covet his smoking-room?'

'Mr Pizzy,' I said, for I wished to ask a question.

'I love the way you say my name, Dora. Some say, "Pitzy". How Italian. Others "Pissy", and well they might. You, you make it rhyme with "dizzy". As well *you* might, given your giddy-making charms. But please call me Bennett.'

'Mr Pizzy.'

'Yes, Dora?'

'Will they really destroy all the stock?'

'Yes.'

'Was any of my work in it?'

'No. I can say that with certainty. Your line of work runs directly between Diprose and the Noble Savages, and is not kept in the shop.'

'So will I be paid for it?'

'Of course. The coffers are not connected either.'

'I have not been paid for a while.'

'And I shall see it gets attended to. But you should not visit here any more. It is not safe. I, or another of Charles's men, will deliver and collect from Lambeth. I shall relish the journey. Oh, but Jocelyn was right. He called you a rum doxy. Now I am sure you are of better breeding, but still, a fine-made wench.'

'Will you excuse me, please, Mr Pizzy.' I stood up, and whispered to Bernie, 'I need to relieve myself.'

'Hallelujah,' she replied. 'And we thought you were too pure to piss.'

'You must not use the privy,' Mr Pizzy commanded. 'As I said, nobody leaves.'

'So where can I go?'

'There's a chamber-pot in the ante-room.' He pointed to a cubby-hole off the top of the staircase.

I stood up, and sidled carefully past Pizzy's knees. I felt his fingertips brush up my legs, then a thumb curled and pressed itself into the top of my thigh. I brought my boot down on the toes of his left foot and did what damage I could with a worn-out heel. At last, a fine purpose for the heels of those unwearable brown boots; would that I had them on now. I did not look back at his face.

But from the top of the stairs, as I stooped to enter the cubby-hole, I could see that his attention was now occupied with Bernie, and no one else could see me from the printing room. I did not even think, but darted down the stairs into the rear room by the alley. The chair on which I had sat this morning was lying on its side; Diprose's chair had been used to gain access to a high cupboard; most of the photographs from the catalogue had been removed, but some remained, ground into the floor, disfigured by footprints and muck.

Alec Trotter was asleep across the door into the alley. I pitied the poor boy for the aches he would feel in the morning. I slid into the shop, and tried the door into Holywell-street, but it was locked.

I went back into the rear room, and tried to reach the bolt without standing on any part of Alec's body, but I could not. And then I noticed that the door was also locked, and the key glinted from the hand on which Alec's body lay. I could touch it, but I would have to unlace his fingers from around it. And then he woke. He was about to cry out when I seized him and hushed him.

'Who's there?' he said, terrified. 'We're armed!'

'It's me,' I said. 'Dora Damage.'

'You can't go,' he said. 'I'm not to let ya.'

'You must. It's urgent. I have to leave.'

'You can't. You'll get us all in trouble. Me ma said. I ain't gonna.'

'There's two shillings in it for you. They'll never know it was you. Look. I'll break this window, and you can say it was robbers. Or rozzers.' I flashed the coins at the boy, and he weighed them in his head. Then he looked down at the key in his hand.

'I can't do it.' I placed first one coin, and then the next, in his palm alongside the key, but at that moment we heard the cursings and hushings of perturbed folk from upstairs, followed by the bobbing halos of candles and oil-lamps coming down. I seized the key, and clenched it in my fist.

'Oi,' Alec shouted. 'Give that back!'

Pizzy arrived first. His smile was gone; however he was going to greet me, I knew it would be with anger.

But he redirected it. Before I could receive whatever harsh words were due to me, Alec Trotter was cuffed round the ear, then caught sharply in the eye by Pizzy's two forefingers.

'Hey,' I started to cry out, and I reached towards the lad, only to find another hand come sharply round from below to slap me across the cheek. Stung, I turned to vent my wrath on Mr Pizzy, but then saw Mrs Trotter, red-faced and stalwart, hand poised to deliver another blow.

'Sit down, Dora, and be quiet,' Pizzy said, righting the chair that lay on its side. I obeyed, glaring at Mrs Trotter and rubbing my cheek.

'Here, take this,' said Bernie with a modicum of tenderness, and handed me a steaming mug of tea. She wrapped a blanket around my shoulders, then set the tea-pot on the table. She pulled Diprose's chair up next to me, and we refilled our cups at intervals, drinking but not talking. I did not want to look around me at anyone. I would not cry.

At length I felt an icy shaft of air, and heard Mr Pizzy, holding the door open into the alley, saying, 'Go on, Dora. Your carriage awaits.'

'Be off with you,' Mrs Trotter said. 'And good riddance.' I fell into the alley-way in an effort to draw my shawl closer, and she called after me, 'And don't be causing any more trouble to poor lads who can't help it.'

I was free at last. What a blessing it was to be out of that horrid building. But I soon faced new dangers, as I put my head down and started to navigate the alleys out towards the Strand. I turned one way, and then the other, but the darkness had put up new walls around me, and I quickly lost my bearings. I remembered the ghost of Holywell-street, so I fingered my mother's hair-bracelet like a talisman, and muttered into myself like a madwoman. Alone except for my imagination, I started to rush and panic. I stumbled over a blanket that heaved with sour breath; a hand thrust forth from it and grabbed my ankle as I hastened past. I tripped, kicked, and pulled my leg out from its bony clutch with the fury of a mother separated from her child, and I ran. Out at last, I fell into the yellow glare of the Strand, and the new fears of the gas-lights as a woman alone in the London streets at night.

Illuminated, I was making a spectacle of myself; in the darkness between the sulphurous pools, I was putting myself at the mercy of unseen terrors. Some sailors stood talking to some men in top-hats, and they looked at me. I knew not where was safest, in the light, or in the shadows.

A solitary cab waited on the road, just at the entrance to the alley-way. It had seen me, for sure, in the lamp-light. I quickened my pace westwards, skirting the pools of gas-lights. But the cab came up beside me, and continued at my own pace, before pulling up ahead of me. The driver hopped down from his perch and landed directly in my path.

When he seized my elbow, I screamed. 'This way, Mrs Damage,' he said gruffly. 'Or didn't Pizzy tell you?' I couldn't snatch my arm away from his strong grip; no one came to my assistance. He shoved me into the back of the cab; I tried to crouch at the door, in order to hurl myself out as soon as I could, but the night did not offer the slow traffic of noon, and the speed to which the driver jimmied his horse threw me back into the seat. I prayed for a sheep to wander into the road from Hyde Park as we raced down Knightsbridge, but the way was clear. And, by the time we turned into Wilton-place and slowed to a halt in Belgrave-square, it was too late.

The driver pulled me down from the carriage, and encircled his rough hand around my waist. I wanted to slap him for his insolence, but the mansion to which he had brought me awed me, and I dared not.

Within, a butler bundled me up an elegant staircase lined with stern portraits, and into a bottle-green office. It was large, but moderately furnished; it did not smell of smoke, or betray the opulence of its owner. It was studious, and reserved; what furniture there was, was orderly and precise, like an officer's room in the nearby barracks. There was a simple writing-desk on one side, a bookcase with a selection of books, and a brown leather couch beneath the window. The only blots in the room were the ink-stains around the well on the desk, and a half-written paper at an angle to the others. I had no idea what time of night or morning it was.

Then a door opened somewhere in the house, and I heard a low rumbling of male voices, and some baritone laughter, and then the door to the office opened, and the butler announced, 'Lord Glidewell'.

Labor Bene – for it was indeed he, Valentine, Lord Glidewell – smiled warmly at me, and clutched my hand by way of welcome. He was a small man, unremarkable in features, wearing a deep-red quilted smoking-jacket, with black braid about his waist, and holding a glass of port.

'Mrs Damage. Sir Jocelyn will be joining us shortly. We are dining tonight. Tell me, Mrs Damage, do you like birds?' His affability was unexpected, given the unconventional manner in which he had summoned me. 'Behind me are some of the finest ornithological volumes you will ever see. I am fascinated too with reptiles and insects; the rarest of the species interest me most. My interests, you will see, are similar to those of Sir Jocelyn's, but mine is a mere hobby, and its subjects have the great advantage of not being human; and therefore, not being able to answer back.'

I forced a small smile, which I believed was expected of me.

'Will you sit, while we wait?'

I perched on the edge of the couch, and asked, 'Lord Glidewell, please tell me why I am here?'

'Why, my dear lady? We have an account to settle, do we not? I have been sent word of your untoward behaviour this past day on this matter.' His courtesy and civility were unmatchable, but the very calmness of his displeasure unbound every nerve in my body. 'To place our entire shared venture in jeopardy with such imprudence only serves to demonstrate to us how remiss we have been in not keeping up our payments to you.'

His voice was so liquid I feared I would slip up on it. I had to be careful what I said.

'Lord Glidewell. My misgivings were not pecuniary.'

'They were prurient, then. Madam, we all have the itch. Only some of us know how to scratch it.'

'No. The prurience is not mine, either. Only that –' But Lord Glidewell had come to stand directly in front of me, and was knitting his brow, such that I fell silent. He began as if by addressing the shadowy towers of the Knightsbridge Barracks through his window, but his words fell into my ears only.

'As a judge, I am no stranger,' he ruminated, 'to the horrors and pleasures of the noose, and other implements of torture. They are,' he gently assured me, 'not suitable for ladies of your skill, and I would not wish you closer contact with them, and neither should you. Do you understand me?'

I swallowed and nodded. His kind voice lulled me. So kind, I could not quite absorb his meaning.

'Ah, and here is Sir Jocelyn.'

'Dora!'

I stood up as the man marched towards me with a broad smile, stopping only to place his glass of port on the writing-desk, before reaching out his arms and kissing me firmly on both cheeks. 'You are safe, dear child! Such a dreadful experience for you to have to undergo. Poor, poor Charles. But you, precious girl, escaped their clutches.' He slid his palms down my arms, took hold of both my hands, and started to stroke my cracked, calloused palms. 'Look at these beautiful hands, Valentine. Our little binding angel; she weaves the softest magic for us, from the most unusual wellsprings of inspiration. Hmmm. You, Mrs Damage, are my *magnum opus*. What a woman we have made of you! I have a gift for you, my angel.' He let go of my hands to pull from his vest pocket a long golden rope, at the end of which was a faceted honey-coloured drop. 'Amber, from Africa.' He smiled, as if at a distant memory. 'I love amber. For me it is like a woman. Did you know, Dora, that amber has a special scent, a *secret* scent, yielded only once warm, and rubbed?' He held the drop tightly in the palm of his hand, and massaged his fingers and thumb vigorously around it, looking at me all the while. Then he knelt down, wrapped the necklace around my neck, and reached behind me to fasten the clasp. 'Can you smell that, Dora?' But I couldn't. I could only smell the spicy smokiness of Sir Jocelyn himself; his velvet jacket yielded a musty perfume, and his mouth the fermenting sweetness of tobacco and fine wine.

'And you must set these into a binding for me,' he proceeded, pouring into my hands ten polished amber nuggets.

'Jocelyn,' Lord Glidewell interrupted, 'I was imparting to Mrs Damage the severity of the day's events.'

'Indeed, Valentine.'

'And I believe you have some information for Mrs Damage? I do not wish to hurry you, but we must return to dinner forthwith.'

Sir Jocelyn stared at Glidewell for a moment, before turning back to me. 'Dora. Darling Dora,' he repeated. I think he was slightly drunk. He sat down on the couch, pulled me next to him, and rubbed my hand some more. 'Dora,' he said again.

'Yes, Sir Jocelyn?'

'Dora.'

But I never knew what he wanted to say to me, for all of a sudden, as if taken by something of a more pressing nature, he stood up sharply, picked up his glass, and left. I heard him mutter to Glidewell over his shoulder as he passed, 'Your dirty work, Valentine, not mine.' And with that he was gone, and the door clicked neatly shut behind him, like the cocking of a flintlock gun.

Lord Glidewell seemed unperturbed. He paused to sip his drink, then smacked his lips together, and paced the room. When he began to speak again, it was with military precision and care.

'I may not be a medical man, Mrs Damage, but as a judge I know how to weigh evidence, and as such I am convinced that Sir Jocelyn will be considered to be the most eminent, radical and life-changing, nay, *epoch*-changing, physician of his generation. I urge you to tender your greatest consideration to what I am about to say.' I sat, attentive, and waiting. 'Did you know,' Lord Glidewell continued, 'that Sir Jocelyn has found a strong and convincing connection between an individual being subject to an excess of sexual energy, and that same individual suffering from epileptic seizures? Ah, I see I have your full attention now. You did not know that, I can tell. I appreciate that this is a very delicate area, but may I ask if Lucinda partakes in, shall we say, onanism?'

'I do not understand,' I eventually said. I had certainly read that term in one of Diprose's books, but I struggled to remember what it meant.

'Well, then, I shall call it by its blunter term. Masturbation. Does Lucinda masturbate?'

I remained silent. I was not going to speak on this subject.

'Do answer me, Mrs Damage,' Lord Glidewell urged tetchily. 'We are most fortunate to have such a renowned expert in his field; it is an interesting and credible theory which is shaking the world of medicine.' He was getting exasperated. 'Has she confessed to any sexual fantasies? Has she made any untoward advances to her father, or to Jack, or to any other men? Does she *frig* herself, Dora? Dora, I ask you to be vigilant, for it may bring your daughter closer to a cure for her condition.'

'A cure?' For certain, I wanted to know about a cure, but I could not fathom how this course of questioning would lead us to one. 'Which is?'

'First, we must diagnose such an excess, as well we might, given the apparent success of her bromide therapy. Bromide reduces sexual desire, *ipso facto*, if bromide treatment is effective, the cause was likely to be sexual excess. We then – or rather, Sir Jocelyn – will have no choice but to carry out the requisite operation. It is termed a *cli-tor-i-dec-to-my*, a clitoridectomy, and is, quite simply, the excision or amputation of the clitoris. Constitutional symptoms such as Lucinda's are increasingly traceable to its irritation and abnormality –' I think I stood up at this point, trembling as the lecture continued '– and the necessity for its removal when much enlarged is increasingly recognised by eminent surgeons in such widely differing cases as dysuria, hysteria, sterility and epilepsy. She will, of course, be thoroughly chloroformed throughout the whole procedure.' I sat down again, then stood once more. 'It will positively cure Lucinda of her epilepsy and render her immune to further convulsive episodes. Have you not seen Sir Jocelyn's treasures?'

'Treasures, Lord Glidewell?' I managed to say, my mind reeling.

'Why, I imagined you two to be more intimately acquainted. He has an entire collection of clitorises pickled in glass jars, along with the renowned "Hottentot apron". I am sure he will reveal them to you should you wish to peruse them.'

If what Lord Glidewell was telling me were true, then all Sir Jocelyn's questing for a better world had disappeared up his own fundament.

'Lord Glidewell –' I was shaking, 'Lord – Glide –' I spat, '– well, if you – or he – or any of you! – lay one finger on Lucinda – I will go straight to the police! You can threaten me all you like, but you will keep Lucinda out of this!' I was shouting now.

Lord Glidewell, on the other hand, stayed unnervingly calm. He was even able to smile at me, as he said, 'And the police will be convinced of the necessity of the operation, when they discover her mother's fascination with sordid texts, and will make the appropriate equation that heightened sexuality must be an inheritable trait.'

I could not say a word; I feared I would swoon.

'Good evening, Dora.' He seized my hand and raised it to his lips, staring into my eyes all the while. He led me out into the corridor, and made to go back into the dining-room, but the door opened before he reached the handle.

A man I did not recognise, in a blue smoking-jacket, with slick black hair, stood at the door. He looked me quickly up and down, before addressing Lord Glidewell. 'Ah, Valentine. I trust you have remembered to impress upon our guest

238

that we are still waiting for an assurance of the loyalty of her mahogany journeyman.'

I knew not which of the Noble Savages this man was, but I had ceased listening. For behind him I caught a glimpse of a long, hazy room, a shining table, men in jewel-coloured velvets, a flame lighting a cigar, a flash of gold. It felt tremendously improper for me to witness this male occasion; it somehow felt more shameful than anything I had seen in any book to date. But I could not avert my gaze, and the men within, too, stared back out at me, laughing in a fraternal code that sneered at outsiders.

I had known these men's inmost desires for months, and yet I was only now seeing them for the first time. My gaze flitted promiscuously from one to the next, as if it were possible to match their countenances with their proclivities. They all held glasses, thick with bloody liquid, and while Bacchus danced amongst them on the table, Priapus, I knew all too well, pranced beneath. Who was it, then, who was hooded like a king cobra? Which of them had been disrobed by the knife at birth? Whose was the fat purple bishop? And whose the spotted dick? Whose curved like a walking stick? And who inched the pipe-cleaner down into the eye of the snake, and who boasted of preferring a goose-feather quill, bony end first, even, and no trimming of the feathers beside?

Which one rampaged for little boys? And who for young maidenheads? Which ones gave, and which received, and who was the lucky one who always found himself in the middle? Who had fucked what of the feast that spread between them? Who had impaled the turkey while its neck was wrung, and who preferred stuffing the ducks? Which one lowered horses onto his ladies, and which one had watched the breath pressed out of one poor unfortunate by a pot-bellied pig?

I exaggerate not. They were all here, I knew, for I had read

239

their diaries, their letters, their stories, and they knew it too, as they watched me watching them. Who wrote the diaries, and who the treatises? Who was tickled by *galanteries*, and who the prints and photographs?

The only one I could place with any certainty now was Valentine. He was the one who hung himself nightly on a silken rope above his desk, in order to elicit forth an orgasm of especial violence, while a valet stood by with a sharpened knife ready to cut the cord at the critical moment.

And was that a woman in there with them, and if so, how many other dusky-eyed houris trembled in the shadows? But no, I was mistaken. It was a man, with flowing, oiled, yellow locks and rouged lips, but he looked so young, and had not the supercilious air of the Noble Savages, that I had to surmise that he was, like me, nothing more than hired help.

And standing in the midst of them all was Sir Jocelyn Knightley, glass still in hand, staring directly at me, surrounded by smoke. When my eyes finally came to rest, they came to him, and I held his gaze with defiance, like an angry, betrayed lover, until and beyond the closing of the door.

The vision of the smouldering room disappeared, and I was alone in the hall, until the butler came for me and deposited me on the doorstep outside, where no cab awaited me, and none troubled me either on my journey home to Lambeth. I may have been leered at, propositioned, threatened, followed even; I knew someone was chasing me, but I outran him, and gave him the slip after Westminster Bridge. But it was as a ghost floating above the streets themselves that I navigated the horrors of London at night. The poisons that coursed through the veins of our society from its crown to its very toes seemed to run through my body too; I felt drugged, and dazed. The king is sick, I wanted to cry, but I had no breath for it, and besides, so are his attendants.

I ran up Ivy-street, oblivious to twitching curtains, and

pushed my own front door open. Greeting me was the improbable sight of Jack in my apron, pan in hand, serving hashed meat to Peter, who sat at the table; Lucinda was carrying the milk jug to the table in her nightdress. They broke off the moment they saw me and rushed at me with words of concern – all except Peter – and Lucinda and I embraced in a moment of peace amid the hubbub.

When she had had enough of being held, the child led me to a chair, and Jack brought me a glass of warm milk.

'There's brandy in it for you, Mrs D.'

'Where've you been, mama? Where've you been?'

'Oh child,' I cried, and stroked her hair. 'Are you well? Your health? Are you well?'

'I'm very well, Mama.'

And I could see that she was. Despite the strains of prolonged absence from her mother, Lucinda had not fallen fitting. For that, I had to be grateful to the man responsible for my absence and pains: Sir Jocelyn Knightley. But I swore that night that I would die before I let that man take his knife to her; his were idle threats only, nothing more, I told myself over and over, and that such brutality would remain the stuff of fantasy in the fictions of his books in such a gloriously free country as ours, under Her Majesty's rule. This was London, not the barbaric outer reaches of her Empire where mutilating little girls was considered normal. This was London; fine, clean, noble London. Wasn't it?

I could not sleep for what was left of the night. I watched Lucinda breathing far away in her dreams for an hour or so, and then I glided into our bedroom. I pulled back the bedclothes at the corner, so as not to disrupt the portion that covered Peter's body, and I lay next to him, trying not to touch him, and to keep my breathing quiet. But I stared at his face in the moonlight, pitted and red like the complexion of a lover of the bottle, so misshapen was it, and I tried to remember what it was like to feel in love with him. Then I got up again and went back to Lucinda, and kept watch, as if I knew my love was not enough to protect her, and that I would have to be vigilant now too.

Chapter Fourteen

Hey diddle dout,
My candle's out,
My little maid's not at home;
Saddle the hog,
And bridle the dog,
And fetch my little maid home.

I wouldn't have noticed her through my bleary eyes if I hadn't let the milk boil over again. The smell was so horrible I thought it was worth letting a bit of London's stink and cold in to compensate, so I went over to the parlour window, took the plants off the ledge, and opened the sash. And there I saw her little urchin face, and her stick-and-bones frame perched on the door-step, as dirty as the step itself which I had not whitened for weeks. She had no coat, no shawl, no scarf even, and her skin was grey and cracked.

'Good morning,' I said to her, half-choking with the dust descending from the window struts.

'Mornin',' she replied. 'I'm 'ere for the job.'

'The job?' I had all but forgotten in the cruel events of yesterday. 'Oh, the job!'

The poor little scrap scarcely looked older than Lucinda, but I reckoned she must have been about fifteen. She stood up quick as a rake that had been stepped on, and I unbolted the front door and let her in. She hovered on the door-mat as I closed the door behind her.

'You'd better follow me in to the kitchen,' I said, waving

my hand in front of my nose. 'Sorry about the smell. I forgot to scald the milk from yesterday. I'm a bit preoccupied, so I'll have to ask you some questions as I work, if you don't mind.' She moved forward the length of one room, and stood in the door-way of the parlour, watching as I wrung out a cloth to clean up the top of the range. I scrubbed with one hand; with the other, I threw the pan into the corner where the beetles and spiders were winning their siege.

'Now, something clean to make the breakfast with. What's your name, dear?'

'Pansy.'

'Pansy. That's a nice name.'

She said nothing, but watched as I busied myself in the kitchen. Unused to a witness at this hour, I muttered under my breath like an old forgetful woman. 'Now where's the . . . ah there it is . . . Put some water in . . . mustn't forget the . . .' As usual, within a trice I had the water boiling, the laundry steeping, the floor swept, and a few bugs moderately intimidated. I thought of going to wake Lucinda, but I knew it was to calm my own fears, and not for her sake.

'Beg pardon, mum, but I was wonderin' if you could say if I 'ad the job or no.'

'Oh, Pansy, forgive me, but you'll just have to wait until I've got the house going a bit. It is early, love, and I was awful late last night.' I poured the boiling water on to the tea-leaves.

'Yes, mum, sorry mum, only I got to go now or as I'll be late for the day shift so as I need to know now.'

'The day shift? Where?'

'Remy's. I need to go now and I'll still be late most like.'

I saw Lucinda standing behind Pansy, clutching Mossie, and eyeing the new arrival. Her hair was still tangled, and her feet were bare.

'Good morning, lovely.' I crouched down and held out my arms to her. She came to me and kissed me, then went to play in the parlour.

'Well, I'll try to keep this brief then. Do you have any references?' I started to butter some bread for Lucinda, and pour her some milk.

She shook her head.

'How long have you been at Remy's?'

'Six months. Three months on nights, now I'm on days.'

'Is this your first employ?'

She shook her head. 'Nah. I was at Lambard's before then.' I knew them; a very large industrial bookbinders, larger than Remy & Rangorski.

'Bible work?'

She nodded. I whistled through my teeth as I took Lucinda's breakfast through and placed it on the dining table. Everybody knew Bible contracts paid woefully, and treated you even worse. It's a rum world, I thought, where white men preached the Bible to chained folk and free, in America, in the colonies, across the Empires. They might say slavery is bad, or they might turn a blind eye, but in order to press a Bible into the hands of the heathen they relied on slave labour back home. Frederick Douglass, I remembered, had words to say on this matter.

'Eat up, Lou. Your bread and milk's here.' I turned back to Pansy. 'What did you do there?'

'Days, first. Then days and nights.'

'Both?'

'Christmas. They make you do it all when it's Christmas. Or just busy.'

'I meant, what work did you do for them?'

'Oh. Sewin'.'

'And at Remy's?'

'Sewin'.'

'Why did you leave Lambard's?'

'I had to, mum. They was bringin' in them new sewin'-machines, an' I din't knah how to use 'em.'

'Why couldn't you get a reference from them?'

'Wouldn't give me none. Said they could pay a girl less than they could pay a woman, so I had to go.'

'But what did they mean by that? You are a girl, Pansy.'

She was twisting one of her feet round on the ball of her foot, and her knee was pointing inwards beneath her flimsy skirt. She looked like a little child. She bit her lip, and looked down at the floor. She was flushing.

'They said I wasn't. See, mum, I got in trouble there.'

I raised my eyebrows.

'It weren't my fault, mum, and I won't be causing trouble for you 'ere. I'm not like that, honest. It weren't my fault, and it were me first time, an' if I was strong enough I'd never've let 'im near me, mum.' We both looked down at the same time, to see that Lucinda had come in. She was holding her plate out to Pansy. She had torn her bread in half and dipped it in milk. 'Is this for me? In't you kind?'

Lucinda looked at me. 'Mama hasn't given you any tea yet, and I thought you looked cold.'

'I am, dearie, I am. Bless yer 'art. But you eat it. I can get meself summink later.'

My head was telling me she had 'whore' written all over her, but Lucinda was forcing me to listen to my heart. Whatever questions I was going to ask – her background, if she'd been in trouble with the police, if she'd ever been thieving or the like – sounded brittle in my ears. My daughter had trusted her straightways, and that was worth more than any reference. I started to lay out Peter's breakfast things, and added an extra cup for Pansy.

'So what happened to you?'

'They made me work the night shift. Them respectable girls never would, but they never believed me when I said no, cos they knew I needed the money, what with me mam dead and ten of us at home. 'E was a backin'-machine op'rator, and 'e made me do it, and got me chavvied up, but I told the foreman, only 'e told me I was a liar, but his auntie knows how to do away with it, if you get my meanin', an' he took me to 'er, and I bled for a month and 'ad the doctor's bills to pay, and I 'aven't bled since, if you beg my pardon, and they told me I never would again, never 'ave me own babies, which they said I 'ad them to be grateful for, no more mouths to feed. I don't mean to tell you this all, only so as you know I'm not gahn to be causin' you trouble. It ain't nice, people thinking you're like that, and doctors comin' and checkin' you fer disease an' that, an' Sally an' Gracie too, and the women in the tenement upstairs, like bein' a whore was infectious.'

'Was that when you left?'

'No, mum. But they don't like a blower, do they? They never asked me to do the night shift again, but I needed the money, so I started to do nights at Remy's. Twelve hours at Lambard's, eight hours at Remy's. Until they said they wanted me "replaced", they said. It was slack time, anyway. Always is, March through July. Now I'm at Remy's.'

'What do they pay you?'

'Eight shillings a week. I'd've got twelve if I coulda used one of them machines.'

I poured her a cup of tea, and cut her a slice of cake. As she sat and ate, I took Peter's tray up to him, then returned, and told her everything: how the workshop ran, about Peter's illness, and Lucinda, and about Jack, and Din, and the terms of employment. I left nothing out; nothing, except the nature of the work that went through the workshop. I outlined what work I needed her to do, and that she could hand in her notice at Remy & Rangorski today if she chose.

Pansy shrugged, and said with a mouth full of crumbs, 'If I'm not there by now, me place will have gone anyway.'

There were so many things I could have started Pansy working on immediately, that it was hard for me to choose where she would be best placed. Eventually I decided she needed to begin right where she was: in the kitchen. As the centre of operations for the household and workshop, it was relative squalor, but I wondered how it compared to where Pansy lived. I showed her where the water came in, and told her the hours that it ran, and how the range worked, and where I kept the salts and soaps, and with that, I slipped behind the curtain into the workshop. I was alone for once: Din had taken some gold-dust back to Edwin Nightingale, and Jack was delivering our trade-card up along the Strand.

At least, in amongst the offensive literature, Diprose still sent me the occasional Bible, or prayer-book, or Sir Walter Scott, so today I could occupy myself with those. I selected a Bible, to pretend for a while that I was back in the early days, when I was still the innocent. The binding would be pale blue satin, and I was working it in coloured silks and silver and gold threads. I planned to depict scenes from the Song of Solomon surrounded by an elaborate border of beasts, birds and fruit, and I turned to the right page and read.

> Song of Solomon:
> I am black but comely,
> O ye daughters of Jerusalem,
>   as the tents of Kedar, as the curtains of Solomon.
> Look not upon me because I am black,
>   because the sun hath gazed upon me.

I was interrupted by a stern rapping at the outside door. I opened it to find Bennett Pizzy standing outside, looking remarkably well recovered from the previous day's troubles and exertions. A large, bruised man loomed on either side of him, neither of whom I recognised from the *razzia*. They pushed past me, although I was gratified to watch them all check at the smell of the workshop.

'Her name?'

'A pleasure to see you too, Mr Pizzy, so soon after our last delightful meeting.'

'Her name?'

'Pansy, Mr Pizzy.'

'Pansy what?'

'Pansy I don't know yet.'

'From?'

'Don't know.'

'Family?'

'Don't know. Mother dead, ten siblings, I think she said.'

'Father?'

'Don't know. You really should . . .'

'Age?'

'Don't know.'

'Previous employment?'

Here I paused. 'Don't know,' I finally said.

'Don't you ask questions before you hire someone?' he asked scathingly. 'Don't you have any sense of responsibility? If not for yourself, for Mr Diprose, for Sir Jocelyn Knightley? Have you quite taken leave of your senses? Have you not even asked if she can read?'

'Course she can't,' I snorted. I stared Mr Pizzy defiantly in the eye. 'Ask her yourself,' I said quietly, and pulled the curtain aside.

With less resolution, as if he were not quite prepared for this, Pizzy walked through into the kitchen, followed by his thickset friends. Pansy was on her hands and knees in the fireplace, with black smeared on her face and neck. She sat back on her haunches as they came in, and looked at me for reassurance.

'You are Pansy, correct?' Pizzy asked. She nodded, her hazel eyes wide and bright in the hearth like a frightened cat on a dust heap.

'Mr Pizzy, beg pardon, but may I – may I tell her who you are first?'

He nodded.

'Pansy, love, these gentlemen are clients of the workshop.

They're not from Remy's or Lambard's or anywhere like that. They just want to ask you a few questions about yourself, so as they'll know who's helping where they get their books done up.'

'Your surname?'

'Smith.'

'Address?'

'Six Granby-street, top floor.'

'With?'

'There are thirteen of us.'

'They are?'

'Me auntie Grace and uncle Raymond, their lodger Dougie, then let's see, Baz, Sally, and Alfie, and Hettie, Pearl, Willie, Frank, Ellie, and Sukie.'

'Brothers and sisters,' I interjected to Pizzy.

'Nah, not all of 'em,' Pansy explained. 'Sally's married to me brother Baz, and Alfie's their baby.'

'And you all live together? Separate tenements in one house?'

'Nah, one tenement, three rooms. There's twelve on the floor below us.'

'Where did you work before?'

'Remy's.'

'Why did you leave?'

'Saw the notice in the winder.'

'The notice?' Pizzy looked at me. 'What did it say?'

'It asked for a girl, to do sewing and folding and nursing an invalid and – and – domestic chores.' Pizzy was still staring straight at me. I held his gaze, but I could not keep the horror from my face.

'Thank you, Miss Smith. Good day.' And with great charm, and a raise of his hat, Pizzy marched back into the workshop, and without so much as a click of his fingers, his two henchmen picked me up by the arms, and dragged me behind him, and threw me on the floor, and one of them yanked my arms behind my back, and I saw Pizzy out of the corner of my eye unravel a piece of rope from the pocket of his coat, and then he crouched down, and ripped off my cap, and pulled my hair upwards so hard my head came off the floor.

'You told me she couldn't read,' he hissed into my ear. One of his men took the rope and tied it tight around my wrist. 'You told me, you little bitch, that she couldn't read. What else have you lied about, hmmm?'

I tried to shake my head, but it was impossible, and my throat was so stretched that I could scarce get a word out, only tiny, high-pitched squeaks. Pizzy stood up, and with the point of his flashy leather boots started to kick me, in the ribs, then in the stomach, then in the hips, and I cried out from each as if they were the stab of a knife. Then he pulled my head up higher by the hair, and my chest and back hurt from the angle and the tension, and I knew he was waiting until I could bear it no more and only then would he slam my head down into the sawdust and floorboards.

Only then, we heard a quiet voice above us, saying, 'Actually, sir, she's right. I can't read.' From the corner of my eye I saw Pansy, who flinched as she finished speaking as if waiting for the blow to fall on her next. 'I got me brother Baz to come and read it for me,' she said quickly, still cowed. 'I knew the word "wanted", but only cos I'd seen it on a poster about me dad.' Pizzy lowered me gently to the floor. 'An' we lived round the corner, so it wasn't far fer Baz to come read it fer me. You can go an' ask 'im if you like. 'E's on the market, selling ches'nuts. Tall fella, scar on his face, inked-up arms, by the Vic.'

Pizzy was standing straighter than a hat-pin, and his hands were curled by his side. I almost pitied him; men don't like being caught doing wrong, especially to a woman, and by a woman. And blow me if I didn't even find myself wondering how I could make it easier for him; we women have received an impeccable training in accommodation from our own mothers. We also know the wrath of a man who has been shown up to be wrong, and it is often nastier than simple anger, so it was not surprising that I feared what he might do next.

One of the men undid the rope, and I put my hands underneath me and pushed myself to standing; the pains in my side stung sore.

'Would you like a cup of tea, gentlemen?' I asked, as calmly as I could. The other man picked up my cap and gave it to me; I raised my arms to fasten it on to my head, but my sides wrenched at the movement, and my head went black at the pain.

'No, tea will not be necessary,' Pizzy finally said in a weak voice. Then, a bit stronger, he said, 'Bill, Patrick, go, wait outside. Pansy, you may leave too.' She dared not look at me, but turned straightways and went back to the kitchen, ensuring the curtain was fully across behind her.

Pizzy couldn't look at me either, which was some small satisfaction.

'I trust I did not hurt you too much, Mrs Damage,' he said to the bench, not to me. 'Although let me tell you, it was not without due caution. In a business like ours, one cannot be too careful, and this must serve as a warning to you.'

'I have had sufficient already, Mr Pizzy,' I said.

'Where is the nigger?'

'He's on an errand.'

'He and Pansy are under your jurisdiction, along with whosoever else the fancy takes you to employ. If any of them reveal anything to anyone about the trade at Damage's, we will hold you personally responsible. I have been instructed to tell you, yet again, that if you are not able to find a meaningful way to ensure the nigger's loyalty to you, you must dismiss him without further ado. Have you?'

I shook my head miserably. 'Perhaps you could suggest to me how I should go about it.'

'It is not that difficult, Mrs Damage,' Pizzy said, exasperated.

'You have women's wiles. You must find a weak spot, a secret, something you can use to blackmail him with. Use your charms. And if he is immune to those, you must use whatever means you have. A little espionage, a little subterfuge.' He walked out into the street, where Bill and Patrick flanked the carriage. He ascended, buttoning up his coat as he climbed, then turned and said casually, 'And Dora. Do something about that curtain. It doesn't do to be overheard by servant girls.'

I would not move from the door until I could be sure he and his men had left Ivy-street. I wanted to get to Lucinda and hug her, and be sure she was safe, but only once I had ensured the carriage had departed.

But it stopped a little further up the cobbled street, and one of the two men – the one who had handed me my cap – got out, and knocked on Mrs Eeles's door, and when she came out he pressed something into her hands. Then he ruffled the hair of young Billy, reached into his pocket, and gave him something else.

And then I realised, in an instant, that the old jade had been spying on me all this time. She had been their lookout, and that miserable boy Billy must have been the messenger, reporting back to Holywell-street on the comings and goings at Damage's. No wonder they knew all about us, of Pansy's arrival, of goodness knows what else. All of it, no doubt. And Billy – who would have thought? Oh, I didn't resent him his role, only her: at least I had been giving him, unwittingly, a chance to get out of her house. I consoled myself with the thought of the motherless little boy with a twisted face and broken glasses, running away from the House of Death, and the ghost, no doubt, of his mother, at full pelt. I was, in some small way, glad to be of assistance.

Suddenly I could see, all around me, the disintegration of my place in the community. I had tried to ignore the details: that Lucinda no longer went to play in the streets with the other children; that people had stopped knocking on my door with a loaf of bread or a basket of eggs; that neither did I make a large stew and take it to someone else's door like I used to; that people had even started to turn away from me in the street. I wondered what they had heard from Mrs Eeles, or Agatha Marrow, or others, and what they knew of my running the workshop, and even whether they knew of the books that I bound.

Then I saw myself as if from a distance, and wondered what I would think of myself, a young woman with a crippled husband, who received a regular train of different, well-dressed male visitors, and her resultant new-found wealth. I did not flaunt it – I had never worn those fine scarves, kid boots, the parasol and the fan – but Lucinda's lovely blue coat can't have escaped their notice. And if what had happened to Pansy were true, in the spirit of self-preservation, no decent woman could have afforded to know me any more.

I closed the door and found Pansy peeping into the workshop from behind the curtain. When she saw I was alone, she pulled the curtain right back and swung herself inside. She was holding a warm bread-and-water poultice in a damp flannel.

'Y'all right? Let me have a look at ya.' I lifted my smock, and she put the pack on the worst of my bruises. 'Maybe we should get the doctor in to put some leeches on ya. Could do with half a dozen. Look at the state of ya.'

She wiped my nose with a handkerchief, and I saw that it was bleeding.

'No doctors, Pansy.'

'Nah? Don't blame ya.' She rubbed some pure extract of lead on each of the larger injuries, and set about covering the worst of them with bandages. She had a big grin on her face. 'I knew you was all right, mum, straight from when I saw the parsley in your pots.'

'Parsley, Pansy? I didn't know I had any.'

''Swot me mam always said. "Where the missus is the master, the parsley grows the faster."'

She had nearly finished when Jack returned, having finished delivering our cards.

'Crikey, Mrs D, what happened to you?'

When I told him, he hung his head wretchedly. 'I shoulda been 'ere, Mrs D. I shoulda. You need me to pertect you, in this line o' work. You mustn't be alone without a man again, Mrs D.' The tattooed skull on his arm grimaced up at me, and seemed to nod in agreement as Jack hammered his fist on the table. For all his gentleness, there was strength and meanness in his skinny arms.

'No, Jack,' I protested. 'It won't happen again. And Jack, this is Pansy. She's working with us now. She'll help me in the house too. She's fresh from Remy's.'

'How d'y do?'

'How d'y do?'

They could have been brother and sister, I thought, as I watched them bob up and down nervously at each other. Both had brittle, bony exteriors, but there were wounded birds inside those cages that needed more careful handling than either of them had been used to.

The other wounded fellow, by which I mean Din, did not return that day, or the next, which troubled me somewhat. Could Diprose have meant what he said about capturing him and sending him back? Had he been killed by some nigger-hater, or a gang of youths, in a back-street in the Borough? Had he been ravished to death by Lady Knightley and her lustful ladies? Given that she would be nearly eight months' pregnant by now I doubted it, but the thought at least brought a sorry chuckle to my throat.

At least I had Pansy now, I thought, if Din never returned to sew and fold for me.

Pansy's worth, however, was so immediately apparent in the house over her first week with us that I started to doubt she would ever get close to the workshop. She found for me a pail of cheap enamel paint and set about banishing the staleness and soot from the dingy kitchen. She wrapped brown paper around a hot coal, and applied it to the candle-wax; then she made up a mixture of fuller's earth and turpentine, and rubbed them over the remaining candle-grease stains, and where the oil-lamps had spilt. She cleaned the oven and the flue, polished the steel with bathbrick and paraffin, and black-leaded the iron. And she waged war on the bugs by scrubbing the floors with carbolic, and filling up all the holes in the mortar and cracks in the floor with cement. (She got the cement from the road-diggers laying new sewers outside; I watched her with fear as she strutted over to them, but the way those men obeyed her, no one would have thought she was so recently the victim of unsupervised lust.)

She bathed my wounds daily and rubbed my bruises, just as she saw to my smocks, aprons and floral dress. Lucinda watched her in wonder and interrogated her all the while on what she was doing.

Pansy also treated us to home-cooked, love-cooked food. With friends in the highest parts of the market in New Cut, she was soon dishing us up breakfasts of eggs, bacon, kidneys and mushrooms, and for supper we would have kedgeree, or grilled fish with potatoes, or a nice piece of tongue. Even I had thought that poor folk didn't know how to cook, that they were happy to make do with stale bread and cold meat, even when warm soup was not hard to come by. And it was not without misgivings that I ate her lovely food, for I wondered what the rest of her family at home had to eat, in what little time she had left over from her chores here to cook it.

But even Pansy couldn't reduce my load of washing to one wash-day a week, although she breathed new life into my stale linen. She cut and sewed the bed sheets sides to middle, and made sure Peter had a fresh set every other day, and Lucinda and I every week.

She arranged for a carpenter too, to come in and build a door to replace the flimsy curtain separating the house from the workshop. He came straightways – Pansy had an impressive knack of getting people to do what she wanted – with his tools and several large planks of wood, and was sawing and banging and fixing into the evening. I expected the Noble Savages and Holywell-street would be informed of his arrival and activities, but I was only carrying out their instructions. I also ensured that the door had a strong lock on it too, and only one key, which I kept round my waist between my skirts.

And Pansy blackleaded the grate and whitened the front steps, and as Jack arrived at work one morning he whistled in wonder that the establishment had been made to look so respectable once more. 'If only they knew, mum, if only they knew!'

'Are you calling this place a whited sepulchre?' I said, and he winked impudently at me.

'No, Mrs D, wouldn't dream of it.'

Din returned on Saturday morning, a week and four days after his disappearance. I should have been angry at him; an employer would have stamped his foot, interrogated him, and demanded suitable recompense for his absence. But I wanted instead to throw my arms around him, to make sure he was well and that he had not had some dreadful misfortune or accident, and to express my relief that he had not been deported by Diprose. And so, of course, caught between shoulds and wants, I did nothing more than offer him a polite welcome, present him with some Bible manuscripts for mending, and slip inside the house to fix my hair more neatly under my cap.

'Oos that fella, mum?' Pansy asked me in low tones as she wiped the dust off the banisters. 'That coloured fella?'

'That's Din, Pansy. Din Nelson. He helps me out with sewing and stuff.'

'American?'

'Yes. He was a slave. He was bought by the Ladies' Society for the Assistance of Fugitives from Slavery, and they asked me to give him a job.'

'Only I know him.'

'Do you? How?'

'Not sure. 'Is face looks familiar, but I can't fink where from. Never mind. It'll come to me.'

I had to wonder how many men of colour she was familiar with; I knew so few I would not misplace their faces. But our distant thoughts were interrupted by Peter, giggling in his armchair, and reciting to himself, 'There was an old man from Tobago, Who lived on rice, gruel and sago . . .', before collapsing into such paroxysms of mirth he was unable to finish the limerick.

By mid-morning I felt as if my cool welcome and immediate removal from Din's vicinity had not been terribly polite. I attempted to rectify this by going over to the sewing-frame and asking, 'I trust you achieved your business during your absence?'

'Thank you, ma'am, I did. And I trust my absence didn't overly inconvenience y'all at the bindery.'

'Bindery?' I said. 'What an interesting expression.'

He shrugged. 'It's what we call it, back home.'

'Bindery,' I mused. 'I like it. I have always found "workshop" to be rather functional. And "atelier" is too pretentious. "Bindery." How simple. Like a bakery, or a brewery. Yes, I shall call it that from now on. Thank you, Din.'

'Pleasure, ma'am.'

I watched as his fingers threaded the sewing-frame, and wondered again what it would feel like to touch his skin. Mere intellectual curiosity, I persuaded myself, like wondering what hay might be like to sleep on. It was something that I might idly muse over, but never actually consider doing.

'Mrs D, we're short of boards. Shall I run to Dicker's and get some?' Jack called.

'Of course,' I said. I rummaged in the drawer for some coins for him.

'Nah, he'll give you credit now,' Jack said.

'Really? What good news.'

And I watched Jack take off his apron and leave, before realising that I actually needed an extra pair of hands to hold the leather down while I pasted.

'Din. Would you mind stopping what you are doing for a while, and helping me with the leather?'

'Sure, ma'am.'

He came over to the bench and placed his hands on two opposite corners of the leather while I worked the paste into it. It was important that the leather did not slip, which would smear the paste onto the good side of the leather. I tried to concentrate. Din's head was bowed, and he appeared nonchalant, but to me it was unbearable.

I could smell him. He smelt of smoke and soil, not like dirt but the soil of the earth itself, sweet and damp, like the smell that lurks between moss and bark, or bark and tree-flesh. I was drawn by the smell of him, mixed with the sweet, dusty odour of leather and sawdust around us. I wanted to sniff him deeply, to bury my nose into his flesh and breathe him noisily in.

Instead, I held my breath. Half of what I desired? I was doing the exact opposite of my desires. And then I knew that he was holding his breath too, and he was answering me, and smelling me too, and I felt a stirring inside me, and my secret longing urged like a vapour towards him and pressed itself into him without me, as I stood still, and rigid.

'Din. Please, repeat for me the quotation from Ovid's *Amores*. I have been struggling to remember it.'

' "*Suffer and endure, for some day your pain will be of benefit.*" '

'"Suffer and endure . . ."' I repeated, quietly. 'Is that a particular philosophy of yours?'

I felt him smile, although I did not look up into his face, for it was too close to mine.

'It is indeed, ma'am. My favourite motto. For it is about hope. You see, before, ma'am, since my people were first enslaved, there was no hope. Instead, you had to defer your hope to the kingdom o' heaven that was meant to await you in the next life. You know the song. You'd be escorted there by bands of angels, on winged chariots. It was the only hope we had, and you had to believe it, or despair. Without hope, how can a man live? But now I don't believe in that no more.'

'Why not?' I was growing hot from the fire in his eyes as he spoke.

'Because I am startin' to believe in something else. I am startin' to believe that there may be hope in my lifetime. There are signs round every corner that the end of enslavement is near. I have more hope than ever before, that the kingdom o' heaven can indeed be now, and that today can be the day o' change, for ever. But then again,' he conceded, 'a boy may have strange opinions about all things Christian when he come from a country that says slavery is the will o' God.'

He chuckled, and kept talking, but I had stopped hearing his words and was just listening to the music of his voice, knowing as I did all the while that the leather was fully pasted, that I could keep him at my table no longer, and that I didn't know how to tell him.

So I listened to him talk again, until he had talked himself out, and we lapsed into silence, and I eventually said, 'Thank you, Din,' and released the pressure on the leather, and didn't dare watch him as he returned to the sewing-frame.

Later that day Pansy came up to me again.

'I've remembered it now. I know where've seen 'im before. 'E's a fighter, mum.'

260

'A fighter?'

'Yeah. Dahn the tanners. 'E brought Baz back one night, all cut up and bleedin'. 'E couldn't even walk. It was 'im what brought 'im back.'

'Back from where, Pansy?'

'It's a fighting-gang. They're all at it. Dahn the tanners, at the weekend. Well, used to be the tanners' yard, now they do it in a drill-shed somewhere. Or outside.'

'Who does it? Is it a prize-fight?'

'Nah, nuffin' so legit. They just beat each uvver senseless.'

'Why? Is it sport?'

Pansy shrugged. 'It was the tanners what started it. Now it's anyone. Men from the barracks, costermongers, all sorts. Roughs and bruisers, all of 'em. They get well mashed up.'

'Bare-knuckle?'

'Mostly. Only they sometimes do a challenge with the tanning tools. Leather-ligging's Baz's favourite, when they do it with leather straps. Metal bands, they use, too. Or worse. They use all sorts, the tanners; they've got these big metal triangle pins, and all them pokes and knives. But they don't do it all the time, or it'd be murder. Baz once had to fight this big Irish fella, who was a shedman.'

'A shedman?'

'The one whose job it is to pummel the leather, to soften it. And d'you know what they use to do that?'

I shook my head.

'This bloody great stave with two 'eads on. Baz couldn't walk for a month. 'E got whipped that night.'

'Whipped?'

'Yeah. There's this bloke with a long leather whip, who whips 'em if it all gets out of hand, before one of 'em gets killed good and proper. You sing small for a while if you've been whipped.'

'Are you telling me that Din gets involved with all this too?'

Pansy shrugged again. 'Far as I know. 'E brought Baz back,

I remember that much, the night 'e got whipped. Does 'e come in 'ere lookin' all mashed sometimes?'

'Yes, he has done. Pansy, could you find out for me?'

'What?'

'Well, if there's anything about Din I need to know. Anything that . . . doesn't reflect too well on him.'

'All right, mum. Only, it don't reflect well on all of 'em, if you don't like that sort of thing.'

'But is it legal?'

'Oh, it's legal enough. Wouldn't get any rozzer down there, at any rate.'

'It's just . . . I need to know more about him, something he might not tell me if I ask. Do you understand me?'

'I think so,' she said doubtfully. ''E's a lucky fella, 'e is, landing this job with you.'

'Maybe. But he hasn't had much luck before that.'

'It's a sight better than anyfink I've ever 'ad. Wish some royal bird would have bought me and landed me a job when I was down on me luck at Lambard's.'

'Peter?' I whispered. He was lying in bed, staring with glassy eyes at the ceiling. 'Peter. We must get you out of bed today. Pansy wishes to change the sheets.' I spoke slowly, hoping some of it was going in. 'Peter. You have not been out of bed for days.' I took a flannel from the press, dipped it in some water, and wiped his chin, his cheeks, his brow.

He muttered something, but I could not hear him.

'I don't understand,' I said, and held one of his ravaged hands. He turned and looked at me through rheumy, yellow eyes, streaked with blood. Even his tears seemed to be red.

'I have not been good to you,' he said slowly.

'Oh, but you have,' I replied merrily. 'You have been a fine husband. It is I who has not been the best wife a man can hope for.'

He stroked my hand, then raised his head.

'Your ring. Your wedding ring. It's gone.'

I started at my hand, and for a moment felt like a drunk woman who wonders where she has left her baby.

'Did you sell it?' he asked sadly.

Then I remembered it was still in pawn.

'It's . . . it's . . . I take it off to do the work.' I wondered if it was too late to redeem it. But then again, I still had nothing to redeem it with as I was yet to be paid.

Peter started to cry, low and soft. 'You are no longer my wife. You no longer sport the sign of our marriage.' He was not accusing, or angry, just resigned.

'No, Peter,' I said quickly. 'The work is the sign of my true commitment to you. I have saved your name.' But I knew I had soiled it. 'Is that not the greatest way a wife can serve her husband?' I hated myself for these lies. I wanted to apologise to him, and ask his forgiveness, but possibly the lie was better for one in his condition. I did not know any more what was right or wrong. I simply wanted to wrap him up in a blanket and carry him to a place where there was great beauty, where he could lie down in a field, smell the corn, and watch the butterflies flutter colour through the air, and know that he was safe.

'Am I dying, Dora?' he asked.

'We all are, Peter,' I said quietly. 'Only some will get there sooner than others.'

He placed his other hand over mine, and closed his eyes. 'A pearl of a wife,' he said. 'A pearl.'

I leant forward and kissed his wet lips, then sat next to him with my ringless hand on his chest for a while. His body never twitched or turned, but weighed the mattress down like a rock. Silence was better than lies, at least.

I let him sleep a while longer while I worked in the bindery. Then Pansy came in to tell me he was stirring so we went upstairs together, and helped him out of bed and into Lucinda's room, where he lay down on her cot and moaned for some more Drop.

'I'll bring it for you when I've helped Pansy make the bed.'

'Now,' he groaned. 'Now!'

So I descended for the bottle, and when I brought it up he grabbed it from me and swigged. I had never insisted on the measuring-spoon; it would have been impossible to start now.

I joined Pansy in the bedroom where she was stripping the bed. 'Anything to tell about Din?' I asked quietly.

'Nuffink. Not a jot. Baz told me nuffink. They're all as bad as each other, seems. If you're wantin' to shop 'im to the coppers . . .'

'That's not my intention, Pansy. I just need to know a bit about the side we don't see at work. You know what it's like.'

She looked doubtful again, and slightly suspicious. I decided I would have to take a different approach. But I was sure there was something about these fighting nights that would serve my purpose. It was getting urgent, too.

My troubling was interrupted by a noise from Lucinda's bedroom. I rushed in to find Peter lying flat on his back, clutching at her bedclothes with claws of terror, and staring at the ceiling.

'What is it?' I asked.

Beads of sweat clung to his face. The bottle was on the floor. I picked it up quickly, fearing it had spilt, but it was empty and there was no mess.

'Peter. Have you drunk the lot? Peter?'

I tried to remember how full it had been. His eyes were closing. I let him sleep.

Chapter Fifteen

Friday's a day that will have its trick,
The fairest or foulest day of the week.

The volume of work was abating as we got closer to Christmas. Soon we had precious few books to get up into leather, except, of course, for the photographic catalogues, which remained in a stack by the wall, a tower of Babylon taunting me in tongues I could not and did not wish to understand. I had achieved no victory over Diprose – they still had not paid me – and I wondered how desperate I would have to become before I would give in to the work they proffered. I had thought that working like this would save us, that I was being the best wife I could be, but in truth, I wondered if I were any better than a prostitute. I felt like the ghost of Holywell-street, trapped in endless gas-lit labyrinths of vice and filth, and unable to find a way out into daylight.

It was when Mr Skinner arrived again, and with only the curtest of greetings and a 'thankin' ya werry much' pocketed our remaining proceeds, leaving us with nothing to buy food even, let alone stretch to a little extra Christmas spending, that I started to worry. I took a meagre bag of gold-dust to Edwin Nightingale, who offset it against my outstanding debts with him, but would not give me cash. I became angrier in the workshop; I snapped at Din, and at Jack, and I shouted at Pansy.

'You know your hours,' I reprimanded Din one day. 'They are less than Jack's, and still you cannot keep them.'

'I know.'

'Why do you leave me every Friday?'

'I have other business.'

'Which is?'

'I cannot tell you.'

Oh but you can, I thought. And I know anyway. Other business, indeed. I tried to find another way to pry.

'Din, sometimes, you come in here . . .' How was I to say this tactfully? 'You look . . . You look . . . as if you have been hurt. You come in here all black and . . .' Oh my, what a turn of phrase.

'. . . blue, ma'am? Yes, we folks do bruise, but it's harder to see.' He continued working. A curse on my haste.

'So where do you go then, of a Friday, Din? What is your other business?' But I was not getting anywhere, so I added, 'Or are you ashamed of it?'

He said nothing.

'Are you happy here, at the bindery?'

'Happy, ma'am?'

I could not stop myself. 'Are we not enough for you, that you have to take on "other business"?' He stayed silent. 'A-ha! Then it is us you are ashamed of! Are we too shameful for you, Din?'

'Shameful, ma'am?'

'Is it not degrading for you – to be working on – *this*?' Still I did not know if he knew the true nature of the work here, but my anger pushed me. But still he did not react. It provoked me further. I was what was shameful here. 'And for a *woman* as well?'

He lifted his head from his work, and met my gaze. 'Shame?' he answered. 'There is no *shame* here. You run a highly respectable business, ma'am.'

'Do not mock me!'

'I do not.' He tilted his head, and closed one eye, as if to scrutinise me with the open one. He looked amused.

'Respectable,' he repeated. '*Respicere*. To look back at. To regard. To behold.' He was grinning now, and I was confounded. 'Respectability is only how folk see you. I only know how I see you, not how they do. To me, ma'am, you are indeed respectable, for here I am beholdin' you.'

His words winded me, and I paused, unable to go back to what I had said, or forward to what I wanted to say. This was not where I had intended to be. Finally, I replied, 'Then you cannot worry that I may not think you respectable. Am I not beholding you too?'

A moment passed between us, like the air that waits between the bell and the clapper as the clock strikes the hour, before I turned away. If words were nothing more than dressings on our true selves, then the not-saying, the silence, was an undressing, and I was shivering. But I dared not allow the man's beholding warm me up, although I knew it would. It would stoke fires that would rage beyond my control, and consume me in their heat, all for the sake of a bit of warmth. No. How dare he behold me. How dare he ridicule me, mock me, play with me, undress me. I was his employer; he was my slave.

If the man would not tell me where he went, all I had to do was follow him. I would know, then, and I would have power over him. I believe now that that was what I wanted most: power over the man. For in the face of those strange feelings within me that he engendered, I was powerless.

I also had the leisure to undertake this plan, given the troubling lack of crates descending on us from Holywell-street. But it would require some preparation, so I ambled up Ivy-street, plotting my pursuit of Din, and knocked at Mrs Eeles's door. She opened it quickly, only to discover to her disappointment that it was the whore of Ivy-street. She left the door open, as a sign that I was to continue my supplication, but hid herself entirely behind it.

'Mrs Eeles,' I said to the empty space. 'I beg your forgiveness for broaching you on such a sensitive issue, only I have today received news of the passing of a business acquaintance of my husband . . .'

I had not appreciated how little she would be able to resist. Her head poked round the door, so she could show me how well her brow was knitted out of concern. 'Oh, you poor, dear girl. Did you know him well?'

'Passing well, yes. But I do not ask for pity. It is his widow for whom I feel sorrow, and his eighteen children.'

'Eighteen!' Now a hand appeared, raised heavenwards. 'The Lord giveth, and yet He taketh away. May He bless the poor, bereft, little ones!'

'The funeral is on Friday and . . .'

'. . . you wish for weeds?'

'Sadly, yes. I am in need of a mantle, and the weeping veil I gave you in lieu of rent back in December last. Just for one night. I shall be leaving around five o'clock on Friday, and walking to my destination. I will return it to you clean and fresh on my return.' I could see she was noting the timing in her head, and I hoped she felt it would not be worth sending Billy to follow me. I knew not where I could give him the slip on the way to the tanneries.

She went back inside for a moment, and left me on the threshold. I did not turn around, but could feel I was being watched by Ivy-street. Eventually her hand wound its way around the door, holding a large black bundle of crêpe and wool. I took it, and bobbed a curtsey, even though the hand couldn't see.

'I am ever so grateful, Mrs Eeles. Thank you.'

'And here are some gloves for you,' came the unexpected words, and the other hand thrust out two limp black gloves at me. I half-expected a third hand to appear with a jet cameo, and a fourth with some ribbons, but I was grateful for what I had, and fled with them back to the workshop.

My time in the bindery with Din on Friday was fraught with tension. I trembled constantly at the thought of what I was to undertake that night, and how best to explain myself should he catch me. But in truth, my trembling was for other reasons. For I was starting to worry that my desire to touch him was not out of any intellectual fancy – which is what I had told myself – but from a compulsion born within the pit of my being, which threatened to stretch my fingers out without any intercession on behalf of my brain. Each time I passed him a folder or buffer, it was as much as I could do, as I withdrew my hand, to will my fingers to clench into a fist, as if I were deliberately trying to hammer the air instead of impress his flesh onto their tips.

Idle fantasy arising out of our irreconcilable, innate differences, I kept trying to convince myself as I struggled to work. That much I knew from the literature Diprose had supplied me with, which declared that black men want white women because they are everything they have been told they can't have. The argument reversed would imply that I only wanted him because he was black; Lady Knightley and her Ladies were proof enough of that. No, books were no help to me here. The only book that showed the lust of white women for a black man was *The Lustful Turk*, but then, he was a Turk, not an African, and the Dey at that, and so prodigiously endowed that, allegedly, no woman brutally awoken to her sexuality by such a weapon could ever resist, once pain had transmuted to pleasure. So I could hardly look to it for guidance. Nowhere could I find a book that would help me: this was not the sort of thing one would find on the shelves of Mudie's Select Libraries. A delusion of love, Dora, I told myself over again. An unrighteous lust, Dora.

I announced, very publicly, to Jack that I would be leaving the bindery early, that he must lock up, and that I expected he would leave on time. At a quarter to five I went into the house and put on the long black mantle, the veil and Mrs

Eeles's gloves. I put on my boots, but beneath the finery their sorry state was more evident than ever: my toes were completely exposed, and there was hardly enough left of the eroded sole to keep in the pages of *The Illustrated London News*. In haste I pulled my new brown boots from under the bed, and persuaded myself that tottering in heels would be preferable to freezing in ruins. I laced them tightly, then bid farewell to Pansy and Lucinda, all the while listening for the door of the bindery, and then it came, and I sensed Din's shadow passing the house as he left.

I could not see Billy the Nose anywhere, and by the time we got to Waterloo Bridge I knew I was not being tailed, which left me free to concentrate on following Din at a distance, and to worry about where we were going, for it was clear we were not heading to Bermondsey. Besides, I was worrying about the weather. Crêpe did not like getting wet. The gummy, tightly wound silk threads would shrivel in the rain, and the veil would be ruined, along with my plans, and Mrs Eeles's pleasure.

But then I had another thing to worry about. I could hardly count the times I had crossed this bridge watching my toes go in and out under the hem of my skirts, and each of those times I had longed for smart new boots to keep the rain out and my toes warm. Now I had them, and their efficient clip clip clip gratified my spirit but grated my feet, which were soon blistering all over.

As we reached the Strand, Din stuck out his arm, and a green omnibus marked 'BOW and STRATFORD' ground to a halt, so I quickened my sore pace to reach the vehicle before it pulled out again. I fretted about whether I had the exact fare in my purse, so as not to draw attention to myself when paying, and where I was to sit: not on top, in this fine mantle, but if I sat inside, I risked being cheek-by-jowl with the man I was stalking.

I could not hear what Din said to the driver as he paid his

fare, but afterwards he placed his hand on the wheel rim and leapt on top of the bus, as if he were hurdling a gate, which meant I could comfortably and appropriately ride inside.

'Same as him,' I whispered to the driver, and proffered a shilling.

'You what?' the man shouted.

'Same as him,' I repeated. 'I'm getting off where that man's getting off.'

'The nigger?' he said loudly.

'Yes,' I hissed. 'Please, be quick.' He took my coin, and I climbed across the knees of the bowler-hatted clerks on their way home, and sat where I could see the movements of Din's legs on the knifeboard, so I would know where to dismount.

The other passengers stared at me as if I were a pickpocket. But I remembered from before that this was indeed how people looked at you if you were wearing a veil; their inability to see your eyes offers a false reassurance that you can't see theirs. I forgave them their insolence; there was precious little else to look at on this grey Friday evening, other than the strangers with whom one was sharing a space that was even smaller than our box-room. I could not see much in the fog outside, except the shapes caught in the yellow pools of gaslight, so I spent the journey keeping half an eye out for Din, and half an eye out for maltoolers. Clerks descended; clerks got on again.

Finally Din's legs straightened: he had stood up, and was about to descend.

'Excuse me, excuse me,' I whispered, and 'I beg your pardon,' until I was at the top of the precarious steps and, even though the bus was still moving gently, I had to jump or lose my prey. I staggered on the curb from the unfamiliar heel height, and clutched onto a lamppost for support. But where was Din? I spotted him turning the corner into another street, and I hastened after him. I had not thought this far ahead, of the folly of tottering on cobbles, wearing a long mantle and fine boots through streets where there were no sweepers for what lay in my path. It disguised me insomuch as it was not my usual costume, but it drew attention to me too.

I lost him here and there in the misty gaps between street-lights, but I could hear him whistling, and when I could not, a couple of women standing by a shop, arms folded, shouted out, 'Scrub your gob, Uncle Tom,' and I caught up once more with his springing stride, which had not faltered. Then an urchin skipped alongside him for a bit, singing 'nigger, nigger, nignog' at him, before chancing upon a puppy to stop and torment. Occasionally someone nodded at him; a few greeted him openly. 'Dinjerous!' an older black man with a grizzled beard said to him, slapping him on the back. I noted the wider range of complexions than I was used to; there were more black people, more Indians, more Orientals, and indeed more women on the streets of wherever we were now.

Then Din strode over a large stretch of cobbles to a public-house that stood in the centre where two roads forked. I could only stand and watch as he disappeared into a space next to the main door, and down a stairwell. I could not go in alone. I was rooted to the spot, and suddenly conspicuous.

I tried to pretend I was waiting for someone. I pulled the mantle more closely around me, and noticed the cold. I could not go home yet, but I had not found anything out. 'A-ha, Din! So you went to a public-house!' It wouldn't really suffice.

But as I was troubling myself, Din's face appeared, smiling, in the gloom above the stairwell.

'You not goin' to follow me in, lady?' He came through the doorway and started to walk towards me, holding out his hands. 'You come all this way, and you want to miss the party? I can't leave a lady standin' out.'

'How on God's earth did you know it was me?'

'I'd know you anywhere from your gait, for all those foolish boots.' He took me firmly by the arm, and I shrank at his touch, then relaxed into the warmth and firmness of his grasp, which was as welcome right now as a warm brandy and milk.

'Where are we?'

'Whitechapel,' he replied. 'Come on in.'

'Can I?'

'It's not good, no. I was close to roundin' on you all the way. But I'm not angry no more. You're stupid, though. If I leave you up here, you'll be dead when I get back.'

We descended the steep wooden staircase – Din gripping my arm above the elbow – and I used both hands to lift my skirts. We reached a room in the cellar. 'You would do well to leave your veil on,' he whispered.

Inside were congregated about ten people; most, but not all, of the same hue as my escort. Two were of the fair sex, although whether that was a suitable title for a woman whose skin was blacker than Din's, I was not altogether sure; Sir Jocelyn, no doubt, would have had some words on the matter. Din found me a seat in the shadows at the back of the room where he left me, and went to roam around. He waved at some of the occupants, placed his hands on the shoulders of others and patted them warmly, and chatted to still more. Occasionally, while talking to someone, he would gesture back to me, and his companion would look at me, and nod.

I was more nervous than when I was following him on the streets. My hands were clammy inside their gloves, and my armpits too, despite the cold. Nobody seemed to look at me for long, but one of the women had a baby on her lap, and the baby was staring hard at me. I was grateful for the veil, and wondered if Din would offer me his protection, should his colleagues demand the removal of my disguise. I wondered when the fighting would start.

'Back to our business here,' a tall man with a red hat said, with a gesture to the minor disruption of our entrance.

Quickly the discussion grew, and the atmosphere in the room was as serious as death. Most of what they said passed me by completely; names of people and places were tossed around, some I'd heard of before, others which were completely new to me. Someone mentioned Freddie: Freddie Douglass. Harpers Ferry. John Brown. The conversation heated up. Shouts were thrown, fists pounded tables. But this was not sport with a rabble of tanners. What was it then? An abominable brotherhood? A satanic sect?

'South Carolina is gonna secede. We have to strike there.'

'Our scouts are in Mississippi,' a small, scruffy white man said. 'All our people are there. South Carolina will be impractical, impossible.'

'South Carolina is where it's at. Barnwell Rhett is our man, not Davis. We be fools to miss it.'

'We be fools to try. Mississippi will go too, believe it. We still go for Davis.'

'He's saying he ain't gonna. He opposes it in principle.'

The speaker was swooped on by half his listeners: 'But in *practice*, fool?' 'You believe him?' 'Watch Mississippi pull away.' 'Watch and wait.'

The argument did not abate when the landlord brought in a tray of beer, which he distributed amongst the guests. A few took their glasses from him with a nod and a smile, which he reciprocated; the tall man with the red hat ignored him, and the drinks too. The landlord lingered for a while, listening to the debate, then left, seemingly unperturbed by, or accustomed to, the rising tension. There would be a fight, I was sure of it.

'He's right,' said the white man. 'It's stepping up, and we must step up too. Strike while the iron's hot; strike while the President's fresh.'

'You're wrong. It's too dangerous now. We shoulda nailed him earlier. He'll get too big soon . . .'

'. . . an' bigger if Mississippi go too.'

'The bigger the better.'

'So nail him now!'

'We don' dare . . .'

'Sol is right, but for the wrong reasons.' This was Din speaking. He stood up, and the room hushed. Din. My heart beat loud and I grew hot with fear. What was his role here? Was he some cat's-paw, or a ring-leader, or a stooge? 'We go for Davies. But we don' kill him. Davies is the mos' importan' man in the South, an' we can' have blood on our hands at this time. We revert to the July plan.' His accent was more pronounced than ever; I had never heard him talk like this. He made to sit down, but nobody was going to let him.

'You change yo' tune, Din, little man! What's gettin' you?'

'Nothin',' he said, rounding on his accuser. 'I jus' think . . . we're wrong to use violence.' I was stunned by his authority. No one yet had elicited such a reaction. It was deafening. There were hisses from some, boos from others, gasps of surprise, and even a few cheers by yet others.

'Wrong to use violence! Do you hear the words of Dinjerous Din? Wrong to use violence!'

Din started to talk again, his voice low but solid. 'Kidnap him and hol' him hostage. Bring the country to its knees. Hol' it to ransom.'

'I'm hearin' you, Din!' shouted another man from the corner.

'Give him a taste o' captivity; and kill him if our demands aren' met,' Din continued.

'Kill him first! Kill him first!' someone else shouted amidst the rising hubbub.

'Silence y'all!' Din was standing in the centre of the chaos. 'We take; we don' kill. We bite; we don' kill. We strike; we don' kill. Why?' The fuss started to die down around him. The man was a great speaker. 'Cos we wan' time. Time to take our demands to the Senate, and time for them to consider them. There is too much blood already on our hands.' Then he added quietly, 'I know that more'n all.'

'Din, you have been baying for blood since you joined us!'

the man called Sol said. He had a warm face; he looked tired, and old, but I liked him already. 'What's changed, brother?'

'What's changed? What's changed is that I know I'm a fighter. We're all fighters here; an' we can' fight if we are dead. I ain' gonna risk a hanging without trial. I ain' gonna risk that. The day I risk a hangin' will be the day I know I am seen as a citizen of the United States, and that I be granted a trial for my wrong-doin'.'

'You're a coward, Din. A cheap chicken-heart.'

'You wrong me, Adam, you *wrong* me. Remember New Orleans? That was nothin' short of a suicide mission, but I took it. I will die for my people and my country. *If* I believe it is the right action. But now, it's changed. You can smell it too. And Jefferson Davis is mo' use to us alive than dead. Don' misun'erstand: I could pull the knife on the man if I wanted to. I could kill any man who says he'll uphold slavery at any cost, includin' the cost of the union. But if I am to lead the team o' hostage-takers – and I have been chosen by you, all o' you – I will feed that man the finest foods and wines three times a day an' mo'; I will treat him in his captivity like an African king – nay, an African god – if it will secure freedom for ev'ry nigger under the sun, and under grey skies too, for that matter.'

'We chose you, Dinjerous Boy, to hijack the man,' said the man in the red hat, amidst nodding faces. 'We did not choose you to decide. If we wan' you to kill him, you kill him! What's change' yo' tune, bogus boy?'

I was trembling so hard the veil must have been bobbing visibly to the entire room, although no one was interested in me. I was sharing a room with a renegade group of fugitives in a tiny corner of an unimportant district of London, yet here the plans to overthrow the entire remaining centuries-old institution of slavery were being laid down. The secret I had hoped to procure in order to barter with Din for his loyalty was proving larger, more horrific, more noble, than I had ever, ever imagined.

And here Din faltered.

'What's change' yo' mind, for you, hmm? Bin seein' too many pretty ladies, hmm?' A peal of laughter went round the group; some of them looked over at me.

'Leave her out of it,' Din said.

'But you brought her here, Din-din. Did yo' ask? Don't nobody bring no one here without askin'. Who are you, precious girl?' Red hat called over to me. 'Stand up. Let me see your pretty face.'

There was more laughter; I wished I could have pleaded with my eyes to Din to know what to do.

'Leave her, Jon-Jo,' Din commanded.

'You makin' me?'

'Yes I am. The lady will be no trouble. No trouble at all. She's got enough dirty secrets of her own to worry about. It'll be easy for me to keep her quiet.'

'Make sure you see to it, brother. Personally.'

'Oh, an' I will.' He threw one more glance over at me, and with that, the attention shifted away from us, and I exhaled, and Din too, by the look of him. He chewed the skin round his fingers as the conversation turned elsewhere, but he did not look back at me.

I concentrated hard for the rest of the evening, and I learnt a lot. I learnt that it was one thing to leave America if you're black, and quite another to get back in again, and I heard the pros and cons of route A (Cunard, the Great Western, steerage and Ellis Island), versus route B (cargo, trade, contraband and stowing-away). I heard news about sources of funds, timing, different ways to get messages safely to the mostly Quaker families closest to Davis's homestead who had offered their support. Only by listening hard could I forget about myself; slowly, my trembling subsided, and the meeting, too, started to relax. Eventually Din came over, and offered to escort me home.

'You not comin' to the tan-pits, Dinjer Boy?' someone called, but Din shook his head. We climbed the stairs together, knowing that we were leaving something of a stir behind us, and stood outside in the dark.

'Don't take me home. You are going to the Borough.'

'So? You goin' to Lambeth. I will survive the journey; you might not.'

I was grateful, in truth, for it wasn't safe for me. Besides, I knew I needed to explain my presence there, but the questions poured forth as we walked, and I believed my interest compensated for my transgression. I knew nothing, and wanted to know every how, why and wherefore that had brought Din to that dingy basement in Whitechapel.

So he told me, on the long journey back to Lambeth, about the many slave insurrections that had been tried and which had failed, and the difficulty in co-ordinating uprisings across the country. For a full-scale revolution, he told me, a critical mass of insurgents had to be reached: the big ones – Gabriel's Rebellion in 1800, Southampton County in 1831 – were not big enough. They might have raised awareness of the sufferings of slaves, but only served to increase fear of the darkie. He told me too of John Brown, a white man, who nearly succeeded, seizing a hundred thousand muskets and rifles from the arsenal at Harpers Ferry in Virginia just a few years ago, with the intention of galloping south with them to arm every slave he met along the way, but he failed.

'Why? There must be millions of you, Din, enough for several armies.'

'Do you know, ma'am, what slavery does to you? Do you think all slaves are always poised for a rebellion, watchin' an' waitin' for any chance to rise up an' conquer? Liberty's been so long gone now, folks are scared of it. Slavery makes you dependent. It's a drug you're forced to swallow, a drug that lays you low and strips you of all your dignity. If you ain't got dignity, you ain't got nothin' to fight for. There ain't gonna be no wholescale rebellion, only isolated escapes here an' there. You can't tell a man to give up opium once the doctor has made sure of his addiction. You can only destroy all opium around, an' help the addict find something better.'

'So, why are you planning to take someone hostage?' I asked.

'Call it a new approach. It's radical, an' it's simple. Can you imagine white folks allowin' a man like Jefferson Davis to become a martyr, to die at the hands of niggers?'

'They said you changed your mind; said that you wanted murder before.'

'I did, for a while. But now I'm not so sure.' He fell quiet, and I did not know what to say. My body was suffused with some strong feeling for him, and it ached for reciprocity. 'This way, America will be forced to listen; they will rewrite the statute books.'

'Do you really believe that?'

'Yes. And no. Ain' nothin' sure when you've been a slave. But it won't be much longer. I can feel in my bones that a war is imminent. Yet too I wonder if it will ever happen. I promise you now, ma'am, I will die tryin'.'

'I believe you. But I do hope you won't.' Oh, but I curled into myself, for my trite words could not say the half of it.

'It's what I live for, ma'am. Once my mamma died, I had nothing else, except the freedom of my people and their children. It is all I live for. It is how I love.'

Love. We were here at last. He had said the word. I probed him gently. 'I do not understand. How is it how you love?'

'Is love not only sacrifice? Do we not give up those we love, in order to prove to them that they are loved? My mother gave up her freedom for me; I gave up my chance of freedom for her. I only know love for what we lose by it.'

And I was lost myself, for I started to realise then what what I wanted with this man, and knew that I would never have even half of it, and was not sure that I even deserved it.

Eventually I was too tired to ask any more, and he had spoken enough. We sat in each other's silence on the omnibus home, and barely looked at each other. I kept my veil on; it was easier that way. After all, I was meant to be returning from a funeral, and whatever little reputation I might have in the neighbourhood would be lost entirely if I were seen publicly with a black man in the small hours of the morning. But he was my protection too; I was safe from the drunkards, the leering swells, the policemen, the beggars. I did not for a moment think I might be at risk from him.

I put my finger to my lips when we neared the front door of 2, Ivy-street, and motioned to the door of the workshop instead, for we would be less likely to wake the household that way. I pulled the key from my skirts, and put it in the lock, my mind full of the evening and what I had learnt of this man, when I discovered that the door had not been locked. The door had been left open. For how long? And why?

I pushed the door slowly open with my fingertips, and waited on the threshold as my eyes adjusted to the dimness. Din sidled past me, and lit a candle.

No one was there.

Had Jack forgotten to lock up? Unlikely, for such a responsible lad. So what, then? Who? And were they still here, somewhere? We paced round the workshop, with increasing confidence as we discovered no one under the benches, or hiding in the booth, and no disturbances to the work on the tables, or in the presses, or in the crates. Jack's apron was on the peg; his coat was gone. And, most importantly, the new, heavy door was still locked between the workshop and the house, and the only key for it was hanging beneath my skirts.

I pulled it out and unlocked the door, then crept into the kitchen with the candle. Through the gap into the parlour, we could see a dwindling fire flickering its red light onto Peter, who seemed to be sleeping. I tiptoed upstairs: Lucinda was sound asleep in the box-room. I glided downstairs. Din was hovering around the new door, as if unsure whether the potential danger of the situation justified his setting foot in my house for the first time. I motioned to him to go back into the bindery.

'Do you want me to stay?' he whispered once we were out of the house. 'I'll sleep here, on the floor.'

'Yes, I do. But not because I'm scared. Because I don't want you going back to the Borough at this time of night.' I went over and locked the door to the street.

'I can fend for myself.'

'But I'd rather you didn't have to. Be safe; don't put yourself in danger when you can avoid it.' Or is that impossible for you, I wanted to add. I went back into the house and collected some blankets; I handed them to Din at the door of the workshop.

'It won't be too comfortable,' I said.

'I've slept on worse.'

'I'll have to lock you in, but here's the key to the street if you need to get out.'

I decided not to disturb Peter, but stoked the fire to keep him warm; I would be rising in only a few hours, and I would move him into our bed then. It was just as well, for I was wakeful with frets and perturbations: the revelations of the pub basement in Whitechapel, the mystery of the unlocked door, the presence of Din's sleeping body in such close proximity to mine. I slept on my side, with my hands tucked between my thighs for comfort.

I rose at five as usual to start the morning chores before Pansy arrived. Peter was still in his chair, and the fire was low. I picked the blanket off his knees to wrap round him better when he stood, to discover that his legs were cold, like pink-veined marble, such that there was no warming to be had from any blanket. I checked his face. His eyes and mouth were wide open, like a pig's head on the butcher's stand.

'Peter,' I said sternly, as if he were a child playing games with me. 'Peter!'

I did not know when the spirit had left him; had I checked on him properly before turning into bed I might have discovered something then that could have saved him. I grasped his lifeless hands; they caused him no pain at last, and I squeezed them and squeezed them as if they were bellows, as if through them I could breathe new life into him as into the dying fire.

Chapter Sixteen

My father left me three acres of land,
  Sing ivy, sing ivy;
My father left me three acres of land,
  Sing holly, go whistle and ivy.

We kept the curtains closed all the while; Pansy and I washed his body by candle-light, and we patted him dry with towels and finished him off in front of the fire. I shaved his face, and cut a piece of hair from his head, which I tied in a knot and placed in a box on the mantelpiece, where the clock had been before I sold it to Huggitty. But even if we had still had it, I would not have known the time at which I should have stopped it. Pansy said Peter had bid her farewell as she left last night. She also said that Jack had still been in the workshop.

We wrapped him in a sheet and laid him out on the floor under the windowsill. I sent Lucinda to hang Peter's blanket over the mirror in our bedroom, and Pansy out into Ivy-street to tell the neighbours.

'Can I be of service?' Din asked, as he brought his breakfast plate in from the workshop.

Yes, you can hold me through my grief; yes, you can go away and leave me for ever, I wanted to scream both at once. I had not expected so extreme and immediate a punishment for my unnatural urges.

'You may go home, Din. We shall not be working today.'

'As you wish, ma'am.'

'Oh, but Din?'

'Ma'am?'

'Go and tell Jack, won't you? See what's happened to him. Pond Yard, up past the Vinegar Works, by the river. Lizzie, his mother is.'

Jack. The coincidence of his disappearance with Peter's death troubled me. I never doubted the boy his love for my husband; even my suspicious mind did not dare imagine that he might have been in some way responsible for this. But I troubled that there was something further to this than I could see. I fretted that we might find Jack dead today too, for all I knew.

Mrs Eeles passed Din on his way out. She scarcely seemed to see him or me as she hunted round to find where I had hidden my husband.

'He's gorn!' she lamented, clutching her hands at the air. 'Our dearest Peter! Gorn! What a suffering befalls us all before the day of reck'ning! Where is his body?' I gestured to where he lay under the window. 'What, no coffin yet? But least you'll be able to bury him nice,' she added, finally locking my eye, 'what with business and that.'

Oh, I had not thought that far. Of course my Peter could not have a pauper's funeral, but we had not a penny spare.

'You'll be wanting horses with plumes and all, won't you, and mutes, and shall I be coming with you to get your blacks dyed? Black Peter Robinson's we could go to. At least to get some mourning trimmings for that dreadful old frock of yours.'

But then I remembered the finery: I would pawn those impractical brown boots and the cream silk scarf, and the empty hamper, the parasol, the hair comb and fan. They would come in useful after all.

'It's all so expensive,' I said wearily. 'What do you think we'll need? Four or five guineas at least, for a plain burial?'

'A plain burial?' a deep male voice said behind us. 'My finest bookbinder shall have nothing of the sort.'

We turned to find Sir Jocelyn Knightley standing in the front doorway, doffing his hat. 'A plain burial, Dora, for your dear husband?' He held his arms out to me, one hand still holding his distinctive silver cane with the red ball top, but I did not stir. Lucinda came downstairs slowly, clutching Mossie, and eyed him carefully.

'Little Lucinda,' he said. 'I am so sorry, poor child. There are no words.' Then all of a sudden, off the bottom stair, she launched herself at him.

'Don't!' I screamed at her, and at him, but the rogue crouched down and seized her, and she buried herself deeply in his chest. 'Don't,' I repeated, more feebly. I had not imagined I would let him touch her ever again, but I could not stop this.

'There, there, precious girl. Cry all you must. But your mother is dry-eyed. Does she not cry, Lucinda?'

Lucinda shook her head from within his coat.

'I am not afraid of tears, Dora,' he said, looking up at me.

But I had no tears to shed. My chest was crammed with grief, but it would not be released. Besides, I feared that if I started crying I would not stop, and I certainly did not want to give Sir Jocelyn cause to comfort me. Lucinda pulled herself away from him and started to wrap herself in me. I was so wretched with misery I could scarce summon up the requisite loathing for him.

'I heard word,' Sir Jocelyn said, standing up slowly. He pulled himself up on his cane, and pressed into his waist with his other hand: his stab wound, I remembered. 'I came as quickly as I could.'

'Why?' I said, my mouth clenched.

'Why? Theodore – Dr Chisholm – is away in the country shooting, and I am unaware of any physicians of note in Lambeth.' He raised an eyebrow, as if challenging me to dispute him. 'Lucinda, take Mossie, and go and play in your room.' The girl slid from my arms, and obeyed. 'Come, let me see the body.'

I led him over to the window and carefully unwrapped the sheet from Peter's corpse. Sir Jocelyn laid his cane down, and crouched next to him. Mrs Eeles was peering over my shoulder; whatever she thought of me, she was relishing this.

Peter was cold and heavy as stone: more solid, even, than when he had been alive. We watched without flinching as Sir Jocelyn examined him all over, cut him with a scalpel in places, and put a tube down his throat. He asked me many questions as he worked, and I answered frankly, even when it came to his consumption of laudanum. Sir Jocelyn pulled himself up on his cane again, and asked to examine the remaining bottles of Black Drop. He sniffed them, before placing one in his bag.

'I shall issue you now with a certificate of death,' he finally said. 'There is no need for an autopsy, and you would not wish for a coroner's interference, would you?'

'Not if you say so,' I said doubtfully. I could not speak my worries, for Mrs Eeles's presence.

He pulled out a printed form from his bag, sat down at the dining table, and wrote for several minutes. I rolled Peter's body back up in the sheet, while Mrs Eeles watched. Pansy returned, and busied herself in the kitchen.

'Now, you must leave the funeral arrangements to me,' announced Sir Jocelyn.

'But I cannot . . .'

'But of course you can. I insist.'

'Is that really . . . proper?'

'I shall take care of it all. There is to be no argument.'

'Well, Sir Jocelyn, if there's—'

He held up his hand to silence me. 'You have more than enough to worry about, you poor dear girl. I am glad to see you are well supported by your community.' He nodded at Mrs Eeles. 'A finer neighbour than Mrs Damage one cannot hope for.'

Mrs Eeles was in trouble, and making peculiar noises. Clearly she did not quite know where to put herself in the presence of Sir Jocelyn: if she truly thought that I opened my legs to men like these, she was realising now the true perks of the trade. Torn between arch disapproval of my whoring and the thrill of breathing the same air as a full-blooded aristocrat who would even pay for the finest funeral to which she had ever borne witness, she sucked her teeth and fretted her hands. 'Nor a finer tenant,' she eventually affirmed.

'Indeed. Would that they were of your ilk around Berkeley-square, Dora. Now, may I ask, Dora, if it is not too inopportune a moment, if you have given thought to cremation?'

'Oh, merciful Father!' swooned Mrs Eeles, and I feared she might collapse. 'No, no, no!'

'I espouse it as quite the modern thing: it is hygienic, and it hastens the natural process of decomposition. Ashes to ashes, Dora, is considerably quicker than dust to dust.'

'Is it not rather barbaric?' I asked nervously, one eye on Mrs Eeles, who was clearly revising her opinion of the gentleman.

'We can learn from our Eastern brethren in this matter, who consider cremation as the only option in a hot country, and for religious purposes. Not that I am condoning their related practices: I would not wish to see Mr Damage's good widow immolate herself on her husband's funeral pyre!'

'I – I – do not believe it would have been Peter's wish.'

Sir Jocelyn held up his hand. 'I need hear no more. It shall not be.'

Mrs Eeles righted herself, and smiled approbation at me. I realised, having been so long out of her favour, that I did not much prefer being in it either.

Sir Jocelyn packed his bag, collected his silver cane, doffed his hat to us, and left. I hurried after him into the street, as much to escape Mrs Eeles as to air my troubles to Sir

Jocelyn. I checked we were out of earshot of Mrs Eeles, then spoke quietly.

'Sir Jocelyn?' I knew I would never forgive myself if I did not ask.

'Dora.'

'Does it – does it look at all suspicious to you?'

'Suspicious?'

'Like – like – like *murder*?' I barely mouthed the word, but it seemed to echo up the whole street.

Sir Jocelyn paused and seemed to be examining the side of our building before saying, 'Not evidently. There was no blow to the head, no stab in the gut.' Then he dropped his voice and said pointedly, 'But suspicions may be alerted to one who had the inclination and ability to poison him with opium for many months. I doubt you would wish that to come out, Dora?'

'Oh!' I gasped and put my hand to my mouth. 'But I didn't! I didn't!'

'I know, I know,' he soothed hastily. 'But best not to draw attention to the possibility, eh?' Then he kissed me on the forehead, and departed. I rubbed the spot vigorously; he was a swine, and a dangerous one, and I owed him so much – and so little, too.

I went back into the parlour and straightways looked at the certificate he had left on the table. Under 'Cause of death' was written: 'Congestion of the brain and heart: severe rheumatism leading to brain fever and *morbis cordis*.' Would I ever be free of my obligations to this man?

Later that day, Din returned.

'I found Jack's mamma, at home, as you said, but she wouldn't talk to me. She said she'd speak to you about it all, if you would be good enough to come see her. I told her of your misfortune with Peter. She sends condolences, ma'am.'

'Din?'

'Yes, ma'am?'

'You got the impression from her that Jack was still alive, didn't you?'

'Indeed I did, ma'am. Just she would not say where.'

'Should I be troubled, Din?'

He shrugged. I thanked him, and dismissed him until further notice. I could not think of business at a time like this, although I knew I would have to soon. I wondered if I should send the police round to Lizzie's; I banished the thought the moment it entered my brain. Jack was a good boy, that was one thing I could be sure of.

The men in black came to measure Peter that afternoon, and returned with the coffin the following day. Having placed him in it, they covered the box with a fine black pall, which they fixed with bright brass tacks, and moved it into the centre of the parlour, so that there was scarcely any room left to live in. They brought too, much to my embarrassment, a fine black woollen dress, which was soft and warm and fitted me perfectly, along with a new long weeping veil, and a pair of black gloves, all with the compliments of Sir Jocelyn and Lady Knightley. Mrs Eeles was beside herself with wonder and envy, especially as I still had my old veil in my keeping, and owing to her.

The chief undertaker informed me of the details of the funeral, which was fixed for the coming Thursday at Woking, given our convenient proximity to the Necropolitan Railway. I sent telegrams to those of Peter's siblings for whom I had details: his brothers Tommy and Arthur, and his sisters Rosie and Ethel.

'Shall you be attending?' Mrs Eeles asked me anxiously. She had hardly stayed away from the house these last few days, not believing her luck at having a fancy funeral so close to home. 'Hard to say what's best to do, nowadays.' She could not help but stroke the sleeve of my mourning dress, even as I was wearing it.

'What is your opinion, Mrs Eeles?'

'You may think me modern, but I think us women should be there. It might not appear seemly, for us so to sit by the gaping maw of the grave, but we work our hardest getting the poor soul ready for it; why should we be deprived the internment itself? And I will go with you, if you choose, if you wish not to be the only woman there and therefore something of a conspicuousness, if you get my meaning.'

'In truth, Mrs Eeles, if I do not go, who else will?' I sighed. 'I am hoping his brothers will attend, but my father is dead, and so is his. Who of the book trade will attend?' I did not mention Jack, or Din. 'Precious few, I imagine. Peter does not deserve to be put in the clay without witnesses.'

I was glad not to have mentioned these concerns to Sir Jocelyn, or he would have offered to hire extra mourners, no doubt. As it was, thanks to his lordship, Peter got the finest funeral this part of Lambeth had ever seen. The bells started tolling early on Thursday morning for him, and the procession arrived at nine. He got eight horses, each with a black plume, and a shiny hearse adorned with gold scrollwork.

Mrs Eeles, Lucinda and I followed the coffin out of the house, where, to my shock, two mutes were standing on either side of our door, stiffer and more inert than the trees flanking the Knightley's front door in Berkeley-square.

'Hello,' I said to one of them, just to be polite. 'Thank you for coming today.' But their faces stared ahead, as marmoreal as figure-heads on a gravestone, even though the massive crêpe ribbon on their staffs flapped in the wind, and kept hitting their faces.

The pall-bearers lifted the coffin into the hearse, and the three of us followed it to the steps of the station just round the corner. Nora Negley, Patience Bishop, Agatha Marrow and the rest of Ivy-street stood in their door-ways, watching us go past in a silence that I hoped was out of respect. It must have made a good spectacle. Did these good folk of Ivy-street think I had paid for this all out of the proceeds of prostitution, I wondered. Were they mocking me in my grief for my apparently cuckolded husband? I was strangely glad of Mrs Eeles by my side in the face of their stares, torn though I knew she was.

As we ambled, our three blacked heads were sorely outnumbered by the wealth of black plumes nodding to us from all corners of the hearse and on the heads of each horse. But we were joined at the Church of England platform by Din, and by our former journeyman Sven Ulrich, who squeezed my hand tenderly and offered me sweet words of sympathy, and by Peter's older brother Tommy. Arthur, he said, could not get leave from the Church. It struck me that I had possibly caused offence by not asking him to take the service; I did not think to be offended that he had not offered.

There were three classes – First, Second and Third – for both the living and the dead – and we were in Second. Peter would have approved of the middle way; Sir Jocelyn was a clever man. He did not attend, despite having borne the cost, although I was relieved in part. However, just as Peter's coffin was being loaded onto the hearse car, Mr Diprose turned up and breezed into the passenger carriage with us, fresh from prison, and with a notable spring in his step. He uttered the usual words of condolence, only in French.

The person who was most conspicuous by his absence was Jack, dear Jack, who had worked for Peter for six years. Jack, who hadn't seen his father since he was eleven, and who treated Peter as a respectful son would a father. How could Jack miss this day? Jack was not playing truant; something bad must have happened to him. My gut ached as I thought of him, and I still could not help but wonder what his disappearance might have to do with my husband lying cold in his box. I felt for him like a mother for a son; I clutched Lucinda's hand tightly, and wondered at this pomp and ceremony for our dear departed, when there are people left behind in this life who are suffering and abandoned. I looked at the fields and trees flashing past the windows of the train, and wondered who this was all for, really, who we were trying to console with such funereal ostentation. Even Peter, I would wager, would have disapproved if it had been bestowed on anyone else. I felt removed from the outward display, from the vanity of it all; my grief bore inward. I did not wish to show my pain to the good folk of Ivy-street and get their approval for it. I wished to suffer it alone, and know the knife-edges of grief, and guilt, and not have them appeased by my neighbours' self-satisfied nods, or the clutches of Mrs Eeles's hands.

We arrived at Brookwood an hour later, where we received a simple, short service in the chapel. When we drifted out again, it felt only natural that Mrs Eeles, Lucinda and I lead the pitiful handful of mourners through the avenue of birch trees to the graveside, and not an eyebrow was raised at our sex. I was glad to be seeing where Peter would be laid to rest, and that it was proper. Brookwood was indeed a splendid place: everyone got a plot to themselves, even if one was in Third Class, and there were plenty of watchmen and high gates and fences. I knew he would be safe here. Burke and Hare might have been relegated to the role of bogeymen with the passage of time, but resurrection men still stalked the pages of our newspapers, and our nightmares. I did not want my husband dissected, even by the likes of Sir Jocelyn Knightley. Strange to think that so fine a physician could only become so by chopping up dead, possibly snatched, bodies, but such was the way of the world. Strange, too, the thoughts that wander through one's head on the way through the quiet eeriness of the cemetery; I tried to shake the vision of Sir Jocelyn's knife penetrating Peter's cold flesh as we approached his graveside.

To distract me I looked up at the clouds, and the slender, leafless birch trees flexing in the wind; even grief and the severity of the occasion did not prevent my work-addled mind from perceiving the trees as giant whips, flexing in the wind as if the clouds themselves were fluffy bottoms waiting excitedly for flagellant attention. I lodged the image in the recesses of my filthy brain, with intentions to inset a watercolour on vellum of this very row of birch trees topped by fluffy, *derrière*-like clouds, into the morocco binding of my next whipping-themed commission. For this was how my mind worked now: I could not see nettles growing in the hedgerows without thinking of whipped fundaments, could not hear of a nunnery without thinking of a group of cats licking each other as if they were bowls of milk, of the Irish without thinking of their antics in the sheep-fields, and, worst of all, of the Italians without thinking of corpse profanation, which of course brought me back to the cemetery at Woking, and the interment of my poor Peter, whose body was just now descending into its pit. Earth was shovelled back over the coffin, until I could no longer see it. I rubbed my hands together to keep them warm, and felt my fingers through my black gloves and the place where my wedding ring should have been.

'Wery sowwy, Mrs Damage.' It was Skinner, at my elbow, leering at me, with a thick-set, squat man by his side, like a mastiff, whom I presumed was Mr Blades.

'That a man could pass on without settling 'is debts in this lifetime is indeed a twagedy,' said Skinner.

'Oh, a twagedy,' echoed Blades.

''Is debts are now yours, madam. Wha' a legacy.'

'Wha' a legacy,' came the echo again.

'They always were, Mr Skinner. Good day to you, Mr Blades.'

'My lady.' The mastiff touched his cap and grinned; he lacked his front teeth, but his canines on either side were sharp and brown.

'Yeees,' Skinner said with gratification. 'I 'ear business is booming. Just as well your 'usband agreed to step up the repayment schedule afore 'e died.' He thrust a paper up into my face as I grabbed Lucinda's hand and stalked round to the other side of the grave. I did not see them merge back into the the trees and gravestones, but heard Skinner's voice like a ghost chasing me, 'Lookee 'ere, it's in 'is own 'and. In 'is own 'and . . .'

Chapter Seventeen

I saw a ship a-sailing,
A-sailing on the sea,
And oh, but it was laden,
With pretty things for thee!
There were comfits in the cabin,
And apples in the hold;
The sails were made of silk,
And the masts were all of gold . . .

Christmas crept up on us unawares after Peter died. It was just another trouble to add to the empty tea-caddy: the worry about Jack, Skinner's threats, the chores, the battles of getting fires going on freezing mornings, the coaxing dry of frozen washing, and the cold fingers of grief and loss that gripped my heart and stole it of all sensation. I wondered if I should start work again in the bindery, even just to pay the butcher's bill for Christmas, but there was, in truth, little to do, which troubled me too. I kept meaning to return my old veil to Mrs Eeles, but put it off for fear that she would ask me not only for the current rent but also for the two months' rent the veil initially bought me. No doubt she would have strong opinions about my returning to work, given that I was meant to be in mourning for a year and a month. A man who had lost his wife would be expected to mourn for a month, for it would be assumed that he would need to get back to work. But what of a widow who needed to do the same?

But I could not avoid her for ever, and on Christmas Eve

she came knocking on my door with false concern and a breezy smile, just to ask how I was getting on.

'Well enough, thank you.' I did not want to invite her in, but it was cold out on the door-step. 'Oh, Mrs Eeles, I must give you back the veil I borrowed,' I said, quickly, meaning to hand it over and send her on her way before she could settle herself down.

'Oh, no matter, dearie,' she said casually, pushing her way into the house. 'It's always handy to have a spare one.' But as I was closing the door behind her, we heard the noise of a carriage rattling into Ivy-street; Sir Jocelyn's brougham lumbered towards us, patterned with frost, and stopped outside the bindery. The gentleman was not within, but his driver started to unload first one tea-chest, then another, and then a third and a fourth, while I unlocked the door to the workshop.

'Excuse me, Mrs Eeles. I wasn't expecting a delivery.' She folded her arms as I rummaged for the key in my skirts. 'Books?' I asked the boy, but he shrugged his shoulders.

'Not this one, anyway,' he added, as he pulled a large, narrow, rectangular box out of the interior.

'Is that,' Mrs Eeles started to say, stumbling towards us, visibly disturbed, 'that isn't, is that, could it be, a corset box?' Her voice reached a shriek.

'A corset! No, it can't be,' I remonstrated, but I could not deny that it was distinctly of the right shape. That, and the fact that it said, 'Elegant Line Corsets' on the top, with a picture of the back of a woman, hair piled up on top of her head, admiring her elegant line in the glass, in which her frontal glories were fully reflected. 'Hygienic and comfortable', the box declared.

'A corset!' Mrs Eeles repeated, in horror. 'Well, I never knew the like!'

'But I don't want it, Mrs Eeles,' I protested. 'I don't want it,' I said to the boy. 'Really, I don't.' I thought quickly, to counter her shock and disapproval. 'If it is one, Mrs Eeles, would you like it? You can have it, in lieu of rent.'

Mrs Eeles's nose wrinkled slightly as she leant forward to inspect the box closer. 'Is it a mourning corset?' she asked, tentatively.

'Are there such things?'

'I read of one once. All trimmed in black and edged in black satin. Why, even the stitching was black silk. It must have been quite a sight to see.'

'Well, I'm sure it must be, given that everyone knows that I am in mourning.'

I opened the box carefully. Unfortunately for us both, it was a simple ivory corset, with a cuirasse-bodice, trimmed with lavender lace. I hastily put the lid back on.

'Just give me the money, then,' Mrs Eeles snapped. 'I need the last two months by Christmas,' she called over her shoulder as she stamped her cold feet back up Ivy-street.

At least I would get a pretty penny for it at the pawn-shop, I rued, as the boy ascended the carriage and trundled away. I settled down to the boxes in the bindery, in the hope that their contents would prove to be more practical. With the claw of a hammer, I levered out the nails of the first, and prised off the lid. I did not want to see vile catalogues. I put a hand inside and pulled off the straw padding, hardly daring to look. My hand reached first a bottle, and then another, and then some more: in total, six bottles of fine wine and two bottles of port. In the middle was a vast, warm lump wrapped in hemp wadding. I pulled back the hemp, and tore through the wax paper. It was a goose, and it had been roasted. The thoughtfulness of my benefactor extended even to the details; he had realised my range would never fit a goose inside. I found its cavity: it had been stuffed, too.

The other crate contained a ham, a Stilton in an earthenware pot, a mature Cheddar in a tawny rind, some fat Muscatel raisins, a jar of figs in syrup, a box of honeyed dates stuffed with almonds, a tin of candied lemons, oranges, pineapples, plums, and some fresh winter pears, Ribston pippins, grapes, and pomegranates.

'For Lucinda', read the tag of a parcel, which I placed down carefully on the floor. For her also were several brown packets of bromide.

'For the able apprentice Master Jack Tapster', was a bottle of single-estate whisky.

'For the maid of all work, Pansy Smith', was a new bonnet, with blue ribbons.

For Din, there was nothing, but that was of no surprise.

And for me, was a sumptuous, brown silk dress, the colour of caramel, and of my boots. It had cream petticoats, and a central black rose at the bust-line, with pleated sleeves and cream lace edging.

Unlabelled, but I presumed for me too, was a small cardboard box, containing something I would not have been able to recognise even six months ago. Due to my rapid education in such matters, I was able to work out (within only a few minutes, at least) that they had a contraceptive function (the words '*Ballons baudruches*' on the side of the box would have given it away to a Frenchman, who would have needed less help than I in their recognition anyway). I had never seen them before, given that they cost over a pound each, and were only available to those with connections. I could not help but be shocked. Sexual relations whilst in mourning was as bad as, if not worse than, actual adultery. I would not be unfaithful to Peter's memory. Noble Savages indeed.

And finally, there was a book, bound in full aquamarine morocco by Zaehnsdorf himself, with marbled endpapers, entitled *A History of British Birds, Indigenous and Migratory*, by William MacGillivray. It bore an inscription on the ivory endpaper:

To Mrs Dora Damage,
a fine and rare species,
with respect at Christmas time,
Valentine G.

I ran to get Lucinda and Pansy, to show them the sight; it was as if Christmas in some fine town-house had come to pass on the workshop floor.

'For the love of – !' Pansy said, as I gave her the bonnet.

'And this is for you, Lou,' I said, giving her the parcel.

'For me? Who's it from?'

But I could not answer her as she pulled the paper off, to reveal a pretty doll's tea-set, with a tea-pot, coffee-pot, milk-jug, sugar-bowl, and four cups and saucers, all painted with violets and forget-me-nots.

'Mossie's got to have some!' she said, breathless with delight, and raced off to find her doll. When she returned, she blithely invited Mossie to tea, and together they poured and drank, and made polite talk that was as one-sided as my tea with Lady Knightley.

Pansy was at the looking-glass trying on her bonnet while I busied myself with the other crate. It was full, as I had both hoped and feared, of unbound manuscripts. I wished that Jack could have been with me, to investigate their contents first. I took out the top one, and opened it. It was reasonably benign, as were the subsequent ones. Also included were three Bibles, and a letter from Bennett Pizzy requesting more pretty albums and fancy journals: 'your superfluous nonsenses have proved irresistible to ladies and their menfolk', he wrote.

So it seemed that Damage's was back in business, and back to normal, if normal is what one could call it. I wondered again at this absurd world I had found myself in; a world in which my patrons bought me mourning finery, and yet knew I would have to continue working as if I were not in mourning; a world in which my neighbours expected me to behave like a widow, but knew I would behave like a widower. It was, as always, about a woman's visibility. I would walk the streets in my mourning attire as a woman, but at home, behind closed doors, I would work like a man.

Wedged down the side of the crate, I found a large manila envelope. I prised apart the seal, and reached inside, where I found papers, a great many of them, all identical, longer than my hand, black ink on white paper. The words 'Bank of England' in an elaborate typeface, were printed across the centre of the notes, and the portrait of Britannia was in the top left corner. It promised to pay the bearer on demand the sum of five pounds. I had never seen paper money before; it seemed as unreal as the photographs had become to me, or as real. Eighty fivers. Four hundred pounds.

I pulled out the accounts book and totted up what I was owed. It was all there, for all the work I had ever done for Diprose, and for the contents of this new crate at least. It would pay off my debts with Skinner and Blades completely. It was a fortune.

First I went to Mrs Eeles, and handed her over three of the precious fivers with a 'Merry Christmas' and a smile as sweet as sherbet, and did not look back to see her face as I hurried out of Ivy-street. Then I went to the pawn-shop and redeemed my wedding ring, and enquired as to where I might find Messrs Skinner and Blades. A further couple of hours was spent traipsing from gin-shop to petty sessional court, bottle-shop to auction-house, knocking on all manner of seedy doors and asking of a great many harassed and worn folk until I found Skinner, who offered to relieve me of the money there and then, only I insisted so on a solicitor, and although it were Christmas Eve we finally found one of good note, and the matter was settled for ever with a counting out of my precious papers and a flourish of his pen.

It was fair to say my feet were sore but my spirits somewhat lighter when Din came by that evening to find out how I was faring, and when I would be opening the bindery again for business. I took him to the drinking-house on the corner that evening. It was Christmas Eve, after all, when otherwise respectable people could drink here without a stain on their character, even a woman in mourning, and we stood amongst the husbands with their wives, the legal clerks and the tradesmen, amidst the cries for porter and juniper, ale and stout, and the exhortations to 'sluice your gobs, for it's Christmas after all'; and we drank awhile and I pondered my peculiar fortune.

'Come and dine with Lucinda and me tomorrow, Din,' I asked him as he escorted me back home. The festivities were passing me by – the strolling carollers with their black lanterns, the brass bands bedecked with holly, fir and laurel, the cries of 'mistletoe' from the little girl-sellers, the crowds still pouring into the poulterer's, the butcher's, the grocer's, the itinerant vendors with scrawny little ducks and geese still alive, albeit barely, pecking at the meagre grains in the mud – and I felt the need to spend the day itself with people about whom I cared. I bought a ha'pennyworth of mistletoe, then I stopped at one of the penny-toy men, and bought a handful of tin soldiers, several pairs of brightly coloured knitted gloves, and a mouth-organ. At another one, I bought a box of paints and a paintbrush, and a monkey whose arms and legs leapt in the air when one put one's thumb into the base.

But Din shook his head, and said that he had other plans; but beyond spending the day with those I had seen in the basement of the pub in Whitechapel, eating roast beef at the Christian alms-house, I could not imagine what they could be. So I sent him home with a side of goose, some ham and cheese, a bottle of wine, and fruit. Then I handed him the gloves and the mouth-organ I'd bought from the pedlar. 'And this,' I said, as I put an envelope in his top pocket, 'is your Christmas bonus.'

'Thank you ma'am,' he said, and turned to leave me.

'Ain't you going to give me a kiss under the mistletoe, then?' I said in my best Cockney. A little sprig was drooping meekly from my hand.

He took it from me, raised it over my head, and gave me a little peck on the cheek. 'Have a fine Christmas now, won't you?'

'And give your friends my thoughts for the season,' I called to his departing back, and watched as he lifted his hand from his parcels, and waved his farewell.

We are bound to be happy at Christmas, whether we feel it or not. People exhort it of us several times a minute, and being a good girl, and one always to do what I am told, I felt it insolent to defy them. Yet neither was I relinquished from the need for cheer by dint of my widowhood: too much pity galls, like too much rain.

Din left me to a warm house at least, filled with unexpected fineries. Pansy had tucked Lucinda up in bed, clutching Mossie to her breast. I pressed the soldiers and some more gloves into Pansy's hands, and sent her home in her new bonnet with another envelope of money and some more victuals from the crates. Then I drifted around the parlour, alone. I thought several times of going into the workshop and starting on the newly arrived manuscripts, out of force of habit, and something to do.

This loneliness is only to be expected, I tried to console myself, what with my husband so recently passed away. Only I knew I was not missing Peter at all. This was a different kind of vacancy. I was richer than I had ever dared dream, and yet I felt bereft and alone to my core, and it was not an obvious bereavement.

I thought of Din, and the way I got him to kiss me, and what a chaste little kiss it was. I was ashamed of myself. Our minds keep secrets even from ourselves. Had it really been so obvious to those at Holywell-street? How had they found me out, when I was still denying it to myself? But now that I lacked the pressures of survival to keep my real feelings at bay and a man in the Windsor chair – even a sick man who needed nursing like a baby – Din's absence came crashing in.

I had to work, I decided, just to blot out these worrying revelations bursting inside me like fireworks. I headed for the new crate, trying not to look at the sewing-frame where he used to sit. But I could not help myself. I ran my fingers along the wood; I picked up a needle. I tried to remember the gentle words we used to exchange right here. I craved him; now my belly was filled, I could feel it all the more. It was a different kind of hunger.

I tore myself away from the frame, pulled out a manuscript from the crate, and scanned it to see what treatment it required. Oh, but it was revolting, too. Revolting, yet deeply sad; poignantly paradoxical, that such literature described the most intimate thing we could do with another person (or admittedly, people), in the least human of terms. There were no people in these books, really; only parts. The stories weren't about union with another at all; they were about individual fantasies, self-serving indulgences. They weren't generous or free-spirited or embracing; they sought to exclude, to diminish and dominate. There was no pleasure, unless it was denied to some as much as it was enjoyed by others. And, as my existence was founded on my complicity with the production of these texts, what hope for the satisfying emotional life I so craved? You can only have half of what you desire, my mother would say; and if financial security was the half I was being granted, my emotional self needed excising.

In the morning, as the parish bells rang and the roads teemed with parishioners who were better dressed than usual, I tried on my new brown dress, even though it would be a year yet before I could go into half-mourning and wear it. I took off my cap and cuffs, then slipped out of my smock and chemise. I would not try the corset; the dress was enough of a novelty for one day. I pulled it on, and reached behind myself. With various configurations of arms up over my shoulder and under round my waist, I was able to do up enough of the fastenings to see how the dress became me. I pulled the blanket off the Psyche in the corner of the room, and although I could scarcely see my reflection through the dust on the glass, it was enough to make me shriek with alarm.

'What is it, Mama?' Lucinda came running, tea-cup in one hand and Mossie in the other. 'Oh! You look – beautiful! Mama! Here, let me help you.'

Beautiful? Is that how I looked? My neck, shoulders and even all the way down to the rising curve of my tiny breasts were completely exposed. Aristocratic women might have presented such splendid *décolleté* every evening, and in front of gentlemen too, but I had never felt so undressed. Beautiful? Bony and scrawny, like a sad old chicken, more like.

'Mama, look at the blisters on your hands,' Lucinda said. The finery of the dress threw up my imperfections as my smock never would. 'Your shoulders are hunched. Ah, now you are holding them back, like a proper lady. You should wear this all the time. You look ten feet taller!'

I seized the black-and-purple feather fan, and held it in front of the lower part of my face, with only my eyes peeping over, and my arm crossed my body to cover my neck and breasts. But such a presentation only served to hint more at the nakedness beneath. I tried to look only at the dress, and ignore the flesh rising above it. It was designed to be worn over a corset, the way its curves flexed, but even without a corset I could not deny that my waist looked good in it.

I threw the blanket back over the glass, and in agitation paced over to the window, from where I could see the merry-makers on their way to church. They were not the habitual faces of Ivy-street; people were passing this way for a festive change, or had come up to visit family for the day. My eye was drawn to a group of men waiting for their slower companions. Some of them were smoking; they all looked proudly awkward in their Sunday best, stiff and unfamiliar, and not-quite-gentlemanly. One of them – a tall, handsome fellow on the edge of the group – saw me looking, and returned my gaze, which I held likewise. I felt I could stay there for ever, until I realised that someone might stop and look where he was looking, and see me, and judge me for a brazen hussy. I left the window sharply, and came back to Lucinda, but his eyes were still in mine.

I am no longer waiting for my life to begin, I thought, before being seized with a vast sense of abhorrence at myself. A woman in mourning, indeed. I fiddled at the fastenings down my back, and barked at Lucinda to help me, and only felt a lightening when the silk cascaded down to my ankles. I took my chemise and my black dress from the peg, and wriggled into them, my new old skin. I pinned up my hair and pulled on my veil, and my old worn boots, and seized Lucinda's hand, and headed out of the house to join the throngs of church-goers.

I sang the hymns with gusto, as if volume would drown out the rising confusion in my breast, listened intently to the Christmas sermon, nodded at the urgings to charity, and rested my eyes on the evergreen boughs bedecking every arch, window and ledge, as if they might provide me with something on which I could ground my shaky sense of self. I scarcely noticed that my 'Merry Christmas's to Mrs Eeles and Billy, Nora Negley and husband, Patience Bishop and her two sons and their wives and children, and Agatha Marrow and countless relatives, were all shunned or met with frost and pursed lips. For nothing seemed regular to me today. I had not recognised the face that stared back at me from behind the fan in the Psyche. Who was this terrible woman, I kept thinking, who dishonoured her sex, and betrayed her deceased husband and invalid child, by abandoning her position as the refuge, the balm, the angel in the house? I, who had once been a kept wife, was now an enterprising businesswoman, yet my business was illegal, immoral, and disrespectful to women, and any sense of freedom I was feeling at being the bread-winner was skilfully negated by the inescapable traps constructed by the *obsceniteurs*, which bound me inexorably to them through their knowledge of Lucinda's condition and my ambiguous status. At least I no longer had the challenge of finding a way to bind Din to both me and them, but it was not a finding I wished to share with them.

Furthermore, I was not a lady, although I was being dressed like one, at the behest of the richest *roués* of London town; I felt no shame at flirting with a strange man wandering through Waterloo on Christmas morning, and was finding myself drawn to a mysterious, and black, former slave. The Noble Savages must have been having a good laugh at my expense, as if I were some botched Galatea. I knew full well that the rest of the upper ten thousand wouldn't look at me for a fraction of a second, so why should Knightley and Glidewell take such interest in me, and dress me so? I was further away from the ladies these men sojourned with than the wilds of Africa, and far less interesting. The thought of who I became when I put on that brown dress appalled me.

But, I thought, as I sang praises for the birth of our Saviour, I would not be vanquished by what was also feeding me. We best seek the resurrection, not the tomb, I reminded myself, although I would not try telling that to Mrs Eeles.

I did not hurry home after the service; on this sacred day, I felt that my house was more than ever an unholy temple of vice and vanity. Savonarola would have rampaged through it: not only the crates of books that lined every wall, but also my fine dress, my corset, the luxuries that were strewn across every room while I wondered where to put them. Savonarola burnt everything – not just books and art, but mirrors, cosmetics, dresses – and in the end, he was burnt too. Burn or be burnt; what we think we are choosing comes back on us in ways we cannot imagine.

Lucinda and I warmed the goose and stuffing, roasted some potatoes, cooked some carrots and parsnips, and opened a bottle of wine, and as we sat around the table, we managed to make merry. It was a warm place to be, and in so many ways a safer, prouder day than last Christmas, despite our poor dear Peter. But we couldn't help but laugh as I told Lucinda about our first Christmas in Ivy-street, when Patience Bishop had just been bereaved, and we took her round some meat and dumplings, and Nora Negley had drunk too much gin and wouldn't stop singing 'Lipey Solomons, the Honest Jew Pedlar', and Mrs Eeles kissed Peter under the mistletoe. Lucinda was laughing so much she got hiccoughs, so I poured the dregs of the wine into her little tea-set, and I let her have a few sips, and we tickled each other and sleepily sang Christmas carols, until I took her to bed with her protestations that it had been the best Christmas ever, although she hoped the ghost of her papa would not hear her say that from down the line at Woking.

The brown dress lying on the bed mocked me. Little Miss Jackie Jump-Up, it teased, as I folded it up and laid it in the ottoman, in the space left by my weeping-veil. Think yourself the lady, do you? And even when you are out of full mourning, when, now that you are banned from Holywell-street and confined to the workshop and home, do you think you will possibly wear me?

Once the house was still, I was left alone with my emptiness – which I wanted to be filled only by one man – and my compulsion to work to fill the space instead. I went to the workshop, lit a solitary candle, and worked until midnight.

Boxing Day brought the usual procession of dustmen, watermen, grocers' boys, post-boys, coalmen, and lamp-lighters all begging their Christmas boxes, and I was glad not to have to turn even one away. And after lunch on the twenty-seventh, when Pansy and Din were busy at their work once more, I left Lucinda playing in the parlour, gathered my shawl and veil, and finally set off to find Jack's mother.

Without a single look at the sharp eyes glinting at me from behind windows and door-curtains, I walked north-east, towards the river. I wondered if this was the route Din had taken when I sent him to find out what had happened to Jack the day Peter died. I tried to think of my dear husband, but, cruelly, my thoughts kept wandering back to Din, Din here in these streets, Din here on my cheek, until eventually I came to 13a Howley Place, as Din would have done, and saw these same squat little houses with broken windows and paintwork that had peeled so much one could scarce tell what the original colour had been. There were ragamuffins sitting outside these houses in the street. The door to Lizzie's home was wide open despite the cold, so I called inside.

Out from the shadows came a wizened and pinched woman, like a thread of grey dust that had been wafted upright by a breeze. Her eyes were sad and sunken; everything about her was meagre.

'I wondered when you'd come,' she said, as I lifted my veil. Her lack of teeth was only revealed when she spoke, for she never smiled. 'Should've gone and told you meself,' she said. 'But it's been busy, with the little ones, and Jack gone and lost us his money. Cou'n't tell the darkie, no matter what Jack said about him. Cou'n't bring meself to.'

'That's all right, Lizzie. I'm sorry it's taken me so long. It's not that I didn't care – I've been worried sick – but I haven't had a moment, what with Peter dying so sudden and . . .'

'I'm ever so sorry about that.'

'Thank you. It was strange, not having Jack at the funeral. Is he in trouble?'

'Come in. I'll tell ya all about it.'

She led me inside, into a room that had scarcely any plaster left on the walls, and that smelt of rotting floor-boards, rising damp, and decay. A dozen bright eyes peered from the stairs from dirty little faces, most no bigger than

Lucinda, although I knew some were older. There was one chair in the room, and two little three-legged stools.

'Sit down,' Lizzie said to me.

'No, you have the chair, Lizzie. You look weary.'

We both remained standing in the end. The floor was so uneven, due to sinking walls, I felt like a sailor in need of my sea-legs. 'So tell me, Lizzie.'

'We didn't know it ourselves for a while. Should've seen the signs. Should've. Good thing Dan isn't 'ere no more, 'e'd have brained 'im, straight off. Dan would've killed that boy, I'm tellin' ya. That's summink to be grateful for, I s'pose.'

'Why would he have killed him? What's he done?'

'That night, when he left yours. He was arrested, right on the door-step.'

'On what charge?'

'Ugh, Mrs D, that's where it 'its 'ard.'

'Has he gone down for it, whatever it was?'

'Hasn't gone to trial, yet, but 'e ain't got a hope. Ten years, I've bin told. Ten years, 'e's gonna get.'

'Do you mind if I ask you what for?'

She sighed deeply, as if what she was about to say might kill her off finally, and slowly and heavily raised the middle finger of her left hand, which she curled upwards, and then made a sudden jerking movement upward with it. And then I knew, without any doubt, and years of not knowing all flooded with meaning.

Peccatum illud horribile, inter Christianos non nominandum, as I had read in a thousand texts.

'Ten years!'

'Ten years. Still, could've been worse. If it'd been a year ago 'e would've been 'ung!' Her voice was rising, and her hands lifted like shabby angels' wings, as if for all the world she were about to ascend to reach her maker, along with her voice.

'No, Lizzie, they wouldn't have done, I promise you.' I

grabbed her arms and brought them down again, and held her hands to my chest.

''Swot I was told by the Shiv,' she said.

'Who's he?'

'The knife sharpener,' she said, as if that proved it.

'Lizzie, yes, in theory, yes, he's right. They repealed the death penalty for – for – that crime only last year. But they haven't hung anyone for it since the thirties. Trust me, I know these things. It's in the books,' I said, then added hastily, 'I mean, the books Peter used to bind, when he worked for the Parliament, him and Jack. Don't you be troubling your head any further with these things. Ten years, it's better than the noose. Console yourself with that, Lizzie.'

I sank her down onto the chair at last, and looked around at the misery surrounding her, to see if I could find something to wrap around her.

'What do you need?' I asked, but I knew there could be no real answer to that. She was beyond tears, and sat numb in her shock.

'Can I visit him, Lizzie?' I asked. 'Where is he?'

But she shook her head. ''E don' want no visitors, ever, 'e said as much.'

'I'll bring his wages round next week,' I said quietly, then I squeezed her hand and got up to leave. Three little children, all with Jack's red hair, stood in my way.

'Are you gonna bring Jack back?' one of them asked me.

'I wish I could, little one,' I said.

'Cos Mama needs him,' another piped up.

'An' he owes me money,' the third said.

'Clear orf, all of ya,' Lizzie shouted, her last burst of action before she slumped down over the back of the chair like she was dead. 'You can get me some gin, if you really want to help,' she uttered miserably, like a guttering candle, as I left.

I cursed my empty head all the way home for not realising. All that time I'd known Jack, and I had chosen not to read the signs. His lack of care for a sweetheart. His embarrassment at so much of the literature we worked on; and his lack of it for others. And, just as when one has recently been bereaved one starts to see crêpe and jet everywhere one turns, I started to see them everywhere, and realised what I had been over-looking. The boys in sailors' uniforms along the Strand. The post-boys in Holywell-street. Mary-Annes, all of them. Mandrakes. Inverts. Bin-dogs. Sodomites.

Was I disgusted? A year I ago I might have been. A year ago I might not have struggled so hard to understand. Little Jack. He was such a loving, good-hearted boy. Jack and his furtive, secret little life. No, I was not disgusted. Ashamed to say, I was somewhat relieved: relieved that it had only been coincidence that had seen his arrest fall on the same night as Peter's departure from this world. Possibly Peter had witnessed it, and heard the charge being spoken to his apprentice. Peter would have been more than disgusted; he would have been sickened to the core. Possibly that was what tipped him over the edge, into his last bottle of laudanum and onwards along the final journey to his Maker. It would not have surprised me in the slightest.

And as I saw Peter's outraged face, I saw Lizzie again in my eye, crushed by her sense of betrayal, wounding herself over and over by his insult. Mother, I reject your sex, and choose for myself my own.

I met his father, Dan, at the beginning, when they signed Jack's indenture, shortly before he ran off that night after the prize-fight when he pocketed ten pounds. Some say he went to sea. Some say he had another wife in Glasgow, where he lived now. I remember he moved heavily and slowly, like someone who had accumulated grudges since the moment his mother yanked him off her tired breast. A blacksmith, he was, before he turned to the drink, a rough old man, who beat little Jack with iron rods, and threatened to brand him with bars out of the forge, and despaired of him, his lean, wiry scrap of a lad who showed no signs of following his father into the blacksmith's trade. Jack was the only one in their family who could read, and he taught himself entirely from the newspapers he collected from the streets. It was a while before Dan accepted he wasn't going to toughen up his boy through hitting him, that it only sent him off into the corner where the newspapers were stacked, and slowly, Dan and Lizzie's hopes and aspirations developed for him. They grew to encourage his bookishness; they scrimped and saved for his meagre education. Dan came home one night with two books he had proudly nicked from some men in the pub for his lad. One was Shelley's *Prometheus Unbound* (had Dan known it was poetry, he might have taken it back); the other was the 1844 Report of the Metropolitan Commissioners in Lunacy, which didn't tell Jack anything he hadn't already learnt from life by the river, and boosted his confidence in his own intellectual capacity. When they finally signed the indenture for his apprenticeship at Damage's, I remember thinking that Lizzie's heart would burst with pride. Jack would not have to go and work in the blacking warehouse, or on the river; Jack was the great hope for the family.

Poor child. It was a wonder he had survived in Lambeth as long as he had.

Chapter Eighteen

Bye, O my baby,
When I was a lady,
O then my baby didn't cry;
But my baby is weeping
For want of good keeping,
O I fear my poor baby will die.

There was a woman, or a lady, I should have said, waiting for me on the door-step when I returned from Lizzie's house. It was dark already, but I could see in the gloom someone wearing a bonnet that jutted up above her head like a spoon, with pale feather trimmings inside, as if the top of her head were a chick hatching from an egg. The bavolet behind was long and cream-coloured, and around her shoulders was a three-quarter-length dark-grey hooded cloak of softest cashmere. Beneath it was another shawl, this time of fine Chantilly lace, and underneath it a large bundle of lace and silk. Her face was more pinched and her brow more furrowed than when I first saw her, but it was clearly the face of Lady Knightley, like a star that had fallen from heaven, and was troubling itself in the worry of how it could possibly get back up there.

She did not seem to see me, but stood on the pavement, eyes glazed, with several brown leather cases around her feet. She can't have knocked, I thought, or Pansy would have brought her inside by now. Then the crying started from within the bundle of lace at Lady Knightley's front, and I knew without thinking that I had to get her off the streets and into the warm.

'Lady Knightley, what a pleasure. Please, come in.'

But she made no move, and the crying escalated.

'Come in, now.' The fog and darkness were too great for us to be seen from Mrs Eeles's house, but she would soon hear this racket, and be sending Billy off to Holywell-street, or indeed, Berkeley-square. But still she stood, and I started to panic. 'Please, move quickly, now.' I grabbed her arm more forcibly than I had intended, and she leapt at the touch and darted past me into the house.

I ushered her and her screaming bundle away from the windows into the kitchen, where Pansy was cooking griddle-cakes. I pulled the Windsor chair in from the parlour, and waited for Lady Knightley to settle herself gingerly into it. Slowly, as if unaccustomed to such an action, she unfurled a tiny baby from the yards of lace; he was purple in the face. Once free from his swaddles, Lady Knightley held him up at arm's length, and watched him cry. I did not know if she were proffering him to me, or what, but her face betrayed one who was utterly spent, and that always meant danger to a little one. Lucinda cowered behind me.

I saw Lady Knightley's lips murmur something which I couldn't hear, and then, over the din, she shouted, 'For God's sake, take him!'

So I did, and cradled him in my arms, and he was startled into silence for a moment.

'What's the matter with him?' I asked. 'Is he hungry?'

'How would I know?' she snapped at me, and he started to cry once more.

I wiped my little finger on my smock and curled it into his mouth. He sucked frantically on it for a moment, then pulled off in disgust and rage, and howled worse than before. He scrunched his fists and eyes in fury, and opened his mouth wide, his tongue tensing along the length of each scream between snatched breaths, and I wondered at how a being could come into the world with such a quantity of rage.

''Ere, take it, get this dahn him.' Out of nowhere, Pansy was brandishing a bowl which looked as though it held milk with bread crumbled into it. 'I ain't 'ad time to warm it, but don't matter. Get it dahn 'im.'

I perched on the rickety stool, and held the baby as still as I could, while Pansy gently spooned the pap into his mouth. Lucinda scrutinised her every move. At first he gagged, but some dribbled to the back of his mouth, although much went down his cheeks and into the collars of his fine lawn smock. I looked over at Lady Knightley, who didn't seem to care; her head was resting in the crook of her arm, and I could not see her face.

'This can't be the best stuff for him,' I said to Pansy. 'Lady Knightley, what do you normally give him?'

She looked up at me with a vapid gaze. 'What?'

'The baby. What are you feeding him?'

'Are you asking me? Ask Fatima.'

'Fatima?'

'Fatima!' she almost shouted, but the exertion was too much. 'The monthly nurse,' she whispered.

'Where is she? Nobody was with you, Lady Knightley.'

'No. She's gone. Gone. She wouldn't come here. Not –' the word was a struggle for her, '– not – south – of the river, not – to an unknown address. She went. I don't know where she is.'

''Is bowels ain't gonna like this, mum,' Pansy said to me as she spooned more pap into his mouth. 'It needs to be goat, at least, if ain't gonna be heaver-brew. Oh well. She'll find aht in his napkins, soon enough.'

The baby did not eat much, but soon his eyes closed, and I was honoured with the sweet sensation of a baby falling asleep in my arms.

'Bless you,' I whispered, and planted a kiss on his wrinkled forehead. It was soft and downy; the skin of someone who hadn't lived life yet. Lucinda stroked him nervously. His head lolled back in my arm, his eyes and mouth hung half-open, and his breathing became slow and heavy.

'What's his name?' I ventured.

'Nathaniel,' she said without thought, and without looking over at me or him.

'How old is he?'

'A week.'

'He's lovely,' I said, but the silence poured in on my comment, and we sat in the chill of the kitchen as the night fell around us. I waited for Lady Knightley to say something that might explain her presence here, and give me some indication as to whether she wished to stay for supper; Pansy, bless her heart, knew that I needed her, and did not leave.

'Are you – are you passing through, Lady Knightley?' I eventually proffered.

'Damn your impertinence!' she suddenly shouted. 'You dare not interrogate me! I am to stay here.'

'Here? Why?'

'You will not disobey me, Dora!' But this last was almost a question, and not a statement. Her tyranny originated only from her own uncertainties; I had no reason to be afraid of her. 'Not you too. Damn you! Curse the lot of you! I have spent the entire day driving around with that wretched driver sniggering at me, from Mayfair to Belgravia, to Chelsea, to Kensington. I have been to Baroness Temple, and Lady Montgomery, and Honora Williamson, and Victoria Hamilton-Wright, and all the other women of the Society, but Sir Jocelyn has turned them all against me. So now I have come to you. *You* cannot turn me away, it would be the final insult.'

'I am not turning you away, Lady Knightley. I am just rather surprised. I was not expecting . . . I don't expect you shall be comfortable here. Perhaps you have us wrong. Surely there must be somewhere else you can go.'

'Are you delighting in my injury? I will not suffer it. If only Lady Grenville were still with us – she'd not have spurned me – she cared not what society thought!'

'And I'll not spurn you neither, Lady Knightley,' I said softly. 'We shall make you comfortable for the night as best we can.'

'I'll sort a bed out for her, mum.'

'Thank you, Pansy. I suggest you change the sheets on my bed, and I'll sleep in the box-room.'

'Very well, mum.'

I did not believe what was happening; it was not possible that we were the only hope for a woman so well connected as she, and besides, the knock would come at the door soon enough, and Diprose, Pizzy and their men would turn up and take her with them.

'Papa warned me not to marry a man who did not have a country seat,' she sobbed, as if she had not heard me. 'That would have been the safe place to go while this all blows over. I've never had anywhere to retire to once the season is over.'

'What of him, Lady Knightley? Can you go to your father?' I wondered what sort of trouble she could be in.

'Good Lord, no. It would force him into a most ugly position. And my brothers besides. Everyone has turned me away! I would not have chosen to come here, Dora, but where else could I have gone?'

'Lady Knightley, if you don't mind my asking, why have they turned you away?'

'Why? I wish I knew too! Jocelyn has told them all I am mad, and that they are not to associate with me!'

'Why on earth would he . . .'

'I don't know,' she said in a loud, almost bored voice. The hard edge reappeared in her speech when she was not crying. Then she changed tone again, and asked, 'You don't mind, do you?' and I could see from her face it was a genuine question. 'It will not be for long,' she assured me, and I knew she was right, for Diprose and Pizzy were surely just round the corner. 'It is mere caprice on Jocelyn's part, and he will be begging for me to come back. Are we not bonded by the sacrament of marriage? I am much prized; I have borne him a son! I shall soon be back at my rightful place by his side, and afterwards, we shall reward you greatly for your pains – and, it goes without saying, your discretion.'

We lapsed into silence. It was getting late, and Lucinda needed to eat and to go to bed, and Nathaniel was stirring in my arms. 'Lady Knightley,' I attempted, 'what are we to do about feeding him later?'

Lady Knightley was staring around her in a vague daze. 'How peculiar,' she mused. 'You have your store-room as one with your larder, your scullery as one with your pantry, and just one sink for all four functions.' After further bemused perusal of the kitchen, she stood up and paced into the parlour. 'And your parlour is also your drawing-room, and your dining-room!' I heard her say between the rooms. 'Ah, you have a cottage-piano.' She started to play the opening bars of Schubert's 'Adagio in E major'. 'Eugh, it needs tuning.'

I made up my mind what I had to do next, difficult though it would be.

'Pansy,' I said, as she walked past with a pile of sheets in her arms.

'Yes, mum?'

'Would you hold the baby for just a short while?'

She placed the sheets in the corner of the kitchen, and came back to take Nathaniel from me. We exchanged a lingering glance, as if to ask, what is going on here and what can we possibly do about it? 'I won't be long, love.'

I placed a few griddle-cakes in a clean tea-towel, and gave another couple to Lucinda, then I wrapped my shawl around me, and left the sounds of Schubert behind to face the freezing night air. I crossed the road, and knocked on the opposite door. Nora Negley shouted from within, 'I'll be there,' and the goat maa-ed from the kitchen, then the bolt was pulled back, and the door was opened a crack.

'Oh,' she said in surprise. Then her mouth wrinkled with distaste, as she asked, 'What you want?'

'Sorry for the bother, Nora. Only I have an unexpected guest, with a newborn baby, in need of some milk, and I was wondering . . .' and, as I proffered the griddle-cakes up to her, steaming in the cold air, the door was slammed in my face and I dropped the cakes in the street. I returned to the house, and to Pansy in the kitchen, who was cooing at the waking baby.

'Nora won't give us any milk.'

'Pity.'

'What else can we do, Pansy?' We shared another look. 'Do you know a wet-nurse nearby?'

She looked doubtful. 'There's one I can think of, not far, but she got a lotta little 'uns and I can't see she'd want one more. I'll ask her though. Now?'

'Please.' I took Nathaniel from her, and rocked him back to sleep as best I could. 'Take my shawl, Pansy. It's very cold out.' She took it off from round my shoulders, and gave me a little squeeze of reassurance, before wrapping it round her and disappearing into the Lambeth night.

Lady Knightley came back into the kitchen, oblivious to her child in my arms. 'Goodness, but it's cold in here. How can you live in such draughts?' She lowered herself carefully back into the Windsor chair, and we waited for something else to say to each other.

Then suddenly, the composure on which she had such a precarious hold left her altogether; her head and shoulders fell forwards onto her lap as she set about weeping, as if she was going to tip onto the floor and lie there. Thank heavens, I thought, for Pansy, and a clean floor. Only a few weeks ago she would have tipped herself into dust, grease and beetles. I sat and watched as she cried herself out like her own baby;

I knew his stirring would increase to full-blown rage and hunger soon enough, and I hoped his mother's tears would not hasten the process. She cried and cried, and the tears dripped onto the silk of her skirts, and spread there.

'There's a sorry thing, Lady Knightley,' I said, quietly. 'Don't take on so.'

She cried a bit further, then sniffed loudly, then set to crying again, and then the sobs died down, and she sighed, and stood up and wandered around a bit, then sighed some more, and sat down again, and looked at me with eyes that had spent a lifetime being untroubled, and I found myself pitying the weak woman, for not knowing how to live with pain.

'The injustice of it, oh, the injustice!' she wailed. 'He – Jocelyn – he said . . . oh, I cannot bring myself to say it!'

'You don't have to.'

She shuddered further, then sniffed, 'He sent me word this morning that I was to leave, and not to come back! Ever! The child is a week old. My lying-in should have lasted a month, with no leaving the house, no exercise, and a feeding-cup for meals! And now I am on the street, with nowhere to go!'

'You're here,' I said gently, only I doubted whether this was the best place for her.

'Yes,' she said gloomily. 'Oh Dora, it is all too much for me.'

And, frankly, it was all too much for me, too, to fathom this world where blood was thinner than the old school tie, and where those who opened their hearts to slaves from overseas had little time for the needs of one closer to them, even to a mother and newborn baby. Surely she was exaggerating? Maybe she was playing a game with Jocelyn, and had not gone to her Ladies at all, but at the first whiff of his malice had taken herself to the lowest place she could imagine – here, in Lambeth – to see how quickly he would come running for her. She was using me, I was sure of it. I could not help but be sceptical.

We heard the front door open and shut, and two sets of footsteps coming into the house. Pansy had brought a woman with her. She was not a coarse-mouthed fishwife, nor a long-suffering kitchen-servant type, nor doughy and nurturing like a baker woman. She did not have voluminous breasts. She looked composed and efficient, like a nurse, and had a slightly furrowed brow and expression of concern, like one of those ladies who visit the missions, the really squalid ones in the east, not just the ones near Chelsea.

'It's late, you know,' was the first thing she said.

'I do apologise,' I said.

'I'm halfway through the nippers, and I must be back within the half-hour if I'm to get any rest tonight.'

'Thank you for coming out, Mrs . . .'

'Masters. Bess Masters,' she said, looking between Lady Knightley and me as if wondering who it was who needed her assistance. I started to explain the situation, and gestured towards Lady Knightley, and the little baby in my arms. Mrs Masters had a permanent expression of doubt on her face, which I hoped would lift the more I talked, but it didn't.

'I'm awful busy. Got so many babies this time of year, got to get back to them soon too. Not sure I can take another one on.'

'It's only for tonight.'

'Actually, Dora, we cannot be so sure.' Lady Knightley's voice had returned to its usual authority, poised halfway between tedium and wrath. I looked at her in surprise. 'I'm here until he comes for me,' she said simply, as if that explained everything.

'And you will, of course, pay Mrs Masters well,' I said, but she dropped her gaze into her hands.

'I have no money with me. Jocelyn can pay you, but it will be in time. It will be handsome, but in time.'

'Nope. Just too busy,' Mrs Masters said.

'Please.' Lady Knightley's voice was weak.

'She will have money soon,' I said, but Lady Knightley's eyes were still lowered. 'Won't you, Lady Knightley? Won't you?' I was willing it now, more than ever, for in that moment I realised that it was possible that Jocelyn might never have her back, no matter how innocent she was. 'I can pay you,' I said finally to Mrs Masters.

'D'ya not hear me? Too many mouths.'

'So what can we do?' I asked.

'How old's the baby?'

'Seven days.'

'And you gave it any of your own milk?' she said to Lady Knightley.

Lady Knightley shook her head.

'You bound?'

She nodded.

'It might not be impossible to get you going.' I don't think any of us understood straight away, even when Mrs Masters went on to say, 'Let me have a look at you.' And with that, she stood up, and gestured to Lady Knightley to do the same.

'I do not understand,' Lady Knightley said.

'I need you to cast your skin, luvvie. To see if there's any hope in those breasts of yours.'

'I will not do it! What an extraordinary suggestion!'

'Well, you've got to do it. Or the little bugger'll starve to death.'

Bess Masters, Pansy, Lucinda and I all stared at Lady Knightley, and she looked back at us in dismay and affront. We all knew her decision would clarify everything.

So when she stood up and beckoned to Pansy to undo all those buttons and ribbons and stays which Buncie had fastened only this morning, I knew that she had lied when she had said Jocelyn would find her soon, and she had been right when she had said she had nowhere else to go. My confusion and suspicions about her disappeared in an instant; we were well and truly lumbered with her.

She was as good as gold about it when we peeled the binding off her, though she screamed when Mrs Masters rolled her nipples in her fingers and pinched them together. If it had been six months ago I wouldn't have looked; I would have stared at the floor, or into the ceiling, along with her. But I had seen so many pairs of breasts now that I didn't feel the lack of decorum, or the burning curiosity, that would have forced my eyes away from them. I could see it was hard for her, and I was quick with her clothes once the ordeal was over. She was shivering, and had goose pimples all over her ivory skin, and was chastened with the indignity of it.

'Perfect. Got lovely milk in there. Pity about the binding, but do as I say and you'll have fountains of milk. Rub them every hour. Rub them, pinch them, brush them with a soft-bristled brush, ten minutes each side. Give them to the baby to suck, and let him suck and suck even if he's a hungry bugger, and if he screams cos he ain't getting nothing, then pull him off, and feed him milk with a teaspoon, only a bit mind, then put him back on, then feed him a bit more by hand, and then on again.' Lady Knightley nodded, but I knew she needed me to be following it too. 'I've got some herbs here,' Mrs Masters continued, pulling out a bag of dried leaves. She spread them on the lid of the range. 'There's fennel, blessed thistle, borage. And here, here's fenugreek.' I fingered the pyramid-shaped seeds; they smelt of syrup.

'Ugh. Jocelyn brought some back from India. He loves the stuff.'

'I got mine from an Indian family up the road an' all. And beer. Drink lots of lovely beer. It's the hops what does it. But whatever you do, don't eat anything cooked with sage. And avoid onions for a week or two. Give it ten days, you should be on your own.' Then she turned to me and added, 'Let her cry as much as she needs to. Tears help the milk flow. She's gonna be cryin' buckets, an' all.'

The crying started right then, only it was Nathaniel. I

handed him to Mrs Masters, and she said, 'Let's give it a go right now.' She put her finger inside his mouth to get him sucking, then she brought him over to Lady Knightley's dress and tugged it down. She got Lady Knightley to hold the baby while her finger was still in his mouth, then, using her other hand, pinched and tugged her nipple until it stood out like a cigar butt, grabbed it between the knuckles of the hand that was in the baby's mouth, whipped out her index finger, and shoved the nipple in. Nathaniel's eyes opened wide in shock, and he pulled back a bit, so she guided his head back to the nipple and he gave it a lick, then clamped his mouth firmly on and started sucking.

'When did he last feed?'

'About two hours ago. Bread and milk.'

'Good. He's in the right state then. Look at him, he's doing well already.'

'It hurts,' protested Lady Knightley.

'It's gonna,' said Mrs Masters. 'But not half so much as a hungry baby who's sick with the wrong kind of milk. Cry all you like; crying helps the milk to come.'

Lacrimosa, I thought. Tears. And milk.

'I'd better be going soon. Me milk's comin' in again and I've got four mouths waiting for me. But I'll give you something before I go to get you through the night. Pansy, be a love and get me some hot water and a glass.' Then, when she had them, she warmed the glass in the water, quickly undid the buttons of her blouse, pressed the rim of the glass over her nipple, and the milk poured into it as if she had turned on a tap. The glass went cloudy with milk and steam, and when it was almost full, and the flow had slowed, she pulled it away, and fastened up the buttons of her shirt with one hand, using the cloth of the shirt itself to mop up the drops. 'Look at that,' she said with pride, and I thought she was going to drink it, she was salivating so. 'Ain't no better substance on earth. She can use goat after this if she likes, shouldn't need it for more than a week. Make sure she uses it up by midnight, or it'll go bad. That, and the herbs, makes a nice round two and sixpence, don't you think?'

No sooner had I given her the money than she was gone, back to her waiting hungry mouths. I could almost hear the crying that would greet her as she turned into her street.

It was getting late, and I still had things to tidy up. I pressed some small coins into Pansy's hand, even though she wouldn't get paid properly until the end of January, and sent her on her way, and then I went back into the kitchen to relieve Lady Knightley of her now screaming child.

Nathaniel seemed bitterly disappointed with his mother's provisions, and there were tiny spots of blood around the top of her dress. I took him into the parlour and jiggled him up and down for a bit, before laying him out on a blanket in front of the fire, which quietened him somewhat, and he gazed at the flickering shadows it cast, while Lucinda sat by his side and stroked him. Then I went back into the kitchen, where Lady Knightley was still sitting in a droop where I had left her.

'Come with me, upstairs, now.' She followed me and my single candle meekly, and I took her into the bedroom, which Pansy had aired. 'You will sleep here. I will clear all this —' I dismissed the impedimenta of the sick-room with my other hand, '— tomorrow.'

Lady Knightley was looking strangely around the room. 'What curious taste you have!' she said quietly. 'And my, you have so few wardrobes! Oh look, how clever!' She pulled back the drape I had pinned across the alcove between the wall and the chimney breast, to reveal the pegs and hooks and their meagre hangings in darkness behind. In her surprise she seemed quite to forget her misfortune. 'How ingenious! But where do you fit your dresses?' Had she not noticed that my dresses did not trail with the yards of fabric of her own? I did not mention the brown silk one in the ottoman at the foot of the bed. 'And look! No hangings on the bed! But what do you do about draughts? Why, this house is considerably draughtier than Berkeley-square, but still you have no curtains!'

I went over to the chest of drawers and opened the bottom one. It still contained a few of Peter's shirts; I lifted them out and placed them in the drawer above, then pulled the bottom drawer out completely, and placed it on top of the chest. 'And Nathaniel will sleep here.'

She looked down at the drawer, without comprehending at first. Then, as my proposal dawned on her, she protested, 'But what about soot? What about dust? Have you no cot, with draperies? And a cover you can wash? Why, this is disgusting.' Her eyes started to fill with tears, and she looked as if she was going to fall over. 'I had such a beautiful berceaunette for Nathaniel! It had yellow flowers, and cream lace. And my perambulator! It came from France!'

But this is Lambeth, love, I wanted to say to her, where we carry our babies, and put them in a drawer to sleep, but if they're lucky they get a bit more love than in some other places. Not always, but sometimes.

I watched her for a while as she dried her tears on the lace edges of her sleeves, then I helped her out of her dress and into one of my nightgowns.

'You must do something about this,' she said, as she took her petticoats off, and pulled a bloody towel from between her legs. 'Take it, please, and get me another one.'

I folded the towel in on itself, and put it in the chamber-pot to take downstairs. Then I pulled a flannel from the press, folded it, and handed it back to her ladyship. When she was ready, I wrapped her in a blanket, and took her out on to the landing.

'And where is the bathroom?'

I must have looked at her blankly, for she repeated the question.

'There's a tap in the coal cellar,' I said eventually, 'and a hip-bath under the bed. If you want hot water for it, ask Pansy, but please, not on a Monday, which is wash-day.'

We went downstairs again, and I brought Lady Knightley and Lucinda a bowl of soup and some griddle-cakes, and we sat and ate in silence, watching the flames flicker, and listening to the sweet babble of Lucinda to Nathaniel. But soon the baby was crying again, and I picked him up and leant him against my shoulder to rub his back. Lucinda came over and caressed his meagre hair.

'Maybe it's time to feed him some more,' I said gently.

'I can't bear to do it, Dora,' Lady Knightley snapped, 'whatever that awful woman said. Go be a love, get me a teat and a bottle from the pharmacist, and we'll make do with that.' I simply sat and stared at her; her child raged against my shoulder and tried to suckle first the skin on my neck, and then its own fists. It was all too much to take in. 'Get me one, now, or I shall strike you!'

I rose to standing and felt the words come out as a shout, despite myself. 'Strike me all you like, you're using your own tit to feed that child!'

I handed Nathaniel to her, went to the kitchen, took the glass of breast milk off the windowsill, and found a clean tea-spoon. I wondered at myself and what had brought me to shouting at someone of her station, but my anger was still hot. And when I returned, her head was bowed and tears were dripping off the end of her nose, but her chemise was slipped down, and for a while, Nathaniel was sucking her breast with relative satisfaction and quiet. I waited until he started to cry again, and then I pulled up a chair and spooned the the milk into his mouth as his mother held him, then I made her some tea with the fenugreek, which she took obediently despite its awful taste, and we both knew the balance of power had shifted in my favour, and would stay there as long as she was under my roof.

Chapter Nineteen

Blackamoor, Taunymoor,
Suck a bubby,
Your Father's
A Cuckold,
Your Mother Told Me.

The visit from Diprose or Pizzy never came. I wondered if they had been informed but did not care, or whether for a moment we had slipped the scrutiny of the Eeles spies. It did not much matter, either way.

Sylvia (for that is what I was now to call her) spent her first week at Ivy-street living entirely in the past or the future. The present situation and the immediate needs of her child, beyond suckling him, were lost on her. Her milk had started to flow well, and she seemed to gain some small satisfaction from the nursing, but her heavy sighs would startle the baby from his milk-filled dozes. She floated and cried, prayed and yearned, around the house; even the simplest chores seemed to perturb her. She made not a single mention of my Peter, or gave a moment's recognition that I might wish for peace and solace in my time of mourning. She was not interested in what I did all day in the workshop, or even in meeting Din again – in fact, she did not even seem to remember he was now working for me – such was her self-obsession.

She fretted over Nathaniel's linen binder, and insisted on dressing him so: his clothes took up the contents of one of her travelling cases alone. He had a flannel cap to prevent eye inflammations, a selection of cambric gowns and lawn smocks, embroidered or trimmed with muslin and satin ribbons, and woollen shoes. Then there were his Russian napkins and flannel pilches, which had to be laundered separately for reasons of hygiene, and Sylvia's bloody bandages too, while her wounds of childbirth healed, which meant Pansy was at the laundry all day, it seemed. And Sylvia insisted that Pansy starch Nathaniel's clothes as well, and not just with cold potato starch; she made her heat it up in a pan with borax and candle-wax until it jellified, and dip the clothes in, and then iron them only once dry, which taxed the poor girl a whole extra load as well. I told Pansy she could take all the washing out to Agatha Marrow again, which she did, but when it came back she didn't do what I did, and put it all straightways in the press and drawers. Instead, she unloaded it in the kitchen and aired the sheets and clothes in front of the fire, and checked them all over for lice and their eggs. Eventually, I decided, given that money was so good, that we could hire a laundress who would come straight to the house itself, even thought she cost nigh on two shillings. a day, on top of the cost of boiling water, and all the extra soap.

But one could not help but pity Sylvia. It cannot have been easy to go from the upper ten thousand to the lower middle class with such rapidity. She had been bred to be nothing more than a beautiful appendage to an aristocratic arm, helpless but ornamental, and it was not her fault she had not received instruction in resourcefulness in circumstances such as these.

She required my presence each evening to hear her latest lamentations, which quickly moved from sobbing to anger. She would reminisce about her childhood and her courtship with Jocelyn; she would bemoan her recent pain, and strategise how to win him back; everything, in fact, but explain the reason for her eviction, much as I was curious to discover it, and despite my best efforts to draw it out of her by stealth, the direct approach having been firmly rebuffed the first night she had arrived.

'Is he not beautiful?' she started one evening. 'Is Nathaniel not exquisite?' And this single sad thought so quickly precipitated outright indignation. 'How dare he! The monster! Spends his months with naked African women, all saggy dugs and bloody thighs, and yet he would not even attend me in childbirth while I was wearing a chemise, a full petticoat and a bed jacket! Would the man have preferred me to have worn stays as well? He administered the chloroform, then went off to his club for a game of backgammon and a venison roast.' And thence she would meander into her thoughts, which took her any which way. 'Charles Darwin gave chloroform to his wife, and stayed. *And* Charles Dickens! Queen Victoria took it when she had Leopold and Beatrice. Where was Albert?'

'At least you got chloroform,' I muttered.

'There are, I suppose, some advantages to being married to a man of medicine. I could have had my pick of my brothers' friends, but they bored me. Decaying men with their crumbling manors, or stiff rods in the Army, or worse, in business. I chose none of them. Jocelyn told me I had too much sunshine in me for the grey lives they offered. He might not have had the breeding my father required, but I loved him.'

'Breeding?'

'I'm the daughter of an Earl, Dora. Papa told me I had to think of my future, but I had never wanted for anything. I would bring money to our marriage, so why should it trouble me that Jocelyn never quite reached the five thousand a year Papa demanded? Jocelyn had invented some half-credible scheme, some crazy prospective venture, which half-quelled Papa's doubts. But of course it came to nothing. I thought my father secretly liked his wayward son-in-law. His interest in science might have marked him as more upper-middle than upper ten, but Papa loved his sense of adventure, and when he received his title for his exploits in India, Papa couldn't have been more proud. Besides he couldn't fault Jossie's love of the foreign climes. They even went tiger-shooting together in Burma. Jocelyn killed two; Papa didn't kill any, but Jossie gave him one of his, and on the boat back, Papa finally accepted Joss's request for my hand in marriage. They used to joke that I was traded for a tiger-skin; Jossie always said I was cheap at the price.'

I listened, and oh, but it was tedious! The only thing that kept me in check was Lucinda's delight at little Nathaniel, and at Sylvia too, with her wan beauty, her suffering and sighs. Lucinda helped out in every way she could – she brought Sylvia drinks while she was nursing, she held the baby while Sylvia bathed, she helped Sylvia bathe the baby – and was responsible for the first smile to cross Sylvia's face since being thrown out of her own home. I would sit and listen to the woman, but my attention was always on the enchanting games being played on the blanket at our feet, of a happy little girl with a living doll for a playmate.

'So, you have a lodger,' Din murmured one morning as he fastened some cord to the sewing-key.

'You have seen Lady Sylvia?' I queried.

'Hmm-mmm,' he affirmed. I watched, quizzically, as he laid out the shears, and checked the sharpness of the bodkin. Then, almost as if he weren't talking, and I weren't listening, he added quietly, 'But she ain't that much of a lady.'

'Din!' I scolded, as both warning and encouragement. 'You wish to tell me something?'

'Hmm. Maybe,' he breezed.

I sat down on the chair next to him, and started to rub the bodkin against the strop. We would catch each other's eyes, then look away, and giggle, until finally he spoke.

'I told you they made me pose with spears, yes?'

'Yes.'

'An' do the Zoo-loo warrior thing, yes?'

'Yes.'

'Well, that lady likes spears.'

'She likes spears?' Oh my, but I had visions of the Lustful Turk's fleshful weaponry, and I was not sure I wanted Din to continue. 'Your meaning?'

'She had this idea, see, of bein' the white lady captured by savages. She would swoon, and lie down, and pull at her dress, like this, see –' and he tugged at the neck of his own shirt, so that I could see more of his chest, and I found myself looking away, and then back again, '– an' say to me, "No, no, no, you must not kill me!"'

'Why, what were you doing to her?'

'Nothin'! That was what was wrong. She would get so cross with me, an' order me, "You stand there, above me, an' hold that spear so, and point it at me, an' make like you're killin' me!" An' I didn't want to do it. Felt like such a fool. But I did it. "Oh, no, no, no, the Negro is killin' me! Help! Help!"'

'Oh, Din! You're playing with me!' He shook his head. 'Really? What a marvellous story! Sylvia – really – she?'

'Really, she, yes!' Din was nodding.

'The indignity!' I gasped. 'It's outrageous! It's – it's thrilling, and scandalous!'

'Ain' it just!'

The extraordinary memory lingered around us, as Din took the bodkin from me, and tested the point. And there it was again, catching me by surprise: the urge to touch him, and be touched by him. Was this what Sylvia had felt? Did I lack dignity because of it? It certainly was all the more shameful, given that I was meant to be in mourning. But all the more intense, because I was growing to like this man a lot.

'I could always revisit it with her today, only with a real weapon,' he said slyly, brandishing the bodkin and gesturing at the door.

'I fear her appetite is less for frivolity these days,' I chastened.

Din nodded more solemnly. 'There's a baby in there, right?'

'Yes. I don't quite know what to make of it, whether she's a silly woman, or a victim of circumstance.'

'Or both.'

'Possibly you are correct, Din. Isn't it peculiar, that those so recently envied can so quickly elicit pity?' But I was unlike Sylvia, in that his companionship meant as much to me as my desire for him, and each intensified the other.

'And ridicule,' Din added, with poignant resignation.

'And ridicule, Din,' I agreed.

We were interrupted by a knocking from the interior door.

'Dora!' Sylvia was calling.

'Oh my!' I whispered to Din. 'Are you ready to meet her again?'

'As I'll ever be,' he said, casually.

I called through the door, 'What is it, Sylvia?' as I began to unlock it.

'Could you tell me the date, please?'

I swung the door open, and said, 'It's the ninth of February. Why?'

'The Prysemans will be back from Scotland soon.' I waited for her to notice Din, and wondered what her reaction would be. But she continued, dreamily, 'What bad timing my confinement was! Just when people are returning from the hunting season! I must be back in full health by the time the season starts.' She was looking directly at Din now, but her blank face registered no recognition. Then she turned on her heel and disappeared back into the house.

'She has no need to fret,' I said saltily to Din as I locked the door. 'Surely all she does at the season is make small talk with people she doesn't actually really like. I can take her to the market tomorrow for her to practise.'

'You are a wicked lady,' Din said.

'And you a wicked man, for those stories you tell about her. But she did not recognise you, Din.' He simply shrugged.

'Possibly we need to jog her memory. But, to my great regret, I have no animal skins and spears to hand.'

'And, darn, because I left mine behind in Virginia,' Din added.

'How thoughtless of you, Din.'

He continued with his work, but I was not ready to go back to mine. I wanted this moment to last longer. So I found a question I could ask him. 'Tell me, Din, why are you really called Din? Is it a real name? Or were you telling the truth when you said it was that acronym, what was it?'

'Dudish Intelligent Nigger. Of course. Or Dun-coloured Idiot Nigger. Or Dangerous Irate Nigger.'

'No, seriously, Din.'

'Yes, seriously. They would put it in on my papers. DIN. Dangerous Intelligent Nigger.'

'Really?'

He laughed. 'Or I can tell you that it's a word from the Mandingo, my people in West Africa.'

'What does it mean?'

'It don' mean nothin'. But each time I slipped away, I heard a man holler, "Where dat man-Din-go?"'

I had to laugh too. 'You are good at slipping away.'

'And besides, Dora tell me, what is a din?'

'A noise.'

'A noise. See, I been given too many names. The one of my birth. Master Lucas changed it twice. The ones given to you by the other whiteys. Other niggers have had their names changed forty, fifty times. And along the way, they get names like Shame, or Odious. I heard a Master call out across the fields, "Shit, get Dung for me." And they'll keep that name for five years. Din stands for the noise in your head of all your names arguin' at once. I'm going to call any child of mine somethin' wrong, somethin' unexpected, like after flowers, or something. If it's a boy, he'll be tall, so I'm gonna call him Delphinium. An' if it's a cute little girl, I'll call her Daisy.'

'And what if she's a tall girl?

'I'll call her Dora.'

We burst out laughing at the same time, and I felt the unexpected sensation of my eyes watering, but with mirth, not misery, and I bit my lip and scolded myself for this unseemliness. I love you Din, the words teased around my heart. No I don't, my head chastised. I merely appreciated this new and unexpected friendship, which threw the relationship I had with the empty woman in the house into stark relief.

'We all thought Jocelyn had gone mad,' Sylvia exclaimed at supper-time, 'when he came back from the Continent, and wanted his meals served at all sorts of strange times, in the foreign fashion, but Dora, the hours you keep are something else entirely! You have your dinner at noon, and only a frugal repast at nightfall.' I got up at this point, and went into the bindery. Her words chased me there, her voice raised now. 'And as if that were not quaint enough, you still serve your food *à la russe*; don't you know the rest of the world is now dining *à la française*?'

But my head was full of Din, and I stopped hearing her.

Later, however, she knocked on the door, and called through the wood, 'Dora, dear. May I disturb you?' When I did not answer, she added, 'I was wondering if you might like a cup of tea with me, or something stronger.'

'Stronger?' I quizzed. Such an overture was not wholly unpleasant to me. I unlocked the door.

She was standing in the door-way, and shrugged, a small smile on her face. 'I don't know. What have you got?' She was almost skittish.

I was not going to turn down this unsolicited offer of companionship from a softened Sylvia. 'We could make a hot flannel?' I suggested.

'A hot flannel! That sounds marvellous!' She clapped her hands together. 'What is a hot flannel, Dora?'

'My mother used to make it for my father. It's beer, gin, eggs, sugar, and nutmeg. Only, being bookbinders, we make it with egg yolks only, so it's even richer.'

'It sounds disgusting!' Sylvia squealed. 'But it sounds perfect.'

I started to unfasten Jack's apron. 'My father always used to tell my mother, "Just a daffy for me, just a daffy," but he would always drink the lot.'

'And what might a daffy be?' Sylvia asked.

'You shall see,' I replied, as we went into the kitchen. But we had no surplus egg yolks today, as I had not needed to make glair for a while. I picked out the eggs from the basket, and asked Sylvia to separate them, while I went back into the bindery to get a jug of beer. When I came back she was still standing where I had left her.

'What are you doing?' I asked.

'I have separated the eggs.'

Indeed she had: she had laid out the eggs in a perfect circle, so none of the shells touched.

'My apologies, Sylvia. I meant, that one must separate the white from the yolk.'

'And how on earth is one expected to do that?' she asked. I selected two bowls, and started to demonstrate. And as we whisked the whites and yolks, and added the sugar, and the beer and liquor and spices, I felt we were enjoying each other's company. She spluttered and grimaced through her first sips of the beverage, but downed it remarkably quickly, only the alcohol dampened her somewhat and soon she was sighing and fretting and torturing herself once more. Still, I was able to find some vestige of sympathy for her inside me, much as the vision of her begging Din for humiliation started to mock my brain again and antagonise my affection for him.

'Oh, but Jossie must love me still, Dora!' she lamented, as she played with her empty, frothy glass. 'And I love him!'

Yes, you may love him, I wanted to say, but you love him

as you loved that spear, with Din holding it, as a victim loves a villain. And he, he loves you like that too, only in reverse. He loves you as the British Empire loves its conquests, and look what happens when they react, revolt, retreat, I wanted to say. Look at the Fenians; look at the Sepoys. That's how much he loves you.

And then I had to wonder: is that how I felt about Din?

'What will he think? Look at me! I have been reduced to living in the – the – slums!'

'I think you'll find,' I said, hoping that words would obliterate the image of the spear and her white, exposed breastbone, and my own peculiar yearnings for the man, 'that this is the more respectable part of Lambeth.' Peter would be turning in his grave at her words. The grave, I suddenly realised, that this woman had paid for.

'And in such close proximity to whores!' she shuddered.

'There are no prostitutes in Ivy-street, Lady Knightley,' I said pawkily.

'Oh, hark at you, Dora,' she snorted. 'Jocelyn will be horrified when he hears I had to resort to coming here. Look at you in your dull gown! Have you nothing cheerier to wear? What about that black dress we gave you? You depress me.'

I thought of the brown silk dress that lay upstairs in the box-room, and my absurd charade when I first put it on, how it had made me feel such a lady. My cheeks burned with my own contempt at myself.

'Sylvia,' I said quietly. 'We have had a pleasant evening. I beg you not to spoil it.' And so she sunk into her own thoughts once more, and I into mine, but there were too many with Din's name on inside me, so I returned to the bindery to work.

Din stayed later these days, as if he knew I needed the company, what with Jack's absence and Sylvia's presence. Accustomed to his banishment from the house to avoid contact with Peter, Din still never came beyond the heavy wooden door into the house, so he and Sylvia never crossed paths again, but he was my solace and escape when I slipped into the bindery to leave her behind. Our days were marked by periods of intense chatter, and stretches of silence which seemed easy enough for him, but which for me were raging arguments between my heart and my head.

He still left early on Fridays, but nowadays he would ask my leave as a matter of courtesy, and I would of course grant it. And he still turned up some mornings with fresh tar-like wounds to his face, or an eye so bruised it could not see my blushing concern, or injuries to his shins that only betrayed their presence slowly by the steady seepage of vital fluids across the already stained canvas of his trousers.

Din. Din. I love you, Din. Oh, no, I would never say it. But the words crept up from my heart and lurked in the corners of my mouth, as if daring me to swallow them whole, or spit them out, anything but say them. Din.

'I know what you did last night, Din,' I said instead one such morning, only very quietly. I was cleaning a brush, in order to paste the reverse of some leather, and did not look at him as I spoke. But when I received no reaction, I added, 'I thought that was what I would find when I followed you to Whitechapel.'

'You are even more foolish than I thought,' Din said eventually, when the struggle to rig up the sewing-frame became too much for him. 'You willin'ly took yourself to where you would see a bunch of men splittin' each other's skulls and rippin' their skins off.'

'Why do you do it?' I dipped the brush into the paste, and looked at him.

He made a valiant attempt at a shrug. 'Why not?'

'Is it not inhuman, Din?'

He closed his eyes and sighed. 'Perhaps.'

'Does it not reduce you to the level of dogs, or bears, or cocks?'

'Why so interested, ma'am? Do you not know enough about the inhumanity of men?' And here he sat upright, with more determination than his injuries would allow, and directed his one good eye pointedly at me. I swallowed and positioned the leather on the bench. We had never discussed the particular speciality of Damage's Bookbinders; I had not wanted to know that he knew.

He tried to continue with the sewing-frame, but I could see it was hard for him.

'Come, Din. Help me here. It might be easier for you. Hold the leather for me, won't you? Would that Jack were here.'

'You miss him, ma'am,' he said as he stood up and came over to the bench.

'I do, Din. He was very dear to me.'

Din held two opposite corners of the olive-green leather for me, as he had done once before. I was close to his neck; I could see the depth of last night's injury. I should have offered to dress it, but I feared the intimacy. I searched for something else I could say to express my sadness about Jack, but the words did not come out now we were in range of each other's breathing.

As I pasted, Din finally proferred something like an answer to my questions. 'Sometimes, ma'am, I need to feel less than human. But also, it can make me feel *more* human. It reminds me of what I've got to lose.'

'Do you need reminding, Din?' I said quietly, not looking up.

'Maybe we all do.'

'Indeed.' And his statements got me thinking of the pictures in the crates, and I escaped into a new train of thought as if to prove to him that I was not distracted by his presence. 'Do they – they – by which I mean, the Noble Savages,' for there was no escaping it now, 'possibly they need reminding –

possibly they – they – need *these*,' I waved the brush at the crates, 'these pictures, these words, this *violence* – in order to feel more human.'

'Or less.'

'Or less, indeed. I think I am starting to understand you now, Din.'

'We have young aristocrats at the fights too,' he added.

'They come to watch? To wager?'

'To fight. A young Smith-Pemberton, fresh from Eton. A young Gallinforth, trainin' to be an officer,' he said knowingly. 'These names mean somethin' to you, ma'am?'

'I don't believe you!' I said. And yet I did. I could not look up from the leather.

'We've all got our demons. Money don't mean nothin' when you're beatin' the brains out of someone in the East End. They can't do it up West, can they? You'd be surprised who you find there. I don't know many men who don't feel the need to beat somebody else up once in a while.'

'But the tanners: surely they face enough blood in their daily toil?'

He shrugged, then grimaced.

'And they don't do it for money?'

'No.'

'Do you do it because – because the others are white?'

'They're not, not all o' them. Colour doesn't come in to it when you're head to foot in blood. Although bein' black, it don't show too bad much when I'm bleedin'.'

'I would call that a disadvantage.'

'Blood shows them how strong they are. If they can't see it, they feel weak. As long as you can stand the pain, you never let them see how much you're bleedin'.'

I was feeling weak by now; I thought at first that I was feeling queasy at all this talk of blood, but he was leaning slightly further in to me now, and in my head our cheeks brush, and I pull away, and lean in to him once more, only this time slowly, so the hairs on our bodies have to reach for sensation before our skin presses more tightly, and then we move our heads a little, to enhance the tingling feeling, and then my lips find his nose and I kiss it, and my eyelashes flutter like a butterfly's wings across his brow, and I catch close his round brown eyes, and the old scars like fossils in the solid rock of his face, but warm, so warm, and alive, and the fresh wound open and gaping like his mouth into which I am now falling, falling, but I hold on to his teeth, his jagged teeth which are eating my lips, and I hang on, but still I am sinking and drowning and dying for breath, and my chest heaves in the quest for air, heaves and thrusts into him, swelling and shrinking, reaching and fading, and his hands hold me up and he is the pillar which supports me, my column of strength, but then he falls too, down, down, and I look down and see him climbing up my legs, my skirts bunching upwards towards me, he rises and his hands encircle my calves, my knees, my thighs, and still he is rising, and I can't see his face for he is tasting his way blind, up and up, and then I want to come crashing down over on around him, but I don't because it is so sweet here, with his tongue pulsing a nether heartbeat inside me, then his fingers renew the thrust while his mouth sucks, and I well and swell and clutch at the bench to keep me here, on the brink, as long as I can, and my hand seizes something, and I don't know what it is.

And then I saw the brush of paste, and my fingers sticky with cold paste, and the leather that was now fully pasted, and had been all this time, and Din, looking at me strangely, and I knew I could keep him at my table no longer.

A voice that did not sound like mine croaked, 'Thank you, Din,' and he returned, unknowing, to the sewing-frame.

Mr Diprose arrived at the bindery that afternoon. I ushered him quickly into the workshop and closed the door.

'Din, would you kindly go buy me some thread. Here is some money.'

341

I frantically thought about what I was going to say: I had indeed found out some horrendous secret that bound Din and I together, but I was damned if I was going to share it with Charles Diprose. I waved him off the premises, and prepared to defend myself, and Din, once more.

But he did not pursue this tack; he seemed excited, and clearly anxious to get to his brief immediately, although he had brought with him only two things: a piece of leather, and a muslin bag filled with a freshly folded and sewn manuscript.

'*Regardez*,' he said dramatically, as he revealed them to me like a mountebank. 'This is possibly the most important commission of your life. It may seem modest, but you will be paid handsomely.'

I fingered the leather: it was quite rough, and translucent in places, like coarse vellum. Despite myself, I was intrigued. The leather was not particularly beautiful, but tigers and dowries and Sir Jocelyn and the Earl with their rifles danced in my head.

'It must bear the insignia of *Les Sauvages Nobles*, and *Nocturnus*, but no title,' Diprose explained. So it was indeed a commission for Sir Jocelyn.

'Blind- or gold-tooling?' I asked. The skin seemed fitting for a Noble Savage; I wondered if it were the hide of an elephant, or other wild animal, shot on safari.

'Gold.'

'What is this leather?'

'I cannot tell you the exact beast, or from which country it originates,' he answered. 'They are all the same to me. But if you wish to give it a name, by way of reference, shall we call it "Imperial Leather"?' He gave an oily chuckle.

'Do you want it dyed, or natural?'

'*Au naturel*, most definitely. And there is one other thing, Dora. You will not be working on the book itself.'

'I beg your pardon?'

'I have the book here, in this bag, but I am not permitted to leave it with you. You must take the measurements from it now, in my presence, then fashion the binding in its absence.'

'But how will we complete the forwarding process?'

'That is up to you to fathom. A week today, I will return with this manuscript, which you will fasten to the binding, again in my presence.'

I did not answer, for I was thinking hard and fast. This was a new approach to binding, and I knew of no precedent. Strictly speaking, it would be a casing, not a binding, and we would need to leave the cords loose, and forward after the finishing process, all of which was tricky, but not impossible. It would require skill and ingenuity; I wished Jack could have been here to help. I wondered if Diprose knew of his arrest.

As if he could read my mind, Diprose then said, 'And Dora, I need your assurance that only you will work on this. This is not a job for an apprentice. This is a highly secret assignment, and for you alone. You must not even *work* on it in the presence of anyone else. *En cachette.*'

It was not as if I had any choice but to agree. Under Diprose's gaze, I placed the leather in the strong-box, and locked it. Then I followed him out into the street.

'There's three guineas in this for you,' Diprose said quietly as he climbed into his carriage.

Three guineas? I was not sure whether he was playing with me. I raised an eyebrow at him. Three guineas? He spoke the words in little more than a hissed whisper, but I felt the wind carry his words through every open window on the street. I was dumbfounded. This was what men like Knightley paid for a volume like this; what could Diprose be charging him now?

Three guineas.

Yes, I'm Sir Jocelyn's whore, didn't you know?

Really? And I'm Patience Bishop.

And this is my pimp, Mr Charles Diprose.

Would you care for some goat's milk, Mr Diprose? Fresh from the tit, and sweeter than a baby.

A curse on you, Charlie Diprose, and your loathsome money. And the rest of you, with your vile eyes and ears. *Virtus post nummos*, indeed. I am no longer proud of virtue, and I can no longer be shamed by vice; neither impress me. Is not such insistence on virtue only another vice? May you be deafened and blinded by your own filth, if you are not already.

Later that week, I was cleaning the oil-lamps in the bindery in order to start the new commission, when the door opened: I hadn't locked it, as it was after hours. Sylvia glided in silently.

'Can I help you?' I asked.

She approached me with reserve. Although I was wearing Jack's grubby apron, she did not look at me with anything like disdain or reproach. She seemed, possibly, somewhat shy.

'I have brought you a cup of tea,' she said. 'I wanted to apologise to you, actually, Dora. You must think me a frightful pig. I have been here well over a month now, and all I have done is dwell in my own misfortune.'

'You have been rather preoccupied, Sylvia,' I said consolingly. 'It does not matter.'

'But I haven't once asked after you, or your work. Your husband passed away, your apprentice gone, you must be struggling so.'

'I keep going,' I said, 'for Lucinda's sake.'

'Tell me about the slave; tell me about Dun.'

'His name is Din.'

'Silly me! I must have got confused with his colour! Oh, Dora, I do feel awful about it. We knew we were stretching decorum when we asked you to take him on, but I had no idea of the proximity it would involve. Are you frightened at times? You seem so brave.'

'He is a nice man. He is quiet, and well behaved.'

'Yes, but one never knows what they are thinking. You will be careful. You must make sure you never have to be alone with him. I should not like to encounter him.'

'Encounter him? You saw him, here, just the other day.'

'I did? I have been very distracted, Dora. I forget these things.'

'You have also met him before. Or do you not remember that either?'

'Excuse me? When have I met him?'

'He told me you went all the way to Limehouse to find him, at the address he gave to Lady Grenville's maid.'

'Not I! What a ridiculous notion!' We looked at each other as if to await comprehension. And then suddenly, she said, 'Ah! I sent Buncie! With a chaperone, of course. I would not make such a perilous journey. Buncie did it. She's a good girl like that. Goodness, did he think Buncie was me?'

'He did,' I said, and bit my lip. Should I say I knew about the evenings at Berkeley-square?

'Is he of solid build, or is he slight?'

Goodness, I thought, maybe they had a rota of slaves, and she was trying to ascertain his identity through his physique.

'Anyway,' she continued, 'I will have words with the Society to get him moved from here.'

'Really, Sylvia, he's no trouble.'

'Oh, Dora, you may think that you are safe, with your inelegant features, your drab clothes, but to such a one as he, it will not matter if you are suffering from the pox and have lost your nose to the syphilis!' She burst into tears, and covered her eyes with her hands. 'My dear, dear husband. What can he have been thinking of? As if I would betray him – and betray *nature* – like that. As if I would do that a . . . a . . . man of *colour*.'

'Excuse me? I do not follow you, Sylvia.'

'He said I had had an affair! That I must have had! With a – with a – with a man of – colour! That, goodness knows,

I had opportunity enough under the auspices of what he called my Dreadful Society. His son, his baby Nathaniel, is a – a –' here Lady Knightley's voice was reaching a strained high pitch. 'A half-caste!'

'He is?'

'He is! Or at least, Jossie says he is. He said he is . . . he is . . . an unusual hue. To which I protested that he merely bears the sun-flushed cheeks of his father! His colleagues said it was jaundice. But no, Jocelyn was not happy with that. He said the baby's skull sutured closed much more quickly than a white skull should have done, and that this is a feature of the Negroid race, which has a retarded fore-brain, and is therefore less intelligent. And he said other things too, which I can't remember. Only he couldn't prove them, and he was driven sick with lack of proof, and locked himself up in his study to find the answer amongst his books and notes, until he threw me out!' Her chest heaved, and she burst into sobs. 'I protested my innocence. I have only been faithful and true to my darling husband. My soul, I said to him, is lily-white,' here her voice rose to a shout, 'and so is the child's!'

'Calm yourself, Sylvia. Don't take on so, dear. It is not the first of Sir Jocelyn's monstrous theories I have heard. You have more sense than that; you know your own heart, your own actions.' I tried to remember if I had ever noticed anything unusual about Nathaniel's colouring. He was a lovely colour, I thought, like a freshly baked pie-crust. Nothing out of the ordinary.

A suspicion tried to cross my mind, but I dismissed it before it had taken so much as a step. Din would have told me, wouldn't he? The thought attempted to re-enter my head despite my dismissal, but I wilfully restrained it at the edges of my reason.

She dropped her hands to the bench and started fiddling with the tools, as if they might distract her.

346

'Are these how you make the patterns?' she said, sniffing loudly.

I nodded, vigilant and wary. She weighed one in her hand, and traced her fingertips over the brass acorn at the tip. Then she picked up a rose, then a teardrop, the one I used for angels' wings. Finally, her hands moved over to a large, heavy tool.

'I thought you'd returned the Society's coat of arms.'

I waited for her to peruse it further, and when realisation set in, she cried, 'Oh!' then sighed heavily.

'What do you know about that crest?' I asked her.

In a whisper, she said, '*Les Sauvages Nobles*.'

'Who are they, Sylvia?' I enquired. The woman, might, at least, be of some use to me, no matter what she had done with my Din.

'It's a club. A private club. It started with the inner circle of the Scientific Society; now it includes some of their immediate, their most like-minded, colleagues. They meet for dinner every Monday evening, in chambers, or at St James's, or at White's, or sometimes at Berkeley-square.'

'Lord Glidewell is one of them, isn't he?'

'Indeed. You know him? His family has several plantations in the West Indies, three stars to their name in the East India stockholders list, and a mansion in Hampshire.'

'What do they discuss?'

'Oh, this and that. Mostly tedium. The higher specialisations of their scientific and creative endeavours. Theories that may or may not gain acceptance in wider circles. I must confess that I was never entrusted with further confidences about their activities, but neither did I express an interest.'

'What did they do?'

'Well, they didn't play parlour croquet, if that's what you are asking,' she snapped.

And I didn't ask you to come to live with me, I was about

to scream, you and your nigger child! But instead, I waited for her to continue.

'I fear they found me somewhat disapproving,' she said, more subdued now, 'along with all the other wives. Why, even the poor servants disapprove of their Monday evenings. There has been many a valet working for Valentine – that is, Lord Glidewell – who has handed in his notice on Tuesday morning and left without reference by the afternoon. He can never keep them.'

'What else do you know about them?'

'My dear, very little. They mean next to nothing to me. You should hear the way they ridicule the Anti-Slavery lobby, indeed, the Anti-Anything lobby. I overheard them one evening, and my ears still burn at the memory. They were discussing the forthcoming marriage of Aubrey's daughter, Herberta, to a Romanian prince, or a Bavarian count, I forget which, and they were debating amongst themselves about how far East was too far to accept in a son-in-law. Then they moved on to our more Western brethren, when I distinctly heard Jossie say, "My wife, lamentably, is a negrophile; give her a nigger over a Yankee any day," to which Ruthven replied, "Rather an African Negro than an Irish Catholic." And they laughed, Dora, all of them.'

I started to rub at the lamps again, with vigour, my cheeks burning.

'Unfathomable, isn't it?' Sylvia said glumly, presuming to read my thoughts about her husband. Indeed it was, if I thought about it. Here was a man whose fascination with Africa and India was both personal and professional, whose scientific endeavours drove him to calibrate, study and truly endeavour to understand the African and other racial groups, and yet who read *The Lustful Turk*, took Turkish baths, and was more savage than noble in his racial and sexual attitudes. 'But Jossie is by no means the worst of them,' she continued. 'The Noble Savages is, I have always felt, a club based on a shared understanding of – how best to put it? – *cruelty*. It is hard for me to say this, but I believe my husband and his contemporaries have a fundamentally evil streak that needs to be manifested in some way. I must confess to you, Dora, that I have over time grown to be grateful for his Monday nights of hellfire and savagery, for his vicious excesses, for he returns to me on Tuesday morning with a merriness and a levity that is sweeter than sugar.'

When I finally slept that night, the nightmares that visited me could have come straight out of the pages of the books I had bound. First, I was roaming along a row of female body parts suspended in spirits of wine in glass jars, trying to find my own heart. When I found it, I discovered a bite had been taken out of it, and next to it, on either side, were the two castrated organs of the Dey in *The Lustful Turk*. I seized my bitten heart, and ran with it along a corridor into a green room, where Lord Glidewell, clad only in tight black leather breeches, was standing on his desk, underneath a noose. Only it was not Lord Glidewell, but Sir Jocelyn. He asked me with great civility whether I would care to play his favourite game of cut-the-cord, and instructed me to put my heart into his mouth. I did as I was told, but with difficulty, for his mouth was small and my heart over-large, but the effect on limiting his breathing was excellent. Then he handed me a knife; I was to sever the rope just before the moment of ejaculation.

I awoke in horror as he was twitching and thrashing above me, his teeth clenching around my heart, and I stared into the darkness of the box-room, stifling my panicked breathing so as not to wake the others in the house, not knowing if I had killed him or spared him.

The following morning I took myself into the gold-tooling booth in order to prepare the 'case' for Diprose's peculiar commission. His instruction that I should not work on it in the presence of others suited me, for it took me away from Din for the day in both body and mind. The mechanics of attaching the cords to the boards would be complicated: I would have to construct the boards out of one thick and one thin piece of strawboard, instead of one single piece of millboard. Strawboard was softer and less durable, but this approach would enable me to sandwich the cords in between for a secure finish. It was a blessed relief to be preoccupied with something other than my feelings for the man.

It was not hard to prepare, but I found the leather strangely unwieldy. It was stiff to work with, and did not take stretching or glue well. Either it had been very badly tanned – which would have been surprising, given the previous quality of Diprose's materials – or it was indeed the skin of an exotic animal. I traced my fingers over it. It had a strange beauty, and the light played beguilingly on its uneven surface. Several pastings were required.

I did not work on Sunday during daylight hours, but once the household was asleep I started the finishing process. It was very simple – just the Noble Savages' arms and Knightley's Latin pseudonym – but the leather did not respond well to heat and glair, and I had to work long into the night to get a decent finish. I was tired, and worried that I was about to get a cold, or the dreaded influenza. There was also an ache in the pit of my stomach. It did not feel like something I had eaten, or not eaten, akin to hunger though it was.

The church bells rang three times, and I was finished. I wrapped the casing in a piece of red velvet, and placed it back in the strong-box. I cleared up the remnants of leather. There was one particularly wide strip that appealed to me, and I placed it in the drawer of my desk, thinking that I would use it to make a novelty bookmark for Lucinda out of it. The rest of the leather went into the calico bag of scraps. I swept the floor, blew out the candles, and locked up.

And then I recognised the feelings for what they were. I had felt like this before, on Christmas Day. I was lonely: I craved company, gentleness and honesty. I craved Din.

Chapter Twenty

As I was going by Charing Cross,
I saw a black man upon a black horse;
They told me it was King Charles the First –
Oh dear, my heart was ready to burst!

The next day had scarcely begun in the bindery for Din and me, when we were disturbed by a scuffle in the parlour. I opened the thick wooden door to find Pansy and Sylvia having a loud argument, with Lucinda standing anxiously between them, clutching Mossie.

'I en't 'er slave, I en't. I'm working for you, aren't I, mum, an' not 'er. I do what I can to make 'er day a bit nicer, an' I've 'eaved 'er into 'er stays and tugged and primped and preened 'er for hours, but I en't gonna do everyfin' like a friggin' lady's maid. I'm sorry, mum. Your notice said sew an' fold an' nurse an invalid an' a child. Not a toff an' a baby as well. I'm sorry mum, I am. I'll try and do better, I will. D'you want me to leave nah? I'm sorry. I won't mind lookin' after the baby, I won't.'

I looked at Sylvia. Her face was clean, her hair was immaculate and high under the bonnet she had been wearing when she arrived, and her extraordinarily firm figure revealed that she was wearing a corset again. As she put on her white kid gloves, she flashed her eyes up to me from below the feathered brim. Oh yes indeed, the lady was ready to be looked at again; she was back to something resembling her old self.

'We were a mere five minutes upstairs, altering my toilette.

The girl is full of untruths.' Then she said, more softly, 'I'm going back to Jocelyn. I simply asked her to look after Nathaniel for the morning. I will return, of course, in time for his next feed. If he gets hungry, she can give him a paste. That's all I asked. Don't look at me so, Dora.'

'You're going back to Jocelyn? Will he take you back?'

'Your insolence is uncalled for. He needs to see me. He will be missing me, regretting his actions, and desperate for news of me and his son. I will tell him that the jaundice has passed, and that his son has skin no darker than his own.'

'So take Nathaniel with you, to prove it.'

'Don't be ridiculous. It would be a hindrance. I must be able to speak lucidly. And to show him unencumbered how my figure has returned. Besides, it will increase his curiosity, to make him wait.'

I paused, before assuring her that we would indeed look after Nathaniel today. 'It will just be for this morning,' I soothed Pansy. 'I will be able to help you this afternoon, once I have taken care of some business. Mr Diprose is due this morning, you see.' Pansy curtsied. Then I went over to the tea-caddy, and took out half a crown. 'Here you are,' I said as I gave it Sylvia. 'I think you'll need to take a cab, looking as beautiful as that.' I kissed her, and whispered 'good luck' into her ear.

She looked at the coin, and said a quiet 'thank you'. She planted a kiss on Nathaniel's brow, and stroked his forelock with her gloved finger, then left the house.

'Nobody's asking you to leave, Pansy,' I said. 'And don't you dare go considering it. I need you, and I will ensure your happiness so as you stay with me. Why don't you take Lucinda and Nathaniel out to buy some sherbet?' I gave her some pennies. 'There might be some spring greens in the market, even. Take some air for yourself.'

As I waved them out of the door, I could see an old hansom turning into the street. I shut the door, smoothed my hair and adjusted my cap, then hastened through the door into the bindery and locked it behind me.

Diprose seemed unusually pert and dapper this morning, albeit in his habitual ungainly way.

'Tell the nigger to go,' was the first thing he said to me, *sotto voce*.

'Good day to you too, Mr Diprose,' I retorted as I went over to Din to tell him he could leave for the morning.

We watched as he hung up his apron and left. I locked the door behind him, and made a show of checking that the door into the house was locked. Then I pulled the strong-box out from under the tooling-bench, unlocked it, unwrapped the casing from the red velvet, and laid it on the bench.

It certainly did not rank as the best binding I had ever produced. The design was too simple, and the leather was not special enough to warrant such lack of ornament. Still, Diprose proceeded with a ceremonious air. He removed the manuscript from its muslin bag; he kept it closed throughout, so I could only see the spine and end-papers, which were marbled vellum.

Together we fixed the book onto its binding. It was intricate work, and our hands worked closely, holding tension here and tying cords there, but it only served to remind me of the lack of intimacy I had with this man who brought me so much wealth, and so little true happiness, and of the power in the air in this exact same spot when Din held some leather for me here so recently. But the book, when finished, did look remarkably good, and in certain lights, the leather was beautiful, welcoming, and touchable.

Then Diprose reached into his pocket, and pulled out a long, thin strip of metal, like a ruler, which had a small square cut out of the centre.

'Now, finally, I need you to tool an inscription for me. It must be here.' He turned to the back of the book, and pointed to the thin strip of folded leather at the bottom of the inside cover, below the end-paper. 'Let me see . . .' He perused my lettering tools. 'Your smallest font, lower case . . .' He pulled one out of the rack, and experimented with pushing the tool through the square in the metal. 'These will do. A perfect fit. I will need you to tool an inscription, but you must not know what it says.'

'How am I to do that, then?'

'You will draw a grid on the leather according to my instructions, then I will tell you which letter you must tool through this hole in each square; the metal will cover up the words, so you shall only see the letter you are working on.'

'But I shall be able to work out what it says according to the order of the letters.'

'I shall instruct you to tool the letters in a random order.'

'Mr Diprose, forgive me, but it will be impossible to align the letters perfectly like that. Letters are never spaced according to a square grid; I always position them by eye.'

'Mrs Damage, *impossible n'est pas français*,' Diprose cajoled. 'My other bookbinders accept this occasional practice. Do not cause trouble for me, now. Of course I accept some inevitable loss of aesthetic. Come, come, girl. It is the only way.'

So, despite myself, I marked out a grid of twenty-six identical squares, to fit the selected tool size, and Diprose held the metal over the grid, revealing only one square at a time – first in the middle, then close to the beginning, then right at the end, and so on, in random order – instructing me on the letters to use in each square. Having tooled blind, we then had to do the same with the gold.

It was a droll undertaking; its laboriousness amused me. I wanted to tell Diprose that I really did not care what his tawdry little inscription said. But the more we continued, the more intrigued I became. Ironic, I thought, that the procedure only drew attention to what it sought to diminish.

I left out each tool after using it, rather than returning it to the rack, in order to clean them later. I made a mental note of how many times I had used each of them, and those that I had only used once. I would work it out, I reckoned, after he had gone. I would not be hoodwinked.

At length we were finished. My back was aching from the effort involved, and so was Mr Diprose's. I stretched and bent forwards to ease out my back; Mr Diprose grimaced, held on to his waist, and attempted to do the same. He was trying to adjust something at the back of his trousers. I did not look.

'It's just this damn brace I have to wear,' he explained. 'It rubs sometimes.'

'A brace?'

'I would be *un invalide* without it. I have soft bones, bones that bend. I was fitted with it when I first worked in Paris, in my twenties. I met Sir Jocelyn there. It's a fine contraption – steel and leather – but it does cause dreadful pain. I do not complain. *Vincit qui se vincit.*' He stretched his chest out, and released his hands. 'There, that is much better.' Breathing deeply, he returned to the book. 'I am delighted, despite myself. You have excelled yourself, and I am proud of you. It is a particularly splendid day, today.' He placed the book with similar ceremony into the muslin bag, then dug into his pockets, and presented me with three shining sovereigns and a crown. '*Gardez la monnaie.* And now, the remnants, please.'

I was reeling from the coins, shining like three suns and a moon in the palm of my hand, and the instruction to keep the change.

'Mrs Damage? The remnants?'

I placed the coins quickly on the bench, before tipping out the contents of the scrapbag. Mr Diprose and I picked out the remains of his leather from the scraps. I had no spare bag to put them in, but Diprose seemed happy to stuff them into the pockets of his trousers, his frock coat, and his waistcoat.

'You may wonder why I want these back,' he said defensively. 'What I gave you was my only stock of that particular hide; I may wish to re-source it at some point, depending on how well received the binding is. And now, I will bid you farewell, Mrs Damage. *Au revoir*.' He lifted his hat, and was about to go, when he seemed to remember something. He leaned stiffly towards me, a stiffness I now knew was due to his back brace, and I moved my ear towards his mouth.

'This has been one of our more sensitive operations. Tell but a single soul of what you have been doing, and Sir Jocelyn shall not hesitate to undertake another such – *sensitive* – operation, for your epileptic daughter.'

And then he was gone.

I paced into the house, wishing I had not sent Pansy out with Lucinda so I could keep her at closer quarters. I tried to distract myself by returning to the bindery and writing down the letters of the tools I had used before clearing them away. I was angry, I suppose, that he had excluded me from the text, while exploiting my labour to achieve it. So, I noted that *a*, *i* and *r* were used three times, *c* and *o* were used twice, and the single letters were *b*, *d*, *e*, *f*, *h*, *m*, *n*, *p*, *s* and *u*. I also jotted down a reminder that the grid I had marked out was of twenty-six squares: two letters, followed by a one-letter space, then six letters, a space, eight letters, a space, and seven letters. If I had been really bothered, I could have troubled myself over the anagram right then, but it was a sport I would save for another day.

At length, Pansy came through the front door with Lucinda and Nathaniel.

'Mama, Mama,' Lucinda cried as she bounded towards me. 'We saw a puppet show! We saw a puppet show!'

'Well, not quite, Lou, love,' Pansy said. 'We saw them arrive, didn't we? We was comin' back to ask if we could go back for the show, which'll start any moment, but we need some more pennies for them, an' we was wondrin' if that was not too much to ask, mum.'

I looked at my precious daughter and wondered if I dared let her out of my sight again. I knew not of how idle that threat really was. But her eager face could not be disappointed. 'Of course not, Pansy,' I said, as I turned to the tea-caddy. I took out another half-crown, and pressed it into Pansy's hand. 'Take them to the baked-potato man too; we haven't done that for a while. And pick up something nice and easy for tea – some sheeps' trotters, or some oysters or stewed eels.' I looked at her hard, and said, 'Are you sure you can manage this, Pansy? I'm happy to stop and help you this afternoon, with Nathaniel.'

'No mum. We're fine. I just came over funny when she started all them orders at me. Thanks, though. It'll be best to take 'em out anyways, give 'em a nice time.'

I embraced Lucinda again. 'Have a lovely time, darling. Make sure you listen hard to the story, so as you can tell it me later.' Then I turned to Pansy once more, and said in a low voice, 'Keep a close eye on her, won't you?'

I waved them off up Ivy-street. The clock struck twelve, and Din was striding towards them, and me, grinning and waving. He stopped to exchange a word with Pansy, and pulled a flower from behind his back which he presented to Lucinda. Then he tickled Nathaniel in the tummy, waved good-bye to them and started up again with his jaunty saunter towards the workshop. I pulled inside before he reached the house; I did not want to talk to him. I heard him go into the workshop through the outside door.

The house was silent, but I was troubled. I was tired, oh, so tired: the exertions of the past year were catching up with me, along with the strain of Peter's death, and now this constant warring of heart and head. I sat in the Windsor chair, and closed my eyes. I hated Din for an instant. I could hear him in the distance, rigging up the sewing-frame, but once he started to sew all was quiet once more. I could sleep here, now.

Instead, I unlocked the door into the workshop and drifted in noiselessly, towards the chair next to Din's, where we used to sit and sew side by side on his earliest days with us.

'I'm sorry Mr Diprose is always so rude to you, Din,' I said.

He shrugged, and turned the sewing-frame that was in front of my chair towards him, so he would not have to reach too far across me, and started to dismantle the set-up.

'He applies unnatural scrutiny to me. It was why I followed you to Whitechapel. He pressured me to find out more about you, and to find some way of binding you to me.'

'You had no need, ma'am,' he replied, before adding softly, 'for I am bound to you already.'

'I do not mean by dint of the Ladies' Society.'

'Neither do I.'

We fell into each other's silence, only Din tried to clamber out again by passing me an old manuscript that was on the sewing-frame. I took it, and placed it on the table next to me. Then I started to wind the cord onto the sewing-frame. I did not know why I was doing his job, only that I was not tired any more, and I needed something to distract me. His hand went up to meet mine, but still I wound the cord, so he wrapped his entire hand over mine, and kept winding with it for a few turns. Eventually I could bear it no more, and pulled my hand back, and all the way up the length of his arm, and spun round to face him. We kissed – he pulled me towards him with his empty hand, while the hand still holding the thread went to the back of my neck – and I smelt him up close at last.

Unexpectedly, my eyes fill with tears, which stream down my face, and he kisses them, each one, before returning to my mouth, my neck, my chest. I forget about Peter in his grave, about Lucinda and Pansy and Nathaniel on the streets, about Sylvia and Jocelyn, and about myself. Then suddenly I remember.

'Stop!' I stand up so fast that my chair falls backwards. I do not pause to see his face. I push the sewing-frame out of the way and run to the door, find the key hanging round my waist, put it in the lock and turn it. Then I run back to him, and he stands up to greet me, and we kiss all over again.

He kisses my lips, then across my face, and my ear, and he walks slowly round to my back, his lips keeping contact with my skin all the way, and he carefully and unhurriedly unbuttons my dress, and slips it down over my shoulders, which he kisses, each one, before I turn back to him, and do the same to his shirt. It is stained brown here and there, and smells of beer, and sweat, and hedgerows. He takes my chemise off next.

My fingers trace the contours of the skin on his chest. I kiss his neck wound, which has almost gone, although I can see fresh scars on his arms and on one shoulder. I press my body towards him, and slip my hands round to his back. They feel something, and feel it again. A groove. It has me caught; I cannot move my fingers from it. Silky and smooth, a long groove, along which my fingers cannot help but trace. And then I lift my head, and I stare at him. I turn him round, but he twists his head back to look at me. On his back are deep, old welt-marks, like carriage wheels on mud, the entire length and breadth of his back, and the backs of his legs.

'Dare not pity me,' he said sternly. 'Have a look, have a good look. But come back to me, or we both stop now.'

I came back, but I kept seeing them in my head, and struggled to know whether to touch them, or not to touch them, and how to show I didn't care. He kissed me, and he pressed urgently against my hip bone, then towards my centre. The heat from my body seemed to drain towards that one point; my head struggled to reclaim control, and in the conflict, my body lost. I was feeling too much. I feared he would be more than I could bear. My breath was being overwhelmed by a sinister inflation, which threatened to obliterate my ability to inhale entirely. Before it could engulf me, I had to close it off. Instead of feeling too much, I made the choice to feel nothing.

'Forsooth,' I suddenly remembered, relieved that the last year's toil had not been in vain. Then, 'Verily sir, a mighty one.' I lifted my head and strained to latch my mouth on to his ear, like I had read about. I bit hard.

'Ouch,' Din said.

I thrust myself forward and tilted the crown of my head towards the floor, and arched my back dramatically, but it was all wrong. 'Oh, oh, oh, sirrah.' I struggled to remember a sentence from *The Lustful Turk*. Something about 'a delicious delirium'. I stopped arching my back, and started to writhe around beneath him, then lifted my head in search of his ear again. Our skulls clunked together, and our temples throbbed.

'A tremulous shudder, an "Ah, me, where am I?" and two or three long sighs, followed by the critical, dying, "Oh, oh!"' That was it. I tried all those, in turn.

Din pulled back, and for the first time I could see nature's grand master-piece, only his seemed to be wilting. I had not read of that, only of pillars, and engines, and skewers. 'Are you all right?' he asked, perplexed.

'Yes,' I said. 'Are you?'

'Dora. Look at me.'

But I could not meet his eye. Oh, but the sham was more shameful than the real thing.

'What is it? Have I misread you?'

'No,' I said quietly, then I sat up quickly, and hugged my knees into my chest, and sat there like a small curled thing, waiting for the fear to pass. For I'd read of too many fantasies to feel anything other than fictitious myself right now.

'I'm afraid.'

'So am I.'

'But not like I am.' I couldn't tell him of the waves of feeling inside me I had felt with my husband, after which Peter expressed such revulsion of me that he never came near me again, except after vigorous scrubbing with carbolic and bicarbonate. I feared that what I had experienced all those years ago was a cousin of the great explosions, those throbbing, Vesuvial orgasms that I had encountered in close on a thousand erotic books since, which had told me more extraordinary stuff besides on how one should expect to appear to one's man in the throes of *firkytoodling*, or what you will.

But I think Din understood anyway. 'You do not need to do this to yourself.'

'I'm sorry,' I whispered back.

'And don't say sorry.'

But I was sorry; I deeply repented my behaviour.

'Sorry.'

'Let me help you,' he said. He lay me back down. 'Don't move. You are not to move. You may only move when you can't help but move, but not before. If it takes for ever, so be it. If it happens now, so be it. But you are not to move until you want to.'

'I'm scared, Din. I'm not Sylvia.'

'I am glad about that. Because I know where my heart is.'

And I did wait until the movement came over me, and then it was as involuntary as fainting, and infinitely more pleasurable. I do not have a name for what we did; it was not the chaste embraces of popular novels, nor was it the tuneless organ-grinding of Diprose's catalogue of work. It was ferocious, and it was lyrical, and we did it, wordlessly and without name, without 'verily's or 'sirrah's or 'forsooth's, long into the afternoon, amongst the paper shavings and leather parings on the floor, and I knew that I would never again be able to separate the smell of the bindery from the smell of him and what we did that day.

'Would that we could bottle this, and keep it for ever,' I sighed, in his arms.

'You would make a captive of love?'

'No. Just that I am more used to safety than you, and prize it more greatly. If all we had in the world was a square of cloth, you would stick a post up the middle, hoist sail, and ride the wide oceans a-whooping. What would I do? I would grab the edges, tuck them in at the sides, and huddle down beneath it.'

'I don't believe you,' he said, kissing me and stirring me inside again. I wanted to tell him to stop, to never stop, to go away, to stay for ever. 'Why you, Mrs Dora Damage, you're nothin' but an outlaw, just like me.'

'No, I'm not.'

'Oh, but I have seen you battlin' bravely in that world out there.'

'Only because I want to be safe. Safety is an unknown quantity to you.'

'To me, yes, but I want it for my children, and my children's children.'

'And yet I believe you are all the better for disregarding it. I admire you, Din.'

'No you don't. You pity me.'

'I do not. Well, not entirely, at least. And I'm learning not to, besides.'

'Then I admire you your application to your lessons. You are an outlaw, but a highly educated one.'

I laughed. 'You are talking about yourself.'

'Face it, an' embrace it, Dora. You're a fighter. Only you

just don't know it. You even earn a livin' from outside the law.'

'No. I have only swapped one set of rules for another. And curiously enough, they're set by the same people. I hope you never meet Sir Jocelyn Knightley. I fear *he* considers himself an outlaw.'

'I should relish the challenge. Becoming an outlaw is the best response to tyranny I know of. I shall consider him my brother. I have heard you call him a libertine. What is that, other than someone who has been freed from slavery?'

'You do him too well, Din,' I snorted. 'I am afraid he shall consider *you* a scientific curiosity.'

'And what does he consider you?'

'Please don't ask, I beseech you,' I said, knowing that the answer was quite simply, and quite probably more accurately than I had realised, little more than a whore. 'Spank me,' I said instead, surprising myself as I heard the words come from my mouth.

'What?'

'Spank me,' I repeated. 'Here.' I stood up, without wondering for a moment whether I was presenting to him my best angle, and seized the strop from the wall. 'The leather side, not the emery cloth,' I added, as I lay myself across his lap, although this was no time to fear for my tender behind.

'I don't want to hurt you, Dora.'

'Just give it to me. I want to know what it feels like.'

He patted the strop against my bottom, and I giggled.

'Go on, harder,' I said. He raised the strop higher in the air, then landed it against my skin.

'Ouch,' I shrieked, and thrust my pelvis into his lap.

'Did I hurt you?'

'Yes!'

'I'm sorry.'

He rubbed the palm of his hand over my bottom, and kissed it gently.

'Don't be. I asked for it.'

'You have a perfect bottom,' he said tenderly. 'Do you want me to hit it again?'

'No,' I said, wriggling myself around to kiss his face. I think my face must have been redder than my rear. It felt naughty, but appropriate; it was in many ways what I needed, combining both sensation and punishment in the one act, answering my desire and my guilt at once. I was a woman in mourning; I was betraying my husband, and deserved to suffer. I took the strop from him, laid it on the floor next to us, and locked my limbs in his. 'It's just – it was in the books. I was curious.'

'You have to pity the men,' Din said gravely. 'Why is it they think they're bein' dangerous lookin' at a black man with a white woman? Why is that more horrorsome than a fifty-year-old man with a ten-year-old child, or a woman with a goat? Cos it's seen to be the wrong way round; the wrong balance of power. White over black, man over woman, that's the right way, ain't it? Black man, white woman, though, stirs it all up, causes bother.'

'Are you saying they seek out sensation? They want the thrill of possibility?'

'Right.'

'Just like me with the strop.'

'Just like. Cos *they* never lost their dignity, *they* know they'd want revenge if they'd been treated like us. They know what they've done to us, and they're scared that if we get a little power we're gonna get some guns and come runnin' after them.'

'Which is precisely what you've said you want to do!'

'Have to, not want to. I want to live in peace. Ain't no such thing as a free revolution, Dora.'

'Ain't that the truth,' I agreed. I was starting to realise our loving would have a heavy price, although it felt worth every penny. What did Adam and Eve think of their punishment, having tasted the tree of knowledge? I could only remember the wrath and indignation of the Almighty; we were not told whether His first minions felt it was worth it. Was I a white Eve with my black Adam; or was he the black serpent hiding in the tree? I looked around at the bindery and became aware of a crawling feeling across my skin, which sat uneasily with the warmth of his embrace. We had perpetrated a terrible sin; we had violated every moral, social and religious taboo, yet my shame mixed curiously with a wondrous, golden sensation of glory, and I wondered to myself how something so wrong could feel so good. Or was that, how could something that felt so good be so wrong?

'You don't want revenge?' I was starting to shiver with cold. Din fell silent for the first time.

'A little bit of revenge, maybe?' I goaded. His lips moved up and down together, his chin twitched. And then I froze. 'No. Is that what — this — is all about?'

'What?'

'You and me?'

'Oh, Dora, Dora no.'

I sat up and disentangled myself from him. 'Yes! Yes! You horrible man! Go! Get away from me!' I seized my chemise and held it over my nakedness.

'Dora, listen! Way back, back in the homestead, the men used to talk 'bout white women in a way that made my ears burn. And I'm ashamed to say, I joined in, more than most at times.' He took my hands in his, the chemise still bundled between us.

'I don't want to hear it! You, you violator! How could you? I want to spit on you!' Actually, I wanted to vomit, and gouge his eyes out at the same time. 'Was it good, your triumph, your revenge, hmm? Oh!' I shook out my chemise and climbed into it, then searched for my dress.

'Dora, Dora, hush. Do me some justice. Let me finish. What we have just done is nothing to do with triumph, or revenge. I am not those men, I am not the man I was back in the homestead, and I am not the men in your books, either. I have seen – I have seen countless livin' bodies, bodies of my friends, semi-strangled, their backs laid open, every limb mutilated, with veins drainin' and arteries pumpin' out into the soil, and thrashed to within an inch of their life, beyond the point at which every onlooker is beggin' for their spirit to give up the fight and take their freedom. Yet their soul chooses to stay, and their body comes back with it. Life is tenacious, and it is a wonder. The soul loves the body; and if you love one, you cannot help but love the other. I will kill a man who has killed those I love, black or white; but I will *not harm any one of any colour* just because they are of his colour! Do you hear me, Dora?'

I stepped into his arms, my dress still unbuttoned behind.

'Do you *hear* me Dora?'

'Yes.' I believed him, and he was right. There was nothing of transgression or power in our afternoon of bliss. On the contrary, it was a time of healing and forgiveness. In the gloom, we glowed; our union had only made us more beautiful.

'*Odi et amo.*' He turned me round and started to do up my buttons.

'I hate and I love?' I asked.

'I hate and I love: why I do so you may well ask. I do not know, but I feel it happen and am in agony.'

'Ovid?'

'Catullus. Why make love, Dora, if it is not in the spirit of love?' He sat me down again next to him on the floor. He was still naked. 'Our congress is the most precious thing we have; I will never, ever, confuse it with hatred. You're tremblin', Dora. I am sorry.'

'No, *I'm* sorry. I don't know what we've done here today, but it scares me. I feel I know you so well, and yet I don't understand you at all. Two human beings met here today, not just a white woman and a black man. You happen to be black and I happen to be white.'

'An' you happen to be in mourning for your husband,' Din said, and kissed me on the tip of my nose. 'An' I *am* a black man, Dora, and it defines me more than your skin will ever define you. I am black, an' I must fight for its recognition an' acceptance, an' for the freedom of my country.'

'But this is what I do not understand. It is not *your* country. You were taken there, or at least your forefathers were.'

'It's the land o' my birth.' He rolled onto his back, and stretched his arms above his head. I wanted to kiss his armpits, to stretch myself like a cat along the length of him. I loved his nakedness. I was no longer afraid of his body, only of the rules that surrounded me.

'So?' I answered. 'It does not have to be the land of your life! You are free here. Would you stay with a mother who tortured you? You would leave, and find someone else to love you. Why stay with your motherland, when all she can do is abuse you?'

'I am bound by my past, an' the past of my race.'

'You have a responsibility to your future, and the future of your race.'

'Who are still in captivity in the land of my birth. Tell me, Dora, the opposite of slavery?'

'Freedom.'

'Is it? Could be. Or is it mastery? Self-mastery, I mean. Or are they one and the same?'

Self-mastery. I thought about the books of our lives, the choice presented to our souls at birth by St Bartholomew. Freedom has its responsibilities; we are bound to write our books well.

And then we heard the noises in the sitting room, and it was more of a commotion than Pansy and the children would ever have made simply by returning from a puppet-show. I laid a finger on Din's lips, and he clasped it and kissed it, before seizing his clothes and dressing quickly. I watched as he went over to the bindery door, raised his hand, and fled into the night with the silence of snow, on which we had to leave not a trace.

I turned the key quietly behind him, then I unlocked the door into the house, and slipped back inside my life. I rubbed my eyes, rearranged my hair and dress, and apologised for falling asleep in the workshop.

Sylvia was slumped over to one side in the armchair; Nathaniel lay loosely in her arms, busily sucking at her breast. Her dress was undone at the back, and was crushed and creased below her arms, and the top of her corset jutted up and under her breasts, pinching the skin, her flesh rubbed raw around it.

Pansy and Lucinda were standing watching her.

'May I go now, mum? I was gonna stay, to help out with Lady Knigh'ley, but seein' as you're 'ere . . .'

'Yes, Pansy, you may go. Thank you, love.'

Lucinda went into the kitchen and brought Sylvia a glass of water. Sylvia raised her head and looked, bewildered, at it, before taking it and drinking it down in one gulp. 'Thank you, sweet,' she said quietly, and patted Lucinda's shoulder. Lucinda leant on the armchair, half-kneeling, watching Sylvia nurse Nathaniel, and waiting to be of assistance.

I went upstairs and pulled a couple of clean handkerchiefs out of the linen press. I brought them back downstairs, and handed one to Sylvia. She took it, but crumpled it into a ball in her fist. I pulled up a chair next to her and waited for her to talk.

'I'm not going to cry,' she said solemnly. 'I am going to be like you Dora. Besides, I am too tired to cry.'

'Was Jocelyn at home?'

'No. But Buncie let me in. Despite strict instructions to the contrary from "my master". Her master! I told her she had no master, that I was her mistress, and that I would be coming home, and she bobbed and said her by-your-leaves, but that her employer was Sir Jocelyn and – well – you understand. She let me in, which was, I presume, beyond the call of duty. I will not get her sacked for it, at least. I went first to my morning-room, and it was bare. Stripped bare, save a few meagre furnishings that I never liked. As was the nursery. No berceaunette, no lace, no rocking chair, no toys. And my bedroom. He had packed my possessions into boxes. "Will you send someone for them, ma'am?" Buncie asked me. "How can I?" I replied. "I have no one to send. You must work on Sir Jocelyn to find it somewhere in his heart to despatch them to me." I gave her your address. Dora, he has removed all trace of me and the baby from the building. To add insult to injury, he is using the nursery as a packing room, to organise his expedition equipment, for he is leaving for the Zambezi. This has not been planned; he gave me no indication of this throughout my confinement. It takes months to plan these trips, months.'

'Will he divorce you?' I asked.

'Oh, Dora, you're so modern! Don't be ridiculous!'

'Well, he could. He only needs to claim adultery.'

'So what if he does? He will keep my entire fortune. He brought not a penny into our marriage. Who can say what will be the caprices of his goodwill? He could give me some-thing, or nothing at all. I don't even have enough to arrange for the return of my possessions. They all belong to him now. Buncie treated me like a madwoman. He's told them all that I'm insane. She thought I had gone to an institution. Appar-ently he had told all my friends, and all his colleagues, that the baby was unnaturally formed, that I went mad because of it, that I'm in an institution. That's why they all turned me away before I had to come to you.'

'So he clearly doesn't want to divorce you,' I said.

'Why?'

'A divorce cannot be granted if the wife is insane.'

'Are you trying to cheer me up? Because it's not helping.' She sniffed, and blew her nose on the handkerchief. 'Dora, it was as if I had never lived in that house. There was no sign of me at all. It belongs now to a bachelor, and is dedicated exclusively to the higher realms of science and anthropological study. And his books.'

Which hardly belong to those realms at all, I wanted to add.

Chapter Twenty-one

Hickety, pickety, my black hen,
She lays eggs for gentlemen;
Gentlemen come every day
To see what my
black hen doth lay.

We came together whenever we could over the next five days. Some mornings we would make a valiant attempt at work before succumbing to the inevitable; others we would be kissing and disrobing as I was turning the key in the lock behind him.

I learnt more over those five days about the inner workings of our hearts and bodies than I had done in over a year of binding erotic texts; I learnt things on which the books could not inform or instruct, written as they were solely to arose and shock. I learnt that my lover would start soft and vulnerable in my fingers, yet within seconds he would grow and strain against my grip as if outraged at the constraints of my fingers. I learnt of the parts between the parts, the soft rims of the body at the meeting points of the more obvious sensory places: by which I mean the skin above the inner thigh at the top of the leg, before flesh spills and splits, soft and dewy like that between the back of the ear and the hairline, or the front of the earlobe and the whiskers, the crease under the breasts, the crack at the base of the spine. I learnt that it is possible to relax and tense one's muscles simultaneously. I learnt, as my lover surged with delight at a tongue deep in his ear and elsewhere, that it is not only women who like to be penetrated. I learnt that a man's bag of jewels is not fixed, but empties and fills, is carried high and drops low, according to my caresses and the body's secrets. I learnt that there is always one more part of the body for the tongue to probe, for the fingers to engage. I learnt that mouths that start off dry with nerves and anticipation soon overflow with juice, just like the nether orifices: an abundance of drinks. I learnt that my lover's eyes deceived, for when he was close to his limit it was as if he had moved away from the windows of his face into his inmost self, yet it was at such times that he was closer to me in spirit than ever. I learnt that pleasure is not only a final flourish of spending, but also a slow ooze throughout the course of our union, that sticks where it touches and weaves long, shining threads between my thigh, my navel, my breasts, like a spider's web of love.

And I learnt to keep my eyes open – why were they always closed in the books? – whether I was up close to his skin or beholding him half a body's length away. For I learnt that it is not just the men who like to look, as I sat myself up on my elbows or twisted myself round, the better to observe my lover's attentions. But I learnt too that men have the better view, as Din pulled himself up and back, hands on my hips to control the movements, and watch and smile, then look back into my eyes as if he could transfer the image to me that way. And he would place a candle between my thighs, and gaze and gaze and smile, and I learnt at last what my best angle was.

But the books never told me either that the more we did this, the greater would grow the urge to tell him that I loved him, and I wondered if that urge grew in him too, but somehow I doubted it. It was always the men, in the books, who said it first, and always beforehand, to convince their unwilling victims into the act, and never afterwards. I may have defied the books in many ways, but I knew I would not, could not, say it first.

Sylvia needed me every evening of those five days, which was just as well, for it was after hours, in the aftermath, that I found it hard to reconcile the shame prickling over my skin with the impetus to dance and run riot with fulfilled desire. I would sit in the tin-bath and pour icy water over my guilty, spent flesh, but I was torn: I wanted to rid myself of all traces of him, as much as I wanted to smell of him for longer.

The sixth day was Sunday, so the bindery was closed. But on the seventh, he did not come back to work.

I sat in the empty room, ennerved first by anticipation, and then by confusion, anger, and at times, relief, over the next few hours. I held myself tight in the waiting, as if any sudden movement would shatter the tentative and fragile bowl containing these new sensations, and disperse their memory for ever. I tried tidying as I waited for him, as if I could impose order on what had so recently been a temple of pleasure, or a boudoir of vice, I was still not sure which.

Presently I wandered into the kitchen, where Pansy was sorting the washing, and we heard noises in the parlour. Sylvia had opened up the dining-table with the spare leaf, and was trying to move it over to the window.

'I'm going to change the piano with the bookshelf, too. And do you like the scarves I've draped everywhere? I think it gives the room a certain freshness, don't you think, Dora?'

I shrugged, as I watched her struggle with the table.

'Aren't you going to help? Are you just going to stand there? If you will not help me, I will help myself.'

So I came over to the table, but as I placed my hands on the edge she gave it one almighty shove, with the full weight of her anger behind it, and it screeched towards the corner.

'You see, I don't need your help at all.'

And so I retreated once more into the bindery, and tried

to busy myself with work. I knew I had not made much headway on the crates that arrived after Peter's death, what with Jack being gone. I pulled out a stack of manuscripts, but I did not want to disband them and rig up the sewing-frame. I could not shake Din out of my head that way. I would have to ask Pansy to take over the sewing, in Din's absence. I fiddled around on a piece of paper with a few designs, and willed the day to go quicker, and passed it as in a fog.

My yearning for Din was as intense as Peter's had been for laudanum. The pain of not-having transcended the immediate satiation demanded by those lustful Turks. It brought with it its own thrill, which gratified me in the face of the strutting women of Lambeth, the respectable old women of Ivy-street. How free were they all, really? And what of Knightley, and Glidewell, and Diprose, and their lot? Libertines, were they? It felt as if Din and I were the only true Libertines in London society. The conversations we were yet to have; the parts of his body I was yet to kiss; the pouring ourselves over each other and languishing in the smells, the tastes, the heat. Dora, he said. Dora, he called across my fantasies. I cherished the way he said my name. ~~Dorra~~. ~~Dawra~~. ~~Doorra~~. It defies transcription. It leans on the 'do', and dwells on the 'r', richly mouthed, with a full pucker, like an Englishman would never do. *Dooarra*. He felt my name fully in his mouth as he spoke it. My name felt at home there, as if it were basking on the bed of his tongue, in an exciting new room. It felt safe there. *Dooarra*. Yes, my beloved Din.

Oh, but I needed to distract myself with work, before I succumbed to brain-fever. There were some sewn manuscripts ready for forwarding. But we were low on leather, and I could not send Jack to the tanneries to buy some more. I would have to go myself, but some other day, for what if Din arrived just then to find me gone? I ferreted around in the drawer for scraps of velvet to appliqué on to another binding, and came across the single strip of Diprose's special leather which I had saved. It was too late to return it, and he would never have known I had it. I had nothing better to do – everything else seemed like a superfluous nonsense at a time like this – so I thought that I might as well play. I measured the scrap with an angle, and cut it into a perfect rectangle, and then I tooled it into an elegant bookmark for my daughter.

What next? Not the books. No sewing, still. So I tried the anagram of Diprose's inscription. I scrutinised the grid of squares and spaces, then wrote out all the letters, first in alphabetical order, and then in random order.

a, a, a, b, c, c, d, e, f, h, i, i, i, m, n, o, o, p, r, r, r, s, u

n, c, o, a, r, b, c, s, d, u, h, i, m, a, i, o, p, e, r, i, a, r, f

'Birch' and 'houri', I found straight away, as well as 'farce', 'hide', 'chief', 'epic' and 'opium', all of which seemed very appropriate, but I did not need any four-or five-letter words: the grid demanded a word of two letters, followed by one of six, one of eight, and finally one of seven.

Two-letter words were easy: 'is', 'am', 'of', 'us', 'no', 'in', 'he', 'as'. I had thought that the tool I had used farthest to the left had been a 'd', but could not be sure. I had used no upper-case tools, so could not tell which letter had started the sentence that way.

Six-letter words were: 'mirror', 'riches', 'porous', 'prince', 'honour', 'heroic', 'french', 'purism', 'parish' and 'humour'.

Seven-letter words were: 'currish', 'ciphers', 'informs' and 'horrors'.

Eight-letter words were: 'abidance', 'academic', 'conspire' and 'horrific'.

When I found '*soir*' and '*horreur*' I wondered if the inscription was in French; when I found '*a priori*' and '*primus*', I wondered if it could be in Latin.

In short, I was none the wiser. I started to doubt my memory. Had the space been here, and not there? Had I really used 'a' three times, or just twice? Surely I had used 'e' more than once?

I gave up.

I pulled out my account book, which seemed a more sensible distraction, and settled down to my accounts.

I knew we had made a substantial profit, but I had not appreciated that the total would near seventy pounds. It was enough for a guillotine, even. But I had better things to spend the money on; I would continue to oil and steel the old one. I set aside a portion to put into savings for Lucinda, extracted Din's and Pansy's wages, then I took out of it a month's wages for Jack, and then I doubled it, and added another three pounds, and put it in an envelope to take to Lizzie.

Jack, dear Jack, Jack the Skull. I stared at the place where he used to stand behind the bench each day, and felt it tingle with love, real and pure and requited and unrequited, and lust, real and dirty, and I felt a flicker of understanding, that he was no different from me and Din, that we shared our own sense of joy and shame, bliss and guilt, and the feeling that we were different from the world out there, who would never love us the way we needed to be loved. And I thought of all the other men who traipsed through here with their higher and lower desires, their nobler and baser thoughts, and I wondered if we were all one and the same.

That evening, Sylvia sat at the newly positioned table writing a list, muttering to herself.

'Valentine, first. Then I need to find Aubrey. Yes, Aubrey will know. And Theodore, of course, if he will speak to me. I could send a letter to Charles, but that may take a while. Dora, congratulate me on my plans. I will grill them all, and find all Jossie's sins. There must be – must be – some mistress in Paris, some concubine in Africa. Where was he on his birthday last year? With some doxy in a bawdyhouse, no doubt.'

'And you think they'll tell you? The other Noble Savages?'

'Of course they'll tell me. They'll tell me everything. They'll tell me . . .'

'What?' I prompted.

'What?' she quizzed me vaguely.

'The Savages. What will they tell you?'

'What it is I need to know.'

'Which is what?'

'Dora! I can divorce him, if I can prove adultery in the first instance, together with bigamy, incest, or cruelty, or desertion, or rape, or sodomy. So, adultery first. Shouldn't be hard. Incest is out, thank the Lord, and rape, and sodomy.' I might have raised a querying eyebrow, but she did not see. 'Bigamy is always a possibility, in those evil lands he frequents. And cruelty, hmmm.'

'Desertion?'

'Strictly speaking, I left him. But that's a detail. We would still have to wait two years, though, until it counts as desertion.'

'But Sylvia, what rights would these give you over your property?'

'I will be able at least to inherit and bequeath; so whatever my father deigns to leave me would come to me. And anything I might earn in the future. Not that I'd actually consider working. So, cruelty. Oh curses! It doesn't exactly look promising, does it?'

'You could always claim he was right, and that you were adulterous, and then he could divorce you.'

'Oh, Dora. Imagine the shame.'

'Any less shameful than what you have been reduced to?' She pondered for a while. 'On second thoughts,' I continued, 'I have probably advised you ill. For if he divorces you, on grounds of adultery, he gains custody of Nathaniel.'

'He would not claim it. He hates the child.'

'Wouldn't he? Not even to spite you?'

'He loathes him, Dora.'

'Not as much as he loathes you.'

'You evil bitch! Hush your vile mouth!'

And then a thought crackled painfully across my brain, and I wondered why I had not realised before. I had no reason to believe the woman, or Din, for that matter. He had intimated as much about her soirées, only I wanted to believe him when he said that he was never touched *in that way*. But her ladyship's excessive protestations against Jocelyn's accusations only aroused my suspicions, and my cheeks flushed with anger, and no, surely not, with *jealousy*. Might it be true that Nathaniel was not Sir Jocelyn's child after all? Was it possible, could it be, that Nathaniel was *Din's* child?

I turned aside and caught my breath, as Sylvia scribbled beside me. Had she known him in that way? Had she possessed him? How blind I had been! How I had chosen to ignore the awful possibility! I looked at her with resentment and mistrust. I was vexed, and did not know what to do. I felt the urge to strike her.

Had she carried his child for nine months? Had she had what was mine? Had she been there first?

Did you molest unsuspecting black men? I wanted to shout at her. Did you ride a black cock and impregnate yourself with coloured seed? I was burning inside.

I watched her as she wrote, this woman, who allegedly worked hard to secure the freedom of the most exploited race on earth, and yet delighted in making them her own slaves – sexual slaves – of sorts. What a perfect match she was with her contradictory Sir Jocelyn.

And then we heard Nathaniel awaken upstairs, and start to holler.

'Oh, Dora. Do go and look in on him, for I am quite weary.'

What did you do to Din?! I wanted to scream at her. But, to save myself from any rash action, I willingly fled upstairs and picked up Nathaniel, and placed him on my shoulder. I tried to angle him in the moonlight, to see what colour his skin really was, but we are all shades of grey at night.

'Are you my Din's baby?' I cooed at him. 'Are you my little Din? Ooh, what a din you are making. Ooh, what a din Din made here. Ooh, and do you want some din-dins? Din-din-din-da-din-dindin.' And so it became a silly song, pounding though my heart was, and he was soon quiet but alert, and looking round at the dark shapes thrown by the moonlight around the room. I placed him back in his drawer. 'Din-din-da-dindin.'

What with Jack, and me and Din, and Sylvia here too, I was indeed running a veritable atelier of transgression. I should have written on Pansy's advertisement that those who trod the straight path in life need not apply. Was the road to Damage's really such a crooked one? The streets outside looked straight and Roman, but Roman indeed was the dwelling to which it brought one.

The following morning I did not unlock the workshop at all. I knew I could not face Din now, were he to show, yet neither could I face another day without him. Curses on him. Was I really no better than all the other Ladies of the Society, in my desire for the man?

I wanted better things from today. I put the money for Lizzie, and some to buy leather, into my purse under my skirt, and then thought again, and took the bookmark with me too. I went to the grocer and ordered four weekly deliveries of food to Lizzie's house, which cost the equivalent of a month of Jack's wages. Then I went up to the river, and gave the other month to Lizzie in cash, with the futile plea that she didn't spend it all on gin. And finally, I headed off to Bermondsey once more, to the tanners.

I did not go to Select Skins and Leather Dressings, but went instead to Felix Stephens. It was smaller than Select Skins, with only a handful of customers, and I waited by a stack of hides to be served. Curious, I thought, how being a women renders one both conspicuous and invisible at the same time. But soon, visibility won out, and a man came over to ask me my business there.

'I've come to settle the account of Mr Peter Damage,' I said, and was led into the office at the back. The man showed me into a chair, then went to the other side of the desk, from which he pulled out two large ledgers. He rifled through the first, then the second. He did not hurry, but was efficient and calm, and I warmed to him. Eventually he turned both ledgers round to me, and talked me through each item and the date of purchase, before ringing the totals owed in red ink, and adding them up.

'You can pay half plus five per cent, or a quarter plus seven per cent, now. Up to you. How'd you like it?'

'I'd like to pay it all, please,' I said, handing over the full amount. He seemed surprised at first, but happily counted through the notes and coins, placed the cash in to a money-box, and wrote PAID IN FULL across both pages of the ledgers.

'And now, I was hoping you could have a look at this for me.' I pulled out the bookmark and gave it to him.

'What is it?'

'I don't know. That's where I need your expert eye.'

He fingered it with courteous disdain. 'It's a botch job, that's for sure,' he said dourly. 'Look at this flay mark. Done by an amateur, I can tell you that much.'

'I thought that was a vein.'

'No. This line, here, is a vein, which shows me that it wasn't bled immediately after slaughter. It must have been left for quite some time – means the blood had time to putrefy in the veins.'

'So possibly it had died naturally, and was chanced upon in the wild, by someone who thought its skin would be nice to use for a book.'

'Possibly. Whatever happened, it was left for some time. The skin should have been removed and cured within minutes, especially in a hot climate.'

'And how would they cure it?'

He started to relax a little, with the chance to show off his skill. 'You'd hope the leather you'd buy over here would be brined, or wet-salted. But brining is expensive and you need quantities of hide to wet-salt. So I think this has been dried. The oldest way known to man, but it's an uneven, unpredictable, uncontrollable process. This has probably been laid over stones, as it's dry in patches. Done by a cheapskate, that's for sure. 'Straordinary, really, that you've got it at all – leather like this usually stays in the poor countries, as no right-minded man here would buy it. Good tanning is a hard job, madam, that's the truth, if you think about it; it ain't easy, drying a hide just enough to stop it rotting, without making the leather all hard and inflexible. But this is plain shoddy; whoever did this should be brought to task. Brings the industry into disrepute, if you think about it.'

'I'm sorry to trouble you with it,' I said. 'I don't know why I've brought it to you at all, really, only that I'd never seen the like before. I've already pressed my procurer about it, but he told me precious little about where it came from. I thought at first that it could be a type of pigskin.'

'Yes, you are right there, tanned pigskin is notoriously poor. But it's not pig.' Here he seized his magnifier. 'Look, them follicles are not arranged in that distinctive triangular pattern, and they don't go all the way through to the reverse, like the holes left by pig bristles. No, it's not pig.'

'And the follicles are random, so I knew it wasn't goatskin,' I added. 'And it's not dense enough for cowskin either, or oily enough for sealskin. Although that could be to do with the inferior tanning, which I had not considered before you mentioned it.'

'No, it's not sealskin.'

'Could it be lambskin?'

'Possibly. But what a waste of a good lamb, to spoil it so in the tanning.'

'Could it be doeskin?'

'Unlikely. Look how irregular the grain is. It's a puzzle, really it is. Leave it with me. I like puzzles.'

'I'm afraid I can't. But I thank you for your time. While I am here, may I trouble you for some morocco? I will pay now; I don't want to keep the account open.'

And so he helped me to some more leather, and I bought four fine hides, which he rolled and tied nicely for me, and I was grateful for his help and attention, although I was even more grateful to be leaving behind the bloody streets of Bermondsey and the stink of pure.

When I got back that afternoon I set about paring the leather and cutting the boards for several more books. I could no longer afford to be nervous about the forwarding process. I had just started to hammer the spine of one particularly loathsome edition of *Venus School Mistress*, when Sylvia glided in. I had not thought to lock the door.

'Come, Dora. You work so hard. Another hot flannel is in order, I think.'

'No, Sylvia, I do not feel like it today. Oh, don't . . . !' But it was too late. Sylvia had picked a book out of one of the crates, and was opening it. 'No, Sylvia! Please.'

'Dora,' she retorted, holding the book loosely in one hand, but looking straight at me. 'Don't "please" me. I know all about Jossie's books.' And you know all about my Din, too, you bitch, I wanted to shout. She turned back to the book, opened it properly, and said, 'Oh! Oh my!' before snapping it shut. She eased herself down onto Din's chair by the sewing-frame, and flapped the pages of the manuscript over her face like a fan. 'I thought I knew. One has to excuse a lot when married to a medic. Still, I suppose these are not a million library shelves away from his anatomical text books, are they?'

'Sir Jocelyn has a fine collection of anatomies, indeed,' I concurred. Could she really have slept with my Din? She seemed so prim. I didn't want to believe it. 'I wish my Peter had had the chance to peruse them,' I said, to shake my thoughts off their coupling. 'Peter bound some of the great anatomies, but the Galen, and the Bourgery, why, he had not seen the like.' I could see Sir Jocelyn's shelves in front of me as I spoke.

'Jossie loves his books. He loves me too, Dora.'

'Of course he does,' I reassured her. She couldn't have done it, could she? Something was awry, here.

She had started to hug herself, and stroke her shoulders as if imagining his caresses. 'He always loved my shoulders so, my back.'

I could see the title of Sir Jocelyn's finest anatomical tract, Vesalius's *De humani corporis fabrica libri septem*.

'I miss his kisses, Dora. I miss being loved.'

Something was tapping at my brain. Vesalius. Anatomies. What was it? Or was it just Din?

'How do you cope without it, Dora?'

Without what? Without Peter? Or without Din? What was she saying? Anatomies, weren't we talking about?

Then suddenly the fog lifted. I riffled on the bench for the paper on which I had scribbled my musings about the anagram. *De humani corporis fabrica*. It was a perfect fit.

'The things he used to say when he touched me. He could have been a poet.'

I felt as if some invisible hand were strangling me as I struggled to make sense of it. The casing could not have been a binding for an anatomy text, could it?

De humani corporis fabrica.

'*Le peau de ma femme*,' Sylvia said softly, and my blood froze.

'What?'

'*Le peau de ma femme*,' she repeated. I remembered the words in amongst some letters I had bound, in Glidewell's hand. Glidewell to Knightley.

De humanis corporis fabrica. Literally, on the fabric of the human body. Bodies. Mine, Din's, Sylvia's. I went back to the Latin, but I knew enough of how the brains of these gentlemen worked now to sidestep logic and accuracy. I knew what the inscription was trying to say about the binding. I turned to Sylvia, and said softly, 'Tell me about the *peau de ma femme*.' Don't talk to me about Din, now. Something more horrific is afoot.

'My shoulders, Dora. I was telling you. Jossie used to kiss them and tell me that no woman had finer skin. My skin was the nonpareil of everything. He even corresponded with Valentine about the smoothness of my skin: this Dutch paper, he would write, is smoother than the *peau de ma femme*. This perfume smells like the *peau de ma femme*. These flower petals are as soft as the *peau de ma femme*.'

'To be so prized . . .' I murmured. Comprehension was a painful thing. My suspicions about Din and Sylvia were only that – suspicions. Here, I was facing something more indisputable about her husband, something I knew to be true. *De humani corporis fabrica.*

'Oh, how he would kiss them!' She giggled. 'Oh, Dora, he would say, oh, he would say, that he wanted to bind a volume of the finest love poetry in the skin from my shoulders after my death, so he would never have to be parted from their smoothness. Never be parted! He never wanted us to be parted, Dora. Dora!'

De humani corporis fabrica.

The defiance I had been feeling no longer supported me, and I finally crumbled.

'Dora!' I heard Sylvia scream. 'Dora!'

The sobs heaved out of my chest, and I lurched and stumbled into Sylvia's horrified, outstretched arms. She held me close, but her thin arms offered little succour, and besides they might have wrapped around Din once upon a time. It was my mother's arms I wanted, and my sobs were tearless.

I felt my supper rise in my throat, my body revolting at myself, and at the world to which I was so inescapably chained.

De humani corporis fabrica.

I tore myself away from Sylvia, and, shaking with anger and grief, I grabbed the book she had put down and threw it at the wall, as if it stood for all the ignoble books for which I had been responsible. I strode up and down, grasping my hair, and wrenched my face from side to side as if searching for a way out.

'Dora!' I heard Sylvia scream again. I saw her as if through a veil; she reached out for me again, but I could not stand her or myself any more. I wanted to bathe myself, to scrub myself with the toughest brush from head to foot, but the water would not run again until tomorrow morning, and even then I knew I would never feel clean again, not until I had ripped every inch of skin off my sinful flesh.

And then, in the far recesses of my troubled soul, I heard a distant knocking, and I was dragged up from the depths of my misery into the present moment and to the awareness of a call from behind the outside door of the bindery. I stared like a horrified animal at Sylvia, and watched as she made to open it, but I flew to it before her, and threw the door open.

I saw Din standing there, as in a far-away dream. He was excited. He started to talk at me. He spoke so quickly, I could not hear him.

'Dora. Mrs Damage,' he said, uncertain how to address the lover from whom he had absented himself. Sylvia is here too, I could have said, to taunt him. Who would you prefer?

I shook my head, as if to dislodge the water in my ears after a swim, like when I was a child back in Hastings, but it did not help. Still I could not hear him clearly, only through glass, through worlds, or dream-states.

'It's happenin', now. War is breakin' in my country. I have to . . .'

And then his words screamed clearly into my ears as if the water had cleared, the glass had shattered, the dream had broken.

'I have to . . .' he repeated.

'Go!' I screamed back at him, as if completing his sentence for him. 'Go away!'

His face faded from me, and then swam back into focus.

'Go!' I screamed once more. 'A war? I have enough blood on my hands already!'

But still he stood there. He was questioning me, and I was not to be questioned. I wanted to be obliterated, but his presence was making me more real. I needed him to walk away from me, so I could vanish with him.

'Please. Leave me alone!'

De humani corporis fabrica. Made of human skin.

And have you fucked us both into the bargain?

And then I closed the door on his approaching foot, arm, face, feeling the resistance of his flesh until the latch finally found its hole, and I bolted the door and felt him disappear. But he did not take with him my self-loathing, which took me straight towards the bottle of Black Drop on the dresser, and soon I did not know if Sylvia was still watching me, or had gone away with her own miseries.

Chapter Twenty-two

Dancy-diddlety-poppety-pin,
Have a new dress when summer comes in;
When summer goes out,
'Tis all worn out,
Dancy-diddlety-poppety-pin.

'Oh my, how clear it suddenly becomes! Dora, do you know what *sati* means?'

'*Sati*? The immolation of a Hindoo widow on her husband's funeral pyre. It's been illegal for some time.'

'It still continues, in the more rural, out-of-the-way places in India. Jocelyn told me so.'

'Why would he torment you thus?'

'Torment me? Why, he was assuaging me! I hated his long absences, and he would lecture me on the barbaric practices that went on in the darkest corners of the world which he, and only he, could put a stop to. He told me he had to go, in the name of civilisation. To stop the Africans taking a knife to their little girls in the name of chastity; to stop the Hindoos from burning their widows in the name of fidelity; to stop the . . . oh!'

'Do go on!'

'It is hard for me. And that is why I must explain to you, Dora, for I heard Jocelyn boasting to someone – Valentine, Charles, Hugh, whoever – that he would rescue a brave and beautiful widow from *sati* – from her husband's funeral pyre – and immortalise her for ever in the greatest scientific and

388

literary work of the century! Surely ... but I had presumed that this meant the woman would become the basis of a phrenological study! That she was a biological curiosity to him. That there must have been something in her cranial shape and general physiognomy that predisposed her people to barbarism, that it was Jocelyn's duty to discover. This I had so nobly assumed! I would never have thought to take him at his word!'

Is this the intrinsic worth, I wondered, of the human body, to be so reduced after we are gone? And what leads a man to reduce it so, in the name of exaltation? Is he so severed from our source that he must sever more in his quest for wholeness? We tear down trees and rip up animals for our books; we kill elephants and destroy forests to make pianos on which we make music to soothe our souls; small wonder the music is so plaintive, with ivory yearning for its life back. But what when the materials are from amongst our own? For the exaltation of his own fleshful library, Sir Jocelyn had stripped this woman of more than her clothes.

I thought of the books of our lives, and I prayed to St Bartholomew for the opportunity to erase the last few pages of my life and rewrite them. St Bartholomew. And then it dawned on me. He had been flayed alive by Astyages for converting his brother, the King of Armenia, to Christianity. He was not merely patron saint of bookbinders, but of tanners, cobblers and leather-workers besides. Was this a macabre prank? Or was this a tradition whose origins ran deeper and bloodier than I could imagine? I could only think of the St Bartholomew's Day Massacre, the slaughter of thousands of innocents for their differences, and the power that continues to be wielded by the most unworthy.

'Dora. Dora. Calm yourself, girl. What are you doing?'

'What does it look like I'm doing?'

'Well, why, then? Why are you doing it? That's a perfectly reasonable dress. It might be last season's, I'll grant you, but it will last you many more. It's presentable enough.'

My scissors ripped through the seams, and soon I had sixteen pieces of brown silk of various shapes and sizes, and two large pieces of cream silk. I sorted through them until I found what had been two sleeves, and two bodice-sides, then I smoothed down the rest on to the table, one on top of each other. Then I grabbed the cloud of brown and cream silk in both arms, and took them into the workshop. 'Dora! It won't bring her back!' Sylvia shouted after me.

But what else could I have done? This is what I had learnt to do in times of adversity: work. But it was not so much 'working' as 'working out': the bindings were not as relevant as the plan I needed to formulate. One thing was for sure: it was better to have Sylvia on my side now than against me. I would cease my suspicions about her and Din. I laid the pieces of brown silk down on the bench and assessed the number and sizes of journals and albums I would be able to magic from them.

I dissected the parasol, discarded its stem and spokes, and turned the pale blue silk into an embroidered pocket-book, trimmed with its own point-lace. I striped ribbons of cream silk from the scarf over the brown silk of the dress, for several albums. The tortoiseshell top of the hair comb became a buckle on the edge of another brown silk volume, and I fashioned a fastener out of silver wire so it would snap shut. The purple feathers bedecked the ivory silk of the petticoats; the black feathers sprayed around the black rose from the centre of the dress's bodice in an unusual and beautiful centrepiece on the cover of a scrapbook. Everything – except Lucinda's coat – was sacrificed to the alchemical process that provided me with a frenzied focus, as if in work I would find the answer. The work consumed me, and for a while consumed my guilt, and the immoral life I had been leading.

But as I sliced up the silk and wrapped it around the boards, I could only think of the poor unfortunate whose skin had been used for the binding. It was a woman, it had to be. Was it the Hindoo widow, dragged from the fire? If so, how did she ultimately meet her death at the hands of her so-called saviours? I was angry; angry for her ignominious demise, and angry for my unwitting role in furthering her dishonour. I had read of it in a thousand vile books, but I had not realised until this moment how closely allied were anger and desire. And as in every one of those books, my desire was indeed to violate the one towards whom I felt anger. I wanted one thing only. Revenge.

Go to the police, an inner voice called! Pah! To what effect? Look at Charlie Diprose, prancing out of his cell a week into what should rightfully have been a four-year sentence! If that odious man could slip so fluidly out of the hands of the law, why should I imagine that Sir Jocelyn Knightley was any less untouchable?

If only I had known before Diprose brought me the leather. If only. I would have burnt it in the fire before it left my hands to deny the twisted pleasure of so diseased an imagination. If only. And what if. What if I could find out where the book was now? What if I could retrieve it? I could destroy it myself. I could go to Holywell-street – in disguise? I could send . . . who? I could break in . . . I could break in to Berkeley-square? I could send Sylvia back one last time? I could . . . I could . . . I could not think of a single reasonable plan, and the brown silk kept turning to skin beneath my accursed fingers, and I retched, and swooned, and burned with rage and impotence.

My anger was my consolation, though. I thought of Lizzie, whom life had taught that there was no point in getting angry, for nothing would change by it. Anger is a luxury for those who still have hope, who still have dignity; those who have neither, those like Lizzie, know not to waste their energy on anger.

I tried to annihilate the book from my thoughts by focusing

on the women who might own these silken journals. I didn't want to give them to a bookseller who might prove to be another Diprose. I wanted to hand them out on New Cut and Lambeth Walk, throw them from Waterloo Bridge to the mud-larks, walk up the street and give them to Mrs Eeles, Nora Negley, Patience Bishop, Agatha Marrow. Write them, I would scream at them. What are we to write, their faces would ask, looking as blank as the pages within. Your dreams, I would cry. Your thoughts. Your fantasies. Yours, and yours alone. In your own voice. Not constructed for you by Mr Eeles, Mr Marrow, Mr Bishop or Mr Negley, dead or alive. Author your own body. Walk your own text. Is it not constantly being read anyway, each time you walk up the street? You read mine often enough.

Ha! I rued. Would it could have been so. For more likely than not, I knew that every one of these brown-silk beauties would be bought by some rich roué, and some would go to appease the wives, and some would tickle the fancy of the courtesans, and the brothel-keeper would keep her illicit accounts in one, and the dilettante would sketch his naked mistress in another, so ha! Ha to my noble thoughts! And so the world goes, and so our bodies rot and turn to dust, to gold, to nothing. Welcome to Damage's Bindery. The Whore of Bibliolon.

For, once again, more than for peace of mind, I was working, still, for money. The chinking of coins saw me through every fold, every stitch, every cut and every paste, for money was what would see me through, and time was running out.

For one thought sounded clear in the morass of confusion. I could no longer continue to work for Charles Diprose and the Noble Savages. Which would mean that I would break our unwritten contract. Which would mean that London – possibly even England – would become unsafe for us. I needed money to do what I knew was inevitable.

I would flee with Lucinda.

I would find Din before he left, and together the three of us would go to the only place we could possibly go together. America.

'You must be insane! Insane!'

There is no hope; no, for I have loved strangers, and after them will I go.

'Sylvia!' I had figured that the remarkable and rather beautiful change that had come about in her since Jocelyn's final dismissal of her would have opened her to a more sympathetic understanding of my plight. There was nothing else for it, than to broach the issue. 'Sylvia,' I repeated, more softly. 'Is there something behind your anger?'

'I do not follow you.'

'Is there something you wish to tell me about your relationship with . . . with . . . Din?'

'Your intimation, please?'

'Nathaniel,' I whispered, but immediately wished I hadn't, suspicious fool that I was. Of course she would deny it, but I had not appreciated with how much vehemence.

Her mouth fell open, and her eyes widened, and she looked as if she would hit me, but instead she slumped on to the chair and said, 'Not you too! Do you mean to say you have not believed me all this time? Do you accuse me too?'

'Sylvia,' I said gently. 'I know about your evenings with him. I know about the spear.'

'Pshaw!' she said. 'It was not only me. We all have our curiosities. But as if I would take it any further! Dora, you revolt me. You are worse than Jocelyn. But then, you really *have* slept with a black man, so of course, you suspect everyone else of having the same letches.'

There is no hope; no, for I have loved strangers, and after them will I go. Where had I read that recently?

'And you! You, leaving for America, with him! I have

393

never heard anything so mad! I should call for a doctor immediately!'

I remembered the quotation. It was from the book of Jeremiah.

'What you are saying is an abomination! You disgust me! Never in my wildest dreams!'

'Be that as it may, I persist in thinking it would be safest for me to leave. But I am concerned for you, and leaving you behind.'

'Dora, Dora darling. Let me talk some sense into your feeble little head. I do understand, really I do, or at least I think I do, that your Black Prince may now be to you some darling thing with kinky hair and velvet skin, but let me tell you in no uncertain terms, painful though it may be, that in time he will revert to type. I have learnt more than I care to share with you through my work with the Society. They may be our brethren, but they are not our equals. To such a man, his wife is by custom his slave. She is nothing more than a tiller of the ground, a vessel for more children than nature can cope with, and an outlet for his rage!'

'Sylvia . . . !'

'He will kill you, one day, in a savage attack! Or he will take another wife! Or, heaven forbid, wives plural! And Lord, knows, he may not be a bachelor now!'

'Sylvia . . . !'

'Dora! You are very naughty!' She opened her eyes wide and dared me to interrupt her again. When she continued, her voice was calmer, and she had changed tack. 'Dora. There is one reason above all others why I would never have relations with a black man. And that is, that in so doing, one foolish white woman endangers all other white women! Think of your American sisters! Your impropriety will have completely changed that man's expectations of them; their safety has been jeopardised, by you! You! Your actions have served to weaken the very Empire! I have absolutely no idea why you would want a nigger for a lover anyway.'

'And you never did?' I retorted, despite myself. Even if Din wasn't Nathaniel's father, who was to say that she didn't have her way with one of the other slaves bought by the Society? I settled on that as the most likely explanation; it soothed me better, at least.

'Oh!' she exclaimed again, and then her tears started, and I did not move to stop them. I did not even fetch her a handkerchief. 'Oh Dora, forgive me! Forgive me! I am an evil, evil woman! My words are wrong, and I am ashamed! I speak only out of fear for myself, and a deep, and I fear, fatal, disillusionment about love.'

'Well may you say that now.'

'I guessed about your feelings for Din,' she continued, 'a long time ago. But I wish you well. I know you must leave me, and I am sad about that; you showed me unusual kindness in my time of greatest distress, and I fear you are not just the only friend I have, but the best friend I could hope to have. Do you believe me when I tell you I love you?'

I had no answer. I didn't know what I believed of what she told me any more.

'And that I love Lucinda? Look how I love Nathaniel, now that I have embraced my role as his mother! How could I not love Lucinda, who loves him so? Do you not know that?'

'I do,' I whispered.

'And know then, that I wish you well. For I do love you, Dora, and I love Lucinda. So, can't you see, that I cannot bear for two people I care about so deeply to be going to a country racked by civil war! Don't you see that you and Lucinda and Din will be torn apart by more enemies than you can possibly imagine? Have you no eyes, no ears, no worldly wisdom, no common sense? Or has love so deluded you?'

But despite Sylvia's sentiments, I went to Mrs Catamole's boarding house on Borough High Street, but the woman was out and her girl did not know of her tenants' whereabouts.

I left a note for Din, but heard nothing, so Friday found me hailing the omnibus at the Strand and returning to Whitechapel. I willed it to quicken its slow crawl through the traffic, and the moment I got off at Whitechapel I ran through the streets, my veil obscuring my vision. It was harder this time, for then I was following Din, and not logging landmarks and street signs. But I told myself over and over that I would not be too late. It was hard enough, I knew, to find the right ship, with a decent-minded captain, and once he had, she might not sail for weeks. I would not be too late.

And yet again I asked myself as I ran, bumping into passers-by, who spun round to watch me with affront, whether I truly loved the man, or whether I saw him as my way out. But I knew that every black face I saw in the crowds made my heart leap in expectation, and I also knew, despite everything that Sylvia had said, and anything she might have made that man do to her, that the moment I saw the real Din I would fall in love with him all over again, even though every inch of my body was already possessed by love for him.

I skidded on the cobbles on the corner opposite the pub, for I came upon it sooner than I had expected. The door was open at the top of the stairs. Who would be below? And what would I say to them? They would recognise me from the veil, at least. I opened the door. It was dark within, but I found the first step and started to climb down. I held my breath; the cellar smelt musty.

I had reached the halfway step when I knew that what I was doing was ridiculous. But it wasn't until my foot landed on the grainy cement on the bottom that I knew for sure. There were shapes in the darkness, but they were the forms of barrels and kegs, boxes and crates. I quickly went back up and stood outside. Then I turned and went through the other door, into the pub itself, and pushed the veil back over my head.

If those within had stopped their talking and turned to

stare at me, I wouldn't have been aware of it, for I steeled myself against their gaze, found my target and marched towards him, barefaced, without hesitation. The landlord was filling a glass for a customer; his head kept disappearing from view behind a crowd of dirty barrel-like backs.

'G'is a cuppa lightnin',' someone bellowed.

'Excuse me,' I announced, and yanked at each back, each waist, with my gloved hands. They pulled back as if stung; some chuckled when they saw me, some gawped. But in time the backs parted, and I reached the cherry-wood bar.

'Where's Din?' I shouted at the landlord. I had seen him, of course, but he had never seen me. 'Din. From downstairs.'

'What you wanna know for, then?'

'He works for me.'

'Not any more he don't.'

'Have they left?'

'Yup. Every last one.'

'Where to?'

'Why should I tell you?'

'Because I'm asking you.'

'What's in it for me?'

'Have they gone to America?'

'So you know then?'

'I came to a meeting, last November.'

He stopped pulling the pint, and placed the glass down on the bar, then he wiped his hand on a glass cloth and did not seem to hear the orders coming from around me.

'They left for Bristol on Wednesday.'

'So quick?'

'It was Din that did it. He said they couldn't stay another day.'

'So could he still be in Bristol?'

'Only if he misses his ship. It was going to be tight anyway. It leaves on the morrow!'

And then he turned away from me, and poured the quart

397

of porter, the quartern of gin, two pots of heavy brown, and a dog's nose, which he dumped on the bar with a 'damp yer mugs, gen'emen', and the backs closed on me again, and hefty boots trod on my fine ones, and I hunched my shoulders together as if I were folding myself in half, and I slipped out from between them, and into the night air.

My mind still clutched on to hope, and resorted to logic. They left on Wednesday. Would they have found lifts? Or had they the money for a train? Either way, they would only arrive in Bristol today at the earliest. But it would take me another three days from now, too. I will send a telegraph, I thought. I will go to the all-night office at St Martin's-le-Grand, or West Strand, even, if I could face it, and send a telegraph – but to where? And what would I say?

I would tell you, I thought, why I pushed you away in my fear, why I did not draw you closer, for support; why I told you I had blood on my hands, when I had only held a dry epidermis in all innocence. I am not a murderess, I would say to you, only the murderer's unwitting assistant. I would tell you all this.

I could not, of course. But what if I had? Would he have stayed? No. He would have gone anyway, to fight for his country. Would he have let me come with him? No, not if he had had any sense. But at least I could have kissed him farewell, stood on the quay, and waved him off with my handkerchief, praying for his safety. But what of that? Would that have helped either of us any? He would always be an absence.

Danger lurked between every pool of gas-light on my way home, but I did not fear it. My only fear was that I would live to face the rage and despair that was consuming me. I felt my aloneness and insignificance, and shook with anger and pain, and, ironically, it was my pain that protected me from harm. For it was as if my affliction left marks in the air as I stumbled over Waterloo Bridge, and even those of malevolent bent saw it, and left me alone to my misery.

*   *   *

'Wake up, Dora! Dora, wake!' Sylvia was shaking me. Her hair was messy. I could see that, which meant that it was light. Which meant that I had slept in. I tried to remember why.

'The postman has been. He brought this!' She was brandishing a letter. 'I did not find it at first; I was hiding from that dreadful Charles Diprose.'

'Diprose was here?' I said, sitting up in bed. 'Why?'

'I don't know,' she said, disinterestedly. 'I didn't want him to see me here. I stayed upstairs. Listen, I want to read you this.' I reached for my shawl, and started to think about a cup of tea. 'It starts, *Constance*. That's my second name. He used to say he appreciated its sentiment more than Sylvia, which was too pagan for him. But I digress.' I was trying to concentrate, but it still felt so early. ' "Know that I have little care for your desires, but should it be desirous to you, I will grant you a divorce. It is, quite literally, immaterial to me, not that your not insignificant dowry was ever why I first foolishly fell in love with you. Out of the goodness of my heart and way beyond anything expected of me by the courts, I offer you an annuity of three hundred pounds. I refer the matter now to my solicitors, Messrs Krupp and Tadyer, who will be dealing with it on my behalf given my imminent removal to Africa. Your speculations are dangerous and serve you ill; now you have no need to harbour such vain fantasies, and I trust you shall release them as our marriage too is relinquished. My wishes to you are of the very best variety. Yours &c, Jocelyn." '

'No mention of his son,' I said to her, as I reached for my dress.

'None whatsoever,' she replied.

'But I doubt he would have left you an annuity if you had not had him.'

'Do you think not?'

'I think not.'

399

Sylvia sighed. 'I used to think he was quite the Renaissance Man.'

'Resurrection Man, more like. He holds a candle to the devil. Or is that too harsh? Let me be more precise. He is, in fairly equal proportions, a third despot, a third idiot, and a third coward.'

'And a third insolent,' Sylvia added.

'Come, let's go downstairs. I need some tea.' I pulled on my boots, and descended, with Sylvia following me. 'Lucinda,' I called, as I reached the bottom of the stairs. 'Lucinda?' But she was not in the parlour, nor the kitchen. I looked out into the street, but she rarely played outside any more, and besides, it was too early for that.

'Sylvia, have you seen Lucinda?'

'Why, she opened the door to Charles. She can't be far. I simply couldn't face him, Dora, now that he knows we know.'

I did not need to check the door; I knew it was ajar from the coldness breezing through the house. But I felt an inner chill. 'We know what, Sylvia?' I asked, but I knew the answer before she replied; the woman was more foolish than I could ever have anticipated.

'It was the perfect answer,' I heard her protest, as I threw my veil over my head. 'It was my way of claiming cruelty – admittedly, not to me, but to the poor trollop he saved from the pyre, which is an indirect form of cruelty, isn't it? Adultery would be self-evident to any judge, in the face of that, don't you think?'

'You *told* him?' But my wrath was slowing me down. 'No, don't answer me!' I seized my shawl and gloves. 'Tell me, was he in a carriage?'

'Yes, I think so. Oh, Dora, did I do wrong?'

Your speculations are dangerous and serve you ill.

I was running up Ivy-street in the direction of the river by the time I got to wrapping my shawl about my shoulders. The cold wind slapped my cheeks awake, and soon I was pushing my way through the Saturday-morning market goers, tradesmen and stallholders, until I was free to break into a run once more. The carriages, however, were moving apace, and I held out little hope of finding the one I was after. I knew I would have to cross Waterloo Bridge, but then I did not know whether I should head for Berkeley-square, or Holywell-street.

Luck would have it that the traffic had slowed to a halt at the approach to the turnstile by the bridge, and I was able to peer into each one as I passed, all the while scanning up ahead of me for one that I might recognise. And then I saw a dirty brown hansom that I had seen before, and there was her pale face pressed up against the glass. The cab was parked at a slight angle to the line of cabs waiting to cross the bridge, as if it were not quite in the queue. It seemed to be waiting for me. Her mouth opened when she saw me, and I waved to her, and she lifted her hand. I was nearly there, nearly with her.

It was nature that led to me to throw myself into the carriage and seize her in my arms; reason might have persuaded me to stay outside, and negotiate her return to me. But I was inside before I knew it, and holding her, and she me, and she cried into me. And before I had a chance to look around me, we lurched off our feet and had to sit down, next to the other occupant of the cab, for the driver was not paying his fare to cross the turnstile, but had turned the cab round and we were now heading eastwards at quite a lick, towards the Borough, and we were prisoners, I realised at last, of Mr Diprose.

'Where are you taking us?' I demanded of him.

He simply held up his hand to silence me. '*Chaque chose en son temps.*'

'No. you will tell me now! You have kidnapped my child; you must tell me what you mean by it. Lucinda, tell me what the man said to you.'

'He said we were going on an adventure,' she whispered from around my waist.

'And we are, Lucinda, we are,' Mr Diprose said. 'Now, conserve your spirits, for we have a long journey ahead of us.' And with that, he folded his arms, leant his head against the wall, and closed his eyes.

I tried the doors, but they had been locked from the outside. I banged on the roof.

'Let us out, boy!' I shouted. 'Let us out! Stop and let us out!' But I received no reply. 'We do not wish to be here! Stop!' I yelled again. Then I shook Mr Diprose awake, and shouted at him, 'Stop the carriage, you blackguard! Tell me where you are taking us.'

He picked my hands off him with disdain and turned his head further away from me. I peeked out of the curtains, but I did not recognise any of the streets or landmarks. We were certainly in the poorer districts of London still, south of the river, and, I presumed, still heading east. I did not remember crossing the river. I patted Lucinda's hands, and told her silly stories, and she even laughed once, but I was sorely vexed inside.

At some point, as we were nearing out destination, Diprose awoke.

'Now if you would be so kind as to enlighten us, Mr Diprose . . .' I ventured.

But still he remained silent, and soon the cab pulled to a halt, and we stumbled out onto the pavement. The scene that greeted us was beyond anything I had seen before, even up by the river, or beside the tanneries. I knew not where we were, but I could tell straight away it was a neglected place of tears and no pity. Every building was broken; wood and bricks clung forlornly on to crumbling beams; rags and planks patched every window which had never known glass. Strange scents hung in the air – fried fish, mixed with a spicy sweetness, and rotting waste – and faces yellow as the gas-lamps shuffled dejectedly along the uneven streets.

The door upon which Mr Diprose was knocking was distinctive from the surrounding drabness, in that it was streaked with a vivid blue paint, and a square of cloth depicting a red, scaled dragon entwined with an orange fish was nailed to the centre.

'If this is an opium den, Mr Diprose, we shall not enter!' I said as resolutely as I could muster. I had heard of these places.

'Hush, woman,' he said, for the door was opening, and a very small Oriental woman, little taller than Lucinda, was smiling at us from behind spectacles. She pressed her palms together and bowed deeply, then led us up a precarious flight of stairs to the upper tenement.

The room was filled with a sweet smoke, but I could see through the haze that it was surprisingly clean and neat, like the woman herself. She gestured to a low bed, piled with cushions. I wondered where the aroma was coming from. It was not unpleasant. Despite myself, I sat down on the bed. That smell. So strange. I tried to pull Lucinda towards me, but Diprose sat hastily in her place next to me, and I watched as the woman held out her arms to Lucinda, and the child went to her.

'Lucinda, come to me,' I said wearily. Why was I so tired? She did not seem to hear me. As long as I could see her, I thought, she will be safe. 'Why are we here?' I asked Diprose.

'We are going to see Sir Jocelyn,' he casually replied.

'Not, not, to operate!' If I had had the strength, I would have gasped and clapped my hand over my mouth, but my arm would not move.

'Why, yes, you are right. To operate.'

'You – are – evil!' My speech was slurred. I tried to stand. 'Let us out! Lucinda!' Still, the smell. It was taking something from me. My reason wafted on the syrupiness of the aroma. I was losing something to it.

'Be calm,' I heard him say. 'Sir Jocelyn is not going to operate on your daughter.'

'But you said . . .' The smell was pungent, like fresh honey, or that confection, that contentment-of-the-throat confection that Sir Jocelyn gave me, only more concentrated. I was finding something about the situation strangely amusing.

'He is going to operate on *you*.'

I tried to tell him that I did not understand. I think I started to laugh. It was absurd. How extraordinarily funny it seemed.

'Sir Jocelyn,' Diprose continued, 'has finally conceded that I have been right all along. Exposure to exciting material has rendered you dangerous and troublesome.' This, of course, only added to my mirth. 'It is time to calm your uterine fury with the surgical amputation of your clitoris.'

I don't think I stopped laughing. Like a eunuch in a harem, I thought. Mutilate me, so I can serve without threat. My hilarity grew. Was this what they called hysteria? In which case, Sir Jocelyn's diagnosis was correct. So, what are you waiting for, Charlie? Operate on me!

That saccharine gas must have been piped from the noxious exhalations above the river of Lethe, for as I drank in the ether, I was transported to the depths of a valley that ran the length of the border between sentience and death. I rose upwards every once in a while, and was able to peer over the valley sides in both directions, either towards death, or towards the world I was leaving behind, but I was quickly dragged down again to the valley floor, where I languished for I knew not how long.

But I saw visions when I rose, on which side of the valley I could not tell.

An ochre-hued man with a conical silk hat and a long robe.

A room, suffused with an almost spiritual concentration, empty except for a bed on which a woman was lying, face down, her legs bare and spread apart.

A long stick of bamboo, with a fan of thin needles stuck into the end like a fantastical bookbinding tool.

A small, bespectacled woman carrying a tray of bowls.
An ivory hammer.
Lucinda, calling for me. 'Mama, Mama.'
Silence.

Chapter Twenty-three

A long-tailed pig,
Or a short-tailed pig,
Or a pig without any tail;
A sow pig,
Or a boar pig,
Or a pig with a curly tail.
Take hold of the tail
And eat off his head,
And then you'll be sure
The pig-hog is dead.

I found my cheek pressed against crisp white sheets, in a wet patch where my mouth had been drooling. I was lying on my front with my legs apart, just like the woman in my vision, and staring at a wash-stand. The room was dark, but the moonlight was shining through the window, directly onto the mirror that backed the wash-stand. The mirror was surrounded with tiles, which were patterned intricately with cobalt and white designs. The moonlight brought the faces in them to life: the ovals were eyes, the swirls between them noses. I used to play this game with the old wallpaper in my bedroom as a child, which was enhanced by water stains and peelings.

I became aware of a burning sensation somewhere around the lower regions of my body, and struggled to recall where I had been. Lucinda, I thought. Where was she? I lifted my head to see if she was in the room with me, and my pelvis groaned with the effort. I laid my head back down on the bed. At least, I rued to myself, it was not Lucinda who had had to undergo this, and I felt my body flood with a curious sense of relief, and gratitude even. I wanted to laugh again. Peace, at last. Where was my shame? It had been removed, excised from my body. I had been suitably punished. Ah, the relief. Relief at last.

Slowly and with tremendous fear I worked my hand down between my body and the bed. I tugged at my skirts, and pulled enough of them up by my waist to be able to get my hand between my legs. I didn't know what I was expecting to find. Bandages stiff with blood, presumably. But there were none. My thighs were smooth, and not sticky with drying fluids. My hair was still as it should have been.

With trepidation, I placed the very tip of my middle finger where my clitoris used to be, and waited for it to descend into an excruciating mess of tissues, a raw savage wound, and recoil in agony and disgust. Oh, but I was angry now. This was the seat of my new-found sexuality. This was where Din had been. This was where I found myself. And now it had been taken from me.

But it hadn't. I touched it gently, and then more firmly, and it answered me willingly with its usual golden rush. I pulled my finger away, not comprehending. This wasn't right either.

The pain, I started to realise, was coming from my behind. I pushed upwards on my hands until my arms were straight and my trunk almost upright, and twisted my head to see. My skirts were still covering my bottom, so I reached round and yanked them upwards. But it was too dark; no light fell on the bed. In the darkness I passed my hand over the skin of my bottom. It was a series of raised dots and small welts. It stung, like a scrape.

I stood up slowly; my head felt surprisingly clear despite my recent stupor. I twisted again to get a look at myself in the mirror, but I could only see myself from the waist upwards.

I stood on the bed; I was the right height now, but out of the light. I got off the bed, and pulled it laboriously a couple of feet towards the mirror, and stood on it again, directly in the shaft of moonlight. I pulled up my skirts once more, twisted round, and over my shoulder could see that the moonlight was illuminating my bottom perfectly.

On the left cheek it seemed as if someone had painted an ivy wreath, in the centre of which was a portrait of a young woman with a snub nose and an indoor cap and ribbons. She looked not unlike me. On the right cheek, someone had painted the insignia of the Noble Savages, and the word *Nocturnus* underneath.

I rubbed at the artwork with my finger. It was too sore for me to press firmly, and when I examined my finger in the moonlight I could see that not even a smudge of paint had transferred on to it. Comprehension only dawned very slowly. I knelt on the bed, with my bottom in the air, for I could not sit down on it.

I had, I finally realised, been tattooed.

What had he, 'Nocturnus', said, in my bindery? 'Strange to think we find such beauty in the posthumous scarification and gilding of an animal's hide. He had said that tooling was like a tattoo, on dead skin.' What else? Of course. 'I have left instructions in my will to bind my complete works with the skin from my torso, with the scar left by the spear wound resplendent across the front panel, and the tattoo round my navel on the back cover. Is it not a fine way to achieve immortality?'

One cannot tattoo leather, I thought to myself, only living skin.

My magnum opus, he had called me, in Glidewell's study. I had not thought to take him literally.

My skin was being prepared to become the leather for a future book.

I would be Volume Two.

*　　*　　*

This, surely, was a knowledge I was never meant to possess. Does a tree know of its life beyond the papermill? Had the buffalos, crocodiles, goats, calves I had so casually used known of their destination? Or was only I to go to the slaughter with this horrific awareness of my future reduction? I, who was once woman, was to become a book covering? *Sartor Resartus*. The binder re-bound. Was I nothing more than the beasts of the field, air, swamps, prairies, which I now would join in death?

And when would that be? Would I be permitted to live to a ripe old age, and die of natural causes, after which Sir Jocelyn would come and claim my hide? Not likely. It was reasonable to surmise that, pretty much as soon as my skin had healed from the tattooing, I would die. I would, more precisely, be killed.

A key turned in the lock, and the door opened. 'Ah, she is awake,' Diprose said, as he entered, with Sir Jocelyn close behind him. I glimpsed the corridor beyond them, and realised that we were back in Berkeley-square.

'Good evening, my dear Dora,' Sir Jocelyn said.

'Lucinda,' I said. 'Where is she?' They did not answer me. 'Take me to my daughter.' They took an arm each, and led me like this out of the room, and down the stairs. I wanted to spit in their eyes. 'Please,' I begged. 'Tell me where Lucinda is.' I was really scared now. We passed maids, dusting cornices with long feather dusters, and Goodchild, carrying a tray. None of them flinched at the sight of me. We went into Sir Jocelyn's office.

A large leather trunk and two smaller wooden crates stood in the middle of the room. Many of the shelves were empty; the floor was strewn with papers, books, and the parapher-nalia of scientific exploration waiting to be packed: sextants, telescopes, microscopes, compasses, even a portable bath. Was it here that they would kill me?

'Be seated, Sir Jocelyn,' Diprose said eagerly, and rubbed

his hands together. 'You, over here,' he said to me, and pulled me to the corner of the room behind the anatomy model. Vesalius's *De humanis corporis fabrica libri septum* was still on the shelf; I spotted its large black and gold binding immediately. 'Now, lift your skirts.'

'I will not, Mr Diprose!' I said, in a rage. 'I will not!' I clutched his hands with my own, and dug my flaky nails into his flesh. He only smiled, and grabbed at my skirts. I pushed his hands down again, and kicked his shins with my boots, then seized his greasy beard and yanked it firmly downwards, such that his chins bumped onto my collarbone.

'Come, come, my little sauce-box,' he chuckled. 'You shall do me some damage, tiger.'

How dare he laugh? I scratched upwards into his eyes, but he jerked his head out of the way, caught both my hands in his, then forced them down behind my back.

'Possibly you enjoy antagonising me. I suggest you learn a little *obéissance*.' His chest pressed against mine, his black whiskers scratched my cheeks, and his breath was hot and smelt of whisky. I could see the fur on his tongue, the gold of his molars.

All the while Sir Jocelyn sat and watched us from the other side of the room, as if observing one of his fellow travellers subduing some gibbering native in order to carry out an anatomical study.

'Well, Charles. I see you are struggling to unveil your Galatea to me.'

Still holding my hands tightly, Diprose was able to turn me round, but as he tried to lift my skirts again I kicked him sharply in the shins, and he howled with pain. He was not deft, or agile, and he was too old to have any real strength. If I continued to struggle, I thought I could hold out.

But as I kicked backwards again, he intercepted my ankle with his foot, and I fell forwards. He would not relinquish his grip on my hands, so he stumbled on top of me, and we collided with the anatomy model, which crashed to the floor too, and we were a mess of limbs and organs, chipped paint and bruised bones, and Diprose was sitting on my back. He had my skirt up, and started to investigate my bare buttocks.

'Good, good,' I heard him say, and felt his finger following the inky wounds. 'Sir Jocelyn, I shall trouble you to attend to us here, for I cannot persuade the termagant to come over to you willingly.' I heard Sir Jocelyn rise, and slowly pace over to us. He picked his feet carefully over the scattered pieces of his precious anatomy model.

'You are evil,' I hissed, at them both.

'I prefer "exceptional",' retorted Diprose, still squatting ignominiously on me. 'Sir Jocelyn, regard.' Sir Jocelyn's feet were by my head; I could bite his ankle, I thought, if he takes half a step towards me. 'May I present to you the cover of your next *oeuvre*.' I beat my fists on the floor, and tried to buck him off me. He was a dead weight. Sir Jocelyn was silent for a moment. 'Quite exquisite, Mrs Damage,' Diprose continued, 'if I may say so,' he said, as if congratulating a lady on her flower arranging. 'And they are healing so quickly. Only minor scabbing. It won't be long.'

'What in the devil's name have you done, Charles?' Sir Jocelyn eventually said. His voice was low and urgent, as if his teeth were clenched. 'Get off her.'

Diprose's weight shifted on my back, crushing my ribs into the floor. Then he stood up, and I breathed out heavily, and pushed myself quickly up to standing, arranging my skirts.

'Come, Sir Jocelyn,' Diprose said hastily. 'Could there be a more appropriate way . . . ? Just think of the beauty . . . The perfect accord with . . . The pricelessness . . .'

'Of what, Charles?' I could not read Sir Jocelyn's face.

'Come, Sir Jocelyn,' he said again. 'This time I will prove to you I'm no circus master. You shall know that your masterpieces are not made from white pigskin, unlike those shrunken heads and miniature mummies in the street shows.'

'All this, because I didn't believe your feeble inscription.' Sir Jocelyn had started to laugh, shaking his head. 'Really, Charles, you have excelled yourself this time.' He wiped a tear from his eye.

'Why, thank you, Sir Jocelyn.'

'You idiot, Charles,' Sir Jocelyn snapped.

'But, Sir Jocelyn, you told me to dispose of her,' Diprose protested. 'You have always referred to her as our whore. Before I throw her into the Thames, I thought I might as well get our money's worth. So they will discover that one of the many prostitutes' corpses they find today has been flayed. *Qu'est-ce que cela peut bien faire?*'

'I said that I believed she was coming to the end of her employment with us, and that we had to find a reasonable way of disposing with her. Reasonable. Not barbaric.'

'Dispose of . . .'

'Yes, but I didn't mean kill her! Relinquish. Remove. Not rub out! And reasonably, too.'

'So what are we to do?' Diprose asked. I looked from him to Sir Jocelyn, and back again. My future was held in their decision. Sir Jocelyn walked towards me, looking me up and down.

'I always thought you were too scrawny, Dora,' he said at last. 'Charlie, couldn't you at least have found me a woman with an arse that had been fattened on the cushions in the Dey's harem? The perfect quarto, you said? Mrs Damage's arse, I'm afraid, will cover little more than an octavo, and a crown octavo at that.'

Mr Diprose's vile mouth broke into a smile, then a laugh, and soon the two men were chuckling heartily at my demise, and I knew I had no ally in Knightley.

'Never mind,' Sir Jocelyn continued. 'She shall be our perfect pocket-book!'

'And as for her daughter,' Diprose adjoined, laughing so hard he could scarcely get the words out, 'there's no pleasure like the ploughing of a first edition.'

412

Quicker than the men could follow what I was doing, I ran to the wall and seized one of the tribal spears, feathered with orange and yellow. It came off easily in my hand, and I hurled myself with it towards Mr Diprose's shaking back. I rammed it in hard. It met with resistance. I saw his round, purple face turn to me with surprise; his eyebrows were lifted, and his wet little mouth grinned over his shoulder at me. I battered the spear into him again, this time into his side, and then, now he was facing me fully frontal, into his chest. Still nothing. He was still laughing, and looking at me in wonder. Possibly the spear was blunt. Again, and again, I hammered it on to him, fear growing with every blow, from every angle I could, until he simply caught hold of the shaft and held it upright to keep me from attacking him further.

'I had not thought until now how fortunate I am to wear this wretched back brace,' he said superciliously. ' "*The advantages of scoliosis as a life-protector.*" Another treatise for you to write, Sir Jocelyn.'

But before he could finish smirking, the spear was removed from him and he was flattened against the wall with the same spear across his chest, before any of us knew how it had happened. But then it became obvious, for the man holding the spear across Mr Diprose, the man whose face was pressed up against his, eyeball to eyeball, and threatening to crush the very life out of him there and then, was Din. Din, holding the spear, the same spear he had brandished at Sylvia's bosom.

I did not stop to think how he had managed to be here; instead I ran to the wall again, and seized the another weapon, which had a short shaft but a long blade, and without testing it with my fingers ran with it straight towards Diprose, but this time I aimed for below his brace. He saw me coming, and there was nothing he could do, for his arms were pinned by the spear. I landed it directly into the softness of his crotch. Oh yes indeed, this one was definitely sharp. Fabric and flesh yielded. Diprose screamed and quailed. Blood was dripping from the spear, and from Diprose, onto the tiger's head on the floor at our feet. I knew what I was capable of, and what I had to do. I looked at Diprose's pale, shaking face, and knew I had to strike somewhere up here next. I had to find his elusive throat somewhere beneath his quivering chins and beard.

But with every murder there is a moment of possibility, and when that passes, the deed cannot be done. With Diprose pinned to the wall by a stronger man, squealing like a pig, I could pretend I was safe. With every second that ticked by, the moment evaded me further. I was still holding the bloody spear, but did not know what to do with it.

'Kill him,' Din shouted at me. 'What you waitin' for?'

Sir Jocelyn was watching me with the bemusement of a man who has seen too many peepshows, but has finally found a more interesting one. 'Damned if you do, but what if you don't, Mrs Damage?' he asked, cocking an eyebrow at me.

And I wondered then why it was Diprose I needed to kill, and not this other man, who was glowing redder than the devil in front of me. After all, were not I and Diprose both his victims? But I knew the answer before I had even finished the question. What murderous feelings the prostitute dares entertain are reserved for her pimp, not for her clients, no matter how loathsome. Besides, I dared believe, as Sir Jocelyn looked at me, that although his gaze had not the sombre shadow of respect about it, yet it radiated a certain admiration. No, I would let Lucifer live, for his Faustus was the more despicable to me, having chosen his devilish *entente*. The devil, I believed, had no such freedom of choice.

And it was choice that I had here. It was no longer the choosing of a mother for the welfare of her daughter: Lucinda would suffer either way now, with a mother flayed and murdered or hanged for murder herself. My choice was a simple one: good versus evil, virtue versus revenge.

But even though I quickly knew what my choice would be,

I heard Sir Jocelyn say, 'Buy yourself some time, my dear. Give him a taste – or rather, a smell – of his own medicine.' He walked over to Diprose's pocket, and said, 'Chloroform, Mrs Damage.'

Diprose started to thrash again under the spear, as Sir Jocelyn tried to pull the bottle out. Diprose spat in Din's face, and kicked out, just as I had when he had earlier restrained me, and got Sir Jocelyn squarely in the shin. The man buckled slightly, and grimaced, nearly losing his grip on the bottle; Diprose was pinned at the shoulder, but his flailing hand seized hold of Sir Jocelyn's hair, and tugged.

'Charles!' Sir Jocelyn yelled, for it seemed as if Diprose had actually ripped a handful of hair from Sir Jocelyn's head.

'Oh!' I cried. What pain he must be in! And how peculiar he looked, with only a dark shadow over his skull. I blinked, and tried to grab the bottle of chloroform off him in case he dropped it. Chloroform. Of course. It must have been chloroform that subdued me for the tattoo. Chloroform. I would render him unconscious, and delay the evil moment.

And as I uncorked it and was wondering how to administer it, I saw Sir Jocelyn upright again, with his hair as normal, and the strange hairless image of him disappeared. A cloth was what I needed now, surely. I looked around for one, but had none. I grabbed the bottom of my skirts, drenched a section in the liquid, and pulled it up to press it firmly into Diprose's face, my whole body lunging over his as I did so. I think I must have showed my tattoos again, but dignity was the last thing on my mind.

'How long do I hold it for?' I screamed at Knightley, but he shrugged, and seemed to recede from me. Diprose shuddered and panicked beneath my skirts, then he could not help but inspire deeply, and his body immediately went limp, and slumped. Din pressed the spear further into the wall, to keep him upright.

'You can take it away now,' I panted.

'He's bluffin', Dora!' Din shouted.

I pulled my skirts away from Diprose's face; his skin had blistered around his nose and mouth. His eyes were glazed; I pulled his eyelid upwards, and prodded his eyeball.

'No, he's gone.'

Din relinquished his grip on the spear; Diprose's body hit the floor, and lolled over the tiger. And I knew then that I had done the wrong thing; I would never be able to kill him now, a sleeping man, in cold blood. A curse on Sir Jocelyn. Possibly this had been his intention all along.

Sir Jocelyn. What would he do to me now? Would he let me make my escape, for Diprose only to find me and kill me in anger at a later date? Or would he finish me off? As I thought of the Devil, he sauntered out of the shadows, and knelt down next to Diprose. He felt for his pulse. 'He has, indeed, gone, Mrs Damage. He is dead. Congratulations. You have killed him after all.'

Din reached for me, but I would not be held. I waited for Sir Jocelyn to say something, but he did not. Presumably he would now send someone to Scotland Yard. I would be hanged for murder. The inevitability of it stretched out before me. Whatever my claims, who would believe a woman and a black man over a Knight of the Realm? I had killed a man.

'Go to my room, clean yourselves up,' he said, with a calmness that terrified. He opened the door for us himself, and led us down the corridor into a room with pale blue walls. It had a bath in it, and a sink, and a pan with a cistern hung above it on the wall. Din and I stood in the middle of it all, and dared not move.

'Here.' Sir Jocelyn handed us both a small flannel square, and a white towel. 'Come now, act quickly.' Still we did not move. We watched as Sir Jocelyn turned the taps, and the steam rose from the water to fill the room.

'You have piped hot water!' I exclaimed.

'And you have blood on your hands.'

And so we jumped to, and scrubbed our faces and hands, and mopped at the stains on our clothes.

'Now go, quickly, with discretion,' he whispered, holding the door out to us once more.

'My veil, and my shawl,' I said, bewildered, to Sir Jocelyn.

'I do not know. Charles was evidently not intending for you to leave the building again.' Then he said gravely to Din as he passed, 'I suggest you take the lady out the same way you entered the building, so as not to draw attention to yourselves.'

Din nodded, and led me silently downstairs, only we did not turn left at the bottom to go to the front door, but right, to the servants' area, where the flagstones got rougher, and he pulled me into a cupboard as a maid glided past with a candle, then we slipped along further, into the kitchens, which were empty, and out into the area that led up to the mews. But just as we were about to ascend the iron stairs to the gate at the top, Din pushed me into the coal-hole under the street. I could see in the dark at the top of the steps that a woman was pressed up against the gate, and a man on the other side, and they were clearly in some deep embrace, despite the restrictions of ironmongery between them.

Din and I steadied each other on the precarious piles of coal beneath our feet. We must have waited for a quarter of an hour for the amorous couple so to finish their business, and in the interim we, likewise, could not help but find ourselves in each other's arms, our heartbeats clamouring loudly in fearful unison. Our lips and tongues were dry, but it did not matter. He was my saviour and my solace, and I knew that I loved him. But I could not say so to him; I feared it would mean little.

Then we heard the woman tread softly down the steps, wiping her mouth with the back of her hand and laughing to herself, and we pulled away from each other, watched her go inside the house, and crept up the steps ourselves. Din made a foothold for me with his hands, and lifted me up and over the gate, which was as tall as I was, before vaulting it himself, and we dropped into the mews, dirty and black-faced. Din led me across Hill-street, then we ran along Hays-mews and turned right onto Charles-street, from where we could skirt across the south side of Berkeley-square and drop down into Piccadilly.

'We have to find Lucinda,' I said to Din, clutching at his arm.

'Where is she?'

'I don't know.' And I related to Din the events as best as I could remember, breathlessly, as we rushed along the pavement, oblivious to the phantoms and menaces of the London dark.

'Was he Japanese, this man? And his wife?' he asked.

'I don't know. Oriental-looking.'

'It's just I know a Japanese tattoo man, in Limehouse. He is the only, the best. All the slaves go there to get their slave marks changed. That's how I got to know the Whitechapel crowd. I was lodgin' just up from him, and saw all these niggers comin' and goin'. He turned their brands into dragons, or flowers, or patterns.'

'There was a dragon and a fish on the door.'

'It's him. It's him all right. And that was when you last saw Lucinda?'

'I heard her, as I was under the chloroform.'

'Yes. This all make sense. There's only one professional in London. Diprose couldn't exactly take you to a sailor in the backroom of a pub, could he? I'll go straightways, once I get you home safe.'

'You? I'm coming with you! She's my daughter! You might need me.'

'Dora, no. Think. How will we get there? It's too late for an omnibus.'

'I will pay for a cab.'

'Ain't no way you could even bribe one to take you to Lime-house this time o' night.' In the distance we heard a shriek, and the pounding of footsteps that echoed around the stony streets.

'We will walk.'

'And you will slow me. I'll run there. I can run there bare-foot. You're tired.'

'I am not.' I quickened my pace as if to prove it, but I was out of breath now, and we were only at Trafalgar-square, where ashen-faced men in black silk and lace loitered on the edges of the pools of light like vampyres.

'And besides, am I not good at getting secret things out of hidden places? Especially things hidden by Sir Jocelyn.' And with that, he pulled out a book from the waistband of his trousers, and I could see in the gas-light, as we stood in the shadow of the College of Physicians, that it was that horrific book, the one with the hateful inscription.

But still I tried to argue in the face of such evidence of his skill. 'This changes nothing. I'm coming with you.' I took the wretched book from him, and set off at a pace again. 'Why did you take this?' I panted.

'Sylvia told me all,' he said. 'I did not think it fair that those men got to keep it.'

'You spoke to Sylvia?' I said.

'She came to Miss Catamole's and found me. She was worried.'

'She came . . . ? She has some bravery in her after all! You were meant to be in Bristol . . . you were meant to have set sail.'

'The boat was delayed. We heard word to stay.'

'Did Sylvia mention . . . anything else?'

'She told me all.'

'About the boy?'

Din kept his pace, although I was faltering now, and he simply said, 'I do not follow you.'

'Sir Jocelyn is unsure about Nathaniel's parentage. Do you have anything to say to that?'

'No,' he answered.

'I'm not accusing you, Din.'

'Good. Because I have told you the truth. The women touched me. But we did not do *that*.'

But I did not care any more. I only wanted to get Lucinda back safely, and every second I persisted I was still slowing Din down. We could not afford to lose a moment. 'So go, Din,' I eventually said. 'Do not take me home to Lambeth. You will be quicker if you head off now.'

'I am not leavin' you on the streets at this time o' night,' he said, clutching my arm tighter. 'If we hurry it won't delay me over much.'

So we hastened along the Strand, arms locked, and from there he took me home, where Sylvia and Pansy were both sitting up waiting for me. Sylvia hugged me and settled me in front of the fire, and Pansy brought me a hot flannel to calm my nerves, and together the three of us waited into the night and as the dawn spread across the city sky, for Din to return with some news of my Lucinda. As we waited, I told them what had happened. I troubled about when they would come to arrest me, or when the retribution would come from Holywell-street, and whether Din would find Lucinda in time, and if so, whether we should run, and to where.

Sylvia, in turn, told me how she had started to worry when Lucinda and I had not returned; the terrifying realisation that our absence was due to her incautious disclosure to her husband crept stealthily over her, before seizing her entirely in a grip of horror. Her first instinct was to go to Berkeley-square herself.

'Would you really have done so?'

'Yes, I would. In that moment I felt invincible, and that it was my redemption to use that strength to recover you. But

I am no stranger to my weakness. I knew I would not even have been allowed past the front door.'

'And so you went to someone who knew how to slip in and out of your house.'

'Yes, I suppose those soirées had some useful function, after all,' she said ruefully.

'How did you find him?'

'I searched your files for his lodging address. You had made it easy for me.'

She was right. I had only recently checked his address myself.

'He was not there when I went,' I said. 'He should have been on board the boat.'

'The heavens must have stayed him,' Sylvia said, without satisfaction. I could not smile at her, but I felt something akin to deep warmth and gratitude. I knew how hard it would have been for the woman to navigate her way from Ivy-street to Borough High-street, tottering over fouled cobbles, dodging urchins and fielding coarse banter. I had not thought she had it in her.

'And he came,' I mused.

'Of course he did,' Sylvia said.

'It was dangerous for him,' I argued.

'Do you doubt the man's affections for you?' she said. When I did not reply, she insisted, 'You do, don't you, Dora?' But I could not answer.

'Would you really have killed him?' Sylvia asked me gently, changing tack. And I wondered at first what she was asking me, but I knew already that the answer was yes, yes of course I would have, yes, if Sir Jocelyn had not proffered me the chloroform. My choice was between good and evil, and I knew that good would not have served me. And then I killed him anyway, despite myself.

Sylvia was silent for a while, before saying solemnly, 'I believe Jossie knew what he was doing when he told you to chloroform Charles. It is quite a skill. The dose needs to be carefully administered over a period of time; he must have known you would simply smother Charles in it, for one quick, large dose is likely to finish an old man off.'

'But why would he bother to do that, if he saw that I was set to kill the man anyway?'

'That I do not know,' Sylvia answered. 'My husband's mind is more than ever a mystery to me.'

We lapsed into silence, and the waiting, once more. I pictured Din going to the tenement of the Japanese artist, who would be jabbering and gesticulating, with his wrinkled little wife bowing next to him. I prayed Din was right in his suspicions, that their home was indeed where I had been, and that they could tell Din clearly what had happened to Lucinda. And as I prayed, I found myself making strange noises, and I realised I was sobbing out loud, and there were wet tears on the back of my hand when I rubbed my face.

Sylvia stood up and came over to my chair, where she knelt down. 'Why don't you go to your special place, and cry?' she suggested. She stroked my hair, and dabbed at a tear with her finger. I did not know what she meant. I must have looked at her blankly. 'Where do you go to, to cry, Dora?' she asked. 'Everyone has a special place where they can cry safely, don't they, Pansy? I used to go to the bathroom, when I had one.'

'I've seen it. It was lovely.'

'Yes, it was,' Sylvia sighed.

'I do it under the blankets, at night,' Pansy interjected. 'Or when I take the slops out. I have to be quick about it, though. There's nowhere you can cry at home, or in a factory. I do a lot of cryin' when I'm walkin', it's handy cos it keeps the odd folk away. They look at you, cos they think you can't see them if you're cryin', but they won't come near you at least.'

'Do yourself a favour, for once,' Sylvia commanded. 'Go, find yourself a space, and cry in it. What are you afraid of? Tears are only salt and water.'

And I knew where I had to go, and I lay there, in her little bed, and cried until the mattress was soaked through, which was going to be a bore for Pansy, but I do believe it was some help to me. At times, I feared I would never stop. It seemed I had forgotten how to be soundless. My eyes and the patch of skin between my nose and mouth became raw, and I yearned to rub my face on Lucinda's soft hair.

I got up out of her bed eventually, angry at my indulgence. My arms felt heavily light without their usual charge, and a strange sensation ate at my chest. Grief enshrouded me like a mist, as I drifted around the house, picking up and moving around Lucinda's possessions hither to thither and back again. I had to hide Mossie above the wardrobe, for fear I would do her some damage; I took her down again and placed her in the ottoman; I moved her to the coal-cellar. Anything to fill the waiting.

Sylvia and Pansy looked at me as I came through the parlour.

'Sleep, won't you,' I scolded them. But this is a shared grief, their faces said. We are with you, and yet we are not you. We do not presume to know how you feel, and yet we sympathise and feel it too.

And then the front door opened, and Din staggered in, carrying a bundle in his arms, from which a leg fell, and then an arm, and then a cascade of blonde hair, and I rushed to help him put Lucinda down on the rug by the fire.

'Is she alive?'

'Sleepin', ma'am. Safe, and unharmed.'

I knelt down at her head, and rested my hand on her back. 'Where was she?'

'She was with them all along. Mr Diprose gave the woman some money, an' tol' her to keep her until he sent word.'

I shuddered to think what would have happened to her had Diprose decided that she was to be 'disposed' of, like her mother. It would not have been too hard a task, in Limehouse.

And then, just as if it were the gentle awakening of a normal sunny morning, Lucinda shifted herself under my palm, and started to stir. Her eyes opened, and closed again for a moment, and then opened fully. She moved her lips together to moisten them after her sleep, and gave one stretch, and then settled back against me, staring straight ahead with her big blue eyes. None of us dared move. And then she tilted her head back a bit so she could see who it was sitting at her head, and I moved to a crouch so she could see me more clearly, and her mouth broke into a smile, and she curled her fingers up to my face. Then she closed her eyes again, and stretched once more, yawned, and flexed to see the room on the other side of her, scanned the faces of the onlookers, and then turned back to me, and grasped my ribbons in her hand.

'My darling, my darling,' I whispered. 'Lucinda, Lucinda. You're home. You're safe.'

She said 'Mama,' and smiled again, and turned fully on to her side, facing me, and closed her eyes once more. I reached for her hand, and there was no such thing as wrong or right, or sick or well, or noble or savage, or old or young, only her and me.

'Where's Din gone, Mama?' she said, after a while.

I looked around. 'Go see if he's in the bindery, Pansy,' I said. But he wasn't. He was nowhere in the building. 'He must have slipped away,' I said. 'He's very good at that.' I was slightly troubled not to have noticed, or to have extended to the man my thanks, but I had my Lucinda, and as we sat with our hands entwined, and our faces shining, and so many salty tears that one could have been forgiven for thinking that it was like a birth all over again, I knew that, contrary to my mother's ruling, I had, at last, all that I desired, at least until the men came from Scotland Yard to mete out something approximating justice.

Chapter Twenty-four

Who are you? A dirty old man
I've always been since the day I began,
Mother and Father were dirty before me,
Hot or cold water has never come o'er me.

It is July, 1865. I have just had an extraordinary encounter which I need to relate here, for the story seems to have some sort of an ending at last. But first, let me catch up on the intervening years.

I started to write this journal shortly after Lucinda was returned to me, as I laid low, and waited for the knock at the door. The writing kept me busy, and was a vain attempt at making sense of the previous year or so. I chanced upon this small half-bound notebook stashed in a drawer in the bindery: it was a mockery of leather, silk and gold, entitled MOIV BIBLL, but it had beguilingly blank pages, like the blank book that St Bartholomew had intended to give to someone who was to delight under that name in her impending life, only she never showed up, or, possibly, had changed her mind at the last minute, and opted for the book that had been written in instead. Either way, it was if I had got her cast-off, being next in line for a blank book. It was the one book I had bound for nobody else but me, for nobody's perusal, for no purchase, and I realised at last what its purpose would be.

I never saw Din again. Pansy got wind, through her brother, that he had eventually left for Bristol, and thence to America, and although I know that it was his true destination, I could not help but think that it was his sacrifice for me. It may even have been his plan, if they ever had come looking for me: it would have given me the chance to blame the murder on him, this renegade black man. Sir Jocelyn would even have backed me up on it, no doubt, as the only, and most expert, witness. I was aware of what he was risking for me by coming to Berkeley-square that night, and I knew that he would have killed for me. In that way I consoled myself that he must have loved me. For what is love, anyway? Did he not say to me, 'Is love not only sacrifice? Do we not give up those we love, in order to prove to them that they are loved?' But there were times I could not help but feel my victory had been a Pyrrhic one.

But they never did come for him, nor for me neither. As I said, I laid low for a while, scribbling in my journal, and making commonplace books and albums for a stationer's up in Lamb's-Conduit-street, but the knock at the door never came. I scoured the papers daily for news of the Diprose murder. I learnt of the Winner of the Ascot Cup, the Progress of the Building for the Great International Exhibition of 1862, and Paris Fashions for the Summer, but not of what had happened to Mr Charles Diprose. My eyes lingered longer over the reports of the Civil War in America, but they were as missives from a dream state or some distant solar system, and left no trace around my heart.

But one article caught my attention for a brief moment: 'Eminent Judge Dies in Tragic Accident'. It read:

Valentine, Lord Glidewell, the most eminent judge of his time, and the most excellent person from whose hammer justice was meted upon the worst felons of this land, has passed away in tragic circumstances. As the authorities debate the merits of moving the gallows into the penitentiary, and ending the ancient tradition of execution as public spectacle, which can have no place in a modern and civilised society such as ours, the esteemed judge was found hanging from the ceiling

426

of his study in Belgrave-square this Thursday last. It is believed that Lord Glidewell, out of the spirit of compassion and consideration for which he was widely renowned, had determined to understand more intimately what was at stake each time he sent a criminal to the gallows, but this noble experiment had a most tragic ending . . .

But of Mr Diprose there was nothing. Presumably the same contact in the Home Office – indeed, possibly, the same Noble Savage – who repeatedly got him off his obscenity charges, enabled this cover-up of justice too. His allegiance would have been to Knightley, not to Diprose, after all, and there had to be some advantages to having a secret society, didn't there? Possibly Sir Jocelyn donated his body to medical science; they were both, in their own way, fine anatomists, so it was only fitting that Diprose should join them, and save the body-snatchers the trouble.

I found out where Jack was imprisoned, and visited him when I could. He had grown twice the size, and aged as much too, since I had last clapped eyes on him. His hair was darker, and his muscles as big as his father's now. He was quieter, though. A kindly warden brought him some books now and then; that much I gathered, but little else.

After a while, I ventured out and started to earn my living once more. I gave lessons in bookbinding to gentlewomen at a studio in South Kensington: how times were changing! Veritable ladies were choosing to use their idle time in the gentle pursuits of fine handicrafts, and my, they paid handsomely for it. Twenty-five guineas for three months' tuition, forty for six, seventy for twelve, plus materials at cost. But the money was only important in terms of what it enabled me to set aside for Lucinda. There were fears too: I fretted constantly about what would happen if one of my lady pupils were to discover my past. Or worse, if I were to discover the identities of their eminent husbands and find them to be . . .

Eventually, I tired of these ladies, for it was not in my heart so to instruct them. Besides, Din's legacy persisted. I never forgot that day in the bindery when he quoted Ovid at me, or our subsequent conversations in which he revealed his determination to build the kingdom of heaven here, in this life. He was ever true to himself, for that is what I trusted he was now doing in America. And so, too, as an act of love and, in some way, commitment to the man, that was what I had to do here, in England, amongst my own people.

And so, with Ovid's words as our motto, I established here in Lambeth an organisation that rejoiced under the name of 'The Union of Women Employed in Bookbinding'. Pansy, Sylvia and I were its founder members, and we were soon joined by thirty-four others. Our initial costs were funded almost entirely with the money I had earned from Damage's: a nice example, I thought, of converting filth into something more worthwhile and spreading the riches amongst those more deserving of the profits of obscenity. It was a sound enterprise, based on the trades union model, offering support, advice and representation to women in the bookbinding trade, with a target of a thousand members, and a weekly wage of a pound for our girls.

It was Sylvia who suggested I burn the book, the one Din had stolen back for me, the one we now referred to as Jocelyn's Little Black Book. I simply put it in the grate, without ceremony, and watched it flare up. The widow got burnt after all, only not on her husband's pyre, and who can say which outcome was the more barbaric? And then, talking of barbarism, I remembered the photographic catalogues still in their crates, and Sylvia and I burnt them all, one by one, over the next few days. It was a waste of good paper; I would have given them to the poor in their tenements, to burn in their own hearths and keep them warm, had the pictures not been so horrific, but then, if that had been the case, I wouldn't have needed to dispose of them.

But the tattoos, of course, persisted. I did not mind them at first; I felt I deserved them. A clitoridectomy would have been a punishment too extreme for the nature of my crime, but the tattoos felt somehow fitting, the secret branding of a clandestine criminal. Like Hester Prynne, I wore my badge of shame, only further from the heart and closer to the seat of my transgressive pleasure. Only the visuals mocked me: I did not mind so the picture of myself in a wreath of ivy, but the insignia of the Noble Savages rankled and reminded me of the man I had murdered.

It was Pansy who suggested we do something about it. She got a sailor friend to help her, an inksmith who had been responsible for the artwork on her brother's arms. A bit at a time, she inked roses (true love), hyacinths (forgiveness), daffodils (respect), lily (to ward against unwanted visitors), nasturtiums (a mother's love) and of course, pansies (merriment) over my right buttock, until the insignia of the Noble Savages was completely overgrown and invisible beneath the flora.

About a year after Lucinda's safe return to me, in the early days of the Union, we saw a carriage parked at the very top of Ivy-street. It was like Sir Jocelyn's brougham, only shabbier, and the wheels were orange, not red, and it lacked a coat of arms. We were to see it there once every six months or so, never frequent enough for us to remember the last time with any certainty. And if Nathaniel were out playing in the street when the carriage arrived, it would stay there for twenty minutes at a time, sitting, watching the children, until the mothers got wind of it and called to their children to come inside. A pederast, they would whisper to each other, or years later (for the carriage kept coming), we would say a child-snatcher, with the modish hysteria about the white-slave trade, and kidnappers crawling our streets. But I kept my suspicions to myself. I had the fancy that it was Sir Jocelyn, looking from afar at the child he wished were his son. And just occasionally, I spotted Nathaniel, who was growing into a fine lad, with his mother's fondness for excess and drama, standing stock still, and staring back up the street at the carriage, before his mother's fears snatched him out of the way.

And what of Din? Despite all my best intentions, my memories of him crept back. I learnt wilfully to remove all thoughts of him, all conversations my head hosted for me, every moment we had together which my mind wanted to relive, every longing my ears had for his voice, my skin had for his touch, my heart for his love. I did not want Din to become a tormentor of dreams, an invader of hearts; he was only gone, and I was slowly setting him free. Or rather, I was slowly setting myself free of him.

I still used to think about crossing the seas to find him. I was free to go; it might even have been safer for us there. It was Sylvia who told me she had seen the name 'Dan Nelson' in an article about the first black regiment, the 54th Regiment of Massachussetts, and I often wondered if that were him. But, for all my vain fantasies of his leading them on to glory and my meeting him at the edge of battle, I feared I would find him only as a name on a white cross, or maybe never at all. Besides, my life was here. There is hope, I would console myself, for I have loved a stranger, and after him I will not go.

Sylvia became more of a friend than I ever expected, and it was she, of all people, who helped me understand and relinquish my yearnings. She found herself with many an admirer once she started to brave the streets of Lambeth more often, but she never bothered to court them. I thought at first that this was because someone of her standing would have found the thought of a match anywhere outside Chelsea, Kensington or Mayfair as inconceivable, but over time I realised I was wrong. She had, I was to realise, many secret lovers that she picked up here and there. But she had no desire for union with them in anything other than the carnal sense, and she went for considerable periods without any at all. 'Rather no lover at all than a lousy one,' she opined to me. As the former wife of a physician and a bookbinder of erotica, we had enough combined knowledge to ensure she could enjoy these encounters without the threat of impregnation, and with her annuity and my income we lived comfortably without the need to seek out a man on whom to depend, by whom to be owned.

The greatest crime against humanity is ownership, Din had said once. And another time, he had described it as the enemy of desire. Sylvia taught me, over time, to agree with this sentiment. 'My passion for Jocelyn ended the moment I became Lady Knightley,' she said one night when we were both soaked in a hot flannel of the liquor variety, as we shared stories of the men we had known. 'He wanted to own me, and once he did, I presented no further challenge to him. He said I was a dry old stick. Ah, Dora, give me a man who knows nothing of my title, my money, my breeding; bring me a workman, a bricklayer, a mechanic, with strong arms and dirty fingers, who lacks an eye for a conquest and a heart set on ruination, and I shall show you the extent of *this* woman's lust!'

We fell about with laughter and into more flannel, but I knew between heaves of mirth that there was truth in what she was saying. I think we were ultimately both curiously happy to be free of our chains to men; we both knew what it had meant to be owned by a man, and what parts of us it had slowly killed. I had thought that what I wanted was to possess Din, and be possessed by him. But I know now that it would have destroyed our love. I did not want him for a husband, and for us to welter along with our marriage on the inevitable seas of resentment and quiet loathing. I did not want what I had had with Peter. What I thought I desired, would have been desire's undoing.

* * *

But back to today. For we saw the brougham again this morning, at the other end of Ivy-street. It was a different one, but it hovered just the same, watching the children.

'This 'as got to stop,' Agatha Marrow said, and looked at me pointedly.

'Indeed it has, Agatha,' I said, and started to march off up the street towards the carriage.

'No, Dora!' Sylvia called after me. 'It might not be safe!'

I was about ten feet away from the carriage when I stopped, and started to gesticulate at it. I threw a look over my shoulder, and saw that the women were still watching me. I would put on a good show. I waved my arms some more at the carriage, all the while squinting to see if I could see who was within.

'Sir Jocelyn?' I eventually whispered. 'Is that you?'

And then a red glass ball flashed at me like the largest ruby in the world from the window of the carriage, and beneath it a shiny silver cane, and I had my proof.

'I will meet you around the corner,' I hissed, and waved my arms some more, for the benefit of my audience of mothers. 'Go back onto Waterloo-road, then turn into Morpeth-place,' I whispered to the driver, 'I will meet you behind the Wesleyan church.' Then I seized my skirts and marched back down Ivy-street, only turning once, to shout, 'And don't be going and bothering us again!'

But I did not stop to receive the approbation from Sylvia, Agatha and the like. I walked past them, remarking breezily that I was off to market, and would Sylvia mind watching Lucinda for me, and with that I popped into the house, seized my shopping basket, and headed off the other way down Ivy-street, and soon was walking along the main road, which I crossed and turned into the little alley-way that was Morpeth-place, where the carriage was waiting for me. I checked that no one was watching me, and then I ambled round onto the pavement, where I was hidden by the carriage itself, and climbed in.

'Dora,' he said.

'Sir Jocelyn,' I replied.

'Your courage never ceases to astound me. What would you be having with me?'

'I might ask the same of you. Surely it is time you relinquished your attachment with the inhabitants of Ivy-street.'

'When one's flesh and blood live there?'

'Sylvia?' I asked.

'Nathaniel.'

'He – he – is yours?'

'Unfortunately, yes.'

'Forgive me. I was under the impression that you thought Sylvia had been unfaithful.'

'Would that she had. It was bound to catch up on me when I attempted to sire my own.'

'I do not understand.'

And then he pulled off his hat, and tugged at his hair, and it came off in his hand too, and again I saw that peculiar vision I had not comprehended that fateful night in Berkeley-square.

'Must I spell it out to you, Dora?' he said, almost plaintively. His scalp was speckled with dark tufts of close-shaven hair.

And so he told me of his father, a French diplomat, named Yves Florent Chevalier, who married his mother, Elizabeth Talbot, a renowned English beauty, in Paris in the summer of 1825. Two years later Chevalier was posted to the French consulate in Algiers, as diplomatic relations were deteriorating between Algeria and France.

'You have heard the story of the Dey and the flywhisk?'

I shook my head.

'The Dey, as Deys are renowned for so doing, was getting all hot and bothered by an invoice for some trifle, a bag or two of wheat or something like that, some thirty years overdue. My father was in the famous meeting where the agitated Dey got so consternated he frapped the consul with, of all things, a flywhisk.'

433

'A flywhisk?'

'An ornate bamboo flywhisk, such as a eunuch would hover with around a concubine.'

'What happened?'

'Only that the King of France decided to come over insulted, ordered a naval blockade of the entire Algerian coast, and the rest is, as they say, history.'

'Is this the same Dey that features in *The Lustful Turk*? Was that not set in Algiers?'

Sir Jocelyn laughed and seized my hand in his.

'I always hoped it were. What do we have as the likely first publication date of *The Lustful Turk*?'

'1828.'

'Exactly. But the Dey who flicked the flywhisk was called Khodja Hussein. And our fictional hero was called . . .'

'Ali.' The tale was still alarmingly clear in my head. 'But forgive me, Sir Jocelyn. What does this have to do with your parents?'

'Yves Chevalier was in the very room in the palace where this infamous and fateful meeting took place. My mother, alas, was elsewhere.'

'Where was she?'

'They never told me the full story. I like to think that she was the first luscious lovely that the Dey met as he stormed out of the meeting-room, flywhisk still in hand, and that his lusts overtook him . . .'

'Sir Jocelyn! How you speak about your mother!'

'. . . but in truth, Dora, I believe she was found wandering the streets around the palace in a state of undress. I was born nine months later in Paris, after which she and I were returned to England in disgrace, she was thrown into a lunatic asylum, where she lived out her days, and I was sent to her sister, my Aunt Maude.'

'I remember asking you if you had adopted your aunt's surname, on your first visit to the bindery,' I said.

'You remember well. She was a reputable old girl; she had married well, and was widowed young, so under her influence I was able to become a person of reasonable standing.'

'And your father?'

'Yves Chevalier was killed in Algiers in the battle of 1830. My real father is the stuff of my fantasies: you see now why I would rather my mother had been seduced by the Dey than violated by any old common or garden son of Ham who happened to be in the streets of the city that night.'

'Are you telling me that you – *you* – are . . .' I struggled for the words.

'Half-caste. Mulatto. Yes.'

'Hence the . . .' I gestured down at the wig he was holding in his lap.

'. . . hairpiece. Yes. My skin is blessedly pale, but the hair has always been a giveaway.'

I sat silently for a while, trying to comprehend fully what I was hearing.

'So now you know why I was unable to deliver you to the police for killing Charles. Or rather, you know one of the reasons why I would not have done so. We were bound each to the other that night. I witnessed your sin, you mine.'

'I still don't understand. Your sin, as in, your books?'

'No, you fool. Have you not heard a word I have said? My heritage.'

'Your heritage is not a sin, Sir Jocelyn, any more than mine is.'

'That, Dora dearest, is debatable.'

'But still, Sir Jocelyn, how could I possibly have used that knowledge against you? How could it have been an equal threat to the revelation of a murder?'

'You might not have done, but Sylvia would have. It would have been sweet revenge, to ruin my name in society, and all I have fought against the odds for. I have built my very career on the subjugation of my own race, and time after time I

435

have come to the painful conclusion that we are the inferior species.'

'Only because you wish it to be so.' I bit my lip. I had so many questions that needed answering, but where to start? 'You asked Diprose to dispose of me, Sir Jocelyn,' I said solemnly, as an opening.

'Dora, I would have disposed of Charles first if I could have done. You saved me the trouble.'

'Did you know the chloroform would kill him?'

'He duped me into teaching him how to administer it correctly. He said he wanted to relieve his sister of her pains in childbirth. I did not know he was going to use it on you. He deserved it.'

'I always knew you were dangerous.'

'Come now, it was the safest option for us all. I know not of a single surgeon who has been prosecuted for death by chloroform. "Chloroform syncope" I wrote on his death certificate, which was true, was it not? Then I donated his body to medical science.'

'Tell me, why did you want to dispose of him?'

'I was tiring of him. Only he persisted in trying to impress me. The more vulnerable he felt his position in my favour, the more he overreached himself.'

'You did not want that hideous binding?'

'Come, come, Dora. Every medical library of note has an anatomy bound in the hide stripped from a dissected corpse. A well-bound whore gives me no thrills.'

'I was repulsed by it. I wanted revenge.'

'You wanted my guts for garters.'

I laughed, despite myself. 'No. I wanted your scrotum for a nice, soft silky purse, to keep my pennies in.'

'I will leave it to you in my will. No, Charles did not understand sentimentality when it came to choosing his victims,' he said. 'I could not finger your buttocks as I turned those pages. As exciting a prospect as it sounds, you are, nevertheless, preferable to me alive. And I never agreed to abusing my medical knowledge in order to threaten your daughter in such a way.'

'I know you didn't.' I shifted myself closer to him, able to relax at last. Then I whispered, and he bowed his head towards mine to hear me better. 'She would have you back, you know. Sylvia still loves you.' My lips brushed his ears, and I felt him tense. 'This – what you have revealed to me – wouldn't matter now to her. She has left society behind her, and cares not for it any more.'

But Sir Jocelyn would have none of it. He sat up straight again, and fingered the curtains. 'Your attempt is well meaning but futile, Dora,' he said sadly.

'Please, Sir Jocelyn. You have a son together.'

'It is too preposterous even to consider.'

'She loves you, Sir Jocelyn. Or does your hatred for yourself inure you to that?' For is it not, I was realising, a futile endeavour to consider love without love itself? Love viewed from a place of hatred is a painful sight, and only serves to harden the heart against it further. Love seen from a place of hatred, I mused: at last, a fair definition of the literature he had been asking me to bind.

Sir Jocelyn interrupted my reveries. 'There is nothing here for me any more. Did you not hear about the *razzia*? They seized and destroyed all my translations. I passed them through Holywell-street for one night only, and then they were gone. Even Pizzy is still in prison.'

'Why haven't you got him out?'

'He was proving rather tedious too. You had shown us what a relief it was to put Diprose somewhere where even the Home Office could not reach him, and we wished the same for Bennett.'

'And there was I thinking the British Empire stretched to most places.'

He laughed, and continued with his previous train of

thought. 'No, sex is too dangerous these days. My devotion shall be to anthropological studies. I am off to Africa in a month, and I intend never to return.'

'You said that four years ago.'

But his silence spoke more than his words, and I knew that this would indeed be the last time I saw him. Why else would he be so candid with a secret he had kept for so long?

'I am sorry about your tattoos,' he said suddenly. 'They were rather beautiful, though. The image of them is still firmly embedded in my mind's eye.'

'They're not so bad now. Pansy learnt from a sailor, and has altered the insignia for me. It was not an image I wished to carry with me. She always was a fine needlesmith.'

'You could always take your inspiration from Olive Oatman, or those sailors shipwrecked in the South Pacific, and claim you were abducted and forcibly tattooed by a savage tribe.'

'Which wouldn't be too far from the truth, Sir Jocelyn, if you think about it.'

'I shall miss you, Dora Damage. You are the one I couldn't have.'

'I was not aware that you wanted me.'

'Would it have made any difference?'

'No.'

Then he seized both my shoulders, pulled me towards him, and crushed my lips against his. He grabbed at my bonnet, and tore his fingers through my hair, then another hand went to my thigh, then my knee, and tugged at my skirts.

'No, Sir Jocelyn! You may not do that!' But I feared the inevitable. For all our intimate conversation, I was still just another serving-woman, about to be undone by just another aristocrat. I had read of enough of those.

But to my surprise, he nodded and moved away from me. 'My apologies, Mrs Damage. Forgive me.'

We sat in silence for a while. I put my finger to my lips, and felt where he had been, and thought of Din, and Lucinda, and Sylvia and Nathaniel, and divorce, and possession, and the stirrings inside me, and eventually I repeated more gently, 'You may not do that.' Then I added, 'But I will kiss you again. You may do this. Only a kiss, mind.'

And I kissed him, and then his neck, and his ear, and across his cheek, then worked my way back to his lips, which were sweet, wet and golden, before pulling away. It was deliciously unsatisfying, and I flushed with my own audacity.

'So, Mrs Damage,' he said as he sank into my arms. 'You do have a penchant for black men after all.'

'No, Sir Jocelyn,' I retorted. 'I have a penchant for those who fight for freedom. Only you, I believe, are choosing to stay in your chains.'

'There was a noose around my neck from the day I was born,' he said quietly.

'You chose not to remove it.'

'I am a hybrid.'

'You are not Caliban. It is not a calamity.'

He was silent for a while, then lifted his head and spoke again. 'How dare you accuse me of not fighting for freedom. It is all I have ever worked for.'

'It is a peculiar freedom, Sir Jocelyn, which depends on the subjugation of others for its existence.'

He laid his head on my bosom once more, and I stroked the dark, coarse stubs of his real hair. Then I kissed him again, only with an efficiency that betrayed its finality, took the hairpiece from him, and arranged it on his head.

'I must leave you now,' I said. 'I believe we are finished here.' I got up to leave. But before I opened the door of the carriage, I paused.

'What is it?' he asked.

'A thought, Sir Jocelyn. A favour, if I dare.'

'Careful. It will bind you to me.'

'Am I not already? You shall keep my secrets, I shall keep yours, to the grave.'

'Proceed. How I wish I shall never see you again.'

'It's Jack. Jack Tapster. He's been inside four-and-a-half years now. Might your Home Office savage be able to help, now his time is not spent repeatedly releasing Diprose?'

He did not answer me, but rubbed his nose with his forefinger, and turned away from me as if to look out of the window, although it was draped with velvet.

'Good day, Sir Jocelyn,' I said. I picked up my basket from the floor of the carriage, and climbed out. I did not look back as I walked away, for my mind was already with Nathaniel, who really had nothing remarkable about his skin, not in Lambeth anyway, not so as one would notice, and it started to trouble me most deeply, that here we were, two generations later, and there was not so much as a trace of his Algerian grandfather in the boy, not a smudge of brown that distinguished him from me or Nora or Agatha or Patience or Pansy. And let Nathaniel marry one of Jack's red-headed baby sisters, and that will truly be the end of it. But then I wondered whether that was not the way of the world; what I carried forth into the world of my grandparents was negligible likewise.

Or was it? Of course it wasn't. My little Lucinda, dosed up on bromide; my grandfather Georgie Tanner, poisoned in his mental asylum. Three generations apart, same old condition. The blank book of life presented to us by St Bartholomew as we are born is a fantasy; our heritage is our destiny; and who are we to choose which bits of our mother dominate over which bits of our father in the moment of conception?

Thus roamed my thoughts as I strode back towards Ivy-street, but as I crossed Waterloo-road I was aware of Sir Jocelyn's brougham passing me, and rattling off northwards away from me, and I stopped briefly to watch it recede. And when I started to walk once more it was as if the narrow streets of the London map were no longer confining me, that there was something in my step, in the way the basket swung at my side, and in my smile, that felt curiously light and untrammelled, as if all that had hampered me were disappearing along with the carriage, as if it were taking with it a past that no longer served me.

But then it stopped ahead of me, and I felt no need to avert my step, for there was no danger to be had any more. Sir Jocelyn's head reappeared from the carriage.

'Dora,' he said as I neared.

'Yes, Sir Jocelyn?'

He smiled broadly, albeit somewhat sadly, tipped his hat at me by way of farewell, and said quietly, such that I could scarcely hear it over the rumble of traffic and trains: 'Your arse may be a perfect octavo, but your spirit shall not be bound.'

Epilogue

When my mother's publishers requested that I write a preface for the publication of the first edition, I found myself unable so to do. For her past is history, and I cannot preface it. I can only write an afterword, which I agreed to do, for the text is still somewhat incomplete.

My mother had almost forgotten her request of Sir Jocelyn, when, three months after their meeting in the carriage, Jack walked free, halfway through his ten-year sentence, much to his surprise. She gave him Damage's Bindery: he approached new clients, and proved capable, unlike my mother, of steering a course through the con-men and undesirables of the industry. It may not have been the straightest course, but it was the soundest, and kept him closer to the right side of the law than she had ever been.

It may surprise the reader to discover that he and Pansy got married, but it made perfect sense to them and us all. Their affection for each other is greater than between most married couples; her barrenness is no obstacle to someone of his proclivities. They offer mutual love, support and comfort, as do my mother and Sylvia to each other. Neither of them quite got over the men they loved but could not have, and devoted their future to themselves and their children. My mother always disagreed with Dr Acton that women are not victim to sexual urges, but she declared (rather loudly as age superseded decorum) that she would rather have no one than an unsatisfactory lover, and that this was a view she had come to as a result of her late husband, her soldier lover and a thousand pornographic books.

Sir Jocelyn Knightley died in Africa, some time between the 8th and the 14th of April, 1867. Information, and his obituaries in *The Times* and the *Daily Telegraph* were vague, and to this day we still receive rumours of his demise. So far it has been mooted that he fell into the Victoria Falls, got poisoned by a local chieftain, caught one or more of the sleeping sicknesses, marsh-fever, yellow jack, bilharzia and malaria, was stabbed by a loose woman in a city, that it was deliberate, that it was accidental, that it was suicide, and that it was murder. We shall never know the truth, but it was a suitably mysterious ending of which he would have been proud. Africa swam in his bloodstream, and it claimed him in the end.

Sir Jocelyn left Nathaniel his, or rather Sylvia's, entire fortune. The property in Berkeley-square was sold, and Christie's was entrusted with the sale of most of the furnishings, and all the scientific equipment. Sylvia chose, however, to donate his book collection to the British Library, who were possibly too confounded by its contents to refuse. She never found any female body parts pickled in glass jars, and neither did my mother receive a shrivelled scrotum in the post from Africa, much to her relief.

Shortly after, we were to leave behind Jack and Pansy in Lambeth, and set up home in Gravesend, with Sylvia and Nathaniel too, in a small but elegant Georgian townhouse with a large garden. Rumours spread quickly, but having weathered the malicious gossip of Ivy-street, this mere tittle-tattle was nothing but amusing. Of course, the fact they were from London gave them something of a shady patina anyway, as if sapphism, or tribadism, or whatever you want to call it, was *de rigeur* anywhere north of Clapham. The talk did not bother them. Nathaniel and I both went to the local school, where Sylvia and my mother helped out a few days a week. My mother further eroded our neighbours' fears once she offered to rebind the old text books handed down by the boys' public school up the road. She was also happy, too, to do the odd re-bind for those who asked, and it was a constructive way of making new acquaintances, but she did not set herself up seriously.

But the first time somebody brought her a family Bible, she realised that the Song of Solomon still held memories for her, both good and bad. The local vicar told her once in the queue at the butcher's that he considered it to be the height of obscenity. My mother, smiling sweetly, asked for half a pound of kidneys, and never enquired whether he had come across Archdeacon Favourbrook, or the Reverend Harold Oswald, during his early ecclesiastical training in London.

And so to her journal, the book of MOIV BIBLL. After her last entry in it, it was left for many years. But my mother was always one to know how to make a buck from a book, as the Americans would say, and, when the Society of Women in the Bookbinding Trades wrote to her regarding the need to establish a Bookbinders' Benevolent Fund, she wondered at the possibility of sending it out into the world to raise some money. In the end, we decided to split the proceeds between the Benevolent Fund and the Hospital for the Paralysed and Epileptic of London, an establishment in which I have been fortunate enough never to set foot. My mother always said that if my kidnap and subsequent rescue hadn't brought a fit on, then nothing ever would again; and she was right. The nursery rhymes were my idea. Read into them what you will; they are my gift to you.

When she signed her publishing contract shortly before her death, we travelled together to London. The motorcar drove us down the Strand – the new, improved Strand, that is – straight through where Holywell-street used to be, and we admired the curves of the new Aldwych, then, round Trafalgar-square and onwards towards Regent-street; where my mother remembered there had been only one department store, Messrs Farmer and Rogers, where Din had portered, and now there were many. 'Liberty,' my mother read from the lettering above the door. 'Liberty & Co.' But the traffic did not allow us to linger at this peculiar monument; she was unable to spy into its windows to ascertain what type of freedom it might offer – and at what price – within.

I once asked my mother about her own demons, but she said they were paved over like the relentlessness of architecture after this visit to London. I did not believe her. Do we not hold on to our demons, for comfort? Do we not need them, in order to cushion ourselves against the worse demons of others, in this strange and unpredictable world? Gas may have long given way to electricity on these streets, in these establishments, but I defy even the most fervent metropolitan developer to say that it has brought about the triumph of light over dark. One depends on the perpetual presence of the other, just like the trade in pornography.

My mother must have known, better than most, that all the abolition of Holywell-street would achieve was the migration of a handful of pornographers into other premises, and an easier thoroughfare for vehicles and pedestrians to navigate. She died shortly after our visit, in the summer of last year, at a time when pornography had become no longer the privilege of the wealthy, but available from barrows in every market. And although her eyes were failing, she knew that she had seen it all.

Lucinda Damage, Dartford, Kent, 1902

Afterword

While all characters and events in this book are fictional, I have taken several real examples as inspiration.

The London Anthropological Society, which shared many members with the Royal Geographic Society, was at the forefront of Britain's imperial ventures. Its inner circle was the so-called 'Cannibal Club', and its members, amongst others, were Sir Richard Burton, Algernon Charles Swinburne, Richard Monckton Milnes (Lord Houghton), Sir James Plaisted Wilde (Lord Penzance), General John Studholme Hodgson, and Charles Duncan Cameron. It was overwhelmingly Tory and reactionary, and supported research and enquiry into outdated scientific practices and behaviours devoted to securing their place in the world. They were also the most prolific producers and consumers of pornography. At three guineas a volume, and involving arcane, unmechanised methods of printing and binding, pornography was not for the working class in the 1860s.

The pornographer Frederick Hankey owned several volumes of pornography bound in human skin. Richard Burton promised him that he would bring back a piece of human skin from his trip to Dahomey in 1863 (stripped from '*une négresse vivante*' so that it would retain its lustre); fortunately, he failed in this mission.[1] Monckton Milnes wrote in his commonplace book in 1860: 'There is no accounting for tastes in superstition. Hankey would like to have a Bible bound with bits of skin stripped off live from the cunts of a hundred little girls and yet he could not be persuaded to try the sensation of f—ing a Muscovy Duck while its head was cut off.' In the same entry he also mentions Hankey's 'extreme desire to see a girl hanged and have the skin of her backside tanned to bind his *Justine* with'.[2]

The Ladies' Society for the Assistance of Fugitives from Slavery is based on an admirable organisation that did much good work towards the abolition of slavery in America. Frederick Douglass was one of the most high-profile slaves whose freedom was secured by the Society, and there were many fugitive and freed slaves living in the British Isles in the 1850s and 1860s. I by no means wish to suggest that all those involved in the Society were as hypocritical as Sylvia Knightley, but it is fair to say that by the middle of the nineteenth century England was suffering from 'philanthropy fatigue', and such endeavours were often senti-mental and impractical, a balm to one's conscience with little call to action. They gave otherwise idle gentlewomen a certain prestige and, quite simply, something to do. However, the American Civil War provided an opportunity for such organisations to regroup and exert a final push on the institution of slavery, and towards the end of the Civil War they made sent significant contributions to the American Freedman's Aid Movement.[3]

For nineteenth-century white British attitudes to interracial relationships between black men and white women, and the objectified sexual desire for black men as manifested by Lady Knightley, I recommend Ben Shephard's *Kitty and the Prince* (London, Profile, 2003).

Sir Charles Locock, the Queen's physician *accoucheur*, and President of the Royal Medical and Chirurgical Society in London, announced his use of potassium bromide to treat patients with epilepsy in 1857, after a presentation by Edward H. Sieveking (my great-great grandfather) at the Society. In

1861, J. Russell Reynolds published a landmark monograph, entitled *Epilepsy: Its Symptoms, Treatment, and Relation to Other Convulsive Diseases*.

The use of clitoridectomy to treat, amongst other things, dysuria, epilepsy, hysteria, insanity and sterility (which were all believed to have their origins in heightened sexuality) was prescribed and conducted by Dr Isaac Baker Brown during the 1860s, and is mentioned in *The Lancet*. It was vehemently rejected by much of the medical profession, and Dr Baker Brown was vilified and forced out of the London Gynaecological Society.

Dora's dream, of a thousand members and one pound a week for women in the bookbinding trades, was shared by Miss Isabel Forsyth, secretary of the Manchester and Salford Society of Women in the Bookbinding and Printing Trades. It was not realised until 1917.

Many of the erotic books mentioned – and quotations therefrom – are genuine; those that I have invented are as true as possible to the spirit of the real thing.

[1] Fawn Brodie, *The Devil Drives: A Life of Sir Richard Burton*, Eland, London, 1986, pp. 220, 239

[2] Richard Monckton Milnes, *Houghton Commonplace Books*, Trinity College, Cambridge, p. 212, quoted in Ian Gibson, *The Erotomaniac: The Secret Life of Henry Spencer Ashbee*, Faber and Faber, London, 2001, p. 31

[3] See Douglas A. Lorimer, *Colour, Class and the Victorians*, Leicester UP, Leicester, 1978

Acknowledgements

My thanks to:

Anna Balcombe, Emma Cameron, Tara Crewe, Professor Mirjam Foot, Peter Harvey, Dr Maria Iacovou, Eliza Kentridge, Dr Jeremy Krikler, Robert Priseman, Paul Rumsey, Ally Seabrook, Boris Starling, David and Judy Starling, Mike Trim, Guy and Robina Taplin, Jane Wilson; Arzu Tahsin, Holly Roberts and their team at Bloomsbury; my wonderful agent Stephanie Cabot and her team at the Gernert Company.

A complete bibliography of works consulted during the writing of this book would be lengthy and dull, but I must credit Judith Flander's excellent and exhaustive book *The Victorian House*, (HarperCollins, London, 2003) for informing much of the backdrop of everyday life throughout the story, and Lynda Nead's provocative *Victorian Babylon: People, Streets and Images in Nineteenth-Century London* (Yale University Press, New Haven, 2005), which introduced me to Holywell Street and the pornographic industry.

Lee Jackson's ever-growing www.victorianlondon.org is a masterful compilation of primary sources, which held so many answers to my questions about the minutiae of living in London in 1860 that at times I found myself consulting it daily. I would also like to thank Malcolm Shifrind for his fine Victorian Turkish Bath Project, at www.victorianturkishbath.org, and the online expertise of the VICTORIA and SHARP lists, especially Ruth Croft, Michel Faber, Sheldon Goldfarb, Ellen Jordan, Patrick Leary, Jan Marsh, Sally Mitchell, Heather Morton and Michael Wolff.

Finally, I must mention Jeni Bate and Karen Jefferies, without whom my children would have been much less happy while this book was being written.

A Note on the Author
by Boris Starling

Four days after finishing *The Journal of Dora Damage*, my sister Bee (as Belinda was universally known) was admitted to hospital for a long-scheduled operation to remove a cyst from her bile duct.

The operation initially seemed a success, but in the small hours of the following morning her hepatic artery burst, sending her into cardiac arrest.

The surgeons saved her life on that occasion, but she never left hospital again. Seven weeks and two further operations later, Bee died of septic shock. She was thirty-four, and married with two young children.

We held a memorial service for her a fortnight later, on a bittersweet late summer day of swirling emotions. The lovely funeral director who watched over Bee's coffin was, physically if not in personality, an absolute dead ringer for Mrs Eeles. Bee would have been tickled pink.

Several hundred people packed a small country church to say their farewells to Bee; and of all the readings during the service, the one about which people talked most afterwards was the prologue of this book.

'Before we are born,' it says, 'St Bartholomew, patron saint of bookbinders, presents our soul with a choice of two books': a gold-tooled one whose beauty fades under the drudgery of the proscriptive, pre-ordained fate therein; and a plain, rough tome which gradually flowers into a masterpiece as its blank pages are filled in by a soul who lives life according to its own dictates.

There is no doubt as to which of St Bartholomew's two books Bee's soul chose.

Her story was truly one of free will and personal inspiration. She was bottled sunshine, a woman of vital, vibrant, amazing energy; a bright, shining star, a creature of the light, a joy-giver and life-enhancer who lit up the lives of all those who knew her. She loved people not just for their qualities, but for their imperfections and their differences.

Bee was no saint, and would have hated to have been remembered as one. Her wit could be scabrous. She didn't suffer fools, because she, fiercely independent and ferociously intelligent, expected as much from others as she did from herself. She didn't indulge those she felt had let her down; she was quite prepared to jettison friendships she felt were no longer so. And she could be difficult, as can most people who are worth knowing.

Above all, she was that rarest of creatures; someone true to herself, for good and for bad.

For those who knew and loved her, Bee lives on in a myriad of ways, one of which is the book you have just finished. She would have been thrilled that you have read her novel; even more thrilled if you enjoyed it, of course, but equally prepared to have debated its shortcomings with you if you didn't.

The Journal of Dora Damage was a labour of love. All first novels are personal, to a large extent; how much more so this one, when there can be no more after it? There is so much of Bee in Dora, but never more so than when she says, at the end of the prologue, that this book 'conceals the contents of my heart, as clearly as if I had cut it open with a scalpel for the anatomists to read'.

February 2007

Belinda Starling lived in Wivenhoe, Essex with her husband and children and died in August 2006.

A NOTE ON THE TYPE

The text of this book is set in Linotype Sabon, named after the type founder, Jacques Sabon. It was designed by Jan Tschichold and jointly developed by Linotype, Monotype and Stempel, in response to a need for a typeface to be available in identical form for mechanical hot-metal composition and hand composition using foundry type.

Tschichold based his design for Sabon roman on a font engraved by Garamond, and Sabon italic on a font by Granjon. It was first used in 1966 and has proved an enduring modern classic.